MW00626740

SWORD AND SCION

THE CLASH OF CROWNS
BOOK 6

JACKSON E. GRAHAM

YOUNG**OAK**PUBLISHING

Young Oak Publishing LLC
Hayden, Idaho

This book is a work of fiction. The characters, incidents, and dialogue are drawn from the author's imagination and are not to be construed as real. Any resemblance to actual events or persons, living or dead, is entirely coincidental.

SWORD AND SCION: The Clash of Crowns
Copyright © 2022 by Jackson E. Graham
All rights reserved. No part of this publication may be used or reproduced in any manner, stored in a retrieval system, or transmitted in any form or by any means, electronic, mechanical, photocopying, recording, or otherwise without written permission of the publisher.

The publisher does not have any control over and does not assume responsibility for author or third-party websites or their content. For information regarding permission, contact:

Young Oak Publishing LLC
P.O. Box 682
Hayden, ID 83835

Cover design by Uncompleted Canvas LLC
Logo design by KJ Designs
Author photograph by Rachel Stewart Photography

Quotations from (NIV) New International Version of the Holy Bible used by permission of Bible Gateway.
New International Version **(NIV)**
Holy Bible, New International Version®, NIV® Copyright ©1973, 1978, 1984, 2011 by Biblica, Inc. ® Used by permission.
All rights reserved worldwide.
Text set in Times New Roman

http://jacksonegraham.wixsite.com/jackson-e-graham

Library of Congress Control Number: 2022918845

ISBN: 978-1-950917-01-3 (sc)

PRINTED IN THE UNITED STATES OF AMERICA

PRONOUNCIATION GUIDE

<u>Places</u>

Amiranoor (pronounced: Ah-**meer**-ah-norr)
Anehstun (pronounced: **Ah**-ne-stoon)
Edeveros (pronounced: Eh-**dev**-ah-ros)
Fenabor (pronounced: **Feh**-nah-bore)
Gald-Behn (pronounced: **Gahld-Ben**)
Iostan (pronounced: **Eye**-oh-stann)
Norgalok (pronounced: **Nor**-gah-lock)
Qelezal (pronounced: **Kell**-eh-zall)
Rehillon (pronounced: **Rey**-hill-on)
Taekohar (pronounced: **Tay**-ko-harr)
Zwaoi (pronounced: **Z-why**)

<u>Characters</u>

Ayleril (pronounced: **A**-luh-ril)
Eyoés (pronounced: **Aay**-oh-ess)
Gwyndel (pronounced: **Gwin**-dell)
Haeryn (pronounced: **Hay**-rin)
King Fohidras (pronounced: Fo-**high**-dras)
Taesyra (pronounced: Tay-**seer**-uh)

Months for the World of Alithell

Iaudyn
Nósor
Dichán
Biarron
Iaulan
Merchen
Yílor
Thurdál
Aevoran
Rotanos
Rynéth
Bivyn

**Don't miss these other titles by
Jackson E. Graham:**

To my editor.
You helped me sort through the chaos
and celebrate the gems, even when
I didn't recognize them at first.
Thank you for preserving my sanity.

Tell me, river, of the souls you keep
The secrets you hold, the men who sleep
Below your waves.
Tell me, river, of the cloudy day
She drifted away, she went astray
You swept her away
Tho' she begged to stay, you swept her away.

Maviron O'Skei, Fenaboran poet

"For in this hope we were saved.
But hope that is seen is ho hope at all.
Who hopes for what they already have?"
(Romans 8:24, NIV)

"Consider it pure joy, my brothers and sisters,
whenever you face trials of many kinds,
because you know that the testing
of your faith develops perseverance."
(James 1:2-3, NIV)

PROLOGUE

Castle Garifell, Fenabor.
4 years after Norgalok's secession from the Kingdom of Alithell

The sodden cloth landed with a splat upon the fireplace mantle, a dripping corner dangling over the ledge. Wiping the sweat from her brow and the tears from her eyes, the maid snatched up the rag and scoured.

The shadows of a dreary twilight lengthened as the spring rain pattered against the lofty windows of the chamber. Gritting her teeth, the maid worked to the rhythm. A chill seized her and she fell against the mantle in a fit of coughing. The smell of soot—it clung to her nostrils and scraped down her throat like gravel. Chest heaving, she squeezed her eyes shut and fought to maintain her focus.

Stay strong, Cara! That's it, now—keep on!

The fever had grown since last night. Face glistening in the grey light, Cara scoured the stone mantlepiece, wincing as she strained to see. Waves of heat flushed across her skin like rippling fire. Another fit of coughing tore her throat and she dropped the wet rag into the pile of ash she'd swept up.

Cara muttered a curse at the cloth and turned her back, stumbling toward the chamber door fading in and

1

out of her vision. She rammed her toe into the doorframe and fell through the opening. Blinking to clear her double vision, she stood, nursing bruises. In the trembling lantern light, she spotted the white streaks that were split logs and started for them.

The wood scraped her arms like brambles as she took up an armful. Cara returned to the room and began stacking it in the gaping mouth of the fireplace. Her hands trembled, yet she bit her tongue and pushed on.

Hope was earned through hard work—succumb to weakness, and that hope would perish.

As her feverish mind raged, Cara could imagine the master's boot on her stomach. Punishment. It was better to die in her work, sprawled in a heap of ash and soap.

Cara placed the last log and swept the pile of soot into her second bucket. Legs wobbling beneath her, she lumbered out of the room and into the hallway.

Wiping her nose with her forearm, Cara looked down the hall toward the silent doorway at its end.

The baron's quarters. Daghan and the others had warned her. At twilight, when the days withered into night and the owls began their hunt, Baron Falrey O'Dyre attended to his work. Reading forbidden tomes, some rumors suggested.

"'Tis best not to disturb him," Daghan had insisted with wagging finger. The sound of his high, nasal voice echoed in her head.

They want to outdo me. Keep me from impressing the baron with my efforts so they can gain his favor!

Tightening her grip on her buckets, Cara clenched her jaw. How had she been so naive? After years of blind obedience, only now did she suspect their motives.

Exhaling, Cara marched toward the baron's quarters, soapy water sloshing in her bucket. A pungent smell arrested her steps, cutting through the pressure in her forehead. Wiping her nose again, Cara hesitated.

Metal? Blood? Or just lye from my bucket?

She cocked her head, listening. Straining to catch the faint scratch of a pen from behind the door.

Nothing. She frowned. Some nights, she'd heard the baron at his work—books thumping on the desk, the shuffle of his chair as he stood, pacing the floor. He'd grown more distant over the years, more demanding of his subjects.

Cara sniffed, heart pounding. Fire burned behind her eyes and she groped for the shifting doorhandle, water splashing onto her legs.

Her hand grasped empty air. With a cry she tumbled over her bucket and fell against the door, knocking it inward. Her face hit the floor and stars flashed before her eyes. She tasted blood on her lip and struggled to rise, shivering in her soaked, soapy clothes. Cara pressed a hand to her lip to stem the bleeding and stiffened.

Four goats lay rigid on the floor in pools of red— and among them sat the baron, covered in crimson from head to foot. Shaggy, unkept hair hung like rags around a haggard face. His lips moved soundlessly. In the blistering haze of fever, she glimpsed a black figure looming over him, milky white eyes pinning her to the floor. The ghost laughed and seeped into Falrey's skin like water. She recoiled in horror.

"There is no death for Death himself," the baron whispered, his voice tearing through Cara's fevered mind.

His cold fingers were around her throat before she could scream.

1

25th of Yílor, 2211 SE, Asdale

A nightmare? No—this was hell.

The fear of it thickened Eyoés' blood and dulled his senses. His breathing grew ragged, his heartbeat mirroring the steady, resounding clang of the Abbey's bell. As he stared out at the creeping, squirming shapes of the hobgoblins, Eyoés could feel horror spark anew.

Recoiling from the window, Eyoés tripped over the corner of his blankets and fell against the bedpost, head spinning as his heart thumped in his chest. He snatched his father's sword from where it lay and a chainmail jerkin from a chest of armor. With a choked cry, he threw open the door of his room and sped down the spiraling stairs. "Gwyndel! Uwéllor! To arms! *Fight!* Ayleril! We can't let the city fall! *FIGHT!*" he screamed, barely hearing his words echo off the narrow passageway.

Eyoés skidded to a stop at the bottom of the stairs, his wild eyes staring. Servants and court officials fluttered about the main hall like trapped birds, some colliding into him as they frantically searched for a path of escape. Fractured moonlight filtered through the tall windows with a spectral glow. Chairs clattered to the floor around pounding feet. Eyoés caught a glimpse of red hair in the crowd and shoved his way toward it.

Gwyndel, Vakros, and Ayleril clustered about a solitary table, surrounded by a raging sea. Standing at her father's side, Rhoslyn whimpered in fright and wrapped her arms around Vakros' waist. The sight of their horror and bewilderment brought tears to Eyoés' eyes.

Catching sight of her brother, Gwyndel motioned for him to join them. "Eyoés, what do we do?" she asked above the clamor. Eyoés hesitated. He met the eyes of his family in silence, words dying on his lips.

What should he tell them? The sight of the hobgoblins scaling the outer walls had seared itself upon his memory. There was little escaping that scale of conflict. Even during the hapless defense of Ellokon, they'd had the temporary advantage of strong defenses. But with the enemy inside the city walls, defeat was not far off. Eyoés caught Ayleril's eye and knew he was not alone in his misery.

The crowd parted as Uwéllor led the Wardens of the Watch through their midst, golden armor glowing. Several of the gahrim gathered to protect Eyoés and Gwyndel while the others attempted to calm the madding crowd.

Tucking his helmet under his arm, Uwéllor stood at attention. "What is your command, my lord?" he said, his smooth expression offering a vestige of confidence to cling to. The other Wardens reflected their leader's unyielding composure.

Eyoés took a deep breath and combed his fingers through his hair. "We go to the inner ramparts. I need a complete view of the city," he said.

"Shouldn't we stay here?" Vakros asked. "The keep would be the safest place."

Eyoés shook his head. "The hobgoblins won't stop until the entire city is taken. If we stay here, they'll put us under siege, and we're not prepared for that. We need to evacuate before our escape is cut off completely," he said.

Uwéllor put on his helmet with a nod and started for the doors of the main hall. The Wardens of the Watch fell into formation behind him, sheltering Eyoés and the others as they hurried toward the main entrance. Many of the servants and court officials beat upon the locked doors, their voices hoarse with desperate cries for help. Clearing his way through, Uwéllor turned to face the terrified faces of the castle staff. "Wait here and await further instructions," he shouted, his clear voice ringing through the hall like a smooth, crystalline bell. The gahrim by his side opened the doors of the keep.

As Eyoés passed through, he turned. "No matter what happens, remember this—Asdale is not made of walls and paved streets. *We* are Asdale!" he declared, hastening out of the keep and ushering his family out into the courtyard. The Wardens of the Watch spilled out of the keep and shut the door from the outside.

Eyoés sped for the ramparts, scrambling up the nearest stairway with Gwyndel and the others hurrying after him. He skidded to a stop and pointed at Ayleril.

"Shield Rhoslyn. I don't want her to see this," he said. He wished none of them had to.

Ayleril coaxed her from her father's comforting embrace. Vakros squeezed his daughter's hand, reluctant to let go. Ayleril met the man's tear-filled gaze. "She is safe with me," he said. The assurance with which he spoke set Gwyndel at ease. Ayleril escorted Rhoslyn down the stairs, whispering words of comfort.

Eyoés didn't wait to see them leave. Running full-stride up the stairs, he scrambled to the edge of the ramparts and wilted against the cold stone.

As far as the eye could see, the streets of Asdale writhed. The ancient sound of hobgoblin war horns rang out in haphazard bursts. In the darkness of night, all was painted shades of black, blue, and pale white. Several fires glowed orange in the outer streets. Above it all, the peal of the Abbey's bell resounded in the dark, mourning for the city's defilement.

Eyoés forced himself to stand tall despite the twisting in his stomach. He could hear the garrison readying for battle. Tucked in the keep's shadow, the Farradoth burned. The ramparts of these military training grounds crawled as the garrison fought back the hobgoblin siege ladders. The Farradoth had been struck first, and Eyoés knew with a sinking feeling that the knights of Asdale would not last the night.

The Abbey's bell suddenly ceased, and a burst of light drew his eye as the humble building went up in flames. Gwyndel's sobs tore from her throat as she fell against Vakros.

As Eyoés watched his beloved city fall, the numbness that clouded his mind dissipated. There was no reason to fear the opinion of others any longer. No need to gain trust and keep it. No enemy disguised behind the pleasant smile of a friend. His legs grew solid beneath him, and the crisp night air invigorated him. There was only one goal in sight.

Fight to win.

Pounding the battlements with a white-knuckled fist, Eyoés turned toward the gatehouse. "Captain!" he shouted. The man came running, his face blanched. Eyoés seized him by the shoulders. "Listen to me—send a platoon of your best men to build a barricade on the front lines. Set it alight," he commanded, glancing back toward the chaos. "We need to slow the enemy down."

The Captain swallowed. "But my lord, the people are surrendering," he explained.

Eyoés' heart skipped. "What?"

The man pointed down at the city. "We received the news from the front. The hobgoblins are sparing those who surrender, and there aren't many who resist," he explained.

It had finally happened. The people had cracked.

Gritting his teeth, Eyoés turned back to where Gwyndel and Vakros stood, mourning. In the pale light of the waxing moon, their pure grief struck Eyoés as beautiful. And as he looked out over his fallen city, he knew Asdale's people were no longer his people. They belonged to another now. Their sedition had bled his heart dry.

He turned back to the Captain. "Very well," he said. "I'll burn the streets myself. Fetch me three Gesadith lanterns, newly lit." The officer ran back to the gatehouse.

Eyoés turned to Gwyndel and Vakros. "The hobgoblins haven't overrun the northern side of the city yet. The people in the keep—lower them over the north-facing ramparts with the strongest ropes you can find. We must hurry if we're to save them," he commanded.

Vakros and Uwéllor nodded and hastened back to where the Wardens of the Watch guarded the keep. Gwyndel grasped her brother's shoulder. "And you?" she asked, wiping tears from her eyes.

A gust of wind tossed her hair as Gibusil alighted on the ramparts, an unearthly shadow in the moonlight. The griffin's growl brought a smile to his face. He took Fóbehn and its quiver from Gwyndel's outstretched hand. "I'll keep the enemy occupied," he said, briskly kissing her on the cheek and climbing onto Gibusil. The Captain of the Guard brought the Gesadith lanterns and Eyoés fastened them to the saddle.

Eyoés snatched the saddlehorn as Gibusil sprang from the ramparts, almost throwing him clear of his seat. The wind battered his eyes as he hunkered down, watching the town whisk past him. Gibusil banked to the side and Eyoés soared above the front lines, watching the enemy collide with the few who resisted. Wreckage was strewn about the streets, trampled underfoot by some and clambered over by others.

Unbuckling a lantern from the saddle, Eyoés heaved it into the debris with a roar.

The lantern burst in a dazzling flash of light and white flames spilled across the ground, throwing scalding sparks as they set houses alight. Gibusil growled as he passed through the smoke, sparks stinging his feet.

Wheeling the griffin about, Eyoés watched the city he had built burn at his own hands.

2

Stuffed in the corner of a dank, murky cell, Santh Baklyn heard the frantic tolling of the bell and smiled.

He tilted his head back against the wall and closed his eyes, the faint echo of frenzied shouts drifting throughout the dungeon complex. The sentries grew skittish. Even with his eyes closed, Santh could picture them—their soiled boots scuffing across the floor as they fingered their halberds, glancing uneasily down the passageway.

Dark laughter slipped through his widening smile. He straightened, chains clinking as he peered through the darkness to watch them squirm. The guards jumped at the sudden breach of silence. With an oath, one of them rapped the cell bars with his gauntlet and glared at Santh. Shaking his head in amusement, Santh laughed again and sank back into the shadows.

The reckoning comes ever closer, and they can only watch and wait for it to consume them. It must be terrible, realizing you're on the wrong side of history.

Catching the glimmer of a rat's eye in the failing light of a lantern, Santh kicked the unsuspecting creature into the nearby wall, hearing it thud upon impact. His lip wrinkled in distaste and he shifted his position to ease the stiffness in his bones. He embraced the waiting despite his restlessness.

Without patience, true change never comes to fruition. Our victory is inevitable, and I must be content to suffer through its birthing pains.

The faint clang of the bell suddenly ceased. Santh's head shot up and he rose, catching the rumble of stampeding feet. He gripped the bars of his cell and gloated.

Eyoés is no fool. He knows the city is against him. If he's reckless enough to resist fate, perhaps I'll be lucky enough to see him die.

The sudden jingle of armor echoed in the dark. Santh quickly withdrew, fingering the shackles around his wrists. As the sound grew nearer, the sentries stiffened and wheeled to face it. Three Taekoharan soldiers stepped into the lanternlight, their gloves marked with the ranking of lesser officers. The sentries visibly relaxed.

Santh started as one of the officers seized a guard by the face and slammed him against the cell bars. The other sentry let out a choked cry as he was dashed to the ground and slain by his own halberd. Santh eyed the fallen bodies with a disinterested glance as his traitorous allies snatched the keys from where they had fallen and unlatched the cell with a sharp clack.

He stretched out his shackled hands, smiling to himself at the men's eager obedience. He sighed, casting off his shackles as he rubbed the clammy sweat from his wrists. With an amused grunt, he kicked one of the fallen sentries.

"You see, gentlemen, patience is everything," he said.

The deep boom of a crumbling building thundered in Eyoés' ears, drowning out the sharp fizz of burning Gesadith. Clutching the saddle as Gibusil whipped around a corner, he threw up his arm to shield his eyes from the blinding light.

Eyoés squinted, reaching back to his quiver and loosing several hasty shots into the mayhem below. In the erratic light of the Gesadith firestorm, he caught fleeting glimpses of his soldiers in the tumult, lashing out like madmen in every direction to staunch the advancing tide. The enemy went up in flames like torches, clinging to life with screams of terror.

This crazed frenzy was too much for Eyoés to comprehend. A thousand desperate pleas for help clamored in his head simultaneously, all pulling him in a hundred different directions and begging for salvation. Each cry tore a deeper wound in his soul. Paralyzed, Eyoés could only cling to Gibusil and watch the horror unfold.

He ground his teeth and jerked the reins twisted around his fist. The griffin responded effortlessly. Gibusil hurtled into a battalion of hobgoblins, scattering the howling creatures like ocean spray as he swept his claws through their ranks.

Eyoés yelped as a javelin grazed his chainmail in a flash of sparks. He huddled down on the griffin's saddle, relieved he had grabbed the chainmail jerkin at the last moment. Still, it was no suit of armor—one lucky shot, and he would fall into his own fire.

Gibusil scrambled atop a ruined house and took to the sky again. Eyoés unclipped the last of the three Gesadith lanterns from the saddle. He twisted around, catching a fleeting glimpse of the keep through the drifting smoke. Time was running short. Eyoés hurled the final lantern into the enemy's front lines, wheeling Gibusil back toward the keep.

A grating roar chilled his blood as a broad shadow shot over his head. Eyoés pulled back on the reins, heart sinking as he recognized the outline of a dragon streaking through the darkness. He glimpsed the silhouette of a rider on the creature's back.

They've come for Santh.

Gibusil tore after the dragon with a screech. Eyoés drew another arrow, aiming through tears as the wind beat at his eyes. The arrow flew and he followed with another shot without waiting to see if the first struck its mark.

The rider ducked and the dragon weaved to the side, intercepting Gibusil's advance with a whip of its tail. Eyoés wrenched the reins and the griffin tumbled as the monster's barbed tail whistled above their heads. He righted Gibusil in time to see the dragon dive into the keep's courtyard.

Gibusil pounced onto the battlements and Eyoés leaned forward for a better view. The castle staff filled the courtyard in a mad rush for safety. The Wardens of the Watch were overwhelmed, struggling to help people over the wall as Gwyndel and Vakros urged the crowd from behind.

From his perch, Eyoés saw Santh Baklyn.

Santh climbed onto the dragon's back, looking at Eyoés with a smug grin. In a blink of an eye, the dragon took to the night sky and vanished into the western clouds. Eyoés drew Fóbehn to his cheek and aimed to put an arrow in Santh's back.

Rhoslyn screamed.

He looked back to the bustling courtyard and searched the crowd. She screamed again and Eyoés saw her, pressed up against the wall of the griffin stable. Alone. Where was Ayleril?

Several of the enemy rushed towards her with hands stretched out to take her captive. Eyoés spurred Gibusil and the griffin sprang, claws bared and glistening. The men fell dead before the griffin had a chance to strike, and Ayleril appeared next to Rhosyln, materializing from thin air. Eyoés stared, dumbfounded.

His trusted steward was a gahrim.

Reading the look in his baron's eyes, Ayleril flashed a brief smile at Eyoés as Gibusil landed. "I was sworn to secrecy," he admitted. "I would have told you on your deathbed."

Eyes wide, Eyoés sat back in his seat, stunned. "The King himself sent you, all those years ago," he mumbled.

Ayleril nodded. "I once served Eryndál Amberster, and I have served you just as faithfully," he said.

Gwyndel and Vakros pushed through the crowd, rushing to Rhoslyn's side. Pale and trembling, Gwyndel knelt beside her daughter and held her in a tight embrace. Vakros pointed to where the Wardens of the Watch fought back the crazed mob, lowering a few people at a time over the ramparts with rope. "We can't save them all," he said.

Eyoés took up Gibusil's reins. "Open the gates of this inner courtyard. I know a way of escape. I can lead the people to safety," he said, "but we need to make our way to the back side of the city."

Vakros dashed up a nearby set of stairs and shouted a command. A horn blasted above the noise and the gates swung wide. The castle staff rushed for freedom in one mad dash, bursting out of the gates and pouring out into the streets.

Eyoés and Gibusil shot into the sky. Swooping over the fleeing tide, he tried desperately to beckon them, to break through their madness. They were deaf to his counsel. Terror scattered them to the four winds and left Eyoés alone in the night sky. All his years of leadership seemed to mean nothing to them. It crushed him. The neighing of horses pulled him back to the keep. Numb, he landed before the open gate as Gwyndel and the others rode out.

Gwyndel held Rhoslyn close, patting the girl's hand. "I never thought you'd watch your home burn again," she said.

Eyoés hung his head. "Neither did I," he muttered, voice thick.

The Wardens of the Watch assembled into formation as Vakros and Ayleril saddled their horses. Eyoés watched the remainder of the garrison prepare for a final stand and then took to the air again. The riders raced in the griffin's shadow and wheeled their course to the north of the city. The gahrim kept pace with the galloping horses, forming a bristling shield with their polearms. The streets cleared before them as the dazed townsfolk hurried to gather their loved ones and possessions.

Wiping the sweat from his brow, Eyoés looked across the horizon, watching the clouds drift across the stars. He took a breath of cool air and rubbed his drowsy eyes.

"The tyrant flees! Stop them!" voices yelled from below. Their cries sounded murky in Eyoés' ears and he looked back to see a pack of young dissidents charge after them. The Wardens of the Watch turned like a rippling wave and met the challenge with broad shields. The young zealots pounced and the gahrim lunged, knocking the rebels to the ground and resuming their retreat without a single faltering step. Those standing along the streets looked on in begrudging silence.

The riders halted in the shadow of the northern wall. Eyoés landed Gibusil and dismounted. He fished through his pocket and strode toward the sheer stone face, glancing back to see Gwyndel and Vakros' baffled looks. "Appearances are deceiving," he said. Eyoés slipped a key into a chink in the stone and turned. A rumbling groaned within the wall and a broad stone shifted inward to reveal a dark tunnel.

Gwyndel frowned as the realization sank in. "You feared something like this would happen," she said, pressing Rhoslyn against her chest. "Why didn't you tell me?"

Eyoés sighed. "It was too painful. The memory of Skreon's attack was still raw when I oversaw its construction," he answered. He nodded at the dark mouth of the tunnel. "Time is short."

Vakros spurred his horse into the void. Gwyndel followed uncertainly, the Wardens of the Watch covering the rear. Eyoés caught sight of Ayleril and stopped.

The gahrim didn't move from where he stood. "Go on. Flee to Amiranoor. Do not forget what happened here," he said.

Eyoés frowned. "You know this disaster will haunt me—"

"That's not what I'm talking about," Ayleril interrupted. He turned, barely noticing the sound of havoc carried on the wind. "Asdale's fall was due to its own faults, not yours. No, it was here, in the tumult and strife, that you met your destiny. It was here that you became a true hero of Alithell. A man I am proud to have called my friend and ally," he said.

Climbing onto Gibusil's saddle, Eyoés held back tears. "Then you won't come with us?" he asked.

Ayleril shook his head, his face serene. "I will keep the tunnel open for whoever wants to escape," he said.

Eyoés took a deep, trembling breath with one final glance at the city, the white flames of burning Gesadith still flashing amid the smoke. "Farewell, Ayleril," he said. He choked over the words. Throwing himself from the saddle, Eyoés embraced his friend for the last time. The gahrim's hot tears sprinkled his neck. As the sounds of war drew closer, Eyoés climbed onto Gibusil's back and soared into the air.

Eyoés Kingson, slayer of Skreon and Baron of Taekohar, had been exiled.

3

15th of Thurdál, 2211 SE, Hodholm

The soldiery stood to attention the moment Haeryn's foot touched the cobblestone. The clang of their armor brought a smile to his face.

Clasping his hands behind his back, Haeryn paused, his iron gaze passing over them like a thundercloud. His own reflection studied him in return, shimmering off their polished armor in the pleasant summer light. With an amused glint in his eye, Haeryn nodded to himself. "Impressive," he said, glancing back as footsteps drew up behind him.

Beaming, Lord Finn Balston held his chin high. "Herthere's best," he said, twisting his ring as the young knight appraised the levy of troops. "I trust they meet the standards the Baroness has set?"

Haeryn withheld his response. He'd wait to pass judgment until he'd inspected them himself.

Jaaye came alongside, studying the ranks intensely. She paused beside one of the men in silence, eying him from head to foot. She took the glaive from his hands and ran her finger along the shaft. Haeryn noticed the glint of worry in the soldier's eyes as he gauged her reaction.

Jaaye thrust the weapon back into the man's hands with a smile. "If only my men could have such

21

discipline," she said, turning to Lord Balston. "You should be proud." She eagerly pushed on ahead before the Lord of Herthere could express his thanks. Haeryn followed close behind her, content to let her enjoy her moment of peace. After enduring the horrors of Fenabor and the trials of their journey to Rehillon, it was a wonder she had learned to smile again.

"I trust we are to march tomorrow at daybreak?" Lord Finn Balston inquired.

Reality wiped the smile from Haeryn's face. He threw himself into the inspection. These men had not come to Hodholm to flaunt their self-discipline and fine weaponry. They had come to fight—and Haeryn thought himself a fool for losing sight of that fact.

Clenching his jaw, he examined the formation of the ranks, noting the station of the officers and where they were placed. Only one of Rehillon's major towns was represented today. Agnar Crawbrand of Merwic and Gerall Bardmond of Andieff had answered Caywen's summons with enthusiasm, agreeing to rendezvous with the main Rehil force at the ruins of Weomor. Haeryn looked at the colors of Herthere flying over Balston's troops. Though they all shared a common enemy in Falrey, Haeryn wondered whether their zeal would be enough to hold them together on the battlefield.

The battlefield. The thought tore through Haeryn like a windswept tempest. Clenching his fists at his sides, he welcomed the call to action as he fingered the sword buckled to his waist, longing to swing its heft.

This world has rebelled long enough. Falrey's cause is triumphing this very moment. I cannot accept that.

Haeryn noticed Dovarul and Hjarti sitting on the edge of the ramparts, legs dangling in the air as they watched the inspection half-heartedly. They joked quietly to themselves, the sound of their quiet laughter breaking the stillness. Haeryn wrinkled his nose in disgust despite himself. How could they laugh at such a time?

Taking a deep breath, Haeryn lifted his eyes to Hodholm's keep and squinted against the sunlight. He glimpsed Caywen and Beydan upon an upper balcony.

We were all fooled. We believed evil was never strong enough to overcome good. Now see what we've come to.

He shook his head, turning to Lord Finn Balston. "All is in order. Have the officers lead them to the barracks," he said.

We will purge Alithell and build upon the ruins.

Caywen never enjoyed wearing her signet ring in public. As she leaned against the balcony railing, she could feel it weigh heavy on her hand, ever reminding her of the poised image of wisdom and benevolence it projected. Shielding her eyes from the bright sun, she gazed down at Lord Balston's troops. She could almost feel the sun's warmth radiating off their shields.

Will it be enough?

Caywen straightened as she squeezed the balustrade. The sound of playful birdsong on the summer breeze failed to brighten her mood. Her mind drifted, carrying her places she didn't want to go. Places she desperately wished to leave. The pain of Throst's betrayal. The memory of her father's death. The sight of Gwair pitching over the edge into the vacant air below. The looming shadow of a crumbling world. Each horror flashed through her mind like a portrait frozen in time, peeling open old wounds one by one.

With a sigh, Caywen rubbed her face, feeling the ring brush against her forehead. For a moment, she toyed with the idea of tearing it off and flinging it as far as she could.

Father entrusted Rehillon to me. I will not dishonor his memory.

Bracing herself against the balcony railing, she gathered her senses and pieced her thoughts together like stained glass. It was odd, knowing that she looked more confident than she felt. In the wake of Throst's revolt, she had quickly learned the importance of instilling hope in her people. The weight of leadership had matured her greatly—and broken her in the process.

How can I lead in this war when I'm so overwhelmed?

The gentle weight of a hand on her shoulder made her turn. Beydan held her gaze and searched it. "Caywen?"

She gave a weary smile. In light of his temporary promotion to Steward of Hodholm, Beydan had acquiesced—albeit begrudgingly—to the maids' insistence that they trim his hair and beard in a style suitable for public office. He continued to wear his military uniform with pride, the stag emblem of the Northern Guard spread across his chest. Beydan idly shifted his collar. Such formal attire took time to grow accustomed to, though it was an odd look on him.

Caywen sighed. "I'm alright," she said.

Beydan shook his head. "No, you're not. You've been troubled for days," he said, letting his hand slip from her shoulder. "If you are uneasy about my being Steward, I assure you—"

Caywen shook her head and turned away. She tapped the balustrade with a stiff finger. "I'm going to war, Beydan. All I've done for Rehillon is make life more difficult. And now I'm the one to lead them across miles of enemy ground?" she said, as she turned to Beydan. "I'm not equal to this."

Beydan looked out over Hodholm. "We've all made mistakes. But no one can *ever* accuse you of exploiting your people. Don't let the past poison you. And as for war, no man or woman is prepared to face it. None should have to," he said. "We all have a role to play, and some of us are destined to be the titans."

Caywen's mind drifted to Lanyon, envisioning him careening across the fields and forests upon a frothing, sweating horse. "Titans carry the world on their shoulders," she said. "I pray I'm not meant to be one of them."

The scuff of a maid's slippers drew up behind her. "My lady, Torhalla Westulf wishes to speak with you," she said.

4

Tears stung Caywen's eyes as she leaned against the door to Vikar's former chamber, summoning the courage to enter. She squeezed her eyes shut, head against her arm. With his usual generosity, her father had insisted they'd trade quarters, preferring this smaller room to the generous accommodations he'd had as baron. The baron's suite was a symbol of authority—authority he'd passed down to her. Vikar had always wished her to have the best, even if he deprived himself. When she opened this door, her father's face had always greeted her.

Now Torhalla Westulf would greet her instead. In the aftermath of Steinar's attempt to murder his baroness, Caywen had confined his insufferable wife to the unclaimed room till a full investigation could be arranged. The depth of Torhalla's involvement in Steinar's conspiracy against the Northern Guard was still unclear. Tucking a stray hair behind her ear, Caywen hesitated. The guards on either side of the door caught her eye and held their halberds at the ready. She clenched her jaw and opened the door.

The room looked emptier. Vikar had resolved to move most of the furnishings to Caywen's new quarters. Only an off-kilter tapestry was left, portraying the scene of a woman gazing longingly into the distance. Accumulated dust subdued its vibrant colors. The sight of it turned her stomach.

The grand adventure she'd yearned after for years had been nothing like she'd imagined. After the tumult of Throst's civil uprising, her former naivety was now an embarrassment to her. A breeze stirred the red curtain and drew Caywen's eye to the disheveled bed.

Enveloped in the wilting folds of an unwashed dress, Torhalla sat hunched over the edge of the bed. Her blonde hair hung unkempt, piling in tangles atop her sagging shoulders. At Caywen's entrance, she lifted her bloodshot gaze, halfheartedly rubbing at the bags under her eyes. "Please. Caywen—have mercy on me," she said, her voice hoarse and weak.

Caywen's face hardened. "Your husband dragged me across the floor by my hair. And you shared his radical views. I won't apologize for letting justice have its way," she retorted, wheeling toward the door.

Torhalla leapt to her feet and seized Caywen by the arm. "Please listen to me!" she begged.

Yanking her arm away, Caywen closed the door and spun to face her. "Why should I?" she challenged, eyes narrowed.

"Because I didn't intend for any harm to come to you. I didn't scheme with Steinar to assassinate you! I'm not the traitor you think I am," Torhalla replied, curling her arms over her head as her fevered eyes darted about. "Good intentions can still lead to failure. We both understand this. I sought the good of Rehillon and failed. Have you not made such mistakes also?"

Caywen cursed her bad luck. Looking away, she constrained herself. Desperation and cunning were a dangerous combination, one that Caywen didn't wish to prod by exposing her vulnerability. "Mistakes bring consequences. That is reality. Otherwise, we would never learn," she said. "I have no sympathy for those who brush off the consequences of their actions."

Torhalla stiffened. "No sympathy?" she snapped, tugging a fistful of her hair. "Look at me! Why must I suffer for Steinar's wrongs? Injustice does not avenge injustice!"

Caywen restrained the urge to slap the woman out of her crazed stupor. "Your grief for Steinar's death did this to you. I offered you food, and you rejected it," she said. "I don't blame you for that, but you cannot hold me responsible for its effects. Accusing me of oppressing you will not aid your cause or help you see the truth."

Torhalla sank onto her bed. Leaning against the bedpost, she stared at the floor and wrung her hands. The sight of the woman's suffering tugged at Caywen's sympathies despite her disgust. While Torhalla's involvement in the uprising was heavily implied, there was a chance she'd been ignorant of Steinar's lunatic scheme.

Maybe I can still show her mercy without giving her free rein.

Before Caywen could make a concession, Torhalla shook her head and locked eyes with her. Her lip curled in a seething snarl, and her eyes crawled over Caywen. "*Look* at you. Flaunting yourself with such arrogance like a prissy little tyrant," she said, glowering as she leaned forward. "Why do you wring the life out of me? Is it because Lord Ravenstrong crushed you? Or is it simply because your father taught you to be cruel? Perhaps it's both."

Caywen's face reddened. Ice crept through her veins and all thoughts of mercy fled. In one stride she closed the distance and seized Torhalla by the chin. "You're dead to Rehillon—nothing you say or do could hurt me," she said. Wrinkling her nose in disgust, Caywen turned her back and departed, slamming the door behind her.

Torhalla rubbed her sore chin with a bitter smirk. "We shall see," she said.

5

Cinching the leather strap of his spaulders with his teeth, Haeryn slipped on his gauntlets and shouldered the door open, squinting at the sunlight. The garrison saluted with cheerful faces as he emerged from the gatehouse. With a distracted nod, he whisked past and down the nearest stairs to the courtyard. Their gladness at his presence was lost on him. His mind lay elsewhere. Haeryn tugged at the chainmail coif heaped upon his shoulders as it threatened to choke him. Everything needed to be perfect. The day for war had come, and he was ready.

A shout drew Haeryn's attention to horses, soldiery, and equipment assembled in front of Hodholm's gates, waiting to be loosed on the outside world. Looming above the gathering men-at-arms like a burly cedar, Hjarti motioned for Haeryn. Dovarul sat precariously atop the giant's shoulder, bracing himself with a nervous smile. History was being written today, and the familiar pair were making it comedic by simply being there.

Haeryn nodded his thanks to the armor bearer who presented him with a shield. He picked his way through the crowd and stood beside Dovarul and Hjarti, lifting his voice above the sound of tramping footsteps. "You're in a bright mood," he remarked.

Carefully maintaining his balance, Dovarul gestured at the masses hemming them in. "Better to laugh than to hobble around with a long face," he said, scratching under his eyepatch. "Besides, I don't look as ugly when I smile."

Hjarti grinned. "That's why I keep him laughing at all costs," he said. Dovarul chuckled. They always insisted the best jokes were made at the other's expense.

Swooping down from her perch atop the battlements, Thridd landed at Haeryn's feet and nudged his leg. Haeryn knelt and stroked the dragon's narrow head. "Sir Thrynnis always said war brings out the best and worst in men. We'll all see each other differently by the end of this. From the highest to the most lowly," he said, lifting his eyes to the closed gates. "Will Caywen give the order soon?"

Hjarti nodded. "The last of the supply wagons are assembling at the city limits. When they are ready to march, we make for Weomor to join with Lord Crawbrand and Lord Bardmond's troops," he answered. Eyes distant, Haeryn stood. The memory of the ruined castle of Weomor sent a shiver through his limbs—yet still stirred a strange fascination.

Dovarul squinted, peering out over the ramparts. "Last I heard, it sounded like the townsfolk were growing restless," he pondered aloud.

Haeryn frowned, standing as Thridd took to the wind, her six wings beating at the air in a flurry of limbs. "An uprising?"

Dovarul shook his head. "No, thank the Guide," he said, raising his voice above the din of the mustering army. "But they're asking the question that's on all of our minds." The dwarf looked down and caught the young knight's eye. "Lad, here's the truth—no one knows what this war has in store for us. Mothers and children want the assurance that their menfolk will return to them. They want to know for certain that we'll be the victors. In that, we aren't so different, but we are the poor souls who will suffer through the blood, steel, and innards. We all need to be reminded of hope," he said.

Pursing his lips, Haeryn looked away.

Hope is too fragile for the battlefield. Outrage should be our response. Otherwise we won't last.

He mustered a false smile. "I'll see what I can do," he said, his voice distant. Wheeling away from his friends, Haeryn marched toward the ramparts. He said nothing as the soldiers stepped aside to let him pass, astonished by the strength and focus he exuded despite his age. As Haeryn started up the nearest stairway, their stares bored into his back. Good. If words alone could stir men to war, then he would be their paragon.

Haeryn caught sight of Caywen and Beydan as he crested the final step. Above the sound of the gathering army, he detected a growing murmur of voices from outside the castle grounds. Before he could approach the baroness, a familiar hand grabbed his shoulder and turn him around.

Erling looked him in the eye. "You've heard?"

Haeryn nodded. "How serious?" he asked.

Glancing back at the sentries posted nearby, Erling pulled his friend toward the ramparts to offer him a better look. "So far, the disturbance is minimal. But the crowd is growing, and they're seeking reassurance," he explained. "Caywen's not willing to take chances. She fears that if they become riled enough, they might keep the army from marching. She's summoned the castle guard in case of emergency. We can't afford to be late for our rendezvous with Lord Bardmond and Lord Crawbrand at Weomor."

Haeryn peered over the merlons and a crowd of eyes stared back up at him. In the shadow of the gatehouse, a throng of townsfolk huddled together and unleashed their anxieties upon all who could listen, their voices growing louder as they gained confidence. Even from a distance, the fear in their pained stares pricked at Haeryn's focus.

They'll cost us valuable time. Time Falrey will utilize for atrocities. Don't they understand? We can't coddle them right now.

He regretted the thought with a grimace.

If Father hadn't been merciful to me, I would have died in Norgalok.

"Rehils! My kin and allies! Today is a day we will remember for the rest of our lives," Caywen said, her strong voice ringing clear through the air. Woken from his thoughts, Haeryn glanced to Erling and the assembled crowd.

If oratory proves ineffective, then what?

Caywen braced herself against the battlements, holding her chin high with the insistent confidence of one clinging to hope. "Ever since the War of Adrógar, evil has lingered in the shadows—not only in the shadows of this world, but in the darkest corners of our hearts. For centuries, it has awaited the opportune moment to strike, and that moment has finally come. I do not know why we've been chosen to endure this. Why not our ancestors? Or our children's children? I tell you, it is better for us to suffer the throes of war than to abandon our descendants to that fate," she declared. The people stirred.

"I choose to place myself in the path of danger. The men of Rehillon should not suffer alone while their leader looks on from afar. You ask whether we will survive this war and emerge the victors. If I assured you of this, I would make myself out to be a liar. No one knows what the end brings. But if this world should fall, we Rehils will put up such a fight that the enemy will bleed to death even as he triumphs!"

An ear-splitting crack tore through the sky and a gust of air drove into Haeryn's back, throwing him against the ramparts. Debris whistled overhead like arrows, raining down on the town of Hodholm amid a column of smoke. Haeryn winced at the ringing in his ears and scrambled to his feet in a dazed stupor, grasping his bruised ribs as Beydan and Erling helped Caywen to her feet. As the dust settled, Haeryn's mouth dropped.

One of Hodholm's armories—once nestled against the far wall of the courtyard—was gone.

He bolted down the stairs followed by Beydan and Erling. He weaved through the stunned soldiers, darting about to avoid the screaming horses as they stampeded. The men closest to the blast were strewn across the cobblestone, while survivors sought to help the wounded. Fragments of wood, metal, and stone crunched under Haeryn's feet.

He slowed before the smoking ruin, his companions following on his heels. Piles of ash and rubble were scattered throughout the sawtoothed remains. "Who?" he asked.

"Captain Beydan, sir!" a voice shouted. Haeryn turned as a soldier drew up beside them. "Torhalla Westulf is dead," he reported. "We came into her room as she was signaling someone in the courtyard below. She threw herself from her window when she noticed us. We saw a man running into the armory with a torch in his hand."

Beydan's face hardened. Surveying the scene, he twisted the steward's ring on his finger. "Gather the servants for questioning, and pay particular note to those who cared for Torhalla in her confinement. She's convinced one of them to carry out one last act of treachery," he said. Beydan raced back toward the screams of the townsfolk. Haeryn knew what he would tell them. The explosion wasn't a bad omen—just an accident.

Haeryn ground his teeth and knelt. He pressed his palm into the ash and gathered a fistful. In the preparation for the march, the contents of the armory had not yet been distributed among the troops. Duraval bombs, weapons and armor—all obliterated in a spray of smoke and wreckage. Some of the soldiers dug through the wreckage for what they could salvage. Haeryn's lip curled. Torhalla Westulf had reaped the punishment due her, and caused everyone else to suffer along with her.

One final act of disdain.

6

6th of Aevoran, 2211 SE

Blinking to clear the grit from his eyes, Eyoés looked out over the deserts of Amiranoor. Wind swept across mounds of sand, stirring up clouds that twisted and billowed in a silent dance. Slabs of red rock rose from the ground in a maze of canyons choked with sand. Stunted tamarisks offered a paltry relief from the endless horizon. Eyoés licked his cracked lips.

This was the place of his exile.

Sabaah can help us…He must help us…

Falling against the front of the saddle, Eyoés shook his head to clear the dizziness. Sweat burned his eyes. His sweat-soaked shirt clung to his chest and he shielded his eyes with his forearm. Gibusil drifted close to the ground, carried wherever the winds pleased to send him. Gwyndel, Vakros, and Rhoslyn rode on horseback under the protection of a makeshift umbrella of bundled tamarisk branches. The Wardens of the Watch surrounded them, fixated on the navigable route of bare rock weaving between the sand drifts.

No one spoke. Their tongues clung to the roofs of their mouths, the sweltering heat burning away every thought except survival. Torn between sleep and wakefulness, Eyoés was unaware of the passage of time. When his eyes suggested buildings in the distance, he dismissed it. A myth conjured up by the sands and heat. He realized his mistake as the Wardens of the Watch lifted up a cry of joy.

A large plateau of red rock loomed over the flat plain, casting a vast shadow over a broad oasis and the solitary town at its shore. No wall or rampart barred entry—the desert itself decided who was worthy to enter. Mustering his failing strength, Eyoés spurred Gibusil on and the rest of the company eagerly followed. Their arrival did not go unnoticed.

Eyoés felt the eyes of the townsfolk as he landed Gibusil and dismounted. His legs gave out as he touched the ground, pitching him forward. He seized one of Gibusil's saddle straps and heaved himself to his feet. Wiping away the sweat dripping in her eyes, Gwyndel slipped off the saddle of her horse and collapsed into Vakros' arms. Eyoés turned to where the crowd of townspeople stood.

They simply watched, a gust of wind stirring their loose clothing like curtains. Years of labor in the sun had darkened their skin. The scorching heat barely seemed to affect them. Even the children looked on from behind their parents, aloof to the harsh environment.

To them, this was home. To Eyoés, this was an inferno. Considering their reactions, he guessed how desperate he and his companions looked.

Eyoés forced a smile in an effort to conceal his true desperation. "Please. We need shelter. And water. We must get to Tassam," he said, his voice thick. No response. The people's eyes had turned to the Wardens of the Watch, wide with awe.

Uwéllor knelt beside Rhoslyn and offered her a drink of water. "They know we're gahrim," he said, drawing Eyoés' attention to the small abbey placed at the border of the town. The door of the building had been thrown wide open. "They saw us from afar. The few ascetics went to herald our arrival to the town lord."

A commotion rose from behind the crowd, splitting the gathering in two as a small contingent of soldiers appeared. Their fine weapons were clumsy in their hands. Trained soldiery was hard to come by in such a wasteland.

A short, bulky man edged his way through the contingent of bodyguards. His eyes briefly passed over Eyoés and Gwyndel as he turned to the gahrim. As Uwéllor's firm gaze met his own, the man knelt. "In the name of our King and Guide!" he exclaimed.

The Wardens of the Watch gathered around Uwéllor as he motioned for the man to stand. "In the name of our King and Guide," he replied in turn, nodding at Eyoés and the others. "We have guided these here, and we are all in need of shelter and aid."

The man came to his senses and hastened toward Eyoés with a command to his servants. He studied the poor travelers and shook his head. "What a sight," he said, coming alongside and wrapping Eyoés' arm around his shoulder. "How did you manage it?" The man unbuckled a small flask of water from his belt and held it out.

Eyoés took the flask from his hands and pulled the cork. Cool water traced patterns on his dirty cheeks as he gulped it gratefully. "Where are we?" he asked, reveling in the familiar touch of water on his lips. He returned the empty flask into the man's hand.

The nobleman pushed the cork stopper back into the flask. "Sutaquah, I'm afraid. I apologize for the terrible reception—we rarely have visitors, and when we do, they never come from that direction," he said, pointing the way the newcomers had come from. "Sutaquah was once the capital of Amiranoor in the ancient days. But once we became a territory of Alithell, sea trade made Tassam rise in importance. Few bother to cross by land anymore. Due to hazards."

Gwyndel left Rhoslyn with Vakros and staggered alongside. "We're grateful for your hospitality," she said.

The nobleman nodded. "I'm Lord Sarni Benyoun. My father honored guests, as did his father before him. I share my best," he said. "Once you're refreshed, I wish to know why you've come."

Rubbing the soreness from his eyes, Eyoés sagged against the pillow stuffed behind his back. He lifted his eyes, the shimmer of water dancing in the blue and yellow patterns sprawled across the ceiling. After hours in the merciless heat, the cool air drifting over his sunburnt face felt foreign. He propped himself up on an elbow and reached for the cup of water beside him.

In the gentle lanternlight, the walls of the chamber bent and warped to the contours of the small cavern. At its center, a broad, shallow pool rippled silently, save for the gentle bubbling of its origin. The tile floor at the feet of Eyoés' couch seemed to radiate in the glow, sloping down as the pool lapped at it like the tide. Eyoés lifted the cup of water to his lips and admired the place. He could feel the openness of the chamber stretching high above his head.

Fingering the edge of the thin blanket draped over him, he sighed. In the silence of the room, his mind hurried to fill the void.

What becomes of Asdale now?

Even in the midst of the desert, his heart struggled to estrange itself from home. Eyoés gazed at the water's edge, watching it flow across the tiles.

I have seen atrocities and misfortunes reversed. Surely the Guide will do the same again.

The reassurance struck hollow. Eyoés shook his head and laid back on his couch, pulling the covers tight around him in an effort to rest. His heart fell as he bitterly remembered the two young griffins Gibusil and Taesyra had borne, left in the chaos of Asdale's conquest. Surely Santh's brigands would sell them for a high price.

Eyoés laid his arm across his forehead and sighed. He knew Asdale's fate was out of his hands, yet it seized his every thought and made him tremble.

I've been robbed of my home <u>twice</u>. Gwyndel, Vakros, and Rhoslyn have become wandering vagrants along with me. Does the Guide not care?

Even after all he'd seen, there were some things a man couldn't understand. That was the way of things.

Whispers broke the silence. Lifting his head from the pillow, Eyoés looked across the shimmering pool to the other side of the chamber. Gwyndel and Vakros lay exhausted upon their couches, bundled in loose blankets. Eyoés tuned his ear to their voices and pretended to be asleep.

"Rhoslyn is in good hands," Vakros said with a sigh. "You needn't worry about her."

"How much do you think she understands?" Gwyndel whispered.

Vakros paused. "She's six years of age, Gwyndel. Whether she understands or not doesn't make a difference. What are you afraid of?"

Gwyndel sighed. "Our world is growing darker, and I'm a candle. But each day I grow more afraid, more uncertain. The shadows might snuff out the candle before the dawn comes," she answered. The stillness resumed for a time. "I don't want to disappoint her," Gwyndel said.

"Disappoint her? You are no disappointment, my love," Vakros said.

"If only I could be so certain," she said.

"Your heart is what matters, Gwyndel. Without love, even the greatest feats prove meaningless," Vakros said. "Your sacrifices are not in vain."

As their voices fell silent, Eyoés rolled over and threw the blankets aside.

Without love, even the greatest feats prove meaningless...

The aching in his heart gripped him as he watched Asdale's steady decline unfold in his memory. What good had his love for them done? His own people had broken him. Eyoés dipped his hand in the cup of water at his side and wiped his face.

A Hero of Alithell bears the souls of the people on his shoulders. None can accuse me of breaking that promise. But is it worth keeping a promise that could be rendered meaningless by defeat?

Shoes scuffed lightly across the tile floor and Eyoés sat up, swinging his legs over the side of the couch. Lord Sarni Benyoun appeared from behind a pillar, skirting along the edge of the pool as the tails of his tailored robe trailed behind him like ribbons. While clothed in the blessings of aristocracy, the man evoked a certain rustic charm that put one at ease.

As he approached Eyoés, the cheerful expression on Lord Benyoun's face dampened. "Uwéllor told me about Asdale," he said, bowing his head. "I'm sorry for your loss."

Eyoés tightened the belt of his white robe. "I trust Gibusil is alright?" he asked. He was not in the mood to dwell on the tragedy. Not after wrestling with his own difficult questions.

Lord Benyoun politely changed the subject. "Of course. Your gahrim have seen to the griffin's well-being," he said, studying Eyoés with interest. "As Lord of Sutaquah, I appreciate the warning about Falrey's acts of aggression. News is slow coming to this patch of desert."

Eyoés nodded. "I wish we could tell you more. Falrey threatens all of us—but I fear that even if we know his plans in advance, he will play some foul trick on us that will spell our demise," he admitted. "I can't tell you how to ready yourselves for this crisis. I entrust that to you. Until we know better, our only chance is to outrun Falrey." Eyoés stood, smoothing out the blankets of his couch. "Thank you for your hospitality. I must hasten to Tassam before it is too late," he said.

Lord Benyoun laid a hand on Eyoés' shoulder. "You must rest. You'll never make it otherwise. I won't allow such crucial news to perish in my keeping," he insisted. Eyoés studied the man carefully. Then, with a sigh, he rubbed the back of his neck and nodded. As Lord Benyoun departed, he slipped back underneath the blanket.

The fate of the world hung in the balance—and here he lay, watching the storm approach.

Preparations began the next morning. Eyoés cinched the saddle-strap around Gibusil's middle and hefted their supply pack into place. Camels groaned at the rising desert sun, chided by their riders in a peculiar language that hissed like the shifting sands. A hand grasped Eyoés by the shoulder and he turned as Lord Benyoun extended a skin of water. "Thank you," he said, attaching the waterskin safely to the saddle. "Your hospitality is refreshing in a world that's lost its senses."

Lord Benyoun smiled with a humble nod. "The Guide brings us guests on the sands, and we share the blessings we've been given. This is what we've always done," he replied, motioning toward the camels. "They will take good care of your men." The riders wrapped linen shawls around their faces, bantering among themselves as they secured food, water, and tents for the journey. Vakros and the Wardens of the Watch lent a hand where they could while Rhoslyn played in the sand.

Eyoés took a piece of linen from his saddlebags and tried to shroud his head in the correct manner. "A three days' journey to Tassam, you say?"

Lord Benyoun took the linen from Eyoés hand and lent his expertise. "On camel. The griffin should take you only a day if all goes well. Remain on a northeasterly course and you'll arrive at the capital," he said.

Slinging an extra waterskin over her shoulder, Gwyndel rubbed Gibusil's neck. "Dawn is waning quickly. Best to get moving," she said, passing the skin to her brother as she turned to Benyoun. Eyoés caught her nervous glance at Rhoslyn. "Three days. Are they prepared enough?"

Lord Benyoun graciously acknowledged her doubts and placed a reassuring hand on her shoulder.

"These men rove the deserts for weeks on end. Your daughter is in good hands," he said. He studied the Wards of the Watch. "Besides, the gahrim are a blessing in themselves."

Climbing onto Gibusil's back, Eyoés watched Gwyndel embrace Vakros and Rhoslyn as he took up the reins. "I agree. But sometimes I wonder if a blessing is enough."

7

25th of Thurdál, 2211 SE, Weomor

As Haeryn Irongaze ventured into the charred ruins of Weomor, he passed into another world. The smell of mildew hung thick in the air, and somewhere within the labyrinth, a crow's wings rustled as it took flight. Crumbling walls teetered on either side of the abandoned causeway. Haeryn clasped the pommel of his sword, his confident stride wavering. He half expected the ruins to crumble and bury him in rubble.

Haeryn shivered as the soldiers behind him urged him further and further into the maze. Even with them nearby, he could not shake the vulnerability that gripped him. His eyes drifted to the black streaks of ash marking the walls. He could almost feel the flames singeing his skin as he imagined them rushing through the streets. Even the gravel crunching underfoot reminded him of broken bones, bringing unwelcome memories of Kinsfolk sacrifices and their aftermath. While the story of Aunt Gwyndel's escape from Weomor had always chilled him, Haeryn had assumed she'd added a measure of exaggeration to make the story more memorable.

How wrong he had been.

As he passed under a lone archway, he kept a watchful eye on the shadowy crevices and empty corridors among the ruins. He dare not turn his back to them. "This place feels—*cursed*," Haeryn said, eyes narrowed.

Beside him, Erling clenched his fist and looked away. Haeryn pulled his gaze from the shadows and studied his companion. His curiosity died as he saw the emotion in Erling's eyes.

Erling sighed. "The Ravenstrongs are responsible for this," he said, looking up at the ash-streaked walls. "It's not spoken of often. The memory is a stain upon Rehillon's history that is better off forgotten."

This carnage was a monument to cruelty. Haeryn dropped the matter like a hot iron, stopping his ears to the wind whispering through the web of causeways. He felt Weomor's poison touch too keenly. A gap opened in the ruins, and Haeryn slowed to a halt. He caught his breath.

The abandoned tower loomed above them. Black marks streaked down its sides like dried blood. Where the upper reaches of the keep had once kept watch, only crumbled masonry remained, black and jagged against the sky. Haeryn shivered. Gwyndel had once stood there, years ago, surrounded by a firestorm with no hope of escape.

Startled by the sound of Caywen and Jaaye riding past him on their horses, Haeryn hastened to join them. He glanced back to where Hjarti awkwardly ducked under an archway. Dovarul rode with the officers, twisting the reins of his horse as he fixed his lone eye upon the path ahead of him. Haeryn could see he wasn't the only one unsettled.

The causeway broadened and deposited them in the shadow of the tower before veering around the stinking moat at its base. Haeryn wrinkled his nose at the fetid stench of rotting vegetation. He leaned against Jaaye's horse, rubbing at his nose. Across the weather-bleached bridge, a twisted skeleton lay before the gates directly below an uppermost window. A victim of the Phantom League. Haeryn shivered.

That could've been Aunt Gwyndel.

Jaaye squirmed in her saddle, pulling her mantle tight against the chill in the air. Her hand slipped into the folds of her cloak, and Haeryn glimpsed the strange phial of golden liquid clutched in her fingers. As Jaaye turned aside and took a quick gulp, he glanced at Caywen. The Baroness of Rehillon swept her eyes across the ruins, oblivious to her companion's secretive behavior.

Haeryn broke the silence. "Lord Bardmond and Lord Crawbrand may be late," he remarked, brow furrowed as Jaaye choked and stuffed the phial away.

Caywen tapped the saddlehorn and pursed her lips. "By the time Lord Gerall's letter of confirmation arrived in Hodholm, he'd already departed for Weomor. The messenger from Andieff made that clear. If all is well, they'll be here," she said. Haeryn studied her in wonder. The certainty Caywen exuded still struck him as remarkable. Even so, the air of formality surrounding her made it difficult for him to approach her. After the deaths of Vikar and Gwair, that sense of emotional detachment had only increased.

Hjarti's footsteps thundered as he drew up beside them and sat. His stocky limbs pulled inward to avoid touching the crumbling walls. Haeryn braced himself, expecting the giant's booming voice to bring a cloud of dust upon their heads. Hjarti said nothing—no joke to brighten their spirits. Lifting his eyes to the tower, the giant merely stared.

Dovarul dismounted his horse and patted Thridd's head as the dragon landed on the saddle to await his return. "It never gets easier, seeing the consequences of a tragedy," he said under his breath. He caught Haeryn's eye. "Norgalok was even worse. Testaments of this kind of destruction everywhere you look. You were too young to know any better," he admitted.

Haeryn nodded absentmindedly. He would not dwell on it.

The rhythm of marching feet broke the eerie stillness, and all eyes turned toward the sound. A large company of soldiers rounded a bend in the path ahead, packed together like crushed twigs as they fit through the narrow street. Their streaming pennants whipped sideways as the wind shifted, revealing two standards —one of an eagle's head and one of a ram reared to strike. Among the ranks, some of the soldiers wore the emblem of the Northern Guard. Lord Gerall Bardmond and Agnar Crawbrand rode at the head, signaling for the company to halt.

Bardmond approached Caywen with a nod of respect. "I have answered your summons, my lady. The people of Andieff and I are honored to extend our allegiance in the greatest conflict of our time," he said.

Lord Crawbrand gestured to the men behind him. "These confined ruins kept us from presenting our full detachments to you. We left the others with the rest of your army outside Weomor."

Caywen smiled. "Excellent. We will discuss strategy and deployment this evening. In the meantime," she said as she looked out across the gathering, "I wished to speak to the men."

Haeryn clasped his hands behind his back and turned his watchful eye on the ranks. The men stood at attention, some hastily breaking off quiet conversation.

Caywen gathered her words. "We Rehils are one people now. No quarrels will be tolerated in these ranks. You will remember that," she declared. "Once we leave our homeland, other territories will join our cause. Edeveros will be the first. If we cannot learn unity, Falrey will trample us into the mud."

Caywen's eyes narrowed as she held the attention of every soul in sight. "There will be no raiding or looting. Victory does not justify merciless cruelty," she said. "If we are to save this world, it must be with a clean conscience."

Jaaye stiffened, and Haeryn froze as he recognized the angry glint in her eyes. She brought her horse around, nostrils flaring as she glared at Caywen. "Victory belongs to the daring," she said. Haeryn knew what was coming.

Dovarul started forward to break up the confrontation before it could begin. Caywen locked eyes with Jaaye and held out a hand to stay him. She embraced the challenge. "Reckless zeal will only harm our cause," she said.

Jaaye bristled. "War demands the most cruel part of ourselves. No matter how 'distasteful' that might be to your delicate senses," she said, lip curled as she eyed Caywen from head to toe. "I will do *anything* to seize victory. Will you?" The men stirred.

Caywen's eyes narrowed. "Should others pay for Falrey's crimes? Those who've fallen under his spell— should they suffer for his cunning? We save our wrath for Falrey himself, not those who he's trodden upon," she said.

The murmuring of the men silenced Jaaye. Grinding her teeth, she bowed her head as Caywen spurred her horse and motioned for the troops to march out of the ruins.

As the soldiers of Rehillon marched out of Weomor, Jaaye and Caywen led the way, the hostility between them poignant in the silence. Haeryn clenched his fists. Even in her madness, Jaaye had spoken the truth. Caywen's high-minded ideals would never survive the strains of war.

If Falrey fights with iron claws, we must do the same.

8

3ʳᵈ of Aevoran, 2211 SE

The wind whipped beneath Taesyra's wings as the gale shoved her to the side. Huddling low in the saddle, Haeryn corrected their course, teeth chattering. The fierce cold of the windstorm bit through the hood of his cloak, jumbling his thoughts as he fought to tighten the scarf wrapped around his neck. A man on campaign was a man who suffered.

Squinting in the wind, Haeryn looked over the thick column of men marching across the open moorland. The ranks seemed to ripple like waves as the overcast light glinted off their helmets. Streaming banners danced over their heads. The cavalry rode at the fore, wrapping around the front ranks like a bulwark. The archers followed immediately behind.

Haeryn grinned in admiration. They marched for the restoration of their world—and the thrill of it put a strength in his bones that the cold couldn't diminish. It invigorated him.

Haeryn glanced back as the Northern Passage shrank on the horizon. The grand towers seemed small in comparison to the vast stretch of land greeting the Rehil army. Wooded hills spilled out upon the open moors like spread fingers. Through a gap in the hills,

Haeryn glimpsed the sparkling River Myrch. Past its shores, the *real* war would begin.

He urged Taesyra on and the griffin swooped down toward the army. As she landed beside Dovarul and Hjarti, the giant jumped and edged away. Haeryn raised an eyebrow and set the reins aside. "Still?" he asked with a hint of mischief. The giant's enduring fear of birds was ironic.

Thridd landed on Hjarti's shoulder, nudging her small head against his thick neck. The giant reached up and stroked the dragon's back with his finger, watching Taesyra like a hawk. "That beast and I haven't come to an understanding. Not yet. Maybe never," he said, stiffening as the griffin ventured closer.

Dovarul suppressed a smile and patted the neck of his horse. "You're right, Hjarti. Some things never change," he said. Before the giant could reply, the dwarf pointed to the head of the company. Jaaye and Caywen led the foremost ranks at a brisk pace, each taking pains to distance themselves from the other. Dovarul shook his head. "Seems to me our friends are bonding," he said.

Haeryn glanced sidelong at his companions. "They'll lead the army well enough," he said curtly.

Dovarul raised an eyebrow and grunted. "Not for long, I fear. Division will fracture our war effort and pollute the ranks. You would think two clever, mature women would be able to settle their differences. At least until all this is over. We both share a common enemy, after all," he said. Hjarti nodded in agreement.

Haeryn let the matter drop. Running his fingers through Taesyra's feathers, he shook his head softly. His friends had picked the side of prudence. But perhaps it was best to set aside their differing ideologies.

And if we can't agree on what justice means?

Haeryn clenched his jaw and forced his thoughts into other directions.

The Edeverans will help unite us.

He imagined the grand banners of the Knights of the Lance as they rode to the aid of their fellow rebels, with Neifon and Marc leading the way. In this time of crisis, the wisdom of old friends would be more than welcome.

A shout rose from the front lines. Snapped awake, Haeryn caught sight of a scout approaching Caywen and Jaaye on horseback. At his brisk command, Taesyra charged forward and leapt, gliding low as she passed over the army in a blur. Haeryn grunted as the griffin landed roughly beside Jaaye and Caywen.

The scout drew rein. "Edeveran reinforcements approaching," he cried above the wind. As he caught the glint of hope in their eyes, the man shook his head and pointed in the direction he'd come. "You're not going to like what you see," he said, wheeling his horse around to join the rest of the scouts.

No sooner had he spoken than the galloping of hooves pulsed in the earth. Haeryn squinted. Out of the forested hills, a mounted cavalry thundered down toward the Rehil host. Their tattered banners thrashed in the wind like strings. Holding his breath, Haeryn waited for the remainder of the Edeveran host to appear.

Only there was just a small, ragged band.

The mighty Knights of the Lance limped toward their allies, their horses frothing at the mouth as they drew rein. At their head, a young knight sat slumped in his saddle, lifting his bowed head with considerable effort. Haeryn froze. "Marc?" he said, mouth agape as he took in the man's bleary eyes and unkempt hair.

Marc swayed unsteadily, mustering a weak smile before his head sagged to his chest. Several of the Rehil scouts dashed forward and caught him as he tumbled from his saddle. A second rider pushed to the front of the Knights of the Lance and Haeryn paled.

Neifon sat rigid in the saddle, one hand firmly clutching the saddlehorn for support. His stately clothing hung stained and torn upon his slim body. Tears welled in Haeryn's eyes, and he met his friend's weary gaze.

A movement drew Haeryn's attention to the small figure seated in front of Neifon. His heart sank as he saw little Ancelet peering out at the ranks of gruff men. A young child without a mother. Haeryn's eyes widened.

Shivering in the wind, Neifon fought to hold himself with dignity. "Edeveros is lost. Raulin and Roseen are dead, Haeryn. Mithlon and Gahidros have fallen, and we managed to escape with nearly a hundred men-at-arms and some meager supplies," he said. "Hurry, he's right behind—"

Haeryn studied the Knights of the Lance and swallowed hard. "Where are they now?" He caught the snorting of horses on the wind and noticed the fear in Neifon's eyes.

A horde of men and horses crested the hill and drew rein under Falrey O'Dyre's banner. Shouts rang out as the Rehils hastened to formation. Motioning to a scout, Caywen pointed at Ancelet. "Take the child to Hodholm," she commanded. Neifon squeezed the boy one final time before the scout whisked him away toward the Northern Passage.

The enemy merely watched in silence. Haeryn held his breath.

A lone horseman separated from the enemy army and rode forward to the edge of an outcrop. Shielding his eyes, Haeryn frowned and studied the figure intently. Though the distance obscured his face, his manner was eerily familiar. It seemed to Haeryn that the figure was waiting for some sign of recognition.

It hit him.

Santh Baklyn?

A sense of foreboding sent a shudder through Haeryn's body. The utter confidence, the appearance of total control—he could recognize it anywhere. Last he'd known, Santh had been under his father's authority. Now, on the other side of the world, he rode under Falrey's banner.

Something had happened to Asdale. To Eyoés. To Gwyndel.

Nausea struck Haeryn with such force he nearly doubled over. He gripped the saddlehorn. Blood pounded in his ears and he bared his teeth, his thoughts jumbled in a tempest of rage. He yanked his sword free and snatched up the reins. Taesyra sensed his anger and coiled to spring. The odds against them were high—but he welcomed the chance with open arms. It was time to break one of Falrey's poisonous fingers.

I'll beat that traitor to the ground.

With a fanfare of blaring horns, the armies charged each other.

9

In a spray of mud, the spark of war kindled into a roaring fire. The Rehils formed a schiltrom of spears to ward off Santh's advancing cavalry and Falrey's archers loosed a volley. Screams filled the air as the arrows struck their mark seconds before the enemy cavalry crashed into the Rehils, the two armies spilling over into each other like opposing headwaters. Maddened blades glistened like ocean waves and the cavalry punched through the Rehil and Edeveran lines, leaving a wake of dead as they circled back to retrieve fresh lances. The enemy infantry followed immediately behind, closing the distance before the Rehils could recover. The churned mud around the soldiers' ankles turned a deep crimson, seeping out of the battlefield into the nearby grass.

Haeryn became wrath itself.

He drove Taesyra over the men's heads, dodging arrows as she collided into Santh's regrouping cavalry, scattering them like chaff on the threshing floor. Wheeling the griffin around, he set upon the enemy infantry from the rear, driving them deeper into the sea of Rehils and Edeverans enveloping them. Snatching a soldier's spear, he hurled it, pinning an enemy officer to the ground. Taesyra swept her tail into an enemy squadron, scattering their pikes like sticks. Haeryn swerved the griffin toward two enemy riders and trampled them into the mud as the Knights of the Lance crashed into the Falrey's troops from the side. Through the chaos, Haeryn glimpsed Santh.

Hands resting on the saddlehorn, the traitor watched the battle unfold with cool disinterest.

Heaving on the reins with a roar, Haeryn brought the griffin around and took to the sky, hurtling toward Santh. The man took up the reins as the griffin shot toward him.

Santh spurred his horse and galloped into the trees. Haeryn yanked back on the reins and Taesyra ground to a halt before she collided into the forest. He cursed under his breath.

Santh would have to wait.

Caywen's ears rang at the screams of dying men and horses. Her heart pounded. As Neifon and the weary survivors from Edeveros lingered in the protection of several mounted Rehils, the Knights of the Lance charged into the fray—and she watched one of them fall, encircled by a group of spearmen who pinned him to the ground.

Hjarti and Dovarul welcomed the conflict. They tore through the enemy with Thridd leading the way with a scorching column of fire. The Freechildren followed close behind with Jaaye at their head, unleashing years of suffering upon Falrey's soldiers.

Caywen had suffered with them—and she would fight with them.

Feeling the chainmail shirt beneath her clothes, she exhaled and spurred her horse on. The protests of her officers were lost to the din of battle. Drawing her sword, she paled at the bodies of her kinsfolk lying bloodied and broken around her. A small group of Rehils broke away from their unit, pursued by three of Falrey's spearmen, and Caywen's heart turned cold as they were slaughtered before her eyes. The largest of the men yanked his spear free and wiped the sweat from his brow.

His eyes locked on Caywen and her insides turned. "You lost, woman?" he asked, eyes flashing. He bellowed a laugh and pointed his bloodied spearhead at her. "My lady wants some excitement!" he shouted, a venomous grin spreading across his face.

Caywen spurred her horse with a cry and raised her sword. Immediately the men spread out, surrounding her horse as she swung at empty air. A spear darted out and the horse reared with a whinny of pain. Caywen clawed at the air as the horse toppled and flung her to the ground, driving the air from her lungs.

Eyes bulging, Caywen stared up at her enemies. Panic seized her as the men laughed at her helplessness. Gasping for tiny breaths, she reached for her fallen sword as one of the men kicked it away. They peered down with savage grins. She was merely a dying bird to them.

Erling sprang from his galloping horse and rolled to his feet. The soldiers stumbled away as the horse reared, wildly flailing its hooves. Snatching a fallen halberd, Erling struck before the men could unite, cleaving one man's helmet before sweeping another's legs out from under him. Caywen watched dumbfounded as Erling leapt over her and tackled the last soldier. The two of them hit the ground and the man clawed at the young scout's helmet to tear it off. Erling clung to the spearman and drew his dagger, driving it into his collar. The man's grip loosened.

Caywen heaved herself to her knees. As she took a deep, trembling breath, she gaped at Erling. "I'm in your debt," she wheezed.

Erling wrapped her arm around his shoulder and hoisted her to her feet. "And I've repaid one long overdue," he said, ushering her to his horse.

Santh still had not shown his face.

With a crimson wake behind him, Haeryn brought Taesyra around and turned toward the forest. The boughs of the trees hung motionless. Even the wind had grown quiet as the violence unfolded.

Gritting his teeth, he urged Taesyra into a dive, the griffin sweeping her claws through Santh's ranks like a scythe. Haeryn leaned into the wind, letting it surge through his hair. It comforted him, letting loose his anger at the world upon those who deserved it. After months of talk, Falrey's reckoning had finally become a reality.

But where was Santh?

The sound of horns caught Haeryn by surprise. Taesyra banked to the side and he looked out over the battlefield. His breath caught in his throat. Santh's forces withdrew, pulling back toward the hill from which they'd come. Stragglers dotted the muddy fields, scampering over the bodies strewn about like chaff.

Santh's forces are withdrawing! Why don't we pursue?

Haeryn caught sight of Erling riding back from the edge of the battlefield, heading toward the officers and supply wagons with Caywen seated behind him. With another blast of horns, the Rehil forces took flight to the east.

Haeryn's face twisted as he hovered in the air, Taesyra's reins dangling loosely in his hand. He gazed down at the forest's edge, straining to catch the slightest glimpse of Santh. Again, the horns beckoned him. He clenched his jaw. The quick battle had already been costly. Caywen, Jaaye, and Marc could not risk a prolonged engagement after taking losses. No matter their zeal. While he understood it, Haeryn still wrestled.

An agonizing growl seethed past his lips and he wrenched himself away, soaring to rejoin Caywen's fleeing forces.

1◊

Santh crept out from the forest's shadows like a viper from its den, drawing rein as Caywen's army fled to the hills like roaches. He sighed and looked out across the fallen. Ravens had already begun to gather, croaking as they alighted on the dead. Santh shook his head and twisted the reins around his finger.

He couldn't help but pity the rebels for their zealous ignorance. In their devotion to the old ways, the insurgents idealized the past and clung to false pretense. When challenged otherwise, they rushed to arms and fought tooth and nail to preserve the last vestiges of their blindness. Like a man addicted to Ossinder, always seeking to avoid the painful truth. It was times like this that made him appreciate his awareness of the truth.

He was a lucky man.

He clicked his tongue and guided his horse to where his forces gathered. Huddling together at the crest of the hill, they nursed their wounds in the shadow of Falrey's banner. One of Santh's aides saw him approach and rode out to intercept him.

Stroking his horse's mane with a few gentle words, Santh slowed to a halt as the man drew up beside him. "How many men did we lose?" he asked.

The officer frowned and swept his gaze across the battlefield. "Perhaps sixty or less," he replied. "When the census is taken, we'll have a better reckoning."

Santh nodded to himself. "Had we managed to wholly eradicate the Edeverans beforehand, the element of surprise would have been ours," he said. "We will have to be more thorough in the future to avoid ruining our chances." He inwardly chafed at Falrey's unwillingness to place fallen gahrim under his command. Their numbers were few and reserved for his Majesty's main force. Santh clenched his jaw. Under Commander Ros' leadership, the gahrim would remain at Falrey's side with the Baronsguard of Garifell. Here, they would have been put to better use. He was convinced of it.

The aide glanced at Santh and pointed to the distant army fleeing into the hills. "Why did we fall back and let them run? Our forces outnumber them," he remarked. Santh could see the lust for conquest glinting in the man's eyes like forbidden gold.

Shaking his head, he turned his horse away with a sigh. "It is tempting, but we can't risk further losses. His Majesty has devised a far more cunning plan," he said. "For now, we pursue the rebels from a distance. Let them grow comfortable. When they least expect it, old ghosts will come knocking."

The officer frowned. "And if that fails?"

Santh waved the question aside. "Then we close in and drive them into his Majesty's claws. They will be the cattle, we will be the herdsmen."

With a longing glance at the fleeing rebels, the aide spurred his horse and rejoined the rest of the officers to spread the word. Turning back in the saddle, Santh watched the last of Caywen's forces disappear among the hills. His eyes narrowed as he caught sight of the griffin following the Rehils. Even miles from Asdale, the legacy of Eyoés still left its fetid mark. Santh had had enough.

I will finish what I started in Asdale.

11

9th of Aevoran, 2211 SE

Sabaah tossed the bracelet back into the pile of jewelry, suppressing a grin as the fine silver glinted in the sunlight. He shook his head and snorted in mock disgust. "It's no good!" he declared with an exasperated wave of his hand. "I could find a *quality* specimen from Taekoharan traders."

The merchant scowled, leaning against the pillar of his stall with a sigh. "But those shipments come every few months! Why wait?" he countered, locking eyes with Sabaah in search of a new angle.

Sabaah bowed his head in concession. "I am a patient man," he said, tapping the edge of the counter as he studied the displayed merchandise for a fourth time. As his eyes drifted over glinting jewels, he gathered his thoughts. Most other merchants honored his status as a member of the court and surrendered without complaint. This man, however, refused to back down so easily—and Sabaah relished the challenge. There was no telling when he'd stumble upon a catch like this again.

Taking up a different necklace with feigned disinterest, Sabaah let the beads click through his fingers. "How much for this?"

The merchant's eyes narrowed. "Two hundred and thirty."

Sabaah pursed his lips as he examined the ruby inlays. "One hundred and ninety," he shot back.

The merchant grimaced, dabbing sweat from his brow with the edge of his sleeve. "Absolutely not," he said. "Such a price would break me. The lowest I can stoop is two hundred and fifteen."

Sabaah's head shot up. "Two hundred even," he said. The merchant wavered, eying the necklace in Sabaah's hands with longing. Once he saw the uncertainty in the man's eye, Sabaah knew his chances had grown. A flicker of movement drew his eyes behind the merchant stand.

Three little girls peered out from the door of the shop, their tattered dresses hanging like drapes over their shoulders. Sabaah glanced at the merchant, considering his latest offer. It wouldn't have been the first time someone had attempted to put on the appearance of poverty to soften a customer's heart— but this seemed genuine.

The merchant noticed Sabaah's hesitation and followed his gaze. At the sight of his three children in the doorway, the man's eyes widened and he shooed the girls away with his hand. "Go back inside! I'll not have you making us look dishonest!" he said. Sabaah blinked, and the children were gone.

Before the man could apologize, Sabaah extended a hand to silence him. "I will pay a two hundred and twenty," he said.

The man's face softened. "Only ten lower than the original price," he said, studying Sabaah.

Sabaah's hand dipped into his pouch and he placed the coins firmly on the counter. "If you need the Castle Sanctum's aid, don't hesitate. I'll put in a good word," he said. Nodding his head, the man scraped up the coins and tucked them away, watching in bewilderment as Sabaah and his armed escort continued down the street.

Glancing back to the merchant's stall, the captain of Sabaah's guard quickened his steps and shook his head. "That's the third necklace you've bought today," he said, watching as the Hero twirled the necklace around his finger. "All for Kahnna's birthday?"

Sabaah smiled. "She'll appreciate having several options. I've been her godfather for eighteen years now, and I don't plan to stop being generous," he said, glancing back at his companion. "If you're worried about some merchant's pockets, Razeem, I'll sell whatever necklaces Kahnna turns down. The proceeds will go to the poor." The old soldier nodded to himself and Sabaah turned back to the path ahead, weaving around a cart of papyrus reeds as it lumbered through the crowds.

Shaking sand out of his shoe, he took a deep breath of the fresh, salty air drifting in from the coast. In a landscape of arid desert, Tassam was a flourishing burst of color, spilling out toward the ocean. With every year that passed, he counted himself lucky to enjoy it. Canopies of brightly-dyed linen draped over the streets to offer shade. The scent of spices drifted from the windows of lofty adobe houses, and the occasional burst of music meandered through the hum of conversation. Merchants cried out to passersby with arms laden with goods. And like a fine delicacy, the lush air of the delta tied all together, carrying a dampness with it.

Sabaah lifted his eyes to where the rooftops ended, catching a brief glimpse of the ancient palace looming overhead before the canopies obstructed his view. His face brightened. He could almost imagine Kahnna laboring tirelessly within those corridors, immersed in healer's lore. It wouldn't have been the first time she'd forgotten her own birthday.

Her father would have been proud.

Sabaah's smile faded. He slipped the necklace in his satchel along with the others. The honor of being a godfather often obscured the grisly truth that enabled it. He was a fool to think he could keep the memory buried.

They remember. Kahnna weeps in secret. Wisam refuses to speak of it. What am I trying to prove? That I can shoulder both the roles of father and mother?

He glanced over his shoulder to where Razeem studied him. "You're thinking about them again, aren't you?" the man asked, motioning for the rest of the escort to give them space.

Sabaah quickly smiled and forced himself to think positively. "Wisam and Kahnna know I love them like my own children. They *know*," he insisted. He quieted his thoughts before the matter could be brought up again.

He wiped the sweat from his brow before it trickled into his eye. Had the council with the shipmen's guild not detained him, he would've attended to his errands before the heat of the day settled in. With a sigh, Sabaah stepped into a sheltered alcove and gathered his bearings, shielding his eyes from the sun. He hesitated.

A distant shape glided across the sky, wobbling as it grew closer. Razeem followed Sabaah's gaze and frowned. "What is it?" he asked.

As the shape grew rapidly in his vision, Sabaah's eyes widened. "It's a griffin," he said. His stomach sank and he wheeled around to face his escort. "It's not slowing down!" The soldiers scrambled into position, yelling at the crowd to take shelter.

A weak screech echoed through the open air—and the griffin hurtled to the ground in a blur, tearing through the linen canopies like a stray arrow as it clipped the edge of a roof in a spray of broken tiles. The griffin scrambled to slow itself down and land, raking its claws along the adobe walls and barreling through merchant stalls as it came to rest in a cloud of dust in the wide street.

Coughing from the dust, Sabaah darted out of the alcove with his escort following, scimitars drawn. They skidded to a halt as the dust settled, revealing a mass of golden feathers. He gasped at the sight.

Gibusil?

Sabaah gave a sharp command and the soldiers gathered around the fallen griffin. Their haste doubled as they stumbled upon Eyoés and Gwyndel lying slumped in the saddle. He paled and rushed to Eyoés' side, pressing two fingers to his friend's neck. "He's still alive," he said.

"So is this one," Razeem said, kneeling beside Gwyndel. "They're all suffering from heat exhaustion. Baasim, Rusad! Summon a company from the palace guard and tell them to bring the largest wagon they can find. We'll take the griffin to shelter and the poor souls to the palace."

Sabaah cradled Eyoés' head on his knee.

Friend, what brought you here?

Gwyndel woke to darkness and a throbbing headache.

Pressing a hand to her forehead with a groan, she sat up, peering into the shadows. The coolness of the air caught her by surprise. As her eyes adjusted to the dim light, her mind cleared, piecing together vague memories between the throbbing pains in her skull. They had set out for Tassam she knew. After that, she'd lost track of the hours. She stretched her sore limbs as her memory of the crash returned with the haziness of a dream. Her cheeks flushed at the thought. It was certainly not the kind of arrival she'd had in mind.

Grasping her cool, moist blankets, she set them aside gingerly and stood. The shimmer of water drew her attention to a bucket lying at the foot of her bed, accompanied by a dripping cloth draped over its side. Across the room, a stream of light caught her eye and she approached it, her loose white dress billowing behind her. She brushed aside the curtains and immediately squinted as the deep orange light of evening flooded into the room.

She gasped.

A masterpiece of color greeted her. Adobe houses crowded together under the rich glow of twilight, the vibrant hues of the streets weaving among them like the veins of a pied leaf. A scattered flock of seagulls cried out as they drifted above the city. On the horizon, the sun sank gracefully into the ocean, and the rippling waves sparkled like golden lightning. Gwyndel found her eyes drawn to an array of towers silhouetted against the skyline, a sculpted granite hand extending from every spire in supplication. Nestled among the towers sat a collection of domed cloisters. The clang of bells rang bright and clear as the streets settled in for the night.

The Castle Sanctum—the jewel of the East and a refuge of sanity in a crazed world. Even though she'd never seen it, she recognized the place. The sight brought tears to her eyes.

Gwyndel sank against the windowsill, hypnotized. The longer she gazed down at the monastery, the more the fog in her mind dissipated. Her vision sharpened, and the glow of the Sword Imperishable warmed the palm of her hand. Not all the world was lost to darkness—here, the truth lived on. A smile brightened her face. She carried a message of hope. If the Castle

Sanctum endured despite the world's decay, what did it matter if the dying world did not listen to her?

She stepped back from the window and looked around the room. Minuscule designs covered the walls, carved into fine stone and painted on colorful tiling. The soft touch of a red and gold Amiranooran rug cradled her bare feet. Embroidered pillows were scattered carelessly at the end of her couch, and the fine aroma of incense hung in the air. Gwyndel caught the sound of splashing water, noticing a faint glow underneath a nearby door. After all the hours of sweat and sand, Eyoés wasn't the only one in need of a good washing.

The main door clicked open and Gwyndel turned, fastening the belt of her white robe. A young woman slipped inside and shut the door behind her. Her silvery dress, edged with golden trim, glistened as she bowed. Her curly black hair bounced, making her thin, dark-skinned face seem even thinner in comparison. "I see you're awake," she said, striding over to the bucket of water placed at the foot of Gwyndel's bed. "You both slept for hours. Sabaah and my brother feared you had gone past recovery, but I could see the signs."

Gwyndel studied the woman. "You cared for us all this time?"

The woman lifted the bucket with a grunt and carried it to the windowsill, dumping its contents out onto the courtyard far below. "It's no trouble. I'm honored to care for a guest," she said, glancing back at Gwyndel. "I'm Kahnna."

Gwyndel smiled, eying Kahnna's dress curiously. "Gwyndel. If I'm honest, I didn't expect a noblewoman to wait on guests," she said.

Depositing the bucket in a corner of the room, Kahnna caught Gwyndel's eye with a smile. "I've always held a particular dislike for that title. Noblewoman. No matter how many times my brother insists, I prefer to set my eyes on more practical pursuits. Pursuits that can help people," she explained, adjusting her necklace.

Gwyndel collapsed into a nearby chair with a sigh and pulled her hair back into the beginnings of a braid. "Your brother—I assume he's one of the court?" she said.

Kahnna nodded with a laugh. "My brother is Baron Wisam, though many can't spot the family resemblance," she said.

The door to the washroom opened and Eyoés strode out, tying the belt of his robe. "I can finally breathe without choking on dust," he mumbled to himself. He flushed at the sight of Kahnna and fastened another few buttons on his robe. Gwyndel bit back a smile.

Kahnna ignored Eyoés' embarrassment. "Sabaah and my brother Wisam are hosting a feast tomorrow night. You would be most welcome," she said.

Clearing his throat, Eyoés combed his fingers through his hair. "We'd be honored," he answered.

With a gracious smile, Kahnna bowed and started for the door. "But first, rest. Then we'll be expecting you," she said, leaving the room.

Eyoés paused, fingering the upper button of his robe. The woman's tone was probing.

She wonders why we're here. She won't be the only one.

12

10th of Aevoran, 2211 SE

Gwyndel let out her breath as she drew Fóbehn's bowstring to her cheek and sighted along the arrow. Her peripheral vision faded. Fixing a single eye on the straw target, she released.

The arrow sailed from her hand, tearing through the target and disappearing into the sandbank behind it. With a sigh, she lowered Fóbehn and watched the arrow materialize in the quiver, nestled among its brothers like it never left.

Rolling her shoulders to ease the tightness in her neck, she selected another arrow. She'd found a solace in archery as a Forester, seeking out remote places to practice her craft and lay aside the worries of the day. She drew another arrow and released, walking over to the target to examine the hole it left behind. After a long night's rest, her bed had grown tiresome.

"On your feet again, I see." Gwyndel turned as Kahnna entered the indoor archery range with a tray of wine and dried dates. The woman set the tray on a nearby bench and examined the target from afar. "You're not one to rest on your laurels longer than necessary," she remarked.

Gwyndel smiled. "I rest when I need it. Sometimes longer, though I try to stay disciplined," she said.

Kahnna raised an eyebrow and poured a cup of rich wine. "Ambitious *and* honest. It's not often that you find both," she mused. Gwyndel let the compliment roll off her shoulders.

Wandering back to her quiver, she set aside Fóbehn and took up a handful of dates. "I want to thank you again for caring for me and Eyoés," she said. "In these times, there aren't many people willing to welcome strangers and show them kindness."

Kahnna's smile waned as she handed her a cup of wine and poured another for herself. "It truly is an honor. For some, hospitality is more of an obligation that our traditions have made stagnant," she admitted. "I want to change that. I strive for a better Amiranoor."

Gwyndel's brow furrowed. "A better Amiranoor? I've dreamt of this place, of the Sanctum, wondering what it would be like. The clang of the bells, the smell of spices in the markets," she said, popping a sweet date into her mouth. "It's even better than I imagined."

Fingering the edge of her cup, Kahnna sank down on the bench. "Peace is easy to find for some. But not for others," she said. "For me, it's long in coming." She stared at the floor, seeming to shrink in the silence.

Gwyndel wavered. Painful memories of Asdale welled up in the void and the sinking feeling in her stomach returned. She'd fought it off for hours. Yet no matter what she did, books, archery, and conversation only numbed the pain momentarily. Taking a deep breath, she set aside her cup of wine.

Peace. It seems so simple. Why is it so elusive?

79

"I know how you feel," she said, eyes softening as she studied Kahnna, "and you don't need to explain everything to me. Turn toward peace and pursue it, and it will guard your heart."

Kahnna lifted her glistening eyes and mustered a weak smile. "All will be made right for me one day," she sighed, wiping tears away with the back of her hand. "I'm sorry—I don't know what came over me. Sabaah told me about you, your wisdom and abilities. I guess I just wanted to see for myself." She set her cup aside and hastened away.

Gwyndel snatched up Fóbehn and held it out. "Here," she said. "Try a shot. Maybe it'll help you clear your mind too."

Kahnna paused, eying the weapon reluctantly. "I'm unworthy," she insisted.

Gwyndel shook her head. "Please."

Kahnna's eyes lingered on the weapon. Then, smoothing her dress, she took the weapon gingerly from Gwyndel's hand and fingered the bowstring. Pulling an arrow from the quiver, Gwyndel nocked it and pointed toward the target. "Take a deep breath and exhale as you draw. There's no wind or elevation to hinder you," she instructed.

Kahnna took a deep breath and hoisted the weapon, easing into the draw as she sighted along the arrow. She paused, then released the string and sent the arrow hurtling across the room. Gwyndel's hand fell from Kahnna's shoulder and she studied the target from afar. She'd struck the target slightly off-center. "Nicely done," she said, watching Kahnna's reaction.

A wide grin brightened her face.

Eyoés strode through the palace corridors at a clip, his restless mind driving him onward. The fate of Asdale loomed above it all. His mind bent wholly toward it, like a flower craving the sun.

War had begun. Things had been set in motion that could never be undone, and time was of the essence. Eyoés rubbed his tired eyes.

Crystal chandeliers scattered the light like a prism upon the intricate tiling in dancing blues, reds, and sparkling golds. The ceiling itself seemed alive with vibrant patterns, with numerous archways curving overhead. Incense burned on small ledges scattered throughout the palace. This place offered every comfort the desert had denied him, but now was not the time to enjoy it.

Eyoés fidgeted and shot a glance at Kahnna as she led the way. He slowed his pace to match hers, studying her for any indication that she sensed his anxiety.

They're ignorant about Asdale's fall, and the news will come as a shock. Will Baron Wisam come to our aid, or will self-preservation triumph?

His heart jumped at the faint sound of laughter and music further down the hall. The world was deathly ill, and the disease was on Amiranoor's doorstep. Eyoés clenched his jaw. Their way of life was about to shatter —and he was going to be the one who broke it.

Eyoés considered his words carefully. If Amiranoor was to rally in time, assuring the complete support of Baron Wisam Ehnados would be crucial. A disunited people would never rise as one if their leader wasn't wholly dedicated to the cause.

And if he's not popular among the people? What then?

A knot tightened in Eyoés' stomach. He furrowed his brow, trying to recall the contents of his scarce correspondence with the Baron of Amiranoor. Three letters total—and none of them concerning anything more than minor trade disagreements. He barely knew anything about the man, save that people called him a cripple. Eyoés shook his head.

A man should never be defined by his flaws. But Wisam's private nature invites speculation.

Refusing to attend the Assembly of Barons every two years on account of disability and a sickly constitution framed Wisam in a dismal light. As Kahnna approached a break in the hallway, Eyoés couldn't help but wonder whether the people of Amiranoor had come to disregard their own baron.

The wall to their right fell away, and Eyoés descended into the broad chamber. Spots of gold shimmered across the tiled floor as the fading daylight filtered down through a skylight of yellow glass. Pillars inlaid with crystal shouldered the arched ceiling. Stepping around the pillows and lounging guests with quick apologies, Eyoés searched the murmuring crowd and his drifting eyes settled upon a familiar figure.

Nestled beside the musicians among an array of food, Sabaah sat up with a grin. The man's greying hair attested to his growing years, but the few wrinkles on his face only sweetened his cheerful demeanor.

Sabaah rose to his feet with a grunt and embraced Eyoés with a rich laugh. "My brother! I'm blessed to have you here. Welcome to Amiranoor!" he said, holding his fellow Hero at arm's length. His smile broadened as Gwyndel and Kahnna approached. "I'm grateful you've come to visit us, though it was rather unexpected," he noted with a chuckle, embracing Gwyndel briefly and motioning for them to sit.

Gwyndel adjusted her dress and sank cross-legged into a bundle of pillows. "Our arrival must've caused quite a stir. We never intended to make such a scene," she said. She reached out toward a platter of fruit, then hesitated.

Sabaah caught the uncertain glint in her eye and a humored smile tugged at his lip. "The ascetics have already given a benediction," he said. Gwyndel nodded her appreciation and took an orange.

Sabaah fingered one of the tassels dangling from his robe. "Don't worry about your arrival. I don't question your intentions for coming here, and neither will the people. The desert claims many lives. I feared the worst for you both," he admitted, glancing to where Kahnna lingered at the edge of the group. "I'm beyond thankful that my goddaughter saw you through it."

Kahnna flushed and lowered her gaze with a small smile.

Eyoés' smile wilted. Throwing a cautious glance at a nearby group of dinner guests, he leaned forward and motioned for Sabaah to lend his ear. "There's something we need to tell you."

"What's this? Welcoming the travelers without me?" A man's shadow drifted over the group and Eyoés clamped his mouth shut. Leaning against a crutch, the man studied them with a polite expression as he cradled a goblet of local wine in his free hand. In comparison to the vivid trappings of the other guests, his fitted white tunic projected a sense of refined taste. Pricked by the man's silvery grey eyes, Eyoés lowered his gaze and noticed the man's stiff, warped leg.

Rising to his feet, Sabaah placed a hand on the man's shoulder and shook him gently. "My friends, I wish to introduce you to my godson Wisam," he said.

Wisam hobbled forward and pushed his goblet into Sabaah's hand, extending a hand of welcome to Eyoés and Gwyndel. "It's a pleasure to finally meet you, Eyoés Kingson," he said, his curled mustache giving him a look of distinction.

As Eyoés clasped the man's hand, he glanced at Sabaah. For a brief moment, a somber frown dampened the man's infectious cheerfulness. Turning back to Wisam, Eyoés tucked the thought of Asdale away and put on his best face. "I've waited a long time to meet you in person," he said.

Wisam tucked in a stray fold of his crimson sash. "Yes. It's rather unfortunate that my frailty has kept me from the Assembly of Barons. I would rather conduct affairs in person, but alas," he said with a sigh, turning back to Sabaah. "However I am grateful for Sabaah's help managing inter-territorial relations."

Sabaah's head shot up as if he'd woken from sleep. "Yes, of course," he said.

Eyoés paused, eyes narrowed as he studied the two of them. The sense of reservation and formality bleeding from Wisam's bearing and dress clashed with the pain flashing in Sabaah's eyes.

They don't see eye to eye. Something lingers under the surface, driving them apart.

Kahnna stood and folded her hands. "If you'll excuse me, I promised Razeem I'd check on the griffin before nightfall," she said, eying her brother Wisam as she stepped back from the group and started out of the chamber.

Snapping out of his stupor, Sabaah turned to watch her go with a weak smile.

As he eased down into the mound of pillows, Wisam set his crutch aside and took a meager sip of his wine. He gestured toward the platters of food spread out in front of them. "Please. You must be starving after enduring the desert's judgment," he said.

Flashing a smile, Eyoés leaned back against a nearby pillar with a quick glance at Sabaah. He ignored the burning in his stomach and swallowed the news of Asdale's fall for the moment. He could almost feel it sink down into his chest like a lead weight. Clenching his jaw, he retreated into thought and and looked away.

He had to be sure of what he was going to say to them. Of how he was to deliver such terrible news.

As Eyoés snatched up a cluster of grapes, the musicians drew their ballad to a close and transitioned to a lively dance, drawing the eyes of the crowd. Several figures emerged from behind the pillars and swept through the crowd, the ribbons sewn into their sleeves trailing behind them like banners. The music broke and the dancers froze, then exploded into a whirlwind of movement in time to the lively melody. Their turquoise ribbons flowed through the air like water. Several folk tunes came and went amid intermittent applause, but Eyoés heard little through the tumult in his mind. By the time he emerged from his thoughts, the dancers had drifted out of sight.

He knew what he was to say. Eyoés glanced over to where Sabaah and Wisam sat beside him and opened his mouth to speak.

"I've known you for years, Eyoés," Sabaah said, catching his eye. "I might be growing older, but I'm no fool. You did not come here by chance." As he turned to face Eyoés, the shadows aged him. His cheeks had grown hollow and sunken, and grey hair peeked out of the edges of his turban. The sight twisted Eyoés' stomach in a cold fist. He scrambled to gather his thoughts from where they'd been scattered. Wisam's brow furrowed in concern and he waited in expectant silence.

Eyoés caught Gwyndel's eye. "Asdale has fallen," he said.

Sabaah fell back against a pillar and brought a trembling hand to his mouth. Wisam stiffened, his empty wine goblet slipping from his fingers to the nest of pillows. The mask of formality cracked. "What?" he said, his quiet voice barely audible above the cheerful music.

The sight of their grief reawakened Eyoés' misery. Pressing his trembling lips tightly together, Eyoés blinked back tears and looked away. Every last word he had decided upon failed him. "Falrey has seized Taekohar by force," he said. "I fear Amiranoor may be next."

Wisam was the first to break the pained silence. "How long until Falrey arrives in Tassam?"

Eyoés sighed. "Perhaps a month. No longer," he said.

Sabaah grasped his friend by the forearm and met his eyes. "Your suffering to get here was not in vain. We will begin preparations," he said.

Wisam awkwardly shifted to face Sabaah, his crippled leg twisted under him. "I believe I am capable of making my own decisions, godfather," he said. The sharp glare in his grey eyes turned his cordial tone to ice.

Sabaah laughed, incredulous. "The man nearly died coming here, Wisam! Don't insult him with your caution!" he said.

Wisam's response inflamed the raw wound in Eyoés' heart. He glared at Wisam and turned a dried fig over in his fingers. "Do you care to elaborate?" he said, popping the fig in his mouth and feeling the seeds snap between his grinding teeth.

Wisam turned to Eyoés with a nod of respect. "You and your sister proved your courage by bringing this unfortunate news to us, and for that, I am in your debt. But I know what you'll ask of us," he said. "You want Amiranoor to heed the call and join the other territories in war. Am I mistaken?"

Eyoés clenched his jaw. He shot an uneasy glance toward Gwyndel. "We can't defeat Falrey alone. Alithell *must* stand united," he declared.

Wisam leaned forward, his bronzed face glistening with the sweat of the desert's heat. "Falrey's eyes will be fixed on Amiranoor. The Castle Sanctum flaunts the glory of his enemy more than any other institution in the world. There is no greater threat to his power," he said.

An incredulous laugh slipped past Eyoés' lips as he stared back at Wisam. "You're going to pitch your tent and devote your efforts to protecting *yourself*? When the world needs you most?" he asked. The question hung between them.

Wisam frowned. "Falrey wants to conquer *my* homeland. *My* people," he hissed, stabbing his finger into the nearest pillow. "If he succeeds, Alithell's greatest hope and protection will vanish completely. Never to be seen again. The Sanctum must not fall!"

Pushing himself upright with a wince, Wisam clapped and beckoned the nearest servant. The man scampered over the pillows, bowing as he approached his baron. Wisam caught Eyoés' eyes for a final time before he met the servant's gaze. "Bring one of my couriers. I have a proclamation to dictate," he said. The servant paused, swallowing as he glanced at the baron's three companions. The gravity of the situation dawned on the man's face as he bowed a final time and scurried off into the labyrinth of halls. Picking up his empty goblet, Wisam snatched his crutch from where it lay and heaved himself to his feet.

He masked his troubled face behind a polite smile and bowed his head. "Thank you for your company. I assure you—Amiranoor will not fall. Not while I draw breath," he said.

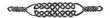

A draft of frigid air made Eyoés shiver as he pushed open the palace doors and strode into the glow of a starlit night. He slumped against a pillar, the laughter of guests and the melodies of cheerful songs fading behind him as the doors swung shut. With a deep sigh, he wandered across the colonnade, watching the shadows of the pillars drift past him.

Perhaps Wisam is right. The Castle Sanctum's a treasure to be defended. Falrey won't suffer its insolence for long. But does that mean we have to abandon the rest of the world to destruction?

It was a painful thing to choose between two tragic outcomes. Shaking his head, Eyoés rubbed his tired eyes. After years spent fighting for Alithell's soul, his heart lurched at the possibility of watching it die.

He caught the outline of the Castle Sanctum against the moon-lit sky. The monastery's spires and bell towers rose high above the adobe houses nestled in their shadows. Eyoés watched the shadows deepen. The embrace of night stripped the life from even the most thriving places, even the most holy places.

An abbey can always be rebuilt. But a distraught people?

Eyoés stopped beside a bubbling fountain and plucked a leaf from a papyrus flower, turning it over in his fingers.

By now, Haeryn and Lanyon will have answered the call to action, and Amiranoor won't be there to support them.

He crushed the leaf in his hand. With a sigh, he leaned back against a pillar and tilted his head back to study the night. A few thin clouds drifted across the moon and wandered over the ocean, breaking apart as the wind shifted. He lowered his gaze to the city splayed out in front of him. A few scattered windows twinkled with light.

All I've ever worked for is crumbling before my eyes.

A horse's whinny caught him by surprise and he whirled to peer into the night. He could make out the shape of a black stallion behind a tamarisk shrub, its rich black coat like a dark cloud compared to the moonlit landscape. Noticing the reins hanging from its bridle, he ventured toward the nearby steps—only to freeze at an acrid stench.

Moonlight shimmered upon bloody stairs. The dark shape was spread upon the steps, stripped and defaced with an chilling precision. Eyoés knelt, his stomach heaving. His hand instinctively fell to his belt, only to grasp at empty space for the sword that was no longer there. It was in the quarters where he'd left it—after all, what threat was there among friends? He'd let his guard down.

He studied the man's agonized face and started in recognition. Wisam's courier. The man had left only minutes earlier, clothed to endure the sands and heat on his journey to Taiseem. Pulse pounding in his temples, Eyoés slipped back into the shadows of the colonnade and ran for the door.

This was a message.

13

11th of Aevoran, 2211 SE

Gwyndel wrapped the blanket tight around her shoulders and settled in to watch the sunrise. All around her, the deep blue of night faded as the morning ripened with an orange glow that set the world afire. She caught the hoarse cries of gulls in the distance. With the tinkling of the Sanctum's bells, the city yawned and the devout rose to prayer. The moment brought tears to her heavy eyes.

The night had been long. Sitting at the base of a pillar, Gwyndel stifled a yawn and rubbed her tired eyes. The fate of Wisam's courier had haunted them all throughout the night. Sabaah and Wisam had meticulously covered all traces of the grotesque scene. She tried to distance herself from it. While they'd taken great measures to keep the incident quiet, the blatant reality of such a barbaric act unnerved her.

I was enjoying Wisam's hospitality while a man was dying in agony.

The guards at the palace gates stirred. Casting aside her blanket, Gwyndel rose and the gates opened as the raging sun crested the horizon. A group of camels entered the courtyard, their riders dusted with sand. She recognized the Wardens of the Watch beside the camels and the tension in her heart loosened. She hastened down the steps and rushed to where Vakros brought his camel to kneel. Sweeping up Rhoslyn in her arms, Gwyndel kissed his cheek. "The journey?"

"Long at times, but Benyoun's men helped us thrive. Had to travel during the night in order to make it to the city gates at sunrise," he answered. "Is Wisam lending his aid to our cause against Falrey?"

Gwyndel's face fell. She set Rhoslyn down as Uwéllor spoke with the Captain of the Guard. "Our rescue may not come from this place of paradise," she said.

"And you saw no one fleeing the scene last night?" Sabaah asked. The tapping of his footsteps quickened as his unease urged him ahead of the others. Even from a distance, Sabaah's slumped shoulders and lowered gaze painted a portrait of distress.

Eyoés nodded, turning to meet Wisam's concerned look. "The poor soul was left to die in the dark," he explained, envisioning the minutes of agony endured in choked silence. To die alone in helpless misery was a fate few men deserved.

In the humid, early morning, Wisam considered the news with careful judgment. The longer he'd considered the courier's death, the more withdrawn he had become.

Eyoés couldn't blame him. In a matter of months, events had unfolded that left much of Alithell scrambling to understand. Weeks worth of thought had failed to provide him much more than a guess as to the consequences of Asdale's sudden upheaval. Only time would tell.

Eyoés' stride faltered and he shook his head. "The courier. He—was immobilized. Unable to run, unable to fight. Mutilated where he lay and left to bleed to death in silence. The entire affair took probably only two, maybe three minutes," he said, the words tasting bitter on his tongue. "In Tassam, of all places. A place renowned for peace!" Wisam stopped, hunching over his crutch like an old man. An uneasy look drifted between him and Sabaah.

Eyoés clenched his jaw. He grasped Wisam by the shoulder and leaned close to his ear. "Are you a man with many enemies?" he whispered.

A tense laugh slipped past Wisam's lips. "The snake pays no heed to the cripple. But a hungry lion doesn't care who he bites," he said.

Eyoés' grip on the baron's shoulder wavered. "You're saying our enemy is desperate?" he said.

"Amiranoor is a zealous place, my friend. Blood runs hotter than the sands," Sabaah said. Glancing down the colonnade, he gathered Eyoés and Wisam together behind a large decorative vase stuffed with broad papyrus leaves. He sighed. "The courier was killed in ritual sacrifice."

The coldness in Eyoés' stomach showed in his eyes. "By whom?" he asked.

"There are those who defy the Sanctum and all that it stands for," Wisam said. "A small cult that still worships the essl."

Eyoés raised an eyebrow. "Essl?"

Sabaah nodded. "Spirits that our ancestors worshipped in their desert hovels. It's been that way since the beginning," he explained. "They believe that, by appeasing the spirits with offerings and charms, they'll earn the privilege to ask them for favors in return. The greater the sacrifice, the greater the favor."

A draft of cool ocean breeze brushed Eyoés' face. Pagans. Leaning against the pillar beside him, he quieted thoughts of Haeryn and threw himself into the solution. "The poor soul was sacrificed on your doorstep?" he asked.

"A curse," Wisam answered, swallowing the knot in his throat. "The boldest move they've made in years."

Eyoés' eyes narrowed. "This cult thinks they're ready for a confrontation. We should give it to them. The Sanctum would lend their aid," he said.

Wisam cleared his throat and caught Sabaah's eye. "One does not appeal to the Sanctum lightly," he said with a slight hesitation.

The baron's few words were handpicked. Eyoés fell silent, eying the two of them. "You have enemies within the Sanctum?" he asked. With fond memories of Asdale's abbey and its Abbot, the reluctance in Wisam's words seemed foreign.

Sabaah bowed his head. "An extreme sect of the Castle Sanctum, devoted to preserving traditional teaching and practice among all of the people. From the highest nobleman to the lowest beggar," he replied. "They call themselves the Searchers."

Eyoés caught the apprehension in Sabaah's tone and frowned. "Amiranoor is a living testament to tradition. Even if a heretic were to come here, I don't think they'd gain much ground," he noted.

Sabaah shook his head. "It doesn't matter. The Searchers will find heresy, sacrilege, and laxity wherever they want to," he said. "I believe they have good intentions, even if they are extreme. But in a den of lions, one must be careful what he dangles in front of them."

Eyoés studied the baron in silence. "So you're afraid to tell them about this curse?"

Wisam straightened, sharing a tense glance with Sabaah. Clearing his throat, the young baron broke away from the group and rubbed his mustache. "I am not afraid of them," he said.

Sabaah's eyes darkened. "Maybe you should be," he said, voice clipped. Wisam held his tongue in willful silence.

Wisam emerged from his thoughts and gripped his crutch. "Falrey is coming. That threat takes precedence over whatever mischief the cult is scheming to garner attention. However, if the Searchers hear of this incident, they will drown us with formal inquiries. We must proceed with caution," he said. The man's tone carried a subtle challenge. A deflection.

"I've already notified the Order of Dawn. They're waiting for us at the fountain," Sabaah interjected, gesturing for the others to follow him as he marched out of the veranda.

Eyoés rubbed his chin and followed Wisam into a wide courtyard. The bubbling of a fountain caught his ear, and the sweet smell of flowers tinged the air as he walked along a corridor of potted plants. Unlike other, well-tailored gardens he had seen, the flowers spilled out of their vases like wild things, sheltering under the shade of several palm trees. A piece of wilderness preserved from the encroaching reaches of civilization.

Eyoés glanced back just as Gwyndel melted into a cluster of bushes behind them. She had insisted on following them from a distance. Should the courtyard killer decide to pry into their affairs, it would be invaluable to have a Forester covering them.

A wide hedge enveloped by sprawling flowers stretched across their path, cleaved in two by an arched trellis. Eyoés glimpsed the shapes of several men through the entryway as Sabaah and Wisam ventured inside. Brushing aside a low-hanging palm branch, Eyoés followed.

A group of soldiers rose to their feet and removed their helmets, leaning their swords against the bubbling stone fountain at the garden's center. Eyoés caught the glint of sunlight upon the studded belts that hung from the discarded weapons. He paused, eying the soldiers as he followed Wisam and Sabaah to a long, empty bench. An air of trust lingered between the soldiers and their superiors. Eyoés remained standing.

Easing down into his seat with a sigh, Sabaah studied the group. "I apologize for the inconvenience of meeting here," he said.

One of the men stepped forward, cradling his helmet in the crook of his arm. "No need, Sabaah," he said, his mouth hidden by the coarse beard sprawling across his face. "I trust your judgment." The man's beady eyes fell upon Eyoés and he nodded, wiping the sweat from his bald head. "You must be one of the poor souls we rescued in the streets," he remarked. His leathery features wrinkled in a quick smile.

Eyoés gave a slight nod in return, studying the man carefully. "These men have earned your trust, Sabaah?" he said without turning his back to the armored men.

Sabaah motioned toward the foremost soldier. "Razeem is the head of the Order of Dawn. It's their task to protect the sanctity of the Castle Sanctum and to keep our baron safe from harm," he explained. "They've taken an oath. I trust them, Eyoés." Razeem inclined his head in quiet agreement. The confidence in Sabaah's voice hinted at the man's competency.

Eyoés eased onto the nearest bench and leaned forward. "You must have been watching the palace grounds last night. Did you see anything?" he asked.

Razeem embraced the question with total honesty. "It happened during a change in the guard. We heard a slight commotion from the courtyard, but by the time we arrived at the scene, you had already reported the messenger's body," he said. "Once the body was removed, I had a chance to examine the grounds for further evidence." He paused, thumbing the smooth surface of his helmet. "This killer is an expert. He slipped past our guards on the palace walls and left the way he came. The only sign of his presence was a trail of faint footprints. That and the horror on the stairs," he said.

Eyoés' eyes narrowed. "Are you aware of how the courier died?"

Razeem didn't flinch at the pointed question. "I am, but my men were not granted the privilege. Sabaah and I were at the scene immediately after you called for help. We wrapped the man in a burial blanket before the others could arrive," he answered. "These are sensitive matters."

Wisam smoothed his mustache, settling beside Sabaah. "So our killer must have been hired for the task," he said with an uneasy glance toward the high reaches of the palace. "Razeem, I value your opinion as a soldier. Do you think this assassin is among the palace staff or from the streets?"

Razeem paused, brow furrowed. "Hard to say for certain. The man's knowledge of the courtyard layout and guard schedule suggests a traitor among the palace staff. But given a high vantage point, the assassin could have studied the courtyard from *outside* the palace grounds," he said, catching Sabaah's eye. "Personally, I believe the murderer came from outside. That level of skill comes with training. It's highly unlikely that one of the castle staff had that opportunity."

Sabaah nodded. "Thank you for your insight, Razeem," he said, catching Eyoés' eye.

Turning his crutch over in his hands, Wisam stared at the fountain, lost in the darkness of his thoughts. "Keep a close patrol and check all passage through the palace gates. Report any suspicious activity to me or Sabaah and await further orders," he commanded, turning to Sabaah and Eyoés. "We need to speak privately."

Razeem threw his arm to the side in a salute and donned his helmet, setting the golden horsetail plume dancing. Eyoés rose from his seat as the man strode out of the garden with the rest of the Order of Dawn marching in his shadow. "How long will you keep them in the dark?" he asked, turning to Wisam.

With a sigh, the baron lifted his face to the sun and rubbed his jaw. "There are multiple essl factions that gather in Tassam. Until we identify the particular one responsible for this atrocity, the Order of Dawn has no target," he said.

The breeze fell silent, and the bubbling of the fountain tumbled into the silence. The cool spray coated Eyoés' skin as he wandered toward it and dipped his hand into the sapphire waters. The heat of the day was growing by the minute as the morning waned. "Where are the shadows in this city? The places where anything goes, and anything can happen?" he said.

Sabaah glanced at Wisam. "The harbor. Most, if not all, of the trade ships coming to and from Amiranoor dock there," he replied, standing to his feet. "I have men there who will spy out the taverns and—"

Running footsteps on the sandy tiles froze the words on Sabaah's tongue. A messenger emerged from behind a monstrous fern and bowed. "My lord baron, the High Rector of the Searchers is at the gate and requests your presence," he said. "Immediately."

14

10th of Aevoran, 2211 SE

Haeryn gritted his teeth as the echoing melody of songbirds gnawed at him. Ignoring the warmth of the sun on his face, he pulled up his hood in an effort to stifle the noise. Restlessness crept through his limbs and implored him to flee to the solitude of the endless woods, far away from the Rehil soldiers marching alongside him. Even now, he could sense their stray looks.

Shaking his head, Haeryn forced himself to dismiss them. They couldn't know his thoughts. Or why their idle glances pricked him like needles. As Taesyra walked among the men, Haeryn risked a glance down at them. They talked to each other, laughed with each other. Even as they marched, the war was lost in the shadow of friendship. Haeryn's heart spiked with indignation.

There is so much pain in the world. Agony. Injustice. Sorrow. How can they forget?

He checked himself. Squeezing his eyes shut, Haeryn ran his fingers through Taesyra's sleek fur. Betrayal. He could feel its sting crawling underneath his skin and dismantling him piece by piece. And all the while, Santh smiled back at him in satisfaction. Haeryn bit his tongue and tasted blood.

Santh had let them go. He'd surprised them not an hour's ride from the Northern Passage, with forces that outnumbered the Rehils and Edeverans combined. Despite having everything in his favor, he'd withdrawn and watched them flee. Haeryn shivered.

We're being toyed with.

Haeryn faced the truth. Asdale was destroyed. Santh's appearance proved that. Haeryn's brow furrowed as tears stung his dry, bleary eyes.

Father is probably dead. And when he needed me most, I was across the world.

He clenched his jaw.

Am I an orphan again?

Gritting his teeth, he pressed a hand tight against his trembling lips. He defied his tears.

Father is not dead. Santh isn't strong enough to kill him. No one is.

Haeryn remembered the story of Asdale's fall to Skreon—of the flames, dragons, and stench of burning flesh. When the world had collapsed into a smoldering ruin, his father, no more than a youth his age, had refused to lay down and die. Instead, he rose to conquer. Haeryn nodded to himself.

He refused to consider the alternative. Lifting his head, he brushed back his hood and dashed the tears from his face. The ranks of the Rehil and Edeveran forces crowded together on the gravel road, hemmed in by embankments on either side as Neifon, Caywen, and Jaaye led them onward. A gentle breeze brushed against Haeryn's face, and he noticed the grass quiver under the sun. Sinking back into Taesyra's saddle, he looked up at the trees.

Maybe he needed the songbirds after all.

"Need some company?"

Haeryn started. Shooting a curt glance at Dovarul, he clenched his jaw. "I'm fine," he said.

The dwarf paused, studying the young knight closely. "Doesn't look that way," he said, looking away to ease Haeryn's nerves. "You don't need to hide, lad."

Stiffening, Haeryn stared directly ahead and tried to calm his quickening pulse. "I hide nothing," he said, immediately checking himself as the words sprung from his mouth like venom.

Dovarul threw up a hand. "Haeryn, I know how you feel. The men do too, though they hesitate to speak openly," he said. "Nobody expected to meet Santh outside the Northern Passage. And that's what he counted on." Leaning out from the saddle, the dwarf caught Haeryn's eye. "Santh let us go. He toyed with us to shatter our confidence and make us feel that we have something to prove. Don't let his schemes trap you," he said.

Haeryn embraced the conversation with a measure of relief. Dovarul assumed their defeat was the cause of his tears.

Perhaps fear for Father's safety hasn't occurred to him yet.

Sheltering in Dovarul's mistaken assumption, Haeryn shook his head. "We've been forced to play the victim. A role I swore to myself I'd never play," he said.

Turning partway in his saddle, Dovarul nodded to where Hjarti and Erling rode in the rear, guarding the supply wagons. "But look," he remarked, pointing. Haeryn glanced back as Hjarti bellowed with laughter, Erling gazing up at him with a bright smile. "Many of us escaped with our lives. To see the sun again. To eat a hearty meal. To hear music. We are not beholden to Santh's ruse. We are slaves to hope, not to fear. And there can certainly be no better victory," Dovarul said.

Haeryn's gaze lingered on Erling and Hjarti. He could see their joy spreading like wildfire up the ranks, brightening the grimy faces of old and young men alike. Snatching up the flask of water strapped to Taesyra's saddle, he downed a gulp and turned away. "Nothing is certain, Dovarul," he said. "The more I see this world, the more I believe that."

A shout rose from the soldiers and Haeryn yanked back on Taesyra's reins, wheeling the griffin around as the men spun to face the embankments on either side.

Elves stood perched atop the steep hills, watching them from beneath deep hoods. Their dark cloaks drifted in the breeze like wings, stretching their shadows across the road. Their silence raised the hairs on the back of Haeryn's neck.

Haeryn looked to where Neifon, Caywen and Jaaye drew rein, the front ranks swallowing them in a schiltrom of pikes to shield them from harm. Taesyra's chest rumbled as Haeryn reached for his sword. His hand stopped short as a solitary figure emerged from the forest's shifting shadows and drew rein, lifting high a banner of emerald green. The sunlight caught the silver emblem of a griffin upon it.

The soldiers exploded into shouts of pride, raising triumphant fists. From the ridge, Lanyon threw back his hood with a beaming smile on his lips and strength in his eyes. Dovarul applauded with fervor and a burst of laughter. The hope in Haeryn's heart surged.

Raising a hand to quell the uproar, Lanyon stood tall in his saddle. "I am Wyndar Alcarthon, and my sword is your servant!" he cried.

15

Caywen had almost forgotten what it was like to see smiles on the faces of her people. The quickening rhythm of a folk tune caught her ear, mingling with the sound of good-spirited laughter around a hearty meal. She smiled as the reedy song of a bowed lyre joined a lute and drums. Blinking against the smoke of a nearby campfire, she watched a group of soldiers spring to their feet and dance. The glow of the firelight shone on their rosy faces.

Here, as they shared a meal in friendship, joy hung in the air thicker than the smoke, drawing men together like family. Standing in the shadow of a gnarled maple, Caywen stood with rapt attention. Moments like this never lasted long enough.

She pulled her wool shawl close to fend off the night breeze. As she took a sip of warm tea, the sound of Lanyon's voice drew her gaze to the fireside. He looked like a ghost in the wavering light, each gesture of his hand casting quivering shadows. Haeryn, Dovarul, Marc, and Hjarti leaned forward, captivated as he entranced them with vivid tales recited from memory. Neifon sat hunched over a leather notebook, writing quietly as he listened to Lanyon's stories. Many carried traces of legend. With others, it was hard to tell. That was the art of it.

Lanyon's return had lifted Caywen's spirits more than she wished to show. Few would have understood. From the shadows, she breathed a sigh of relief that she no longer had to shoulder the burden of leadership alone. Miles of trail grew lonely when your soul ached.

She noticed Lanyon's elf scouts mingling with Rehils and Edeverans alike as they savored the brief respite from the troubles of war. A shared burden united souls. Caywen suppressed a sneeze as smoke stung her nose. It had taken a measure of persuasion to convince her that such a celebration was essential, no matter how small. As she gazed up at the treetops, she could feel the vastness of the forest as it enveloped them.

They were not alone under the trees. Somewhere, Santh and his men camped in this wilderness too. The knowledge of that made her skin crawl. Yet Lanyon showed no fear. In truth, Caywen couldn't remember a time when he had. Still, as she looked out across the sprawling colony of tents scattered beneath the trees, Caywen let her guard down. Her steaming cup was nestled loosely in her hand. Fearlessness brought unpredictable consequences—like a pair of dice thrown in the dust. At times, it lead to unexpected victory. At others, it threw you on your face.

Rubbing her tired eyes, Caywen tried to shut out the memory of her own brush with death. She could still remember the faces of Santh's men that surrounded her on the battlefield. Erling's reckless rescue. Downing a quick gulp of tea, she tuned her ear to another folk tune. Now was not the time to dwell on what could have been.

She jumped as a canvas bag thumped against a nearby log. Erling left the company of friends and strode past, shedding the scout's cloak from his shoulders and tossing it aside in an unkempt wad. Venturing away from the firelight, he passed between two frail pines and was gone.

Caywen set aside her cup and slipped into the night after him. As the firelight danced upon the tree trunks, she spotted Erling silhouetted against the white canvas of a lonely tent. He stilled as he caught the swish and crackle of her feet shuffling through old foliage. Caywen hesitated.

How can I thank him for saving my life?

For a brief moment, she considered him from a distance, then stepped back. "I apologize for disturbing you," she said, turning away.

"Don't leave. Please," he insisted, turning toward her and sitting in the shadow of his tent. Caywen turned back and studied Erling. Moonlight trickling through the boughs shimmered in his eyes as he studied her in turn. As she wandered toward him, Caywen's brow furrowed. The way he looked at her— for a fleeting moment, his face seemed to belong to someone else. Caywen recognized he bore an eerie resemblance to someone she'd once known, but despite her best efforts she couldn't place him.

She sat beside him, her eyes darting away as she gathered herself. "I—I am in your debt," she muttered, twisting a corner of her shawl. She flushed at her lack of words.

I didn't belong on that battlefield. Falrey's men overpowered me without breaking a sweat. And he— only a boy—fought a man twice his size in order to save me.

Erling shook his head and sank back against a tent post. "You owe me nothing," he said.

Caywen caught his eye. "I owe you *everything*. You saved my life and in turn saved everyone under my leadership. You're young. You've only just begun to really experience life. And you risked it all for a noblewoman you barely know," she said, placing a hand on his knee. "Please, accept my gratitude."

Eying her hand, Erling clenched his jaw. "Can I be honest with you?" he asked.

The question caught Caywen off guard. She started, studying him. "Of course," she replied, intrigued.

Erling took a deep breath. "I dreaded the day you'd know my true name, but I always knew it would come eventually," he sighed. "I've kept quiet long enough."

He locked eyes with her. "My father was Fedrik Ravenstrong," he said. "Throst was my half-brother."

Caywen turned to stone. Her stomach dropped, tears burning in her eyes as she stared back at him. The familiarity in Erling's face that had baffled her now made sense. Caywen's eyes widened in dismay. The similarity was unmistakable now. "You look just like him," she mumbled under her breath.

Erling's face twisted in pain. "Please—I have to make things right," he pleaded. "I'm not my brother!"

Caywen looked away, wrapping her arms around herself to keep from shaking. She couldn't bring herself to see his face again—to see *him*. "Why couldn't you cursed Ravenstrongs stay in the shadows? Don't you know what I've suffered?" she snapped, her voice cracking.

Erling leapt to his feet and seized Caywen by the shoulders. They locked eyes. "I've suffered the same!" he said through tears. "In Edeveros, Throst hunted my father down like an animal. He—he took me as a hostage and put a knife to my throat. For two years my heart has melted inside me at the thought of making amends. The least I can do is serve you!"

Caywen pushed Erling's arms away. Disjointed thoughts cut her composure to ribbons and tore open old wounds. She could almost hear Throst's smooth voice coming to her on the wind. Wiping away tears, she squeezed her eyes shut and arrested the panic welling in her chest.

Throst is gone. He can't hurt me anymore. If I keep his memory alive, he will wound me to no end. This has to stop.

She blinked to clear her stinging eyes and ventured toward Erling. "I'm sorry," she said, placing a wary hand on his hunched shoulder. "Throst failed to take away my father and my home. You lost that and so much more. What right have I to reject you?" Erling's eyes glistened as he studied her.

Shaking her head, Caywen let her hand slip from his shoulder and drew away. Her mind cleared as from a dream. She took a deep breath of the cool night air. "This is the chance for our families to reconcile. Once and for all," she said, turning away to leave Erling to himself.

"It is," he said.

16

Snatching up a rock from the forest floor, Haeryn tossed it into the air and caught it with a tease of a smile. He glanced back, watching the last traces of smoke rise from the dying embers up to the stars. The forest enveloping him was a home of sorts, filled with the glow of a warm fire and the voices of friends. Now the night reclaimed the place, the trees once again slumbering in the silence. Thankfully, the warmth of a hearty meal still smoldered in his stomach.

As the chill night air bit through his clothes, the words spoken to the rhythm of the crackling fire returned to him. He pulled his hood over his head. The story of Lanyon's recent travels stirred something within him that he hadn't felt for weeks. Looking at the Alcarthon banner hanging from a trail-worn shaft, Haeryn beamed in spite of himself.

Somewhere, out in the wilds beyond, Santh waited for them. In the morning, their predicament would be no better. Yet with Lanyon now at their head, something had changed. Their fear was dissipating. Fingering the stone in his hand, Haeryn tossed it upward again and caught it. Santh was not prepared for what Lanyon would deliver. And that made him grin.

Haeryn cast the rock aside. He could make out the shapes of the other tents scattered beneath the trees, organized by battalion. In the distance he saw Taesyra's large silhouette as she kept vigil at the camp's edge, waiting for his return. The woods beyond were silent and spilling over with shadows. He didn't pity the watchmen who kept their vigil there, swallowed by the dark.

Stifling a yawn, he considered the quickest path to his bed. He ventured to the forest's edge and plunged into the shadows, skirting along the outer reaches of the camp. As he walked under the lonely boughs, a mouse fled through the rustling underbrush and stirred the crickets from their beds. His eyes shot up to an owl's shadow drifting overhead in complete silence, flying deeper into the thick woodland. He paused a moment to admire.

A shadow moved to his right. Haeryn froze, enveloped in his cloak, peering out from within the cover of the trees. Creeping over a rotten stump, a lone figure surveyed the surrounding woods before plunging deeper into the wild. Haeryn's brow furrowed. As soon as the figure turned its back to him he stole after it.

Clambering over the rotten stump, he ducked behind several scraggly bushes and laid atop a cluster of rocks to further conceal himself. He pushed aside a warped branch to get a better look. The figure stumbled to the edge of a small glade and fell against a tree, sliding down the trunk into a miserable heap. The shimmer of polished glass caught his eye, and he shrank back into cover as the figure threw back her hood. Jaaye.

She shot wary glances at the forest around her, then stared down at a phial in her hands. She yanked the stopper with a curse and downed a large gulp. Squeezing her eyes shut, she tilted her head back against the tree trunk.

She was—crying. Haeryn's mouth twisted in an awkward grimace and he rubbed his eyes, glancing back the way he had come. He watched her. She stirred restlessly, rubbing her arms to ward off the cold night. The moon drifted out from behind a cloud and made the tears on her cheeks sparkle. He could see the look of torment in her darting eyes. It gripped him. Propping himself up on his elbows, he crept forward. It seemed Jaaye hadn't brought her glaive. Considering what he was about to do, he was glad.

Haeryn held his breath and darted out, throwing back his hood. Jaaye yelped and scrambled to rise. Grabbing her shoulder and shoving her back down, he snatched the phial and stepped back.

He locked eyes with her. "What's this?"

With a strangled cry of frustration, Jaaye lunged to reclaim her precious possession. Haeryn darted out of the way and she tripped forward, falling in a heap and clambering to her knees. "I don't need your questions!" she growled.

His face hardened. He sniffed at the open phial and frowned. The liquid inside was odorless. He looked around. "What are you doing out here? What is this?" he asked again, tapping the phial with his finger. "You've skulked about long enough."

Jaaye's shoulders caved. She curled up and held her head in her hands. Haeryn took away the glass stopper and plugged the open phial. He tensed, fist poised in case she pounced. Desperation had colored her every word and action since they'd met, and Haeryn remembered her wild frenzies with a pounding heart. He couldn't see her face, and for a long while, she kept silent. He grew cold as her shoulders slumped in defeat.

Jaaye's hands clenched into fists as she peered up at him. "I'm dead, Haeryn. A shell of lies," she said. A shiver crept up his neck as the starlight glinted in her bloodshot eyes. He'd never seen defeat on her face before, and it frightened him more than her savagery.

Haeryn's hard look faltered. Gripping the phial, he knelt beside her while keeping a safe distance. "What are you talking about?"

Jaaye buckled under the question. She avoided his steady gaze, wincing as if it burned her. Her head fell to her chest. She threw a wounded glance at Haeryn. "My innocence died the day I discovered that phial in the fields, though I didn't know it then. Such a pretty shimmer. Whatever was inside almost seemed alive."

She straightened with a shudder, pressing a fist to her lips. "Mother said I was getting slack in my chores. I was strong. I could survive her taunts and cuffs. Father tried to protect me from her, but he could only do so much," she said. "Mama took to me with a club after I brought friends home one day. No one was supposed to know about the Ossinder we grew. I should have fought back, but that night I felt so worthless that I drank from the phial in hopes of poisoning myself. Instead, I was filled with a reckless courage. I fled the farm in the night and never went back. Only I found I needed that phial from then on."

Pouncing on Haeryn, Jaaye seized a fistful of his sleeve before he could jump out of reach. "The warrior everyone sees is no more than a frightened girl. I live a lie!" she confessed. "Mama was right. I'm nothing. A cowardly whelp of no use to anyone." She stared at the phial in his hand, her face twisting with yearning and grief. The cloak she'd always worn was a bravery she didn't actually feel.

"Drinking this made you brave?" Haeryn asked, glancing up as Jaaye nodded. He straightened, tracing the spiraling filigree designs upon it with his finger. "I've heard of things like this. Used during the War of Adrógar to fortify wounded men on the surgeon's table. This one must've been left behind," he remarked. As he turned the phial over in his hands, the ornate designs upon its rim sparkled silver and gold in the moonlight. It seemed heavy in his hands now under the weight of its misused blessing.

Jaaye snatched the bottle away. Yanking the stopper free, she stared into it. "I don't care about history and all that rot. All I care about is what this can give me," she said. Before Haeryn could stop her, she downed the rest of the golden liquid and tossed the phial at him with a hollow sigh. "It'll be full in the morning," she noted. "It always is."

Haeryn's baffled stare turned her eyes away. He stuffed the bottle into his pocket. "Aren't you tired of living like this? You're too brave for slavery," he said.

Jaaye shook her head. "I'm a coward, Haeryn," she said, pointing at the bulge in his pocket. "*That* is the courage everyone sees. Without it, I can't fight. And when there's nothing to fight for, my life means nothing." Haeryn had no reply for that. She trembled, sobbing. Curling up to shield herself from him.

The sight of her misery enraged him. She had been born into adversity, as he had. Destined to suffer the consequences of bad fortune and trapped in an endless cycle from which there seemed no escape. No freedom. No strength. No love. Life had whisked her off her feet and stolen her hope.

As he looked into her raw eyes, Haeryn saw himself. An imperfect reflection, but a reflection nonetheless.

Frowning at the lump in his throat, he squeezed her shoulder. "Life is cruel. But it also has its joys," he said. "I've felt life's dagger in my heart too." He shut away the nightmare of Norgalok before it showed. "If we're going to rise from the ashes, we have to do it together."

17

Lanyon drew rein in the shadow of a rotten tree and dismounted, ducking under a stray branch as he emerged from the natural alcove. "This is it," he said, nodding to where the ground sloped down to the forest's edge. "We enter Ledale on foot to blend in with the crowds."

With a grunt, Dovarul dismounted and peered down the slope with his one good eye. "Last I heard, Ledale was loyal to King Fohidras," he said as he led his horse to a nearby thicket. "We should be in good standing there."

Haeryn slid from Taesyra's saddle as she crouched, curling up in the thick underbrush to rest. Glancing sidelong at Lanyon, he strode to the edge of the ridge and peered down into the hollow, planting a foot on an exposed rock to steady himself. He spotted a deer trail winding down the hill through the thinning trees.

Shying away from the edge, Haeryn turned back to where they had come from. The faint crackling of broken twigs and underbrush caught his ear. Had he not known of their presence, Lanyon's elf scouts would have passed for nothing more than a small flock of deer. Haeryn took a step back, his gaze sweeping back and forth. The silence with which they drifted through the thick brush still unsettled him.

He tapped the scabbard at his waist and turned back to Lanyon. "You saw the tracks on the road. A large force marched through here. What if Santh lies in wait for us at Ledale?" he asked.

Lanyon caught Haeryn's eye as he shouldered his pack. "Santh would have had to cross that gorge several miles back in order to cut ahead of us. Not easy to do with a swarm of brigands," he said, glancing back to where the elves had disappeared into the forest. "And on the slight chance we're walking into a trap, my scouts should flush out any hidden dangers ahead of us. Besides, we three are the only ones entering the city. Caywen and the others will break camp. We can enter unnoticed." Tucking his cloak over his sword, Lanyon started down the hill. Dovarul followed, his arms shooting out for balance as he stumbled over a rock. Away from Hjarti's giant shadow, the toddling dwarf was a lonely sight.

Haeryn pursed his lips and itched his jaw, turning back to where Taesyra lay basking in the sunlight drifting down through the branches. He stooped to grab his satchel and whistled to grab the griffin's attention. An amused smile broke across his face as Taesyra perked her head at the sound of his voice. "Don't go anywhere," he said.

For a town of scholars and philosophers, Ledale was a dunghill. Sidling along the edge of the streets, Haeryn stepped over a pile of filth and threw a withering glare at the window above. A sharp, unpleasant reek tingled in his nose and he stifled a sneeze. Women of ill-repute stalked among the drifting crowds with leering smiles, and as Haeryn gathered closer to Dovarul and Lanyon, he noticed a young pickpocket swipe an unsuspecting man's coin pouch.

It was a miracle that the place had gathered a reputation for intellect. Especially considering the likes of Mairwen of Ledale and others of the local philosophical tradition. Apparently the scholars kept to their books and left the rest of the place to rot.

Haeryn wrinkled his nose and caught Lanyon's eye with a pleading look. "Please tell me we're not staying here," he said. Dovarul chuckled.

Lanyon stifled a smile and glanced over his shoulder. "There are plenty of loose tongues in a place like this. Listen for information—and watch what you say," he instructed. Spotting a tavern nestled between two off-kilter houses, he gestured at it and marched off through the crowd.

Haeryn's eyes narrowed and he dragged himself after Lanyon. Internally, he cursed the crowds gathering under the long shadow of the city lord's dilapidated keep. With the horde of crass townspeople pressing around him, he kept his gaze lowered. Nothing in this city was worth looking at.

He flinched as Dovarul prodded him. He turned to shoot an irritated glare at the dwarf.

Dovarul's eyes were turned upwards to where Falrey's banner was perched triumphant over the sickly streets.

Haeryn's stomach heaved. He locked eyes with the bull insignia upon the banner, transfixed by its sordid crimson eyes. Eyes stained with blood. He flinched as a hand grasped his shoulder and pulled him further into the crowd. Lanyon pulled him into the shadow of a nearby building and threw his hood up. A trumpet blast rang through the streets and the crowd parted. Haeryn's stomach turned inside out. They'd stumbled onto an execution.

Lashed to stakes like kindling, over a dozen people thrashed and screamed against their bonds. Their cries did nothing. Gathered around the victims, Falrey's soldiers stood unmoved, flickering torches in their hands. The sound of their victims' whimpering raised the hair on Haeryn's neck.

The pyres were lit at the second trumpet. Flames surged upward in a sudden roar that made Haeryn jump. Pleas for mercy morphed into screams of agony as the stench of burning flesh and Gesadith stung his nose. He fought back the urge to retch as the flames crept up their charred, writhing legs.

Dovarul bowed his head. "Poor souls," he said.

Lanyon clenched his fists. "They resisted Falrey's conquest of Ledale. Now human torches," he said. "We must hurry. The city guard will keep them burning long into the night." Turning away, he disappeared into the crowd. Dovarul took Haeryn's hand and pulled him away. The echoing shrieks numbed Haeryn long after the sight was hidden by the crowds.

He stumbled after his companions, barely seeing the ground in front of him. The townsfolk of Ledale continued on with their lives, watching the death of their own kinfolk with nothing more than a wistful shake of their heads. They had no sympathy. After all, why should they pity criminals and rebels?

It was a callousness Haeryn knew personally. He rejected the notion in rage.

I'm not that cruel.

The sound of Lanyon's voice caught his attention. Retreating to the edge of the street, Lanyon surveyed the town as Dovarul and Haeryn gathered around him. "We'll have to do this discreetly," he said. "We go to one tavern and see what we can learn. The executions will undoubtedly cause talk."

Haeryn stiffened. "That's it? We're just going to collect rumors?" he growled.

Dovarul nodded. "Santh is on our tail. We don't have the time or resources to retake the city. The best we can do is gather knowledge quickly and quietly," he insisted. Pulling Lanyon aside, the dwarf leaned close. "What if the people keep a close watch on their tongues?" he asked. "If we linger too long, we both arouse suspicion and delay the army's march."

Lanyon paused. "Pray that we scrounge up something useful and leave before we're discovered," he whispered. He turned. "Where's Haeryn?"

18

Haeryn pushed his way through the crowd, pulling his hood further over his face as he lingered in the shadow of an empty doorway. He studied their faces, his mind racing as his eyes drifted. The screams of the dying rebels began to wane as the smoke choked their cries. Blinking back unwelcome tears, Haeryn embraced the wildfire burning inside him, letting it scorch and consume him from head to toe. For weeks, he had marched with Caywen, Lanyon, and the others in hopes of taking a stand.

He was tired of waiting.

Glancing up to where Falrey's banner flapped high above the town, he gritted his teeth and marched into the street with fire in his steps.

Lanyon and Dovarul are content to let things play out. I'm not.

He caught the eyes of several passersby, only to watch them scurry away under his hard glare. Veering away from the crowds, he slipped into a side street, tramping through filth with barely a thought. There was no place for such petty concerns when greater matters lay at hand. Falrey had his chance to cause pain. Now it was his turn.

The sound of voices arrested his steps, driving him into the entryway of a moth-ridden tailor shop. Deaf to the half-hearted greeting of the shopkeeper, Haeryn peered out the door into the narrow causeway.

Three men rounded a corner and came into view. Haeryn bristled at the sight of Falrey's insignia flaunted on their surcoats. He squeezed the doorjamb with white knuckles and his flinty stare fell upon one of them. The younger soldier, listening to his two elder companions with the eager ear of a gullible child. Haeryn's stomach hardened as the young soldier fumbled with his halberd. He withdrew into the shop before the three men could see him.

With a smile and a pat on the back, the two older men left their young companion with a command and a joke. The brotherhood between the brigands turned Haeryn's stomach.

The young soldier paused, looking around to orient himself. Haeryn's face darkened.

Fool.

When the youth's head was turned, Haeryn slipped out of the tailor's shop and shut the door behind him. In two steps, he dashed forward, twisted the halberd from the soldier's hands, and shoved him against the nearest wall. Slumping to the ground in a daze, the youth stared up at him. The enthusiasm in his eyes had turned to terror.

Haeryn's lip curled in disgust and the soldier's face blanched. He seized him by the arm and dragged him into an alley. Ripping the open-faced helmet from the boy's head, he threw it aside and crouched in front of him like a wolf about to spring.

His eyes narrowed. "I can't abide murderers like you," he hissed, seizing the young soldier by the jaw and locking eyes with him.

The youth trembled in Haeryn's grip. "Wh-who are you?" he stammered.

From within the shadows of his hood, Haeryn bared his teeth. "Someone who wants answers," he replied. He pulled aside his cloak to reveal the knife belted to his waist. "Speak quickly, and speak truth. Or you won't speak again," he said. "Where is Falrey O'Dyre?"

The young soldier's eyes widened. Tears welled in his eyes as he scrambled for words. "He—he's marched east," he said.

The youth stifled a whimper as Haeryn seized him by the hair. He leaned close, eyes flashing. "What cities have fallen?" he demanded. "Speak!"

The soldier flinched, squeezing his eyes shut. "I don't know," he said.

Haeryn wrenched the young soldier's hair. "Liar," he hissed.

With a sudden burst of courage, the youth punched Haeryn in the jaw. "I'm only a footman! But I would rather die than betray my king!" he exclaimed, scrambling to his feet.

Haeryn lunged, grabbing a fistful of the soldier's surcoat and throwing him to the ground. With a growl, he planted a knee on the youth's chest. Eyes wide with fright, the soldier fought to free himself. Haeryn drew his dagger and pressed it to the boy's throat.

He lifted his head and took a deep breath. "Do you smell that?" he asked, his voice deathly quiet. He pointed in the direction of the town square, his face darkening like a storm cloud. "Your king is burning people alive. I will make him pay for it." He slapped the soldier across the face. "What cities have fallen?"

The soldier winced, blood trickling out of his lip. "Kinroft," he croaked. "Then Auxwood in Anehstun."

Haeryn seized the man by the collar. "What drew Falrey to Kinroft?" he asked, luring the man to speak further.

The soldier looked at him with tears in his eyes. "There's a rumor that Baron Vedis has a cache of Duraval bombs. The boys say the king's going to blast Kinroft to the clouds!" the soldier answered, raising his hands to ward off the blow.

Haeryn planted his fist against the youth's jaw with a solid thud. Pulling his hood over his face, he fled into the shadows.

"We're looking for a friend of ours—a young man, on the verge of manhood, about this tall," Lanyon said, grasping a stranger by the shoulder only to be greeted with a withering scowl.

The Crimson Mark held the man's gaze for a moment, then shoved past him. Ducking into a market courtyard, he caught sight of Dovarul as the dwarf approached a group of seamstresses plying their craft.

Lanyon rubbed his stiff neck and leaned against a nearby hitching post as he gathered his focus. Ledale was a busy place. In an instant a man could find himself alone here, separated from his companions by the shifting crowd.

But Lanyon couldn't shake the feeling that Haeryn's disappearance wasn't an accident. Haeryn was often—unpredictable.

Lanyon straightened as Dovarul wandered away from the group of women. Pushing himself away from the hitching post, he pulled Dovarul aside. "Any luck?" he asked. His stomach twisted as Dovarul shook his head.

The dwarf flipped up his eyepatch and itched the scar underneath. "I'm going to kick that whelp in the rear when I find him. We came here in secret. Now we're talking to *everyone* in this filthy town," he said, peering up at the Crimson Mark from beneath his hood. "I'll reckon a guess as to what's going on in Haeryn's head right now."

Lanyon could only imagine. Spotting a grimy urchin weaving through the nearby crowd, the Crimson Mark snatched the lad up by the collar and set him upon a barrel. "You. Have you seen a youth about this high near the town square? Dark hair, piercing eyes?"

The urchin glared at Lanyon with a pair of beady eyes. Hopping down from the barrel, he dashed toward the street. Dovarul seized the boy before he could get out of reach and dragged him back. "Don't you think about it," he growled, holding out his hand. The urchin wavered, eying him head to foot through a tight squint.

The dwarf's rough appearance won out. Reaching into his trousers, the lad pulled out Lanyon's coin pouch and tossed it aside before tearing himself free and darting off.

Shaking his head, Lanyon raised an eyebrow with a grunt. "The boy's good at that," he said with a hint of a smile.

Dovarul raised an eyebrow. "How would you know?"

Lanyon shrugged the pack onto his shoulder. "I met many people in my wandering days. There was a thief I knew quite well. We ended up friends, oddly enough," he explained.

Dovarul frowned. "You must've led a strange life," he said.

Lanyon's smile faded. Catching the dwarf's eye with a brief glance, he peered over the heads of passersby. "Not unlike Haeryn, really," he remarked.

Dovarul laughed to himself. "I hope he turns out like you did," he said.

"As do I."

Lanyon turned as Haeryn rejoined them. Clenching his fists, the Crimson Mark loomed over him with a glare. "Where were you?"

Haeryn pushed his hood back and met him with a cool stare. "Learning things," he said, turning to Dovarul. "Falrey's taken Kinroft and plans to destroy it. To keep us from replenishing our supplies there. If we get to Kinroft in time, we can save the city."

Shoving past his two companions, Haeryn started in the direction of the town gates. Dovarul shot an uneasy glance at Lanyon and hurried after the young knight. "How'd you learn this?" he asked. Without glancing back, Haeryn pressed on. Lanyon's stomach hardened.

Haeryn's silence did not bode well.

19

23rd of Aevoran, 2211 SE, Kinroft

It would be a red dawn today.

Weaving his way through a stand of aspen trees, Haeryn sprang down into a brush-filled hollow and ducked behind the worm-eaten remains of an old pine stump. He wiped at his cold nose and pulled his hood further over his face. Shapes drifted through the mist-shrouded trees as Lanyon and his men dipped down into the hollow, waiting for Haeryn to return from scouting.

Haeryn emerged from behind the stump and hastened toward them. He could hear the birds above him begin to wake from their slumber with singing. The first light of morning illuminated the forest around him and he glimpsed the griffin emblem of the Alcarthons through a gap in the brush. He altered his course to where Lanyon knelt.

Haeryn fell to his knees beside the Crimson Mark. "No one saw us approach. The sentries atop the wall have no idea," he said. A zealous grin broke across his face as he followed Lanyon's gaze to the lonely cavern awaiting them. "It's there. Just like you said."

Lanyon brushed his fingers through his beard. His eyes narrowed as he surveyed the cavern. "As far as I can tell, the Phantom League hasn't used this tunnel for

131

awhile. There's no sign of a recent disturbance. Still, this is the League's only access point into Castle Kinroft, and Amnedd used to keep at least five Hunters stationed here at all times," he said. "Maybe we'll get lucky."

He turned to Haeryn and locked eyes with him. "Enter quietly and follow the plan. Once the keep is secured, I'll give the signal," he said, his gaze wandering back to the tunnel. "If you happen upon the Phantom League, do *not* let them see you. If they discover you're here, they'll light the Duraval before you have a chance to blink. Understood?"

Haeryn's stomach turned to rock. With a slow nod, he studied the place with fresh eyes. In the growing light of dawn, he saw the city wall through a break in the trees. The old growth of the forest butted up against it, forcing the trees to drive their thick roots underneath the stones. At the base of a grand maple, one of the roots had bunched up into a twisted knot, splitting a large, toothed crack into the lower half of the stone wall. To Haeryn's eyes, the cavity was wide enough to allow two men through side by side.

With a quiet command, Lanyon rose and waved for the men to follow his lead. As they snaked through the brush and into the crevice, Haeryn turned to where Jaaye and several of the Freechildren lingered. He motioned for them to follow and started for the fissure.

The bushes pricking his arms fell away as he ducked into the crevice. Stretching his arms out into the dark, he groped along the damp walls and clambered over the exposed boulders protruding from the floor. He could hear Lanyon and the men ahead of him as their scabbards clinked against the rock walls. Focusing on the sound, Haeryn altered his course to match theirs, his steps jarred and halting as he groped at the walls. His stomach twisted as the darkness surrounded him.

He slipped on a wet stone and lurched forward into the flickering light of torches. Someone shoved a torch into his hand and he made out Lanyon's shadow as his eyes adjusted to the dim light. The sound of dripping water echoed in his ears, and he held the torch aloft, watching the flickering light scatter across the glassy surface of a broad cistern.

His eyes followed the bouncing torches of the men as they gathered around Lanyon. Shrouded in dancing shadows, the Crimson Mark held his torch out before him. A narrow set of stairs emerged from the darkness. Holding a finger to his lips, Lanyon started up the stairs, the wet steps glistening under his feet. Haeryn followed with the men trailing behind.

He watched his footing carefully, but still managed to send a loose stone tumbling into the abyss below. In the utter silence of the cavern, the thought of tumbling into that vast nothingness set his teeth on edge.

A clatter and a cry of terror sent his heart into his throat as a flailing man slipped and disappeared into the darkness.

Lanyon threw up his hand. Haeryn did the same, his heart skipping as he looked up into the darkness. The floor of the castle. No one moved. Lifting his torch for a better view, he caught the Crimson Mark's eye.

Lanyon grimaced as he stared down into the blackness. Then, with a nod, he continued on.

After what seemed an eternity, Haeryn heard the slight creak of a hinge open ahead of him as Lanyon eased the door open. The Crimson Mark stopped, wiping the soles of his boots with his cloak. "Wipe your feet. Make sure your boots are dry before you step onto the marble floor. No footprints," he commanded. The order trickled down the ranks.

Drawing his dagger, Lanyon peered out of the doorway. In a blink, he dove out into the castle keep.

The men poured out of the small doorway, splitting into two groups as Lanyon and Neifon had planned. Wiping his boots, Haeryn left the cavern and squinted at the morning light streaming in through the broad windows. He strode into the center of the room and drew his sword. Men rallied to him, shutting the door to the cistern. He glimpsed Lanyon and his men as they charged toward a flight of upward spiraling stairs. Analyzing the layout of the antechamber with a quick glance, Haeryn started for the central hall.

The castle was quiet. Sidling through one of the pillared archways, he gripped his drawn sword. The lonely sound of their pattering footsteps echoing against the vast ceiling ate at his nerves. Kinroft had been under Falrey's control for more than a week.

This keep should be swarming with guards and servants.

The lack of bustle made him pause. Ducking behind a banner hanging down from a nearby archway, he motioned for his men to stop. They dispersed, hiding behind pillars as they looked to him for further orders. Grasping his sword with both hands, he leaned out of cover.

His heart jumped as two portly maidservants fled down the hall with yelps of fright. Haeryn tore blindly after them, his pulse thundering in his ears. In an instant, he was upon them, seizing them by the arms and bringing them to a dead stop. The two maidservants tumbled to the ground, their sleeves tearing in his grip.

As his men hastened to his side, one of the sobbing maidservants tried to stand. Gritting his teeth, Haeryn pulled her to her feet and met her terrified stare with a suspicious squint. "Don't scream," he demanded through clenched teeth.

The woman blanched and shook her head vigorously. "Never! Never!" she insisted, with a shuddering gasp. "Please—spare Anny! She never slandered him!"

Haeryn stopped. "What? Who?"

At his sudden change of mood, the woman stilled. "You—you're not *his* men?" she inquired.

Haeryn's stomach lurched. His grip loosened. Swallowing, he released both maidservants and turned away from his men to hide his reddening face. "No. We're with Wyndar Alcarthon and his army," he said. "I take it you aren't keen on Falrey either."

Relief flooded the woman's face as she helped her friend to her feet. "The louse should keep his hands off our people," she growled.

Haeryn shot a nervous glance down the hallway. "Where is everyone?"

The maidservant lowered her voice. "Most of the remaining servants are in the kitchen during the mornings. Falrey impressed our soldiers into his ranks and left his own in their place," she explained. "Baron Vedis is being held hostage."

Haeryn nodded impatiently. "Baron Vedis' Duraval hoard. Where is it?"

The maidservant's eyes widened. "You mean it's true? The baron has stored Duraval here all this time?" she asked, catching her companion's look of disbelief. With an exasperated growl, Haeryn nodded again. He felt naked, standing out in the open for all to see.

The second maidservant finally found her tongue. "There's a door in the cellar. Kept under lock and key, it is," she said, pointing down the hallway. "Servants are forbidden, and that's caused a lot of talk. Come!"

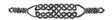

Stars flashed before Haeryn's eyes as he tumbled back into a pile of grain sacks, shaking his head to clear the pain in his skull. He glimpsed the hobgoblin through blurred vision and dodged a second punch, hammering the hilt of his sword against the creature's shoulder. As the hobgoblin staggered to the side with a grunt, Haeryn slipped out of reach and cut him down.

He looked around in a daze. The shouts echoing across the low ceiling of the cellar made his ears ring.

Splintered shelves were strewn across the floor, kicked about as Falrey's guards fought to defend the small sealed door nestled in a dusty corner. Grain spilled out of torn sacks and crunched underfoot. Haeryn willed strength into his aching limbs and dashed into the dancing blades, his men rallying about him as they finished off the remaining guards.

He stood among the pile of slain, prodding one of the bodies with his foot as he wiped his nose with the back of his hand.

A fitting end for traitors.

Sheathing his sword, he pointed toward the door nestled in the corner of the cellar. "Open it," he commanded, glancing back to where the two maidservants huddled together with eyes squeezed shut. "Two of you escort these women out through the hidden tunnel." Two grimy soldiers helped them to their feet and showed them out.

Poor things.

Haeryn folded his arms and sank back against the wall while several of the strongest men threw themselves repeatedly against the locked door. Clenching his jaw, he refused to look further upon Falrey's fallen guards. They were not worth mourning.

The door splintered with a sharp crack, and his men swarmed into the forbidden chamber. Pushing his way through, Haeryn stepped inside. Barrels upon barrels of Duraval stood stacked in neat pyramids across the floor, reaching high above their heads into the vaulted ceiling. The soldiers dispersed through the chamber with whispers of awe, brushing their hands across the cold iron of barrel braces. A thick, oily stench hung in the air. A chill ran up Haeryn's spine.

So much power, all in one place. Waiting for the slightest spark...

A sliver of light drew his eye to the far end of the chamber. He hurried toward it, weaving through the rows. As his eyes adjusted to the light, he noticed several wagons clustered at the far end of the room. He slowed to a stop, lifting his eyes to the large sliding door. He could hear the growing noise of the waking city on the other side. The baron's hoard was hiding in plain sight.

Haeryn drew back. "We can't cart the Duraval out until the city is taken," he said to several of his men. "Stay here while I find Lanyon."

He spun on his heels and bolted out of the chamber, weaving around the slain and racing up the lonely cellar stairs. The castle was almost theirs—he could taste it.

Cracking open the cellar door, he peeked out into the keep. He jumped back as two of Falrey's soldiers passed by in a grim silence. Pressing himself into the corner of the cellar entry, Haeryn froze as their footsteps faded. He crept toward the door.

A hand seized the doorjamb and threw the door open.

Lanyon stepped inside, his drawn sword dangling in his hand. "The Duraval?"

Haeryn motioned into the dank cellar. "The cellar leads directly into the streets. Kinroft must be taken first," he said, facing Lanyon. "Save for a few sentries, these halls are strangely quiet."

The silence broke as a dwarf pushed his way through the Crimson Mark's soldiers. "The enemy is split up across two fronts. A small group of them were entrusted to guarding me. The others are keeping a watchful eye on the public," he explained. "It appears that even the meekest of Kinroft's people are not so easily taken." Haeryn spun to face the newcomer and stared.

The dwarf was blind. His narrow head barely came up to the soldiers' waists, and his fine livery swayed loosely over his distastefully thin body. Reaching out with a cane of knotted wood, the dwarf tapped on the smooth floor to find his way. "Baron Vedis at your service," he said.

Lanyon hesitated. "Falrey put you under guard. How did you escape?" he asked. Now was not the time for diplomacy.

With a blank stare, Vedis smiled. "Never dismiss the influence of a good wine," he said.

Haeryn shot a perplexed glance at Lanyon. He'd heard Eyoés mention Vedis' blindness in the past, but it had done little to prepare him for the surprise. Clearing his throat, he bowed. "I trust you're unhurt," he said, flashing a kind smile. It was only after he'd done it that he realized the dwarf's staring eyes were untouched by his gesture. Inwardly he cringed.

The dwarf lifted his cane and pointed down the hall. "Quickly—I know a way that will lead us to safety," he said, brushing past Haeryn's leg as he shambled down the hallway, cane tapping. "Falrey's vagabonds don't know the half of this place." Several soldiers followed him.

Haeryn and Lanyon followed the dwarf out of the cellar and up a flight of stairs. The sight of blindness perplexed Haeryn. While he'd heard of such things before, the surety in Vedis' awkward footsteps struck him as strange. He shook his head. There was no time to be puzzled.

At the top of the stairway, the dwarf stopped in front of a solitary door. "This way," he said, fumbling for the doorhandle as he removed a key from his pocket. As soon as the lock clicked open, Lanyon threw the door open and raced out, with Haeryn following close behind. A flock of birds flashed past and he skidded to a stop. The streets and houses of Kinroft stretched out before him, bathed in the crisp yellow of dawn. They were on a balcony.

The door slammed shut behind them and they turned.

Blocking their escape, the dwarf chuckled and tossed aside his cane. "Thought you'd be harder to fool," he said, nodding at Lanyon. "The real Baron Vedis met with an unfortunate accident." As the dwarf removed his costume, Haeryn glimpsed the infamous tattoo on the man's neck. Three hooded figures flanked either side of the dwarf with drawn short swords. The Phantom League.

Shielding himself behind his bloodstained sword, Haeryn retreated to Lanyon's side and glanced up at him. A chill coursed up his neck as he caught the bleak look on the Crimson Mark's face. He could hear their soldiers beating on the other side of the locked door. His hands began to shake.

One of the hooded figures stepped to the front and pushed his hood back. As his disfigured, knobby face caught the light of dawn, Haeryn recoiled in horror. The monster of a man noticed his reaction with a misshapen grin. "Knew you'd turn up eventually, Lanyon. Just didn't figure it'd be this easy," he remarked, thumbing the blade of his drawn sword. "One of your men forgot to wipe his boots."

Lanyon's shoulders sagged. He grasped Haeryn by the arm and pushed the young knight behind him. "I'm still wanted then," he said.

The ogre nodded, pointing at himself with his thumb. "Enough to send this Churl," he said through a mouth of splayed teeth.

Studying the figures closing in, the Crimson Mark gritted his teeth. "It's been years since Amnedd's death. The consequences for my disloyalty are long past," he said through clenched teeth. "Why kill me now?"

The Churl snarled with mockery in his eye. "The Ravenstrong farce set the League's plans back a whole year," he hissed. "You know the Code of Conduct. Traitors get the spike. Doesn't matter how long it's been."

The League had set an ambush for them. Haeryn's pulse spiked as Lanyon's hand edged to the horn strapped to his side. "Our army is waiting outside the gates. All I have to do is give the signal and the city is ours," the Crimson Mark growled. A heavy thud on the balcony door drew his eye. "My men are not so easily stopped."

With a dismissive wave, the Churl folded his arms. "Go ahead and sound your little horn. We'll wait," he said. "The League has no preference as to who rules Kinroft. Matters will go on as usual. But *you're* a liability. A wild card that has to be taken out of play."

The assassins sprang. Haeryn caught one of them in the neck with his sword before the others reached him, throwing him against the balustrade. He punched another square in the jaw as Lanyon's horn sounded clear across the city, and he saw the other Leaguers pounce at the Crimson Mark. Pain shot through his scalp as his last attacker grabbed him by the hair and heaved him over the balustrade. Haeryn thrashed, sword tumbling from his grip.

The Leaguer's knife cut through his hair in one slice and Haeryn fell with a scream.

Taesyra's shriek rang in his ears as a sudden force drove the breath from his lungs. Seizing a fistful of the griffin's fur, Haeryn clung for his life. As Taesyra alighted on the balcony, he clawed his way onto her shoulders in time to watch the Crimson Mark yank his dagger from the Churl's ribs. With a twisted grin still plastered on his horrible face, the man slumped to the ground alongside his fellows. Lanyon spun around, sword and dagger clutched in his fists as he searched the dead Leaguers for survivors. With a sigh, he cast aside his dagger and tore his surcoat, pressing the lump of cloth to a wound on his arm.

The Crimson Mark hurried to help Haeryn down from Taesyra's back. "Are you alright?" he asked.

Haeryn swore as he sank against the balustrade, wiping the sweat from his brow with clammy hands. He could care less that Lanyon heard. As the panic began to fade, he noticed the shouts and clang of weapons filling the air. The armies of Rehillon, Edeveros, and the Freechildren swarmed through the streets of Kinroft, plowing through the few ranks of Falrey's men that remained. Hjarti's shout of triumph rang clear as a bell above the cacophony.

Exhausted, Haeryn dropped his head on his arms just as the morning sun crested the highest reaches of Kinroft's keep.

20

11th of Aevoran, 2211 SE

Sabaah shoved the servant's tunic into Eyoés' hands and seized his arm. "Put this on and stay here. I'll go see what the High Rector wants," he said, searching Eyoés' eyes. "Do not let him see you." He dashed down the balcony stairs and out of sight. Ducking behind a potted fern, Eyoés slipped into the tunic and peered over the fronds down into the chamber below.

The hall was quiet. Sunlight filtered through the skylight above and danced upon polished tiles. Wisps of incense tinged the air and rose in tight curls around the baron's seat of state. Wisam placed his crutch against the armrest of his throne. Fastening a belt around his waist, Eyoés heard Sabaah's footsteps echoing below and saw him share a few hushed words with a kneeling scribe.

All eyes turned to the chamber doors. Eyoés could feel his nerves tingle as apprehension electrified the room. He caught a flash of red on the balcony across from him. Gwyndel caught his eye for a brief moment before a thunderous knock made Eyoés' heart jump.

These Searchers are our allies. Our brothers. They should not deserve our fear.

"Enter in peace," Wisam declared, his high-pitched voice cutting the silence like an eagle's sharp cry.

With a low groan, the doors swung inward. Eyoés peered down as the jingling of bells rang out in rhythm. A tall figure floated into the chamber, his smooth gait soundless upon the tile floor. Three others followed behind him, ushered in by guards with heads bowed in humble deference. As the sentries knelt before the High Rector, he extended his hand in silent blessing, the draping sleeves of his dark red cloak drifting above his ankles like pennants. Embroidered upon the hood of the man's cloak was the likeness of a blazing firebrand. A chill crept down Eyoés' arms.

Sabaah bowed, his face masked with pleasantries. "Welcome, High Rector," he said, the purple mantle upon his shoulders swaying as he straightened.

Wisam glanced at his godfather and swallowed hard. "To what may we owe the honor, Kesahdon?"

The High Rector pushed back his hood. He paused, lifting his right hand and putting his forefinger and thumb together in the customary sign of greeting. The stillness returned, awaiting the pronouncement. Eyoés could almost make out the chisel marks on the Rector's hard elven features.

Sabaah's smile wavered at the prolonged silence. "We speak as friends, Kesahdon. As brothers. Will you not tell us your mind?" he asked, motioning for a servant. "Perhaps we can speak over some wine."

Kesahdon raised a hand. "Formal matters demand propriety," he objected, his sharp eyes pinning Sabaah where he stood. "There is a magician in your midst. The brothers and I have heard of it."

Eyoés' pulse quickened.

Wisam's face paled in disbelief. "A magician! I do not allow such evil to cross my threshold. You know I am loyal to our King and his Sanctum," he retorted.

The hooded figure paused, tilting his head and clasping his hands loosely in front of him as he studied them with a cool consideration. A single braided lock of hair dangled from the side of his head. "Two strangers are welcomed into your home and a man is sacrificed upon your doorstep that very night," he said. "Surely you would understand my concern." Gasps of horror rose from the assembled sentries. The lightning bolt had struck home.

The desert air turned to ice in Eyoés' chest.

A bluff. Wielding rumors to lure us into a confession.

He studied the elf from afar, waiting for a sign—anything that would expose deliberate deception. All he found was honesty.

Sabaah and Wisam had taken every measure. Those at the feast the previous night had left the palace blissfully ignorant of the courier's sudden death. The Order of Dawn guarded against an enemy they couldn't even name. The secret had been safe. And yet here it was, thrown naked on the floor from the mouth of a man feared by the baron himself.

There was a loose tongue in the palace.

Wisam gripped the armrest of his throne. "Where did you hear of this?"

A slight smile formed on Kesahdon's lips. Taking a deep breath, the High Rector basked in having caught him off-guard. He bowed his head. "From a humble penitent, whose name I will not disclose," he answered.

Sabaah fought to keep his expression unmoved. "Men lie, Kesahdon. Why should you believe a stranger's word over ours?" he remarked.

The smile left the High Rector's face as he lifted his head. "All claims merit investigation, no matter how insignificant they may appear. Your claim carries equal weight," he said. "But remember my brothers—I swore a vow to preserve the truth, not to shield people from it. Favoritism is the death of justice."

Clenching his jaw, Sabaah knelt. "I swear to you, High Rector, that there is no magician among us," he insisted.

A flicker of compassion shone in Kesahdon's eye. Gliding toward the kneeling hero, the High Rector grasped him by the shoulder. His flinty voice softened. "Do not fear. If your conscience is clean, the Guide will give a sign to vindicate you. Otherwise, you must turn over this magician and be absolved," he said with a small, but generous smile. "I will continue to invoke mercy on your behalf."

Kesahdon stepped back with a courteous bow, painting a circle in the air with his forefinger. "Continue in peace," he said. Pulling his hood over his face, he turned his back and started out of the chamber.

Wisam rose from his throne with a wince, leaning heavily against the stone armrest. "If we find this magician, how will we recognize him?"

The High Rector paused, his broad cape transforming him into a floating shadow. "The penitent said the magician was a woman. A certain Gwyndel of Asdale, rumored to be the Keeper of the Sword Imperishable. A claim I've wished to investigate for quite some time," he said.

The chamber doors shut, and Eyoés looked in Gwyndel's direction. She was gone.

21

Gwyndel threw her pack onto the bed, seizing a fistful of clothes and shoving them into the bag in a tangled heap. She stumbled, kicking aside a fallen pillow as she hurried to where Fóbehn lay propped up against the wall.

Vakros winced as arrows clattered in her quiver. "Quietly," he said. Eyoés could hear the gravel in his voice.

Gwyndel groped through her scant things, and the sight stuck Eyoés' heart like a thorn. She stooped like a beggar, her curly red hair bouncing in tangles about her ears. The sun peeked through the curtains, and Eyoés noticed for the first time white hairs streaking down from the nape of her neck.

Throwing her bow and quiver over her shoulder, Gwyndel hurried to her pack. Her hands were shaking. With a broken sigh she closed the sack with a hasty knot and took it up. She stood in silence, her eyes drifting from Vakros to where Rhoslyn stood.

Vakros rubbed at his chapped lips. "How long must she hide?" he asked.

Eyoés bowed his head. "I don't know for sure. Sabaah said there's a chance she may have to wait weeks," he answered.

Vakros wheeled on him. "Weeks? She's not a criminal!" he said, fists shaking. "The Sanctum is supposed to help us! Haven't we suffered enough?"

Rhoslyn cried in silence, but her mother saw her tears. She knelt before her daughter and embraced her till her arms shook. "I'll be back. We won't suffer like this forever. It'll all be over soon," she said. With a firm kiss on her daughter's forehead, Gwyndel turned to Vakros.

The strength in Vakros' shoulders faltered. Clenching his jaw, he gazed at her through tears. "Why does it always come to this?" he said.

Gwyndel set down her pack and threw her arms around his neck. "I always come back. The Guide always brings me back," she said. When her voice broke, Eyoés felt his heart snap.

Vakros kissed her and ran a hand through her hair. "Rhoslyn and I will be waiting for your return," he said, looking her in the eye. "We will find whoever did this. For your sake and for the sake of our homeland."

With a parting kiss, Gwyndel slipped out of the doorway with her pack in hand. Eyoés buckled his dagger to his side and started after her.

Vakros grabbed his shoulder. "We can't let them get her," he said. Eyoés clenched his jaw and nodded. Action would speak louder than words.

Slipping out of the chamber, Eyoés hastened to Gwyndel's side and locked arms with her. "We're to meet Razeem at the southern courtyard. From there he'll escort you out of the palace," he whispered in her ear.

Footsteps sounded from further down the passage and Gwyndel shied back, ducking into an arched hallway as her brother shielded her from view. While she walked, she gathered her hair in a loose bun and pulled out a simple coif. "Our presence here isn't a secret. If the Searchers have placed spies in the palace, I might be recognized," she said. She cinched a knot under her chin to secure the coif.

A servant turned into the hallway after them.

Eyoés wrapped an arm around Gwyndel's shoulders and his pace quickened. "Keep your face down and we'll make it," he said. He glanced back in time to see another servant join the pursuit.

"They're following us," Gwyndel muttered.

Eyoés slowed as she took the lead. "I can buy you time," he said.

Gwyndel threw him a glare. "Don't make the Searchers suspect you. I can handle this," she said. Eyoés' stomach turned to lead. Bowing his head, he slipped into the first room he saw. He sagged against the wall and closed his eyes.

She's torn away before I can even see her in safe hands.

Gwyndel snatched a robe from a passing laundry-maid and threw it on. With a quick glance backward, she shouldered open a door and stepped out into the afternoon heat. Her pulse pounded in her ears above the drone of voices in the courtyard. Bursts of color caught the sunlight. As far as she could see, attendants drifted from ladders to small awnings with festoons and pennants in their arms. Piece by piece, the festival drew to a close. Gwyndel ducked under a drooping garland as two servants removed it from the archway above.

She came down the palace stairs, picked up a fallen pennant, and tagged behind a group of chattering women. Her heart grew cold at the mention of the Sanctum.

It was foolish to expect their acceptance.

There would be no peace for her here. Or anywhere.

Her eyes scanned the crowd and settled on the bronzed face of Razeem. The man lingered on the outskirts, dressed in merchant's garb as he spoke with a seneschal. Setting her pennant aside, Gwyndel started for him and risked a glance over her shoulder.

Her two pursuers had gained on her. Blades glinted in their hands.

When Gwyndel looked ahead, Razeem was gone. Her mind raced. She spotted a tent stake lying on a barrel and tucked it into her sleeve. She could hear their steps in the sand. As the crowd thinned, Gwyndel's grip tightened around the stake.

"You there! Lend me a hand, will you?"

She jumped at the voice. A waving hand beckoned her back into the crowd and she followed, a cloud of dust gathering around her heels. The spies behind her faltered, peering over the heads of servants to identify the speaker. Gwyndel slipped into the thickest group of attendants and a hand seized her by the arm.

"This way," Razeem said. He ducked under one of the awnings and motioned to two stooping gardeners. They nodded and slipped past in the direction of the trailing spies. Razeem ushered Gwyndel through a maze of potted plants and garland piles. "Once you set foot on the streets, don't waste your time. I have allies among the commonfolk who will help watch your back," he said under his breath.

They stepped into the shadow of the palace walls. Gwyndel jumped as a flock of birds erupted from the parapet above the courtyard gate. Razeem's grip on her arm loosened as he guided her through the open archway. "Head east from here and don't stop until you reach the market. The butcher there will take you in," he whispered in her ear. With a pat on the shoulder, he turned back.

Gwyndel started for the shade of several palm trees. With a pained glance back at the palace, she dropped the tent stake in the dust.

22

The Searchers had declared an inquisition.

News spread quickly, traveling among rich and poor alike till it hung over Tassam like a storm cloud. Commerce in the vibrant streets slowed to a trickle of desperate men seeking daily bread. Musicians clamped their mouths shut and refused to sing the raucous love songs of the common people, resorting to pious hymns or shutting themselves away entirely. The rich commerce of ideas retreated to the cover of night, hidden in the bowels of dank, cold cellars. All suffered. All had ground to a halt.

Under the observant eye of the Searchers, joy was bled dry.

Eyoés stepped into the cool shadow of a towering spire. He looked up at the sculpted granite hand at its summit as birds flocked around it. He paused for a moment, leaning back against the base of a weatherbeaten statue as he soaked in the glory of the broad stained glass window that kept vigils over the steps to the Castle Sanctum.

The murmur of the pilgrims and clergy moving about the Sanctum's courtyard was lost to him. It was the end of the ascetics' midday service. A set of small bells tinkled to signal the official conclusion as a new crowd of pilgrims surged inside to revere the traditions of their forefathers in personal devotion. It was a strange feeling to Eyoés—this sense of piety that radiated in the air like the heat of the noonday sun.

He started up the jasper stairs. As he stepped into the shelter of a sandstone archway, a pair of doves fluttered over his head with grace and alighted on a nearby acacia tree. Several of the pilgrims muttered in hushed words of awe. Eyoés found himself wishing he knew the significance it held to them. In a world steeped in rich symbols, he couldn't help but feel woefully ignorant.

Eyoés joined the crowds as they spilled into the first domed chamber. Beams of sunlight filtered through the windows in colored rays, striking thousands of inlaid jewels set into the archways of the room. Goosebumps swept up Eyoés' neck as he came to a standstill, spellbound. Every wall around him was covered in vibrant patterns crafted from every precious stone he could think of—garnet, carnelian, emerald, ruby, sapphire. A spotless floor of speckled marble stretched out in front of him in all directions, inlaid with gold and jade. Pillars lifted the domed roof high above his head, creating an airy space he had seldom seen before. He smiled as he recognized the similarity to the royal halls of Gald-Behn.

If only Gwyndel could see this.

The thought turned his mind bitter. Clenching his jaw, Eyoés glimpsed a Searcher moving among the crowd and retreated to the shadow of a pillar. Even while dressed in a pilgrim's clothes, he felt like a fugitive scolded before his accusers. Did the Searchers know Gwyndel was his sister? If not, it was only a matter of time. And that time was running out.

The library. His brow wrinkled as he considered Sabaah's directions. Several vaulted hallways split from the main chamber like the veins of a leaf. Eyoés threw a glance to the crowd of pilgrims and hurried across the broad room to a lone ritual fountain. The bubbling water threw a soft, cool spray across his exposed arm as he studied the hallways from a closer angle.

The light drew his eye to long, narrow placards plastered along the archway's edge. With a squint, he could make out the pictograms drawn on them, enveloped by the embellishments carved into the stone. He noticed a pictogram of an open book and started down the hallway it indicated.

The path turned inward, carving deeper into the Sanctum, then suddenly yawned into a cavernous library bathed in the radiant yellow glow of daylight. Eyoés found himself perched on a bridge, with a maze of shelves stretching above him and below him. The odor of incense mingled with the stale, musty smell of old books in his nostrils. Eyoés peered around the corner of a looming bookshelf and ventured forward. He stopped as his foot hovered above a placard built into the floor.

Clergy only. No pilgrims permitted beyond this point.

Eyoés stepped over it. Ahead of him, ascending and descending stairs branched off from a broad platform in the center of the room. The sound of rustling pages echoed and Eyoés ducked behind a pedestal, nearly upsetting the bust atop it.

Golden robes drew his eye as a figure ascended one of the staircases. A silver mask covered half of his face and shimmered in the sun. The man's exposed eye was fixed on the book cradled in his arm, and a peaceful smile touched his lips as he turned a page.

When the librarian's back was turned, Eyoés slipped past and started down the stairway. He placed his steps carefully, listening for movement close by.

If I'm to help Gwyndel, I need to understand her accusers.

He left the stairs on a hunch and turned down one of the rows of shelves. As his eye caught another placard, he stopped.

Sanctum History.

Fifteen feet of bookshelves lay ahead. Steeling himself, Eyoés started with the bottom rows, eyes drifting over the spines as he swept back and forth. He stopped upon several promising leads, rifling through the pages. He returned them to their nests. Echoing above the looming shelves, the wandering footsteps of librarians quickened Eyoés' pulse.

He'd combed the bottom shelves twice before he retrieved a nearby ladder to help him with the upper shelves. Tracing the spines with his fingers, he muttered the titles under his breath. His finger stopped upon one of the books.

"Cult of the Essl: A History of the Heathen"

Eyoés frowned and read the spine again. Looking directly across the hallway to the next group of shelves, he read that placard.

Our Adversaries.

An uneasy tension settled upon him. The thin book was placed alphabetically—in the wrong section.

Someone else is looking into these matters too.

Pulling the book from the shelf, Eyoés took a step down from the ladder and wavered as another book caught his eye. The ladder lurched as he leaned out and took the book in hand.

"Stewards of the Holy Children: The Searchers"

Eyoés stepped down from the ladder. His fingers leapt onto the pages as a librarian passed by on the walkway directly above. While he combed the rough parchment with his finger, Eyoés kept a tense vigil. A particular heading caught his eye and he scanned the sleek script…

Discipline Among the Wayward

As a whole, the legacy of the Searchers has always been fraught with controversy. Since its founding, the sect has witnessed periods of both revival and corruption, leaving many of the faithful in the dark as to what the Searchers truly expect of them. Most Searchers are aware of this. And no facet of their practice has caused as much confusion as discipline.

A Searcher is held accountable for the hearts in his keeping. This understanding has been the essential truth behind all matters of practice. Moderation, however, remained an unspoken, and often unheeded, rule. For many years, the level of discipline wielded among the wayward was dictated solely by the High Rector and his associates.

At the Fourth Council of Al'Tisara, several noteworthy Searchers, including Bal Yfir, were found to have overstepped their bounds in regards to disciplining those under their authority. Of special note was the trial and execution of former Baron Savir Ehnados and his wife Lady Rennai. The former baron and his wife had shown hospitality to a wandering holy man named Dafri, whose esoteric teachings had earned the suspicion of the Searchers.

Bal Yfir, a young rector at the time, sought the matter out deeper than prudence would allow. A tragic series of misunderstandings resulted in a quick trial and execution of the baron and his wife on charges of heresy. Only after the deed was done did the Abbot Behnassos of the Sanctum discover the innocence of the nobles.

Our noble Abbot took swift action to appease the righteous anger of the faithful. Bal Yfir was stripped of his title and rank in solemn ceremony and expelled into the desert to become a hermit. In his stead, Abbot Behnassos consecrated Kesahdon, Bal Yfir's closest aide, as High Rector of the Searchers. All authority over matters of justice was handed over to the Abbot, leaving the Searchers reliant upon the Sanctum's direct order to carry out sentencing.

Due to their sensitive history, the Searchers have been denied the blessing of becoming an official order and continue to remain a closely-watched sect.

Eyoés scurried up the ladder and tucked the book into its place. He hurried down the rows of shelves, coming up short as a librarian crossed in front of him and was gone. Stepping into the light of a sputtering chandelier, Eyoés threw a quick glance at the librarian's back and slunk away. He spotted a sweeping stairway among a long column of desks and started for it as the book's words brewed.

The Searchers answer to the Abbot. Win his favor, and the Searchers will call off the inquisition.

Hope lived still. Gwyndel's case was not lost. Eyoés set his jaw and strength renewed him like a gasp of fresh air. He checked himself.

The Searchers executed the former baron and his wife. The mistake surely won them enemies.

Eyoés rushed for the stairs.

"Eyoés! What are you doing here?"

The harsh whisper stopped him cold. He turned back toward the rows of study desks to where Kahnna sat, watching him in surprise. Crouching behind a chair, Eyoés cursed his luck. "There are things I have to know, and I thought I'd find answers here," he whispered, falling silent as he noticed a librarian alphabetizing the shelves across the hall.

Kahnna picked up her book and wandered in his direction, pretending to read. "You're taking a big risk coming here," she said.

Eyoés raised an eyebrow. "And you?"

Without looking toward his hiding place, Kahnna pulled another book from the shelves. "I'm a healer. Everything I know I learned here. And I've taken vows of allegiance to the Sanctum," she explained. Studying the book in her hand, Kahnna placed it on the bookshelf. Out of order.

Eyoés frowned. "I have to go," he said. With one eye on the librarian, he sidled toward the stairs.

"Eyoés." Kahnna quickly glanced in his direction. "I'm doing everything I can for Gwyndel."

Eyoés paused. He looked back at her with a weak smile. When the librarian turned his back, he rushed up the stairs and was gone.

23

19th of Aevoran, 2211 SE

The air hummed with the life of the sea. It echoed in the cries of gulls and merchants and shimmered on the scales of the perch that peered out of fish baskets with gaping mouths. Docks and boats bobbed to the rhythm of sea shanties in concert with the hiss of waves. This was a song of life, fresh and newly born from the sea.

A sudden squeal startled Gwyndel and a monkey darted around her ankles. Her hand went up to the blue shawl around her head and she leapt aside as a sailor darted past. The monkey chattered and left the man empty handed.

She hurried on, the sand sifting into her sandals and caking her feet. The life of the harbor surrounded her on every side. From the smell of tar and spices to the unwashed sailors and merchants jostling her shoulders, the sea touched everything in its reach. Her ears rang with the sound of it.

Among the crowds, she was nobody.

She ate a dried fig to distract herself from the coarse fabric chafing at her neck and ankles. The discomfort bothered her—the years parading herself as a Forester Liaison had made her soft. The thought of her exile chipped at her confidence the longer she considered it.

This world has changed, and I've changed with it. Can I trust myself still?

She bit her tongue.

Rhoslyn, Vakros, and Eyoés are all depending on me. I just have to approach everything from a different angle.

Leaning against the pier gate, Gwyndel peered above the rooftops to where the spires of the Castle Sanctum reached for the clouds. The Searchers' jurisdiction ended where the dockside community began. Both Razeem and the safehouse watchman had confirmed it. The carefree atmosphere of the seaside market untied the knots of worry in her stomach. Without Searchers breathing down her neck, she could at least sleep in peace.

But the problem still remained. She'd been framed, and the courier's gruesome murder had provided fuel for the fire. Seeds popped between her teeth as she bit into another dried fig. She and Eyoés had arrived at Tassam in spectacle, sure enough, but the imagined link between her and the courier's death cut too deep for mere gossip.

Someone among the court has a loose tongue.

A woman's scream shot lightning through her. Gwyndel spun toward the sound in time to glimpse two men through the crowd, each tugging and shouting over the screams of the woman between them. A crowd began to gather. Gwyndel concealed her face with her shawl and pushed her way through.

"The wench is mine! I won her fair," one of the men protested as the woman tried to tear away from him. He slapped her across the face and flecks of blood flew from the woman's lip. Gwyndel's fist turned white.

The other man's face turned livid. "You crossed me! My daughter was not a part of the bet!" he roared with a thick accent.

The brigand's lips curled back in a toothy sneer and he wrenched the woman's arm to pull her close. "What are you going to do? Blubber at the feet of your priggish clergy?" he snapped. The other man fell silent. Might, not justice, ruled here.

The crowd began to turn back. The woman's whimpers were left to join the crashing of the waves. Gwyndel pulled the shawl over her face to hide the blue glow in her eyes. "I will bargain for her life. Now release her," she said. The words rumbled in her chest as she spoke them, and she saw surprise on the men's faces.

Clutching the girl like a hungry mongrel, the brigand eyed Gwyndel with suspicion. "Bargain? With what?" he asked.

She hurriedly looked for options. Her eyes alighted on a familiar pile of cards strewn across a low table. "You won her, and I'll win her back," she said.

The man's brows shot up and he shoved his prize toward one of his friends. "Or lose, and then I have you both," he said. The crowd surrounded the table as the cards were gathered and shuffled.

Gwyndel settled down onto a threadbare cushion as the cards were dealt. With the crowd of sailors and merchants breathing down her neck, she pressed her doubts into a corner and focused.

Her opponent laid a set of pieces on an X-shaped board and drew a card. He eyed her with a smirk and moved a piece on the board. She ignored him and drew a card. A set of symbols were displayed on it, and she noticed similar markings on the board beside the table.

The crowd's gossip grew dull in her ear. She studied her card, tattered edges and all. Smelled the crowd and the cheap wine on their lips. Felt the warmth of light tingle on her fingertips. With eyes aglow, she let the card tumble from her hand and moved her piece.

The brigand's smirk disappeared. He shot a bitter scowl at the ogling crowd and drew another card. The piece hesitated in his hands for a moment. Gwyndel took another card and answered his move. The man's face flushed and he moved again. She made her final move and dropped her piece on the board with a light clack. To a trusting heart, the Sword Imperishable illuminated the truth of all things.

The crowd erupted into applause. Dumbstruck, the loser shouted his objections, swallowed by the mob as they congratulated Gwyndel on her victory. She rose from her seat and returned the bleeding woman to her father. Bowing her head, she slipped free of the crowd and made for the shoreline with its hissing waves and crying gulls. From the deep shadows of bobbing ships, eyes trailed her.

24

Steam rose from black coffee as Sabaah poured two cups full. "You look tired," he said, picking up the tray.

Eyoés squinted against the crisp morning light reflecting off the pure white walls. Taking up one of the colorful pillows scattered across the floor like stray brush strokes, he stuffed it behind his back and slumped. Slender vases cradled vibrant green papyrus leaves, and the heavy incense choked him. But the bubbling fountain brought some relief.

He took his cup with a weary smile, eyed the room and shook his head. "I wouldn't have guessed you had such luxurious taste," he remarked.

Sabaah set aside the tray and settled down beside the fountain. "It used to be the baron's quarters," he said. "Wisam chose a more humble room. For religious reasons."

Eyoés frowned. "He's taken holy orders?"

Sabaah quickly shook his head. "While he would prefer it, Wisam's bound to the duties of state, but he tries to imitate an ascetic's lifestyle as much as possible. Kahnna, however, has taken vows as a Sanctum healer," he said.

Eyoés took a sip of his coffee and winced as the richness caught him by surprise. He set the cup down after another sip. "I visited the Sanctum's library and read about what the Searchers did to Kahnna and Wisam's parents," he said.

Clenching his jaw, Sabaah set his cup firmly on the tray and rose, stepping over pillows as he closed the window latch. He pulled the curtains without a word. Eyoés glanced at the door. While it comforted him to know that the Wardens of the Watch kept their vigil outside, he knew the state of affairs unsettled them. He'd explained their predicament to the gahrim once they'd returned from Sutaquah. After learning the Searchers were involved, Uwéllor had issued a double guard.

Not only to protect me and Vakros, but to protect the Searchers from themselves.

Sabaah sat and picked up his cup again. "These matters are not spoken of lightly," he said.

Eyoés nodded. "I understand. I'm not trying to reopen old wounds," he insisted.

Taking a long sip of coffee, Sabaah stared at the floor. "The Searchers' interest in Gwyndel has made it difficult for Kahnna and Wisam. It's taken them years to recover from what happened to their parents. They've each handled it in their own way and have taken pains to distance themselves from the Searchers' reach. Until now," he said.

Eyoés traced the handle of his cup with his finger, staring at his reflection in the rich black coffee. His brow furrowed in thought. "I'm sorry. I can only hope that we can remedy the wrongs you all suffered," he said.

Sabaah set his coffee down and wiped away a tear. "What do you mean by that? These things are in the past," he said.

Downing the rest of his coffee, Eyoés clenched his jaw. "Not entirely," he said. He leaned forward. "I stumbled across Kahnna in the library. She was researching the essl cults and looking into the Searchers' history."

Sabaah tensed. His coffee sloshed over the edge of his cup and trickled onto his finger. "Unwarranted curiosity is not a good sign," he mused, swallowing hard. "If the pain of the past is renewed, there's no telling what may come of it. We must keep this between ourselves. I know Kahnna and Wisam will get through this—I'll just keep them distracted with other matters until the storm passes over."

Eyoés paused, considering Sabbah's words. "I hope you're right," he said.

29th *of Aevoran, 2211 SE*

It was the dead hour, when the clouds drifted in front of the moon and a deep silence hung over the harbor, filled with the whispers of the lapping waves. Gwyndel lay motionless on a rickety cot within the safehouse, lost in dreamless sleep. Beside the window, the pages of an open book danced in the night breeze. The streets were silent. But not empty.

Fingers latched onto the windowsill. The open book fluttered as several shadows vaulted in through the window and landed on the floor like drifting feathers. Their cloaks danced as they moved, molding them into a thousand different shapes. Three slipped out of the room and down the stairs, knives shimmering in their hands. Two crept toward either end of Gwyndel's cot.

Their hands shot out and seized her. She woke with a muffled cry as a black cloth was stuffed into her mouth. The odor of strange herbs overwhelmed her, turning her vision cloudy as sleep welcomed her back.

Gwyndel's awareness returned slowly. A glowing speck flickered in front of her as the darkness of sleep took on clearer shapes. First, a candle, drifting back and forth like a fighter studying his enemy. A room, cold and smelling of mildew. Vines splayed over the wall from a crack above.

The candle's reflection shimmering in dark eyes.

Rope chafed at her arms as she strained against them. Her heart spiked at the deep laughter echoing off the walls.

The Searchers—I've been caught!

As her eyes darted between the twisted faces of her captors, her stomach plunged. The way they looked at her like vipers…

The essl cult. The realization struck her like a dropped stone. One of them started for her and Gwyndel kicked at him, nearly upsetting the clattering chair.

"It is a great honor, seeress, to welcome you into our midst," jeered a shrill voice from the darkness beyond the candle.

Gwyndel tugged at her bonds with a fierce scowl. "I'm not afraid of you," she said, the sapphire glow of her eyes gleaming in the darkness.

A lanky figure crept to the front of the group, his face obscured by a white netted veil speckled with crimson. "Nor we of you," he said.

Gwyndel yelped as a blade lashed out three times and sent warm blood dripping down her forehead. A shrill howl erupted from the group and they surged forward, picking up her chair and hoisting it above their heads. Her captors took up a dark song.

How did they know of my gift?

The chair suddenly lurched backward and her stomach upended. Pain speared through her back and she gasped, tears and blood blurring the meager candlelight dancing in her eyes. The smell of acrid smoke snaked into her nose and through her sinuses. A clammy finger touched the cuts on her forehead, and a voice chanted.

By right of this blood sacrifice,
Open thy ears—marked be it thrice
Spirits be pleased—curse to afflict
Render minds by confusion pricked
Tear down, weaken the Sanctum's hold
Restore thy po'er spirits of old
Send this seeress as courier
Carry this curse as sickness dire.

Here lay the Keeper of the Sword Imperishable, helpless against her enemies.

A roar erupted from Gwyndel's lips. "Vehn wass uvinden!" she screamed. The ropes binding her dissolved to ash in a flash of sapphire.

The Golden Tongue. The chants ceased as the cultists shrank back.

Gwyndel rose, gleaming like the stars with the Sword Imperishable burning in her hand. "Vehn wass uvinden. Light has no chains," she said. She swept the sword, and the candlelight swelled into a dazzling blaze.

"Keep your life for what its worth, seeress," the leader's voice growled. "Our triumph is secure."

Gwyndel fumbled for the door as the men cowered, feeling along the ground.

25

"Lady Gwyndel, we've arrived."

With a yelp, Gwyndel startled awake and found herself in a cart of hay. She lifted an arm to shield her eyes from the raging sun and a hand shoved it down. "Stay low. We're passing through the gates," the voice whispered.

Gwyndel winced at the headache pulsing in her temples and twisted around to the front of the cart. Through the haze in her tired eyes, she glimpsed the driver's face as he bounced on the creaking seat.

Uwéllor made a low gesture before she could speak. He pulled the broad-rimmed hat further over his face and avoided the eyes of the gate sentries as they approached. The sight quickened her hands and she covered herself with hay.

A voice called out and the cart squeaked to a halt. Gwyndel froze, hay pricking her face and tickling her nose as she listened intently. Armor clinked an arm's reach away and the butt of a spear thumped along the sides of the cart. She resisted the urge to flinch. After a muttering of voices, she caught the clear tone of Uwéllor's voice. "Hay for the Baron's stables," he said.

"Master Yasef usually delivers the hay himself. Why would he send you?" one of the guards asked.

"Yasef is observing a fast according to the guidance of his spiritual advisor," Uwéllor answered.

The guard grunted. "Wouldn't be the first time. He's rather pious—maybe he should've been an ascetic," he remarked. The other guard laughed.

The cart lurched forward with a groan and the cool shadow of the gatehouse passed overhead. Gwyndel pushed some of the hay aside so she could breathe, then pinched her nose to stifle a sneeze. As the cart clattered over the bumps and ruts of the palace courtyard, she pieced together the haze of her exile. How long had it been?

The days passed roaming the docks had been long. Predictable. Her capture by the essl cult had been an unexpected change. Gwyndel brought her hand up to her forehead and winced. The cuts were freshly stitched.

Keep your life for what its worth, seeress. Our triumph is secure.

Her insides curled at the raw memory and she shivered despite the heat. Knowledge laced their words. Under cover of darkness, they'd taken her life into their hands, toyed with it, and let her go like a hot firebrand. She'd stumbled into the streets and passed out. The gahrim must've found her where she lay.

The cart groaned to a stop. Uwéllor's hand pierced through the straw as he pulled her upright while keeping a sharp vigil. Dusting the hay from her hair, Gwyndel jumped over the side of the cart and hunkered in its shadow. A lone colonnade greeted them, partly hidden by a sprawling tamarisk shrub.

"Go," Uwéllor said, gently pushing Gwyndel along. "My men are over there and will show you the way."

No one was waiting for her in the colonnade. The place was empty, dust drifting across the floor in the afternoon light. Gwyndel clenched her jaw and left Uwéllor behind. Her shadow danced as she raced among the columns. Every brazen step echoed. Her steps faltered for a moment as she saw an arrow being drawn in the dust. Uwéllor's gahrim.

She followed the direction through a doorway and raced up the granite stairs, colliding with a wandering sentry.

The man yelped in surprise as she skidded past him. Brandishing his halberd, he started after her and was thrown backwards down the stairs. The invisible hand grabbed her arm and shoved her down another passage. She ran blindly, the clattering halberd behind her sending her pulse racing. An arm shot out from a doorway as she passed by and pulled her inside.

She stumbled into the dark room and fell against the back of a chair. The door clicked shut and she spun toward the footsteps approaching her with a wild punch. Her fist grazed a jaw in the darkness.

"Watch it!" Vakros whispered, bringing a hand up to his jaw. Sunlight blinded Gwyndel as he pushed aside a curtain. Wincing, Vakros chuckled. "Normally I'd punch back. But for you, I'll make an exception," he said.

Gwyndel blushed. She wrapped her arms around him with a kiss. "Exile doesn't treat love kindly," she replied.

The smile on her husband's face disappeared when he saw the cuts on her forehead. He touched them gingerly. "What happened?" She jumped as the door opened.

Eyoés strode inside, the hem of his loose servant's robe drifting above the floor. "The Searchers are growing restless. There was talk of combing the harbor under cover of night," he said. "I had to get you out of there, Gwyndel, before they—" He froze, staring at the cuts on her forehead.

The look in his eyes put a knot in her chest. Gwyndel nudged away Vakros' hand and fingered the cuts with her thumb. "The essl cult found me. They brought me to one of their rituals," she said. Tears stung her eyes like fire. Vakros' hand brushed her cheek and she fell silent.

Eyoés' face twisted in a scowl and he flew across the room. "You've been used, Gwyndel. But not by the Searchers. Not by the essl cult," he said, catching Vakros' eye as he held her at arm's length. "Someone's feeding the Searchers everything they could ever want to seal their case against you. You're being handed to them on a silver platter."

Gwyndel's breath hitched. "Someone wants me executed for heresy?"

Eyoés shook his head. "No. Someone wants to lure the Searchers with a bait they can't refuse," he said.

She took a fistful of her hair. "Who?"

Eyoés took a step back as he glanced at Vakros. "I have my suspicions, but I cannot say for certain," he said. With a sigh, he faced her. "To lure the culprit out of hiding, you'd have to surrender yourself to the Searchers."

Vakros sank against the windowsill. "Are you mad?"

Eyoés ignored him. He looked his sister in the eye and grasped her hand. "You know I don't ask you lightly," he said.

Fear and duty clashed in her eyes like lightning. Clenching her jaw, she held her brother's hand tight. "I will," she said.

26

Haeryn spurred Taesyra to greater speed, watching the flaxen plains flail under the griffin's beating wings. Squinting against the darkness of the bleak clouds, he leaned forward and strained to see the furthest reaches of the land. Every hill that passed brought him disappointment, but the thundering of hooves droning below the wind reminded him he wasn't alone.

The clouds of North Iostan had spent their tears, it seemed. Haeryn feared to know the reason why. Tugging the hood further over his face, he brought his canteen to his lips to soothe his dry mouth.

It felt strange having his hair cut short. Some would have found it shameful to bear the Phantom League's touch. Nature itself found it a cruel joke, turning his ears frigid. The beating air brought tears to Haeryn's eyes, and he quickly wiped them away.

Perhaps it wasn't only the wind.

At the grim memory of Kinroft, Haeryn growled and threw himself into his work, scouting the landscape of North Iostan. They were close. It had been months since they'd left the Dwarves of Nubaroz to their stalemate with the hobgoblins. Haeryn shielded his eyes and leaned out from the saddle. Shadows played on old wagon ruts cut deep into the plain, scars in the earth. He gathered the reins in his fist and wheeled Taesyra around to signal the others. Hjarti waved in return and the thundering army corrected its course.

Jaw set, Haeryn brought the griffin back around.

We are strong. A family forged in war cannot be broken. Falrey, Santh, and the Phantom League made a mockery of us. For that, they will atone.

A shudder shook him to his core. He'd escaped death by a hair's length, and the shame of that hung over him. How could he have been so careless? Gritting his teeth, Haeryn shot a determined glance at the army following in his wake. A knight kept his word unto death no matter his weakness. Yes, he'd been caught by surprise. And now, he would come back stronger than before.

Haeryn clutched the saddlehorn as Taesyra shot over the crest of a broad knoll and soared down into a low sweep of moorland. His eyes widened and he yanked back on the reins with an oath. Taesyra let out a loud squawk and came to a grinding stop, wings thrashing and billowing as she hovered. Haeryn's face paled.

He'd found the dwarf encampment—what was left of it. Barren plains.

Taesyra eased to the ground as the rest of the army crested the rise and drew to a halt, reins and armor clinking amid the whinny of horses. Haeryn couldn't hear them through the pounding in his ears. As he stared out over the empty moor, he slumped in the saddle as the mist drifted through the grass. They were too late.

A horse trotted up beside him. Without turning his head, Haeryn recognized the rider's sigh. "This is one cruel game of pretend, Dovarul," he said, his voice growing quiet. "How can we call this a war when we win no battles?"

Folding his hands over the pommel of his saddle, the dwarf paused to reflect. He lifted his good eye to where Haeryn slumped atop Taesyra's back. "Don't abandon the fight when the dice rolls poorly, son," he said.

Haeryn lifted a shaking hand to his lips. "Sir Thrynnis never prepared me for this," he said through his teeth. "They're just *gone*."

"None of us were ready," Marc said as he drew up alongside them.

At the sound of the man's voice, Haeryn turned away, unwilling to look him in the eye. Marc was his senior. A knight with great skill and experience. Haeryn couldn't compare himself with him, not the wounds of his own failure were still too fresh.

Marc caught Dovarul's eye. "The greatest victories are those that are the least expected," he said.

Haeryn spun on Marc, tears springing from his eyes as he met his friend's gaze. "We must answer for this!" he shouted, pointing out at the remains of the dwarf camp. "This is not fate! This is failure! And so help me I will settle the score!" Snatching up his reins, he turned as Lanyon and Erling galloped past and rode down into the thick of the empty plain. He left Marc and Dovarul in his wake and soared down after them.

The ground gave a soft crunch as Taesyra landed.

All around him, the land had been scorched. The flaxen grass was gone. Where Haeryn should have seen collapsed tents, only blackened earth remained. Nothing but his memory survived to speak of the dwarves' presence here.

Tearing himself free of the saddle, Haeryn leapt to the ground, clouds of ash rising around his ankles. He turned to where Lanyon knelt. Taking up a handful of blackened soot, Haeryn watched the wind carry it away. "Our friends—turned to ash," he said. He could almost feel scraps of bone and cloth underfoot.

Erling stood beside the Crimson Mark, his face pale as he surveyed the immense breadth of blackened soil. "Dragons?" he wondered aloud. A chill clutched his skipping heart.

The Crimson Mark straightened, sensing the two younger men's eyes fixed on him in hopes of guidance. He frowned. "No dragon could do this on its own," he said, sweeping a hand across the blackened plain.

Haeryn shook his head. "Skreon did it at Asdale. Father told me he commanded multiple dragons that night," he said.

"Falrey has bigger prey in mind than an army of dwarves. My guess is that the enemy set the dwarves' camp on fire during the night," Lanyon said, standing up and returning to his horse to retrieve his waterskin.

Erling's expression turned grim. "Then Brol and the Dwarves of Nubaroz are dead," he said.

Lanyon's eyes flared in defiance. "Not all. These tracks tell a different story," he said, pointing. A wide swath of scorched ground was trampled flat and worn down from many feet. Stopping up his waterskin, Lanyon mounted his horse and took up the reins. "If Falrey saw fit to let some escape, we may be lucky enough to rejoin them further on," he said, digging in his heels and galloping back toward the front lines to discuss the matter with Neifon and Caywen. Erling mounted his steed and caught up to him.

Haeryn took one last look at the charred ground. Squinting, he gazed a ways off, shaking his head as his fears got the better of him. War had a reputation of leaving a man's emotions in tatters.

For a brief moment, he'd thought he'd seen the outline of a large footprint pressed into the earth.

27

Shodric felt like a brand new man.

Hefting the canvas bag of wet-root in his meaty hand, he chuckled to himself and glanced back at the sour faces glaring at him from the rickety tent. Shodric popped a portion of wet-root into his mouth and spun to face them, spreading his arms wide with a grin. He dared them to come—*hoped* they would come. On such a miserable, foggy day, he could use some entertainment.

None moved to challenge him. Shodric turned his back on them. They'd grown wise, it seemed. He rolled his dice in his hand, their blue sides sparkling. Perfect twelves every time. Gently pocketing the tools of his trade, he quickened his steps and lumbered off into the mist-draped woods. With loaded dice and a quick mind, it was easy to make a living.

The sharp tinge of smoke hung thick in the air. Blinking to clear his stinging eyes, Shodric weaved through the mass of tents clustered under the arched boughs of a broad cedar grove. He shoved his way through a group of young men and peered above heads in an effort to find his way.

Through a break in the mist, he recognized the familiar standards of three banners hanging limp in the frail breeze. Amberster. Freechildren. Alcarthon. His lips twisted in a bitter scowl. Snapping off another chunk of wet-root, he wiped the spit from his mustache and gnawed on the sweet tuber. After orienting himself, he started up a steep slope.

The tents around him began to dwindle as he crept along a stony ridge, muttering an oath as he stubbed his foot on a projecting slab of granite.

"I heard that," a voice said, undergirded by a burst of laughter.

He turned toward the sound. A spindly lean-to drew his eye, nestled in a craggy alcove. Clustered around a small campfire, three men watched him with a glint of mischief.

Shodric started for the fire and tossed the bag of wet-root at his companions. "Take a look," he said, smiling as the three men set upon the bag like wolves. "Won it off a scrawny Rehil boy."

One of the men managed to tear it away from the others. Plunging his fist into the bag, he broke off a chunk and stuffed it in his mouth. His eyes widened in astonishment and he beckoned Shodric closer. "This stuff must be worth two weeks wages. Maybe more! Wonder where the Rehil got it," he mused.

Shodric eased himself down by the crackling fire with a sigh. Reaching for his waterskin, he shrugged and popped the cork stopper. "I don't know Joss," he said, downing a mouthful of water to soothe his dry mouth. While he welcomed the long-absent pleasure of wet-root, its side effects were a cursed nuisance.

As he passed the bag along, Joss shot him an uneasy look. "You think the Amberster woman will catch onto us?"

Shodric's mouth twisted in a sneer and he swore, his curled fingers gripping the dirt like claws. "I don't care what that harpy thinks. Her petty edicts are a farce to garner attention and bolster her own self-importance. She can't force discipline on everyone," he growled, shooting a dark glare in the direction of the rest of the camp.

From the far corner of the lean-to, a thin-faced Rehil studied him through a squint. "Caywen Amberster is no fool. I've lived long enough under her rule to know. The Ravenstrong coup tipped her over the edge. Made her stubborn," he said, gnawing on the tip of a piece of wet-root. "I'd be more careful if I were you."

Shodric snorted in disgust. "It's not being careful that irks me, Frey," he said, edging closer to the fire. "Saw the pennants a ways back. Caywen's flying the Freechildren's banner—*our* banner—alongside her own and the emblem of this Wyndar Alcarthon. Its as if we belong to her!" He threw his hand up in a wild gesture. "We're not her playthings! And if that wasn't enough, she expects us to conform to her own high-minded ideals. We were meant to be free!" he exclaimed.

Joss nodded to himself, slipping a hidden flask of ale out of his pocket and taking a sip. "Jaaye understood us. She still does. You've seen how she and Caywen get along. If we hold out long enough, we might see the Freechildren leave this alliance. That'll be the break we need," he said.

As he lingered in the dark recesses of the shelter, Frey fingered the tip of his knife. "That will never happen while that Wyndar Alcarthon keeps fighting for unity," he interrupted.

Joss turned to him and raised an eyebrow. "Do you agree with the rumors? That he's a fraud?"

Frey shrugged. "Can't say. I knew a few Phantom Leaguers back in Rehillon who spoke of a hunter that was out to cripple the League. This Wyndar's spoken of things that sound eerily similar. That's all I know," he said.

Shodric hesitated. As the contempt in his eyes dimmed, he shifted his position by the fire. "Even the League fears him?" he asked, rubbing the back of his neck. Frey nodded, and Shodric's stomach pitched.

The clink of reins and armor made him jump. Joss snatched the bag of wet-root from Frey and stuffed it under his knapsack as he scrambled to his feet. Gathering himself, Shodric rose and turned as several horsemen rode onto the bouldered plateau and halted in front of the ramshackle shelter. His breath hitched and he clenched his fists. The riders wore the Amberster colors.

Adjusting his gloves, the head officer swept a disapproving look over the dirty camp as he dismounted and started toward the three men. His companions hastened to dismount and follow close behind. As they drew near, Joss and Frey stood at attention.

Shodric crossed his arms. He would not stoop so low.

The officer stepped up to them and met their eyes in turn. "I don't ask for your name, and I don't care to give you mine," he said, locking eyes with Shodric. "There've been reports of a band of brigands cheating and robbing at will among the ranks. You look like the sort."

Shodric held his ground. "Maybe we are. Then again, who's to say?" he answered.

The officer raised an eyebrow. "Well, if you prefer it that way," he muttered, glancing back at his men. "Search them." The Amberster soldiers swarmed forward as Joss and Frey scrambled back to escape. Shodric clenched his jaw as he heard the thud of fists. He refused to look back.

Dragging their writhing captives away, the soldiers rifled through their belongings like crows fighting over scraps. Shodric stiffened as one of the soldiers tossed a small canvas bag into the officer's waiting hand. Without breaking Shodric's gaze, the Amberster officer opened the bag and brought it to his face. "Smells like wet-root to me," he said. "The baroness has forbidden it."

Shodric's eyes narrowed. "No harm done. Just something to keep us busy between marches," he replied, cracking a dangerous smile.

The officer's face twisted in outrage. "We fight to save our world, and for that, we need every man at his strongest. Wet-root numbs the mind. Neither Wyndar Alcarthon or Caywen Amberster can afford such a risk!" he yelled, throwing the bag over the edge of the bouldered ledge.

He barely knew what hit him.

Shodric threw a second punch and the man tumbled back, tripping over an exposed rock and falling against a small boulder with an audible crack. Before Shodric could raise his fist again, the men-at-arms pounced on him and dragged him to the earth. One dashed to the still form of his fallen officer and knelt. Through the flurry of arms and bodies holding him down, Shodric saw the lifeless eyes of the officer staring back at him. And as the anger faded, panic sent him trembling.

Murder. A crime deserving death.

28

This would be the second execution Haeryn would see this year.

With the light autumn rain pattering on his hood, he fixed his eyes on the ground and braced himself for the inevitable. The clash of Caywen and Jaaye's raised voices filled his ears like thunder. He kept his distance. Lanyon and Dovarul followed the two women with wary steps. Hjarti had joined them a ways back in hopes of dissuading any rash soldiers who opposed Caywen's verdict. It was better to be cautious, no matter how much Lanyon insisted on the army's loyalty.

Haeryn lifted his eyes to the crest of the nearest rise, an exposed knoll dotted with thick bushes and frail trees. A black-hooded figure watched them approach with a grim expectation, looming over the accused as several soldiers bound his hands and feet. The executioner's forbidding presence could be felt even from a distance.

It was one thing to kill in battle, fighting tooth and nail with your heart beating out of your chest. This was different. Intentional. *Orchestrated.* An execution was more than a death—it was an art, meant to communicate justice and swift punishment.

The weight of it polluted Haeryn's mind. Casting a tense look toward the crowd gathering in view of the executioner, he quickened his pace to catch up with Dovarul. "I don't like this," he said quietly, leaning close to the dwarf's ear as he eyed Caywen and Jaaye.

Dovarul brushed a leaf off his shoulder and wiped the rain from his mustache. He looked up at the young knight with dismal amusement. "That's strange, coming from you," he said. "You seek to bring Santh Baklyn to justice but can't accept the execution of a common soldier?"

Haeryn frowned. "This is different," he said. Dovarul merely grunted in acquiescence. Haeryn's frown deepened and he looked away, leaving the dwarf's remark for another time.

This execution is right, no matter how wrong it feels.

"Your man, Shodric, chose his own fate, not me," Caywen said with frigid directness. "I will not bear the burden of someone else's mistakes." Her stern voice broke through Haeryn's thoughts and shoved him back into the present. She marched onward, her back straight and proud as she stared straight ahead, refusing to give Jaaye the satisfaction of looking her in the eye.

Jaaye stormed alongside the Rehil baroness, tense and coiled to spring. In comparison to Caywen's graceful demeanor, she moved like a cornered animal. As Haeryn recalled her story of tragedy and suffering, it came as no surprise.

Jaaye stared daggers at Caywen. "Shodric has fought with the Freechildren for years! He's earned his keep!" she exclaimed, her glaive shaking in her grip. "We need more men with his passion!"

Caywen marched on. "Stubbornness and a hot temper may be assets for your insurrection, but not here. This isn't a peasant revolt or resistance campaign, Jaaye. This is *war*," she said. "Without discipline and unity, we die." She hurried her steps in an effort to outpace Jaaye and leave her behind.

Jaaye thrust the butt of her glaive into the soft ground and halted. "Times change. Situations change. You can't expect everything to fit your convictions. There are bigger battles to fight than the killing of an officer!" she said.

Caywen ground to a halt. Her back was still turned. "You're not asking for change. You just want things done your way," she said. The anger in her tone brought Haeryn to a stop.

Lanyon glanced back at Dovarul and Hjarti and approached Jaaye. "Perhaps we can find a compromise," he remarked.

Jaaye spun on her heels and gripped her glaive with both hands. "Stay out of this," she snapped.

Dovarul's face turned red and he stepped forward. "Shut your mouth, woman," he said, stabbing a finger at the glaive in her hands. "We don't threaten our friends." Jaaye started, surprised by the dwarf's blunt rebuttal. She backed up a step.

Lowering his hand, Dovarul sighed and shook his head. "What about exile?" he asked, looking to Lanyon for a second opinion. "Let this Shodric keep his neck and take his savagery elsewhere."

Hjarti stopped alongside the group, his heavy footsteps shaking the ground under their feet. "What if Falrey captures him? Torture could wring critical information out of this Shodric. We shouldn't give Falrey that opportunity," he said, earning a scowl from Jaaye.

Caywen clenched her fists. "Disunity is what Falrey stands for. If that sickness corrupts our ranks, we will have won the war for him," she said, turning to lock eyes with Jaaye. "Your unpredictability puts our unity at risk. It's time you decide whether you can be someone we can count on."

Jaaye's face turned livid. Before she could retort, Caywen wove up the winding path to the executioner's mount. Muttering curses under her breath, Jaaye followed her.

The two women marched off. Lanyon shook his head with a quiet sigh and hastened after them. Dovarul grunted to himself and followed while Hjarti lumbered to where the army gathered to witness the coming spectacle. Haeryn wavered, letting the silence of the falling rain and the whisper of the wind through the trees linger for a moment.

He charged up onto the open knoll. The sight of the executioner greeted him like a manifestation of death itself, shrouded in a black sack to mask the man's face. Yet as he passed by, Haeryn saw something in the man's eyes. Dread? Any man compelled by his superiors into such a role might harbor second thoughts. Haeryn recognized the man's look. He felt it himself.

He slowed to a stop beside Lanyon and the others. The accused lay over a log, gazing out across the army watching his demise. In spite of himself, Haeryn scowled in disgust at the sight of him. Shodric refused to look his accusers in the eye.

This was no honest man, condemned without cause. This was a criminal. A swine.

Haeryn lingered back as the executioner joined Caywen and Jaaye at the man's side.

Why did I doubt this man's guilt? I stand with justice.

The inconsistency unnerved him. Standing in Lanyon's shadow, Haeryn observed the unfolding spectacle in perplexed silence.

Caywen approached the ledge of the knoll, gazing out over the crowd of soldiers clustering below. At the sight of her, a trumpet rang out, bringing the army's whispers to silence. As the last bright echoes fled into the clouds, Caywen composed herself. "Friends and allies—doubtless you've heard of this man's crime by now. The charge is murder, and that of the highest offense this army has yet seen. Murder of a superior officer," she declared, lifting her voice the best she could. "Crimes like this are more than acts of anger and rebellion. They turn us all into pretenders—those who fight in the name of truth and justice and yet live in lies and selfishness. If this is allowed to stand, Falrey has won the war, and the deaths of our friends and allies mean nothing."

Opening her mouth to say more, Caywen hesitated. She lowered her gaze as she retreated from the crowd's sight. Glancing back at the executioner, she simply nodded. There was nothing more to say.

With a bow, the executioner took up his axe and started forward. Catching sight of the man, Shodric struggled in a final attempt to free himself. Planting his foot on Shodric's back, the executioner hefted his axe to test its weight. Haeryn held his breath.

A blur knocked the executioner to the ground, his axe flung from his hands. Jaaye yanked Caywen backwards and brought the point of her glaive to her throat. "I am finished with this!" she growled, her crazed eyes darting about.

Lanyon's hands shot out in a placating gesture. "Jaaye, what are you *doing?*" he exclaimed, venturing a step forward.

Jaaye's grip on Caywen's arm tightened and she bared her teeth. "I know you all think I'm a madwoman. A misfit," she hissed, tears welling in her eyes. "But I'm tired of being controlled!" Jaaye had drawn Caywen away from the edge and the watching crowd.

Dovarul and Lanyon moved to either side, trying to come at Jaaye from two different angles. "There's no need for this. Put the glaive down," the dwarf insisted. "We can solve this—"

The executioner's axe bit into blood-red soil. Shodric's dead body tumbled as the guards leapt back. Justice had been satisfied. Jaaye froze, her hand slipping from Caywen's arm as her glaive lowered.

Haeryn tossed the axe aside and locked eyes with her.

Jaaye's face twisted in grief. "You?" she said.

Stepping over the fallen body, Haeryn ventured forward. He held her gaze. "Look at me," he said. "Caywen and Lanyon don't know you. They don't understand your pain. I do." The words hung in the silence.

Jaaye bit back a sob. "Why?" she asked, her voice fragile. Broken.

Haeryn stopped, pulling back his hood. "Because you need to let go of your anger. We are not your enemies," he said, pointing at the others. "We are your family. These people have been a salve to me. Let us be the same for you."

As tears trickled down Jaaye's dirty face, Haeryn looked at Shodric's fallen body. "Besides," he said, "the man had a Phantom League tattoo on his neck."

Haeryn left them in the rain.

29

The palace lay in the Searchers choking grip, and Eyoés found little room to breathe.

He resisted the urge to rub his stiff neck as he kept his seat on a nearby bench, forcefully avoiding the fierce gaze of the Searchers stationed throughout the chamber. Out of the corner of his eye, he watched Gwyndel as she lingered in Vakros' shadow, her arms wrapped around Rhoslyn like a shield. Sabaah sat on the floor, twisting the hem of his robe. The focused stare burning in his eyes aged him. Eyoés could see in them the same fear he felt within himself. He grit his teeth and curbed his indignation. This was no way to live, penned in by fear with the axe of judgement hovering above your neck.

In a small act of defiance, he lifted his head and studied the room. From their posts, the hooded Searchers stood in complete silence as they kept vigil over the few entryways into the room. None moved except for Wisam. Head bowed, he paced fervently across the broad tile floor, occasionally glancing at one of the exits. No doubt his court staff lingered outside, awaiting the outcome of the trial.

After Gwyndel's arrest, repercussions had been swift. While the Searchers had insisted that the inquisition was to be a short one, their meticulous routine grated on Eyoés. The High Rector was late. The baron's staff was confined to a maximum of three rooms within the palace complex, and rumors had already begun to circulate. Gwyndel's unexpected appearance had caught the Searchers off-guard and sparked their zeal into wildfire.

There was no telling the lengths they would go to in order to accomplish their ends, and it left Eyoés watching his back.

In spite of this, Eyoés refused to be cowed. Perhaps it was the injustice of it all. Then again, perhaps it was the dominating presence of the Wardens of the Watch clustered at the far end of the room. Adorned in sparkling gold, turquoise, and silver, the gahrim clashed with the Searchers in a silent contest as they held their partizan spears at the ready. Uwéllor stood at their head, his fearsome helmet and fiery eyes seeming to glow as he slowly eyed each Searcher in turn. Eyoés guessed the head gahrim had placed several of his invisible comrades at the entrances in case of an emergency.

Not that Eyoés expected one. Of all those present, it was clear that the gahrim held the Searchers' respect. Even their reverence. He could see it in the eyes of the Searchers as they studied the Wardens of the Watch from the shadow of their cowls. Had it been otherwise, they would have been forbidden to attend the formal inquiry. Razeem and the Order of Dawn had been denied the privilege.

Eyoés crouched beside Sabaah. "Gwyndel is the one to be tried, not us. Why do they herd us like sheep?" he asked. His eye turned to the Searchers' hands resting on their sabers.

Sabaah took a deep breath. "If they find Gwyndel guilty of sorcery, they will consider us bewitched by her blasphemy. They will question us to see if we are beyond saving," he said, his lips dry and cracked.

"Where's Kahnna?" Eyoés whispered, watching Wisam as he paced back and forth.

Sabaah rubbed his forehead with a sigh. "I don't know. The Searchers sent two of their own to fetch her from her quarters," he said. "At least they have the decency to escort her cordially, like the noblewoman she is."

Footsteps echoed in the hall, and Kesahdon's tall, hooded figure drifted into the room. Eyoés tensed at the sight of him. Like a ghost, the High Rector seemed to glide across the floor as he swept his piercing eyes across those gathered. "I apologize for my tardiness. Abbot Behnassos is ready to speak to the accused. I trust all is in order," he said. As Kesahdon searched the benches, a frown blackened his forbidding expression. "Where is Kahnna?"

Baron Wisam stopped pacing and turned to face the rector. He glanced around, distressed. "Two of your men were sent to bring her here," he replied.

Suppressing an exasperated sigh, Eyoés rubbed his weary eyes. The tediousness of the matter was getting to him. "She may still be getting ready," he reckoned, standing to his feet. "I'll find her."

Kesahdon covered the distance in seconds, seizing Eyoés' shoulder and shoving him backward. He held Eyoés' gaze, a cunning smirk growing on his face. "*You* will wait here as one of my men retrieves her, understood? Your witness may be needed during the proceedings," he said. The coolness of his tone did not bode well.

Eyoés' eyes narrowed. He took a step forward to make his defense.

Uwéllor didn't let him. The gahrim commander stepped between them, placing a hand lightly on Kesahdon's chest. The Searcher locked eyes with him in silence. With a growing frown, Uwéllor motioned in Eyoés' direction. "Eyoés Kingson is a noble man. He has spoken with our King face to face, and his loyal service has confirmed him as *ehmónas*," he said. "He and Sabaah are Heroes of Alithell. They may come and go as they please."

Kesahdon's demeanor changed. He stepped back, studying Eyoés through fresh eyes. "A protector of true teaching, then! It is an honor," he declared with a respectful bow. "Perhaps I have misjudged you. We will see." With a parting glance at Uwéllor, the High Rector of the Searchers spun on his heels and started back to where he had come. As he passed Gwyndel, he caught her eye and motioned for her to follow. "The Abbot will see you now," he said.

Kissing Rhoslyn's head, Gwyndel rose and followed, turning back to catch her brother's eye as she was whisked away.

Vakros stood. "We'll be waiting for you," he called after her. As she left the room, he sank back into his seat and mustered a smile for Rhoslyn. Eyoés turned to Uwéllor with a grateful nod and hurried out of the room in search of Kahnna.

The inquisition tarried for no one.

As the door closed, Gwyndel knew she had nothing to hide. Steeling herself against the stares of the waiting assembly, she stood tall and matched Kesahdon's resolute pace. The rector's eyes narrowed as he observed Gwyndel. Her boldness caught him by surprise.

She pointedly ignored him.

Those who walk in truth have nothing to fear.

Fixing her eyes on the mixed gathering of clergy, Gwyndel clasped her hands behind her back and stood firm. The clergy studied her in silence from their seats upon the tile floor. Every level of the Sanctum's hierarchy was present, their differing regalia separating them into groups. From the dim recesses of the room, the few Searchers watched her closely. The passion for discerning truth from error was written on their faces. Gwyndel met each man's eyes in turn.

As Kesahdon joined his brethren, Gwyndel found her eyes drawn to a stout priest sitting at the head of the group, his white and gold vestments seeming to glow in the gentle light of a nearby window.

Bowing his head in reverence to this elder priest, Kesahdon sat beside him. He adjusted his robe and turned to Gwyndel. "Your name and business in Amiranoor," he demanded.

Before Gwyndel could open her mouth, the elder ascetic in white and golden robes lifted a hand and glanced at Kesahdon. Lifting his eyes to Gwyndel, the man motioned for her to come closer. "Please, sit," he said. The warmth in his voice disarmed Gwyndel.

With an awkward glance at the Searchers and ascetics, she ventured forward and sat. "I am Gwyndel of Asdale. My brother and I fled to Amiranoor to seek shelter and aid in our time of need," she said. "My husband and my daughter are with us as well."

Kesahdon nodded to himself with a hollow smile. "You have been accused of sorcery and blasphemy," he continued. "You are aware of this?"

Gwyndel stifled her indignation. "I am. Such accusations are completely false and unfounded," she said.

Pursing his lips, Kesahdon scrutinized her, probing her weaknesses. "There are those who say otherwise," he said. "One of our spies witnessed you roaming the harbor. You were being trailed by a member of the essl cult."

Gwyndel clenched her jaw.

Kesahdon's brow furrowed. "A palace courier was slaughtered in ritual fashion upon the steps of this very building. Your fellows among the cult were trying to send us a message. We are not intimidated," he said.

The implied accusation brought a flush of color to Gwyndel's cheeks.

She checked herself. "The only allies my brother and I have in Amiranoor are Sabaah and the Castle Sanctum itself," she answered in forcibly calm tone.

Her accuser changed tack. Noting the Phantom League scar on Gwyndel's cheekbone, Kesahdon drew a line across his cheek. "What's the connection? An ally of a *different* sort?"

Eyes narrowed, Gwyndel refused to buckle under the rector's accusations. She reached up and fingered her scar. "It was a warning. My father crossed them when I was a child. The Phantom League is not foolish enough to mark their allies so plainly," she countered. Kesahdon raised an eyebrow and opened his mouth to reply.

Gwyndel denied him the right. She leaned forward, fervor smoldering in her eyes. "I speak the truth and speak it plainly, Searcher," she declared. "I am no liar."

Several of the other ascetics gasped, and Kesahdon started as if scorched. Gwyndel searched their perplexed faces—only to notice a vivid blue glow reflecting off the tiles at her feet. Her heart leapt and she froze under their stares, dousing the Sword Imperishable and stuffing her hand into the folds of her dress. She could still feel her eyes glowing a radiant sapphire.

Kesahdon stared back at her, and for the first time, Gwyndel saw him tremble. "Who are you?" he said in a strained whisper.

Gwyndel shrunk back, words turning to dust on her tongue. Swallowing the knot in her throat, she glanced at the elder priest seated beside Kesahdon. He locked eyes with her. Under the potency of his tear-filled eyes, Gwyndel felt understood. This one was not like the others. Where the Searchers saw a threat, he recognized a blessing.

Gwyndel looked away. In Asdale, she had been labeled a sorceress—a wretch infused with darkness. It had been a painful accusation, but she'd shouldered it with patience. Because of their corruption, Asdale's people couldn't have understood. But here, the accusations stung deeper.

She tensed as Kesahdon rose to his feet, reaching for something hidden under the folds of his cloak. "Impossible," he muttered, face twisting in a fit of terror and awe. "The prophecies never foretold this— *heresy.*" The word left his mouth with such vitriol and spittle that Gwyndel flinched. Kesahdon pushed back his cloak and grasped the hilt of his curved saber. The Searchers started forward as one and Gwyndel sprang to her feet.

"Peace, my son!"

Kesahdon ground to a halt at the booming voice and bowed his head in respect. "Yes, Abbot," he said. Fists still poised to fight, Gwyndel relaxed as the elder priest motioned for the Searcher to sit. As Kesahdon obeyed, the other Searchers retreated to their posts. Gwyndel studied the old ascetic with new respect. The Abbot. She should have guessed.

Lifting his eyes to Gwyndel, the Abbot extended his hands in a plea. "Forgive us," he said, his voice broken in sorrow.

Gwyndel paused, lowering her fists as she cautiously sat back down. "There is nothing to forgive," she said, shooting an uneasy glance to where Kesahdon sat glowering. While she keenly felt his threat, the Abbot's appeal disarmed her.

The Abbot bowed low on his knees. "There is everything to forgive," he confessed. "I've allowed you to be treated with disgrace."

Gwyndel's face softened. "Abbot, I hold nothing against you," she said.

Sitting up, the man shook his head. "Please, call me Behnassos," he said. "It is an honor to see the Keeper of the Sword Imperishable face to face." As he spoke, a tear trickled down his cheek.

Kesahdon couldn't contain himself. Clenching his jaw, he glared at the floor. "The manuscripts speak clearly—'from *his* hand will come tongues of sapphire, cleansing heart and mind with fire.' The Keeper of the Sword Imperishable cannot be a woman," he said through clenched teeth.

Abbot Behnassos turned to face him with the utmost patience. "You misinterpret, my friend," he said, laying a hand on the Searcher's shoulder. "It is from our *King's* hand that the Sword Imperishable comes. The one who is blessed with the power cannot be its source. Our King alone is the source of all good things. Have I not told you this before?"

Kesahdon said nothing. The Abbot sighed and let his hand slip from the Searcher's shoulder. "The obligations of your office have sown pride into your heart. Do not let it kill your devotion," he admonished. Gwyndel averted her gaze in an effort to ease the awkward situation. It was the least she could do.

Frenzied shouts from outside the door broke the delicate silence.

30

The Sanctum was under attack.

The news threw the Searchers to their feet as they whisked the Abbot from the room. None spoke. In the vast, empty halls of the palace, their boots pounded to the rhythm of their speeding hearts. The Wardens of the Watch took up the rear, their broad helmets glinting in the fierce sunlight piercing through the skylights above. With every step, the words of the panicked messenger drove deeper.

The holy texts are being destroyed...we don't know how they got in...betrayal...

Gwyndel's insides twisted as she followed in Kesahdon's shadow. She could feel the precious minutes slipping through their fingers. The Abbot's face twisted in grief and horror and Gwyndel's tears burned in the heat. They both imagined the worst—pages of wisdom, curling in black spirals as fire glowed orange on their edges.

Her heart leapt as Eyoés appeared in the hall ahead and raced toward them. The Searchers drew their weapons and stood their ground. "Stop! Don't come any further!" Eyoés yelled, skidding to a halt before he crashed into them.

Kesahdon leveled his saber at Eyoés' throat. "Out of our way."

A shiver coursed up Gwyndel's spine as she caught her brother's look of alarm. "Eyoés—"

Eyoés glanced back in the direction he'd come from and motioned for the group to fall back. "You're being lured into a trap," he said.

Abbot Behnassos pushed his way through the crowd and laid a hand on Kesahdon's arm. "Vagabonds have broken in and are set on destroying holy texts. We must intervene!" he insisted.

The messenger brushed past Gwyndel and hurried forward. "I escaped in time to bring the news. There's no time to lose!" he exclaimed. Kesahdon nodded in agreement.

Eyoés pounced upon the messenger and threw him to the ground. Eyes wide, the man tried to rise, only to be kicked back down. Gwyndel gasped and the crowd of clergy froze in stunned silence.

Incensed, Kesahdon slapped Eyoés across the cheek. "Are you mad?"

Eyes flashing, Eyoés pointed down the hall. "Take one more step and people *die!* Is that what you want?" he yelled, turning to where Gwyndel gaped at him. "The accusation against you. The courier's death. Kahnna's the one responsible—and she has Fóbehn. I saw her take it." Gwyndel felt the blow land. Every eye turned toward her brother, some with horror, some with outrage. Yet he met their looks with shoulders squared. They didn't know him like she did.

The Sword Imperishable flashed to life in her hand. At her lead, the Wardens of the Watch readied their shields and encircled the Abbot and his fellow ascetics.

Wisam's face twisted in defiant rage and he hobbled toward Eyoés, crutch trembling in his hand. "Kahnna is no killer, you liar!" he roared.

Kesahdon's cold stare transfixed Eyoés where he stood. "Deceiver. I have no patience for you now," he hissed. Shoving Eyoés aside, he marched past.

A whistling arrow tore through his neck and shattered the tile at Eyoés' feet.

The Searchers cried out in horror and scattered for cover. Eyoés dove as another arrow sprayed tile shards into the air. The Wardens of the Watch raised their shields to shelter the Abbot and ascetics. Grimacing as shrapnel grazed his exposed arms, Eyoés glimpsed movement from a small balcony above them. Another wild arrow hit the tile. Kahnna was panicked.

In one leap, Eyoés snatched Uwéllor's spear and hurled it.

A sharp cry of pain—and the dark hooded figure tumbled over the balcony railing. Throwing his shield aside, Uwéllor dashed across the broken tile in a blinding flash and caught the falling figure with one arm, carefully ushering her to the floor. Heart still pounding in his ears, Eyoés fought to gather himself as Gwyndel hurried to Uwéllor's side. Wisam clung to his crutch as his leg dangled awkwardly underneath him.

Eyoés pushed his way through the growing crowd of clergymen huddling around the scene. In one strangled cry, Sabaah's grief touched the depths of Eyoés' heart.

Clutching at the spear shaft protruding from her thigh, Kahnna stared back up at him, face twisted as she whimpered in pain. Gwyndel knelt at her side, fingers bloodied as she inspected the wound. Sabaah pressed his fist to his trembling lips, straining to contain himself. Wisam stood silent at his side, face pale as he looked on.

Catching Uwéllor's eye, Gwyndel nodded. The gahrim seized the spear by the handle and pulled it free. Eyoés flinched as Kahnna's piercing scream echoed through the stone halls. In a flash of blue, Gwyndel pressed the Sword Imperishable against the gaping wound to cauterize it. Awestruck whispers trickled through the crowd of Searchers and clergy.

Eyoés wheeled on them, sickened. "Leave us be!" he shouted. The hushed whispers died and the guardsmen retreated. Shaking his head, he turned back to Gwyndel—and felt wood splinters beneath his boot. He took a step back.

Fóbehn lay in pieces at his feet.

Eyoés fell to a knee and scooped up the wreckage. He turned the splintered limbs over in his hands, the bowstring swaying above the floor. It was pitiful. In the light of the windows, the thin strips of gold intertwined in the nutty brown wood no longer glistened with brilliant light. Jagged cracks fractured the exquisite carvings of vast forests that spread across its length. And among the wreckage, the broken quiver lay in a bed of shattered arrows. The inlaid words upon it were now indistinguishable.

Lips trembling, Eyoés blinked away tears as he looked at Gwyndel. "Fychan," he whispered under his breath.

Sabaah could control himself no longer. "Will she live?" he asked, desperate at the sight of Kahnna's pain.

Gwyndel paused, lifting her glowing hand to study the wound once more. "We'll see. The bleeding has stopped," she said, unable to meet his gaze.

With a roar, Wisam knocked the wreckage of Fóbehn from Eyoés' hands with his crutch. "Look what you did to her! How could you pin her like some soldier on the battlefield? She's devoted her life to *healing*!" he exclaimed. Eyoés turned away from him.

Sabaah stepped between them, turning Wisam around to look him in the eye. "He's not the one to blame!" he retorted, pointing at Eyoés. Falling to his knees at Kahnna's side, he tore the turban from his head. "What were you thinking, child?"

The look in Eyoés' eyes pierced Gwyndel's heart. Squeezing a sliver of Fóbehn in his palm, he glanced back at the body of Kesahdon. "You've avenged your parents, Kahnna. Does it satisfy you?" he asked.

Kahnna gripped her leg and squeezed her eyes shut. Her pale lips trembled, curling in a pained grimace. "Kesahdon got what he deserved," she gasped. "The Searchers will regret what they did to me. To us." As she spoke, her eyes settled upon her brother. Gwyndel saw horror and grief replace the anger on Wisam's face.

There's suffering even here, in the shadow of holiness.

Gwyndel's heart lurched as she laid her bloodstained hand on Kahnna's wound. The young woman flinched at her touch. "You told the Searchers about me. About my reputation," Gwyndel said, locking eyes with Kahnna. "You even convinced the essl cult to mark me so I'd be implicated in their devilry."

Kahnna shrank back from her potent stare. "You— you were the perfect bait for my revenge. Without you, I would never have found peace. Isn't that what you wanted?" she said. The truth seeped through her teeth like poison.

Sabaah's shoulders slumped. Sitting back on his heels, he bowed his head in defeat. "I should have seen this coming. I couldn't imagine you being so reckless," he said, lifting his weary eyes to meet Wisam and Kahnna in turn. "I hoped your hurt had healed."

The pain in Kahnna's face twisted in outrage. "Healed?" she snapped, shaking her head with a bitter smile. "Time could never heal this wound! Some things only blood can heal." Pushing Gwyndel aside, Kahnna rose to her elbow with a grunt of effort and spat at Kesahdon's body. She turned to face the Abbot with an indignant sneer, trembling as she fought to keep herself upright. "You! How could you proclaim peace while brutes terrorize the people you claim to love?" she asked, pointing at the Searchers watching from a distance.

Abbot Behnassos fell to his knees, reaching out to clasp Kahnna's hand. "I have attended to my soul while neglecting the souls of those who most need my help. I have wronged you. Please forgive me," he pleaded, voice breaking.

Kahnna collapsed with a growl. "Never," she said.

"We need to get her to a healer's room," Uwéllor interrupted. He gingerly lifted her, careful to keep the wound immobilized the best he could. The other gahrim gathered about him as he turned to Sabaah and Wisam. "Lead the way." Sabaah leapt to his feet.

The Searchers stepped between them. "What about her?" one of them said, gesturing at Gwyndel with a glare of suspicion. "She evaded questioning and returned marked by the essl cult. If she's truly innocent, she wouldn't avoid us." Gwyndel wiped Kahnna's blood from her hands and said nothing.

Abbot Behnassos held up his hand and the Searchers were silenced. "She is the Keeper of the Sword Imperishable, as foretold in the texts. I pardon her by the authority of the Sanctum," he declared. An angry rumble rose from the Searchers.

Eyoés stood and kicked the broken fragments of Fóbehn. "She is innocent! Why can't you accept that the matter's been settled?" he cried.

Picking up a piece of broken tile, Gwyndel turned it over in her hands as her brother's words echoed through the chamber. As much as they wished to believe it, they rang false. Matters were far from settled.

31

3ʳᵈ of Rotanos, 2211 SE

Eyoés leaned closer to the gleaming edge of his sword, the reflection sparkling in his eyes. He drew the cloth across its length, watching the oil spread across his mirror image upon the blade. After thumbing the edges, he carefully ran the cloth along them, immersing himself in the craft.

Eyoés flipped the weapon over and started oiling the opposite side. He paused as Rhoslyn talked to herself, lost in thought as she explored the room with a child's wonder. Eyoés continued polishing with a trace of a smile.

If only I could see the world like that again.

His oil cloth slid across the blade with a renewed dedication. Even as he focused intently on his work, Eyoés found his mind restless.

Why must I always see the world's decay so vividly? After so long, a man can't help but lose hope.

He set down his cloth and leaned his sword against a table. Sinking back into his chair, Eyoés moved one of the pillows aside, wiping his hands clean.

"You're still thinking about her," Gwyndel said.

Eyoés sighed, hand dangling off the side of the chair. "Kahnna? Yes," he said, watching Gwyndel as she poured two small cups of wine. "I had to try to stop her."

Gwyndel set the pitcher aside and scooped up the cups. "How did you know she was a traitor? She lied to all of us," she said.

Eyoés rubbed his tired eyes. He could still see Kahnna falling with a spear in her leg. "In the Sanctum library I read about how the Searchers executed her parents. Kahnna was there, and the way she spoke to me seemed wrong," he mused. "I've seen what desperation can do to people. What it did to me." He took a cup of wine from Gwyndel's hand. Staring off at the wall, he shook his head. "I could have done more. Maybe if I'd talked to her privately she'd—"

"She would have tried to kill you," Gwyndel interrupted, wandering to where Vakros stood, thumbing through a small book. "Kahnna was blinded by her pain. We came to Tassam to seek refuge, not to stir up conflict. The seeds for what happened were already sown before we came." Eyoés fingered the edge of the table in silence.

Vakros swirled the wine in his cup and took a hearty gulp. "Wisam has sent messengers out to his lords in hopes of amassing an army," he said, turning to Eyoés and Gwyndel expectantly. "In the meantime, we can help him here, gathering supplies and weapons for the march against Falrey. We should repay him for his hospitality."

Eyoés leaned forward. "We've caused enough trouble by simply *being* here. I can't bring myself to meddle in Amiranoor's affairs with Kahnna's treason looming over our efforts," he said.

Vakros' eyes narrowed. "You can't be serious," he said.

Eyoés stood, wandering to the open window. "Since Asdale's fall, Gwyndel and I have leapt from one crisis to another. We need time," he insisted, leaning against the windowsill. "We need to reassess. Lessen the risk of making rash decisions in the future that might endanger lives."

Gwyndel paused, staring into her cup of wine. She set it aside. "What about the aftermath? Word has spread about Kesahdon's death. Surely Tassam's people feel the weight of it. They need encouragement to sustain them through these dark times. They're starting to take sides. A divided enemy is what Falrey wants," she said.

Eyoés turned, looking her in the eyes. "I don't know how much encouragement we have to give them," he admitted. With a sigh, he turned back to the view of the mid-morning sun.

Dust rose on the horizon—and the feeling in his stomach told him who it was.

Their time had run out.

Eyoés tumbled out of the open stairwell and ground to a halt in the middle of the hallway, his pack slung over his shoulder. He whirled back, beckoning the others to him as he started down the hall at a run, his sword bobbing at his waist. Snatching up Rhoslyn, Vakros pressed her to his chest and sped after him, Gwyndel following with her dagger drawn. A group of palace servants yelped in fright as they raced past and disappeared into another corridor.

As they burst into the dining chamber, Eyoés ran to the first guard he laid eyes on and seized the man by the shoulders. "Wisam and Sabaah—where are they now?"

Stunned, the soldier faltered, shooting a confused look at his companions across the hall. "The healer's chamber, checking in on mistress Kahnna's welfare—why?" he asked.

Eyoés shook the question out of the man. "Just take us there," he said.

No matter how many days passed, Wisam still emerged from that room a broken man. Closing the door behind him, he shuffled forward and sagged against a nearby pillar. The sight of Kahnna stretched out on a healer's bed terrified him. He squeezed his eyes shut to purge his mind of the horrible image.

The sound of footsteps startled him from his misery. "How is she?" Sabaah asked, venturing forward like a criminal in disgrace.

Wisam denied him the satisfaction of looking him in the eye. "It will be a slow journey to recovery," he answered.

With a weak nod, Sabaah stood before the healer's door. He held his tongue and stared. His hand reached for the door handle—then withdrew, fists at his sides. Clenching his jaw, he glanced back over his shoulder. "This should never have happened, Wisam," he said. "I should have seen this coming. I could have stopped her."

"I love you, godfather. You raised us both and sacrificed so much for me and Kahnna. Still," Wisam said, "Kahnna would have listened to you. You *should* have intervened." Turning to face Sabaah, the baron held his godfather's gaze. "Perhaps it's time for you to distance yourself. Lord Bandar will welcome you in Taiseem," he sighed, placing a hand on Sabaah's shoulder.

Sabaah merely nodded. "I can only hope time will heal your wounds," he said.

"Wisam! Sabaah!"

The two men jumped at the shouting voice and spun as Eyoés thundered down the corridor with Gwyndel and Vakros in tow. Several stunned guards clustered around them, saluting as they approached their superiors. Sabaah hurried forward to meet them.

Eyoés cut him off before he could speak. "Falrey is here," he said.

Sabaah's face darkened. Wisam shot a nervous look at the healer's door. "How long do we have?"

Vakros stroked Rhoslyn's hair in an effort to calm her. "Minutes," he said.

Sabaah turned to Wisam. "Enough time to mobilize the Order of Dawn and garrison to defend the the palace," he added.

Gwyndel wavered. "The gates?"

Wisam shook his head. "Not enough time," he said, turning to the nearest guard. "Alert Razeem and tell them to gather the garrison to make a stand here at the palace—have a contingent escort as many people as you can to the caves below the city." The soldier nodded and gave a command to his men as they dashed back the way they'd come. Sabaah moved to go with them.

Leaning on his crutch, Wisam seized him by the arm and pulled him back. He nodded toward Eyoés and the others. "Take them to their griffin and provide them with whatever supplies they may need," he commanded. "You must leave Tassam with them."

Sabaah shook his head. "I won't leave you," he said. "You and Kahnna have suffered enough on my account."

Wisam tightened his grip. "I insist," he said. "I'll confront Falrey myself. Perhaps he will be willing to talk terms. Tassam needs to see their baron making a stand for their sake, no matter what happens."

For a moment, Sabaah said nothing. Hanging his head, he acquiesced. "As you wish."

Uwéllor led Vakros and Rhoslyn's horse out of the stable by the reins as Eyoés and Gwyndel climbed onto Gibusil's back. "If Falrey sees the griffin's silhouette, he may have his archers venture a shot. Keep south and stay low," the gahrim said.

Cinching their bulging pack of supplies to the saddle, Eyoés looked down as Sabaah brought his horse alongside the griffin. "We can't just leave Wisam to face Falrey alone," he insisted.

Sabaah shook his head. "He's made up his mind. Our safety is more important to him than his own," he said, watching the townsfolk rush through the street outside. "The crowds will be safe in the caves."

He turned to Vakros and Rhoslyn. "Take your daughter out the Trader's gate. It's closest to the coast and will offer you the best chance of escape before the city is surrounded." Vakros and Sabaah dug in their heels and burst out of the stables with the Wardens of the Watch keeping pace at a run. Gibusil's chest rumbled.

Reaching back to clasp Gwyndel's hand, Eyoés sharpened his focus. "Falrey is but a man. The Guide is on our side," he said. "There's no reason to be afraid." After a long pause, Gwyndel squeezed his hand in return.

She wasn't so sure.

Rushing out of the stable, Gibusil scaled one of the buildings and glided from rooftop to rooftop. Eyoés glanced in the direction of the city's main gate. The dust had settled, and the sound of armor and footsteps sounded clearly above the wind in his ears. As they neared the fringes of Tassam's crowded streets, Eyoés drew rein, bringing Gibusil to a smooth landing atop the nearest house.

Gwyndel grabbed her brother's arm as he started to dismount. "What are you doing?"

Eyoés pulled himself free and hopped down from the saddle. "I need to see this. If we are to free Alithell, I have to see Falrey's strategy for myself," he said, kneeling behind the lip of the adobe roof.

Though the distance and awkward angle obscured his vision, he could make out the wide column of troops streaming into the city at a steady march, a lone rider at their head. Eyoés frowned, looking out at the Trader's gate.

Falrey's making no effort to surround the city. He's simply pushing his way through the main gate.

Movement upon the distant roof of the palace drew his eye. He leaned forward, struggling to make out the figures. "Wait—something's happening atop the palace," he said.

"Armed men," Gwyndel said.

Eyoés turned to his sister. "What else do you see?"

Gwyndel paused, brow furrowed. "They're taking up positions," she said, eyes widening. "Wisam's planning to kill Falrey where he stands."

Wisam steeled himself to take another step. Eyes locked on the lone rider approaching him, he descended the steps of the palace colonnade and fell against his crutch.

The crisp blast of a trumpet rang out and the army came to a sudden halt under the swaying banners of Falrey's insignia. Wisam fingered the hem of his shirt and held his ground.

Seated atop a brilliant white warhorse, the usurper held himself high. Gold trim lined the grey waistcoat that accented his imposing frame, and an ebony crown twisted around the man's head.

Falrey kept his steed at a slow walk. There was no rush. No need to bring matters to a conclusion. Wisam could see the amusement in the man's eye as he drew out the awkward silence.

Falrey brought his horse to a stop when it suited him. He paused, brow furrowed as he studied the baron. "It appears you're alone," he remarked, the words lingering on his lips with perilous implications.

Wisam clenched his jaw. "As barons, we can speak man to man," he said.

Falrey raised an eyebrow. Wrapping the reins around the saddlehorn, he dismounted. One of his soldiers hurried forward and took the horse by the halter, guiding it back to the front lines. "Is this more to your liking?" Falrey asked. Wisam didn't respond.

Falrey hung back, glancing across the city to where the Castle Sanctum stood proud, its towers silhouetted against the sky. "I am an honest man, Wisam," he said, eying the baron. "I am not here to take your place or put someone else in your seat of office." He held the man's gaze with intent. "Ask any of my nobles, and they will tell you with utmost sincerity that I am generous to my friends. I do not wish to see your people go hungry, and I will offer you the finest goods I can spare. All I ask is that you swear fealty to me. Nothing else."

A smile spread on Falrey's face. "Swear allegiance to me, and I will march back the way I've come and leave you with one of my officers. It's simply a matter of words, Wisam Ehnados," he said.

The resolve on Wisam's face faltered. Swallowing, he gripped his crutch and looked back at the palace. Something within him lurched as he pored over the man's smooth words. Wisam turned away and squeezed his eyes shut as he fought back the thoughts racing through his mind. Then, with a conscious effort, he forcefully shook his head. "I refuse your offer, you filth," he said, turning back to face Falrey with a stern look. "Amiranoor is free!" His shout echoed across the palace square.

Two arrows streaked down from the palace roof and skewered the usurper in the chest. Falrey stumbled back with a cry of pain, falling to one knee. His troops raised a shout and started forward, only for their king to stop them with a raise of his fist. Seizing the shafts, Falrey yanked them out with a grunt and cast them aside.

An explosion threw Wisam to the ground as Falrey vaporized into a cloud of black mist and a towering dragon formed from the murk. Digging its clawed wings into the ground, the colossal beast sneered, its lips peeling back to reveal a maw bristling with curved teeth. Its amber eyes gleamed and its blood red scales shimmered.

"So be it," it growled with a snort of hot breath. And with a roar like a thousand screams, torrents of violet flame exploded from its mouth.

Eyoés strained to breathe, chest aching as his heart drove him to his feet.

The palace was gone. Pulverized into a dense spray of singed stone. Liquid flame dripping from its jaws like froth, the dragon leapt into the cloud of smoke and vomited another column of fire with vicious passion. Eyoés gagged as the overwhelming stench of burning corpses filled the air and the monster soared toward the Castle Sanctum. With what seemed like a discordant laugh, the fiend dug its claws into the holy place and ripped it apart, flames pouring from its mouth.

Eyoés sprang back with a shout of terror, eyes bulging as he scrambled to where Gwyndel clung to Gibusil. He clambered on just as the griffin threw itself from the rooftop with a screech.

In seconds, they were outside the city, the dragon's screams a living nightmare.

32

18th of Rotanos, 2211 SE, Thaydale

Haeryn clenched his jaw and stared at the chipped stones underfoot, the eyes of Thaydale's town guard digging into his back like pine needles. He loathed feeling like a criminal.

Eyes narrowed, he flung a cutting glance over his shoulder. They still watched him—a patrol of soldiers scattered among the commonfolk like a horde of roaches as they combed through the crowds. Haeryn pulled his hood further over his face. Even in the height of Asdale's decline, he'd never seen a place like this. Since their arrival, the eyes hadn't left them alone.

Haeryn shook his head. "Excessive security," he noted. Turning to Erling, he frowned as the young scout tugged at his collar and dodged another soldier's potent stare. Haeryn laid a reassuring hand on his friend's shoulder. "Unpleasant memories?" he asked.

Erling shot an uneasy look at Caywen. "Lófroy. Sometimes I can feel his eyes. Looking at me. I know he's dead, but his memory still lives. I wish I could forget him," he said.

Haeryn studied Caywen with a sidelong glance. The march had taken its toll, and leaving the army outside the city wore at her nerves. Nestled between Erling and Lanyon, she stood tall, fists at her sides.

Wrinkles creased the corners of her piercing eyes. Haeryn couldn't remember the last time she'd smiled. The tensions of the war were demanding enough, and with the added strain of Jaaye's contempt, it was a miracle she still stood strong.

Yet it was the sadness in her eyes that worried Haeryn the most. He'd heard his father's stories. For years, he'd pictured a gentle smile on her face, only to find the burden of responsibility had stolen it.

And the inquisitiveness of the town guard wasn't helping.

Haeryn laid a hand on Lanyon's arm. "Your ally here. Can't he meet with us outside the city?" he asked, catching the Crimson Mark's eye as he lightly nodded toward Caywen.

Lanyon's stern eyes softened as he glanced at her. With a sigh, he shook his head. "It doesn't work that way," he said.

Caywen raised an eyebrow. "You needn't worry about me," she said, with the barest of smiles as she caught Haeryn's look of embarrassment. She quickened her steps in an effort to convince. With a reluctant nod, Haeryn dropped the matter.

Rubbing the back of his neck, he looked out across Thaydale to distract himself. The street ahead wound along and down the hillside, rising and falling with the earth like a serpent's trail. Buildings clustered along the curving slopes and spilled down into a narrow ravine, sectioned off into districts by winding streets that trickled from the main thoroughfare. The serpentine walls rose over their heads to the left, overshadowing the few rows of shops cresting the ridge they walked. Two towers like giant cedars stood proud on the crowded hillside, connected by an arched bridge that soared above the slums clustered at their bases. They functioned as the castle's keep—the Brothers, the townsfolk called them.

Haeryn turned to Lanyon and nodded toward the towers. "That's our destination, isn't it?" he remarked.

The Crimson Mark nodded. "We keep that to ourselves. People with business at the Brothers earn a watchful eye on their backs," he said. "The baron keeps his ear close to the ground."

A group of surly workmen brushed past, knocking Erling aside. He stumbled, watching the men disappear into the crowd with a frown. He shook his head and stepped closer to his companions. "These allies of yours, Lanyon—who are they?"

Haeryn pressed the matter freely. "You said we'd linger in Thaydale. Let Santh Baklyn think we've sheltered here. Then corner him from our hidden position on the hill over there," he said, pointing to the craggy rock face in the distance. "We need *all* the information if this will work."

Lanyon silenced them with a cutting glare. "Hold your tongues," he said, scanning the surrounding crowd with feigned disinterest. "The less you know, the safer you'll be if things go awry."

The warning took Haeryn by surprise. "What's that supposed to mean?" he asked. Erling tensed. Caywen's look of purpose was untouched.

The Crimson Mark cleared his throat and lowered his tone. "The last time I spoke with this— acquaintance of mine, we didn't see eye to eye. As a matter of fact, we've differed since the beginning," he explained.

Haeryn's eyes narrowed. "What kind of acquaintance—"

Shattered glass spilled out of the nearest tavern and two men tumbled headlong into the street to an explosion of cheers. Haeryn and Erling leapt back. Lanyon snatched Caywen by the arm and yanked her back as the vagabonds grappled in a cloud of dust. In seconds the tavern's patrons burst out of the establishment and spilled out into the street. The two brawlers scrambled to their feet and stumbled back, breath ragged.

The burly half-dwarf with a blacksmith's calloused hands swore vehemently and nursed a black eye, his bloody nose twisted at an awkward angle. Haeryn grunted as the brigand shoved him aside to give himself more room.

As Erling helped him to his feet, Haeryn turned to the second vagabond. His brow shot up.

The man was a broomstick. While a good deal taller then his opponent, his scrawny legs poked out of his torso like the roots of a withered tree. Haeryn expected his arms to hang limp and broken after such an intense scuffle, yet from what he could see through the crowd pressing in around him, the man circled his swearing opponent with the smooth gait of a predator.

Haeryn blinked, and the wiry figure latched onto the blacksmith's shoulders with a deceptive strength. The crowd's shouts rose to new heights. A roar broke through the noise as the half-dwarf clawed at the fingers poking his eyes, stiffening as a fist pummeled his kidney. Dazed by the speed of the fight, Haeryn stood speechless as the blacksmith fell to a knee and pounded the ground with his palm. The lean fighter relented and released his choke-hold. The match had been far from even. As the blacksmith sputtered behind him, the victor bowed to the crowd's applause.

Haeryn glanced to where a group of soldiers stood on the porch of a nearby inn, watching with amused grins.

What kind of town is this?

The crowd started back for their mutton and ale. Haeryn jumped as a piercing voice fractured the returning stillness.

"Well, if it isn't my favorite idiot!" the thin fighter exclaimed, wiping a trickle of blood from the corner of his grin.

Lanyon left Caywen's side and met the man's embrace with a smile—leaving Haeryn and Erling to look on with incredulous stares. "It's good to see you, Wil," the Crimson Mark said, holding the man at arm's length.

The man cocked his head and raised an eyebrow. "*Baron* Wil Moren, actually. Surely you've heard," he said, displaying the signet ring on his finger with a teasing glint in his eye. "You don't expect me to believe that you're completely ignorant of my achievements."

Caywen's eyes widened. "Excuse me?"

Wil perked up at the tone in her voice and flashed a smug grin her way. "Odd, isn't it? I wonder what mother would say if she could see me now."

Lanyon glanced to where the moaning blacksmith lay curled up in the dirt. "What did he do?"

Wil gratefully accepted a tankard of ale from a good-hearted maid. Taking a deep draught, he turned to look at his former opponent with a look of pity. "I effected a new procedure to sift out dishonest craftsmen. They've given Thaydale a nasty reputation," he said. "I prefer to settle disagreements publicly and effectively, if you know what I mean. It's good policy."

Haeryn stared at the man in perplexed silence.

Downing the last bit of ale, Wil tossed the empty tankard back through the broken window along with a sack of coins. "Come, come. Let's catch up like old times," he said, gesturing toward the prominent silhouette of the Brothers.

33

The door to the baron's study clanged back on its hinges as Wil strode inside with a cockeyed grin. He threw his arms wide with a sigh of contentment. "A palace. My friends, I'm a lucky man," he said, snatching up a goblet and pitcher of wine from a broad oak table. "Put a man in the right place at the right time, and fortune falls into his lap."

Haeryn stepped aside as the others passed by. As he saw the broad rug splayed over the floor, he stooped to remove his dusty boots—only to notice the dirty footprints following in Wil's wake. The baron treated his riches like a sloppy oaf. Shaking his head, Haeryn took his boots off anyway.

Lanyon eased himself into a stiff wooden chair in front of one of the windows. "We couldn't help but notice the patrols roaming the streets. I thought laxity was more your style," he remarked.

Wil leaned up against a small table stand and poured his wine. "It depends on my mood. Law and order makes things easier for me and my staff, poor souls. But playing by the rules *can* get tiresome," he said, setting aside the pitcher as he downed a hearty gulp.

Erling gaped as his eyes swept over the chamber's bookshelves and extravagant furniture. Caywen wrinkled her nose at the soiled rug under her feet and quickly sat.

Haeryn cast a disenchanted look across the room. The soft glow of a bejeweled chandelier reflected off the nutty brown ceiling as it meshed with the radiant glow of stained glass windows. Flecks of dust drifted listless in the air. Velvet-covered chairs were scattered carelessly across the room. Shelves were stuffed to the brim with both volumes of civic records and literature. A stack of loose pages lay precariously on one of the ledges. The place smelled of dust, and from the grey lines tracing the engraved furniture, Haeryn found the baron's lack of cleanliness telling.

Erling shook his head and turned to Wil. "How did you come by this place?" he asked.

Wil nodded with a gleam of pride. "The former baron was a sick man in need of an attendant. I slipped past the guards and posed as a servant. It turned out the baron was a generous man with no heir," he answered.

Caywen's brow furrowed. "So you made a fool of him," she said.

The scrawny man pursed his lips and turned to her in mock consideration. "That depends on how you look at it," he replied. "In the meantime, I don't think we've all been introduced."

Erling stepped between them and extended his hand. "Erling," he said, shaking the baron's hand.

Lanyon came to his feet in an instant and gestured to Caywen with a thin smile. "This is Thora. A well-known orator from Rehillon," he said.

Caywen frowned, then mustered a polite smile as she caught the wary look in Lanyon's eyes. "It's a pleasure to make your acquaintance, Wil Moren," she said.

With a chuckle, Wil bowed. "I can only hope you don't change your mind," he said.

All eyes turned to Haeryn. Fingering the frayed edge of a tapestry, he paused. At the insistent warning on the Crimson Mark's face, his face hardened.

I'm not playing this game.

"Haeryn Irongaze," he said, locking eyes with Wil Moren, "son of Eyoés Kingson."

The baron's brow shot up. "Now *that* is interesting," he said, setting aside his goblet as he studied Lanyon with narrowed eyes. "You must be proud of yourself, Lanyon. Forging an alliance with one of the most renowned knights in east Alithell. I won't ask how you did it. What scheme have you gotten yourself into this time?"

Lanyon's face turned to steel. "There's no scheme. I left that life behind me," he said.

A glinting blade slipped out of Wil's sleeve and shot across the room, thudding into the doorframe. The Crimson Mark barely flinched. Haeryn's heart leapt out of his mouth and he yanked his sword free as Caywen sprang to her feet with a gasp. Erling hurried to Lanyon's side. The Crimson Mark gently pushed him away.

Wil spun a second blade in his fingers. "That was for the last time you lied to me," he said.

Wiping the blood from his grazed ear, the Crimson Mark nodded to himself. "Fair enough," he confessed, unbothered.

Eyes locked on his guests, Wil sat back in one of his chairs with a satisfied nod. "Of course there's a scheme. You've always had a penchant for the impossible," he said, turning his scathing glare on Caywen. "I assume she isn't who you claim." Caywen tensed.

The Crimson Mark held his ground. "You know I can't tell you," he said.

The baron hesitated, brow wrinkled in an incredulous stare. A slow smile built on his face as he shook his head, slipping the knife back down his sleeve. "You're still a man of conscience, then. I'd be disappointed if you'd changed," he laughed, leaning forward. "Now for the question that I should have asked first."

Wil's pointed gaze turned to Haeryn. "You're the honest type. What are you all doing here?" he demanded. The question lingered.

Haeryn stifled a scowl and quickly gathered his words. "Answer me and I'll answer you. How do you want history to remember you?" he said.

Scoundrels thrive off infamy. I can mold Wil's hubris and bring him to our side.

The man's brow furrowed. Wil picked a flower from the vase beside him and toyed with it. As he stared up at the flickering chandelier, he chewed the corner of his lip and tossed the plant aside. "Dangerous question," he said. "Pick another." Haeryn clenched his jaw and took a step forward.

A sparkle of steel caught Haeryn's eye as Wil pointed his knife at the young knight. He shook his head. "I owe you nothing," he said.

Lanyon's eyes brightened as he caught on. He stepped between them with an understanding nod at Haeryn. "Then answer *me*—why, Wil?"

The knife faltered. Wil's scowl faded. Pulling at his collar, he glanced at Caywen and Erling. "Have you told them? Who I am? Who you are? Where we both came from?" he asked. His expression hardened as he caught the hesitation in Lanyon's eyes. "Then tell them, and maybe they'll understand."

"Tell us what?" Erling said, eyes darting between the two of them.

Caywen reached out and squeezed Lanyon's hand. "Tell us the full story, Lanyon," she said.

The Crimson Mark's shoulders drooped. With a hesitant sigh, he sank against the table and rubbed his forehead. "Since the day I was born, my father never let me forget that I was an Alcarthon. A hero, born to change the world. Years passed before I realized what that meant. The world was a broken place, and it was my duty to make it all right. My destiny was fixed, so I ran from it. I fled my father's dreams and became their opposite by joining the Phantom League. Wil and I first met over a dead corpse. He's the son of a boatman and we both feared the weight of destiny," he explained, his eyes kept low.

"Then we both deserted the League. Months after my escape, I stumbled into him during a raid on a Ossinder farm controlled by the League. We roamed the world together, seeking out covert assignments to pay our way," Lanyon said. "Wil and I parted ways in Qezul. We'd gotten ourselves embedded in a conspiracy among the dwarves. I lied to him and made my escape while he walked into a trap. Afterward, I decided that it would be better to die than to make that kind of choice again."

Wil spread his arms with a bitter smile. "We were killers, and look at me now—I've become someone!" he declared, turning to Haeryn with a glare. "That is how I want to be remembered, Irongaze. As *someone*. Your turn."

Haeryn straightened. "We're going to save the world," he said.

Wil Moren burst into laughter. "So you're the ones mad enough to defy Falrey!" he exclaimed, standing to his feet as he wiped the tears from his eyes. "I will admit, I am impressed."

Caywen bristled. "You take us for fools," she hissed.

Wil pointed at Lanyon. "If he's involved, you're not fools. All things considered, you rebels might have a chance. Falrey's stretching himself thin. An army spread across the world is brittle. Strike one place and it fractures," he said, pouring himself another cup of wine. "But then again, poke the wolf and it kills you."

Haeryn frowned. "So you're with us?" The man held up a chiding finger.

"Of course not. Falrey could very well kill you all by next month," Wil said, smiling over the edge of his cup. "I'm merely interested to see how it plays out."

Wil Moren knew they fought for freedom. He was content to watch them die for it.

Fists shaking, Haeryn marched forward. "*You,*" he snarled. He lunged, Lanyon and Erling seizing him by the shoulders. Haeryn barely heard their rebuke through the blood pounding in his ears. Glaring at Wil through a haze of red, he struggled to wrench himself free. "People have lost their lives! Their loved ones! And you care only to please yourself!"

Wil shrugged, pulling a small cord to sound a bell. "That's what makes life interesting," he said. Haeryn roared.

The door to the chamber burst open and several guards swarmed into the chamber, yanking Haeryn away and twisting his arms behind his back.

Rising from his seat with a sigh, Wil set aside his cup of wine. "All of you are free to leave except that one. A spell in a prison cell should teach him some manners," he said.

34

Haeryn pounded the door of his cell with his fist, wincing as the rough wood left slivers. Breath curling in the cold air, he stepped back, staring at the specks of blood he'd left behind. Pitiful. A sorry attempt at change.

Just like the rest of his efforts.

He turned his back on it. Closing his eyes, he clasped his hands behind his head and fought to distract himself. He could feel the emptiness around him—the cold air pouring into his cell, the darkness, the vastness. No matter what he turned his mind to, he couldn't escape the reminder of his quick tongue.

With a heavy sigh, he sank down to the floor. After a long night spent on his feet, the warmth of the sunlight through the barred window was a welcome change. He could hear the city as it came to life with the morning. As he tapped on the stone floor, he glanced back at the cell door. Wil hadn't found it in himself to post a guard. Not that Haeryn saw much value in escape. He'd stood up for the cause and earned his stay by it. He didn't regret a word.

Those who refuse to pick sides in this war will end up dead. We'll see who laughs then.

Haeryn snatched up a pebble and threw it at the door.

Prison can't make me renounce my intentions.

The jangle of keys startled him. He clambered to his feet as the door swung inward. "Finally that braggart came to his senses—"

Lanyon stood in the doorway, the ring of keys hanging loosely in his limp fingers. "You need to see this," he said.

Lanyon's horse galloped through the crowds, forging a straight path for those following behind. From the back of the saddle, Haeryn glanced back, watching the tails of Wil's black riding coat flapping in the wind. In their rush to the city gates, they'd passed Caywen and Erling as they joined the servants in gathering fresh clothes and medicine—and the uneasy look on their faces troubled him.

Haeryn laid a hand on Lanyon's shoulder. "Has Santh caught up with us?"

The Crimson Mark shook his head and pulled back on the reins to slow their horse. As he rounded the curve of the road, he brought their steed to a sudden halt. "See for yourself," he said. Haeryn peered over the man's shoulder.

His body turned cold. "Father!" he yelled, leaping impulsively from the saddle.

He ran to where two gahrim kept Eyoés on his feet. With a groan, he stumbled forward into Haeryn's arms. Haeryn's eyes widened as he caught sight of Vakros and Rhoslyn slumped over in the saddle, exhausted. At their rear, Gibusil trudged through the gawking crowds, wings tucked at his side as he mustered the last bit of his strength.

"Haeryn!"

Struggling to support his father, Haeryn looked to where Gwyndel sat atop the griffin's back, her hair tangled and ragged. "What happened?" he asked.

Eyoés groaned and willed himself to stand, gripping his son's shoulders. Haeryn flinched as he looked into his father's bloodshot eyes.

All he could see was horror.

"Three thousand strong, perhaps four," Eyoés said, rubbing his tired eyes. Falling back in his chair, he took a deep draught of warm ale. Sweat glistened on his grimy face in the light of the chandelier, and Haeryn noticed the tremor in his hands.

The sight made him sick. Turning away to gather his senses, Haeryn studied the patterns in the stained glass windows. The smell of his father's sweat lingered on his clothes.

Wil Moren winced as he eyed his unexpected guest. "You've had a rough go of it. Rest and we'll talk later," he said, tossing a handkerchief onto Eyoés' shoulder.

Eyoés set aside his mug and wiped his face the best he could. "No. I need to tell you everything," he insisted.

Grabbing a nearby chair, Lanyon placed it across from Eyoés and sat, laying a comforting hand on his friend's knee. "Falrey attacked Tassam with three thousand men? Are you certain?" he asked with as gentle a tone as he could.

With a fierce growl, Eyoés threw the handkerchief to the floor. "Absolutely—only Falrey *didn't* attack. He marched through the open gates and confronted Baron Wisam personally," he answered, shoulders drooping as he leaned his head against his fist.

Haeryn swallowed. "No one resisted?" he asked, unable to bring himself to look his father in the eye.

Eyoés clenched his jaw. "Wisam orchestrated an assassination attempt as soon as we saw Falrey approaching the city. The usurper fell to his knees with two arrows in his chest," he said.

Spiders crawled under Haeryn's skin. Turning back to the others, he strode to Lanyon's side. "Falrey's dead?" he asked. His father's uneasy silence killed the hope before it had a chance to blossom.

The door opened as Caywen stepped inside. As Eyoés turned to her, she lowered her gaze. "Gwyndel wept herself to sleep," she said. Another figure slipped around Caywen and closed the door—an older man, his face darkened by the desert sun. Haeryn recognized him as one of the company who'd been among the gahrim helping Vakros and Rhoslyn down from their horse.

Glancing at the others with a tired nod, the man walked to Eyoés' side and sat on the floor, leaning against the leg of the table. "Sabaah, of the Five Heroes of Alithell," he said, placing a hand on his chest with the last strand of dignity he had.

Eyoés reached down and grasped his friend's hand. "We both witnessed Tassam's fall," he said.

Lanyon twisted the Alcarthon ring on his finger. "And Falrey?"

Eyoés gripped the arms of his chair and stared at his feet. "He—changed form," he said, brow wrinkling as he struggled to make sense of his own words. He suddenly stood, eyes bright with the light of a horrible memory. "Falrey transformed into a dragon and razed Tassam to the ground before our eyes," he said.

Silence.

A hollow chuckle rose from Wil and he shook his head. "This can't be Eyoés Kingson. A madman who jumps at shadows?" he said. "Do you really expect me to believe this?"

"I'll never forget the dragon's roar," Sabaah interjected.

Wil rolled his eyes. "Men can't change form. Gahrim, perhaps, but not a human, elf, or dwarf. You two are out of your minds," he said. "The wine's strong in Amiranoor. A long rest and a warm gin will clear your senses." He winked with a smile.

In a single leap, Eyoés seized Haeryn's sword, yanked it from its sheath, and leveled it at Wil Moren's throat.

The baron froze, raising an eyebrow in surprise. They locked eyes. Sword trembling in his grip, Eyoés pressed the tip against the underside of the man's jaw. "I am not a liar. I know what I saw," he said. "I show you the courtesy of a warning."

Lanyon slowly rose to his feet, hands extended. "Put the sword down, Eyoés," he said, venturing a step forward.

Eyoés glared back at him through tears. "Believe us. Tell me you all believe us!" he yelled as the blade drew blood.

Caywen lingered at the edge of the room, watching the unfolding scene in shock. "I believe you," she said.

Lanyon took another step forward. "We're your friends, Eyoés," he pleaded. "No matter what comes, we stand by each other."

Wil cleared his throat. "You've convinced me," he admitted.

Pursing his lips in a thin line, Eyoés clutched the sword. Haeryn trembled at the pain in his father's eyes. He unbuckled his sword belt and held the scabbard out to Eyoés. "I believe you, Father," he said.

Eyoés looked into the eyes of his son, and the sword lowered. Taking the scabbard from Haeryn's hands, he sheathed the sword and threw it to Lanyon. He embraced Haeryn. His lips trembled. "I love you," he whispered into his son's ear.

Haeryn blinked back tears. His mind reeled at the sight of his father's desperation. While he had seen the stresses of leading Asdale affect his father, the utter brokenness he saw now shook him deeper than he thought possible.

He turned to the rest of the group. "We must include Jaaye in this. She needs to know," he said.

Caywen clenched her jaw and bowed her head. "Agreed. This situation is more dire than we could've imagined," she said.

"It is only a matter of time before Falrey arrives at Thaydale. Evacuate the city while you still can," Sabaah said.

Eyoés squeezed Haeryn and released him, turning back to where Wil slumped in his chair, wiping the blood from his neck with a kerchief. "When Falrey comes to you, he will burn this city to ashes. He's surely followed our trail from Amiranoor," he said. "You've harbored his enemies. There will be no quarter, no bargaining."

Wil shook his head. "I'm *not* your friend," he said. "As a matter of fact, the only reason we're all having this conversation is because of old allegiances." He turned a dark look on Lanyon.

Lanyon's eyes narrowed. "You consider yourself neutral, but do you really think Falrey will be content with that? He'll demand your loyalty—the loyalty you reserve for yourself," he said.

Wil paused. Rubbing a hand through his hair, he leaned back in his chair and stared at his feet with a frown. "Falrey's quite the zealot, isn't he? And a monster, as you've so kindly explained," he said, tapping the arm of his chair to an odd rhythm. "Men like that get a thrill out of forcing their zeal on others.

After all, why remain unbiased when you can *make* the world conform to your ideals?"

Eyoés nodded. "Evacuate the city," he said.

Wil pursed his lips and shook his head. "There's no need," he remarked, rubbing his fingers together with a growing smirk. "I have something in mind."

35

"Watch your step."

Holding his lantern aloft, Eyoés clambered over the slimy rock, fingers groping for a handhold. Water dribbled across his arms and head from the stalactites far above. He awkwardly çlimbed over the maze of boulders scattered across the gravelly cavern floor. Drops of water echoed through the vast silence.

At the head of the group, Wil swung his lantern side to side and peered into the dark. He took a deep breath. "Ah, cold, stale air," he said, glancing back at Lanyon. "Reminds me of that job in Nubaroz, with the mines and all."

In the shadows, the Crimson Mark's eyes looked hollow. "Why have you brought us here, Wil?"

Wil lifted a finger to his lips. "Don't ask—you'll ruin the fun of it," he said.

Eyoés clenched his teeth and let out a slow breath to calm his bad temper. Trying to ignore the deep ache in his limbs, he fought to restrain himself. The man's flippant manner did little to ease his exhaustion.

At least Vakros, Gwyndel, and Rhoslyn are in the hands of friends. Caywen, Erling, and Sabaah deserve my thanks when we return.

Loose rocks tumbled in the darkness. Venturing into the halo of orange lanternlight, Haeryn regained his balance and squeezed through a narrow cleft between two jagged rocks. His short hair still baffled Eyoés. While he respected his son's privacy, he couldn't help but wonder what misfortune had caused the unexpected change. As Haeryn found his way among the rest of the group, Eyoés smiled weakly. The quiet, shivering boy he'd rescued from Norgalok had become these men's equals.

Haeryn stopped beneath an overhang carved under the earth by time. He joined his father as he passed by. "Santh ambushed us as we were leaving Rehillon," he said, gazing off into the blackness beyond. "I feared he'd killed you."

The shrill squeak of a startled bat made Eyoés jump. Gathering his nerves, he shivered. "I should have killed Santh while I had the chance. He knew Asdale would fall. Traitors inside the castle set him free, and now I must live with the truth that Taekohar birthed one of Falrey's greatest assets," he sighed.

Haeryn shook his head. "You're not responsible for Santh. He made his decision. And I hope to kill him for it," he said.

Wil set his lantern atop a nearby stone. In the flickering light, Eyoés could make out the cavern's sloping walls. The chamber narrowed into a winding passage and he stooped inside.

As the others gathered into the tight space, Lanyon moved to set his lantern down. "Take one of them along. You'll need it," Wil said, ducking around a rocky corner before questions could be asked. The narrow tunnel hemmed them in as they felt their way along the knobby walls. Haeryn muttered under his breath when he bumped his head on the low ceiling.

The tunnel widened into a small chamber where a foul smell assaulted them. The far wall of the small cavity had broken away, leaving a ledge peering out into a large cavern.

Stifling a yawn, Eyoés sat down and leaned up against the wall, grimacing as a fist of rock pressed into the middle of his back. He watched as Wil knelt on the ledge and gazed out across the expanse. "Alright, we've played your game," he said. "What is this about?"

Wil's hand shot out to silence him. He turned to Lanyon. "Give me your lantern," he whispered. Glancing at Haeryn, the Crimson Mark passed the flickering light.

Wil hurled it into the darkness. It spun end over end as it plunged into the depths, shattering upon the cavern floor. The ground immediately whooshed into flame, illuminating a white carpet of withered skins that blackened and curled as fire spread through the entire cavern.

A moaning growl echoed through the caves.

Ears ringing, Eyoés pressed himself against the craggy wall. With a mischievous smile, Wil pulled Haeryn and Lanyon back into the shadows with him. "Consider this a gift to your rebellion," he said.

A rhythmic scratching rose from the broad chamber—and a giant serpent slithered into the light below. Its blue tongue slipped past its crooked teeth and flicked along the walls. The firelight glistened off its pale white eyes and dark purple scales. It growled again as it slithered over the flames, extinguishing them.

Wil pointed to the rock over his head. "We're in front of the main gate. Anyone who wishes to enter my city walks over this monster's head without even knowing it," he said. "My predecessor discovered it while considering these caverns as a possible escape route for emergencies. Called it the Steward. From what I've seen, the blind creature navigates mainly by taste. I don't know how it survives down there."

Haeryn stared at Wil. "You're mad! What are you thinking?" he hissed, shooting a wary look at the serpent slithering below.

Wil grinned. "There was an old tunnel that connects with the Steward's lair. It's blocked by boulders. We'll need Duraval oil. A lot of it," he said. "Crack open his home, and the beast will retaliate. If we time it right, Falrey will feel its teeth. See if he can survive *that*."

Haeryn pounded on the door with his fist. "In the name of the baron and the King!" he said, glancing back as the regiment of soldiers went door to door.

A scuffle of feet caught his ear and the door opened as the woman of the house immediately stepped into the doorway. Eying Haeryn, her brow twisted in worry. "Yes, my lord?"

"How many in your family?" Haeryn inquired. He managed a glance into the room over the woman's shoulder, glimpsing an old man holding several children close to himself.

The woman shot an uneasy glance at the old man. "Six, including myself. Is there trouble?" she asked.

Haeryn looked away. "Pack your things and stay ready. If the trumpet sounds twice, flee," he said. He moved on before the woman could ask any more questions.

As he started down the street, one of the soldiers hurried to his side. "That's all for this street, sir," he said, motioning to where the other soldiers regrouped.

Turning to where the street withered away, Haeryn nodded and marched toward the nearest alley. In the stillness of the afternoon, he could make out the sounds of the men outside the gates as they planted Duraval charges into the crevices of the rock. The rhythmic tink of picks on stone set the rhythm of the passing seconds.

Fingering the flap of his belt, he looked up at the cloudless sky.

How much time do we really have?

The memory of his father's fevered eyes unsettled him. Haeryn believed his father—and yet his outlandish claims sounded absurd. Had he not seen the look in his father's eyes, he would have dismissed them completely.

But if they prove true…

Haeryn refused to imagine the consequences. As the alley spilled out into another street, he turned to make his way up the steep incline and almost ran into Hjarti's hulking leg.

The giant knelt, throwing his shadow across the small houses. There was no smile on his face this time. "Haeryn, we're in trouble," he said.

Nodding to himself, Haeryn cast an anxious look up the street and quickly motioned for the soldiers to continue on. "I know. Sundown will be upon us before long. We've warned barely a quarter of the city," he said, clenching his fists.

Hjarti shook his head. "Not that. Jaaye and the Freechildren—they're deserting," he said.

Haeryn swung open the barrack door to a barrage of shouts.

Gripping the bedpost with trembling hands, Jaaye yelled at the top of her lungs as she faced Erling with a feral glint in her eye. The young scout stood his ground, stretching out pleading hands as he tried to explain. Their voices met in the air and broke against each other in a chaos of gibberish. Haeryn briefly glanced at the open pack on Jaaye's bed.

He snatched a shoe from the floor and pounded it on the door. "Quiet!" he roared.

Jaaye wheeled on him with a snarl. "Leave me alone!" she retorted, stuffing another shirt into her bag.

With a sigh, Haeryn turned to where Erling stood, shaking his head in defeat. "Give us a moment," he said. Erling wavered, watching Jaaye with a hard glare. Bowing his head, he turned away and brushed past Haeryn as he strode out the open door.

Haeryn closed the door and let the silence speak.

He took a seat on one of the nearby beds as she packed her bag, wiping away tears. "I understand, Jaaye," he said, eying the glaive leaning against the wall. It was a distance away.

Jaaye thrust a spare pair of boots into her pack and stepped back, shooting a glare at him. "No, you don't," she snapped.

Haeryn refused to accept that answer. "In Edeveros, I joined a plot to oust the baron. Galeras Estworth. The law protected his corruption," he said, the memory bringing a bitter twist to his mouth. "I wanted to kill him. To look him in the eyes as he died. My convictions landed me in prison. In the end, Galeras was murdered in the very prison I slept in. My patience was rewarded."

With a bitter laugh, Jaaye wrinkled her nose in disgust. "I'm tired of this," she declared. "Tired of kneeling under that harpy's authority! She stuffed my men and I into these barracks like rats and made us wait for orders. They make me sick. Caywen and Lanyon both!" Pulling the drawstring of her pack, she dropped it on the floor with a thud and turned to where her glaive waited for her.

Haeryn came to his feet. "You're strong. Every time life has tried to break you, you endure. You have nothing to prove," he said.

Jaaye froze, hand outstretched to grab her glaive. For a long time, she said nothing. "The Freechildren are better off on their own," she insisted, voice unsteady.

Haeryn shook his head. "You don't believe that," he said.

Bringing a hand to her forehead, Jaaye turned to face him. "I can't take it any longer," she pleaded, brow wrinkled as tears welled in her eyes.

Haeryn locked eyes with her and grasped her wrist. "Listen to me. Things have changed. You heard my father's returned," he said. He clenched his jaw as Jaaye nodded. "He brought grave news. Falrey can change form."

She paled. "Impossible," she muttered. "How—"

"That doesn't matter. I know you feel overlooked, but this is bigger than us. No matter our weakness, we're there for each other. That's what matters," Haeryn said. "We're a family, and we fight as a family."

Jaaye bowed her head. Pulling her hand away, she stepped back and wiped her tears with a resigned sigh. "If I stay, it's because of you," she said.

36

19th of Rotanos, 2211 SE

Merra, Queen of Norgalok, was a failure.

As her Winterhounds skulked around her reindeer's feet, she straightened in the saddle and fingered the talisman hanging from her neck. Her head spun from sleepless nights. The breeze brought tears to her dry eyes. Through the ringing in her ears, she could hear the dejected voices of her army as they lifted a weary chant in an effort to keep the pace.

The march through Taekohar and South Anehstun had brought the heathens to their knees. Even with Asdale firmly under Falrey's banner, some had resisted. Many of the southern towns had been complacent enough—easy prey for axes. Yet when faced with the thick forest and the summer sun, their victory march had slowed. In their time of exhaustion, the Taekoharans had pounced. Like wolves, they'd picked off the weakest sons of Norgalok, lingering just close enough to watch the army's strength fade. Merra grimaced as her stomach twisted with hunger.

The Norgalokans, terrors of the wasteland, had become prey themselves. They had escaped with a severely reduced number of troops. It was an embarrassment.

Taking a deep breath of the brisk autumn air, Merra relished the grey skies. Her reindeer snorted, leaves crackling under its hooves. As she studied the barren trees, she shuddered, shying away from their twisted fingers.

I've failed to win Falrey the honor he craves. He will exact a heavy price.

A chill spread down to her fingertips. She'd seen what he demanded. Shaklun's sacrifices to Olthroc had proven it to her. Now, with a crown upon his head, no outcry would be safe from his judgment. Merra turned in the saddle and looked across the derelict ranks as they wound through the forest to the rhythm of their lumbering song. Bleary eyed. Filthy. They were all Merra had to show for her efforts.

Grasping her talisman in a clenched fist, she guided her reindeer around an outcrop of rock and trotted up a nearby slope into an open plateau. As she dismounted and walked among her Winterhounds, she gazed down on the valley below. Thaydale waited in silence, draped over the side of a broad hill. From afar, she glimpsed the distant forms of guards patrolling the walls, and yet the city streets looked empty.

A distance from the main gates, a large encampment teemed with life. Above the centermost tent, Falrey's banner stirred in the breeze, with the pennant denoting Santh's division hanging not far away.

Merra's breath hitched. The Winterhounds sensed it and growled, hackles rising. Her men had drawn to a halt, and she looked back the way they had come from

—then mounted her reindeer and spurred it on to the nearest path downhill.

There was no going back. It was time to face her failure.

Merra could feel their eyes upon her as she rode among the tents. As the bedraggled Norgalokans trickled into the encampment, Falrey's men stopped to watch. Some smiled in mockery. Others looked on in pity. Merra felt exposed. Paraded before the eyes of her inferiors as an example of defeat. Holding her head high, she steeled herself.

A powerful gust of wind surged through the tents as a vast shadow soared overhead, wingbeats throbbing in Merra's ears. She yanked back the reins and looked to the sky.

A giant tail whipped overhead and she tumbled from her saddle with a scream. The dragon's head swerved around, its amber eyes locking on her—and her legs turned to water. She bolted. "We're under attack! To arms!" she shrieked, eyes bulging. A hand seized her shoulder and yanked her back.

"Why flee from your greatest ally?"

Merra pushed Santh away and staggered back. Bewildered, she snatched her spear from where it had fallen. "What?"

Folding his arms, Santh cast a calm glance at the dragon soaring overhead. "Must be a shame to know you've missed it all. Falrey is no longer just a king among men," he said with a growing smile. "He is a god."

Merra stepped back. Her face darkened. She shoved the point of her spear at Santh's face. "Don't take me for a fool," she growled. A gust of wind nearly knocked her off her feet. The ground shook and a rush of hot, stinking air made her gag.

The dragon loomed over the encampment as its clawed wings dug into the earth. Its lips peeled back in a twisted smile of bristling teeth. "Welcome, Merra," the beast said, its booming voice grating like grinding millstones.

Trembling, Merra dropped her spear. She recognized that voice.

The dragon laughed at the sight of her terror. "There is no need to fear. Your loyalty has earned my respect," he said, his eyes flicking to where the Norgalokans looked on in horror. "Your march did not go as planned, I assume."

Merra paled.

The dragon held her gaze, then disappeared as a cloud of black mist swirled in its place. Falrey stepped out from the mist's depths, tugging at the cuff of his raiment. The crown upon his head gleamed a radiant orange, fading to an ebony black as the mist dissipated. "Mistakes are integral to who we are. They shape us. Make us stronger," he said, glancing over his shoulder to the silent walls of Thaydale. "This city is ours. I have seen to it."

Striding between Santh and Merra with barely a glance, Falrey started for his tent. "Come. I've already summoned Commander Ros, and there is much to discuss," he said.

37

Atop the Brothers, Eyoés braced himself against the tower battlements. He clenched his jaw. In the distance, ranks upon ranks of shields glittered in the autumn sun just outside the city walls. Above the sea of polearms piercing the sky, the banner of Falrey O'Dyre flew proud. The bull's red eyes stared at Thaydale with bloodlust.

Wiping away the sweat stinging his eyes, Eyoés turned his back to the enemy and faced his friends. Dovarul stared at his feet. Lanyon stood stalwart as he gripped the pommel of his sword. Sitting upon one of the merlons, Haeryn gazed down into the city from their perch atop the Brothers. Eyoés couldn't bring himself to look Gwyndel in the eye. With the terror of Amiranoor's slaughter seared in his memory, he didn't know what to expect.

All the things I've never had the chance to say...

He looked southward. Toward Gald-Behn, the land of hope.

The Guide must do something.

The hatch in the floor opened with a clang as Wil Moren hoisted himself onto the platform. "Everything's ready. All we need is for that churl to get close," he said, his eyes gleaming with violent zeal.

"Be careful what you wish for," Eyoés said under his breath.

Lanyon didn't take his eyes off the enemy. Reaching for the horn at his waist, he grasped it tightly. "If this fails, we won't have much time," he said.

Peering over the battlements, Haeryn looked to where Gibusil and Taesyra perched on the bridge joining the two Brothers. "Then we won't let it fail," he said.

Dovarul twisted the lacing of his chainmail shirt. "Where is he?" he asked. None wished to answer.

The skies were torn in two by a roar that Eyoés felt in every bone of his body. Cutting through the clouds like a knife, the dragon swooped down over the city and spewed fire from its jaws. The towers swayed on the shaking ground and a wide swath of the city was blown to pieces in a column of violet fire. The torrent cut off and the dragon circled for another pass. Wil Moren leaned over the battlements, gaping in shock. Gwyndel held onto her brother. Eyoés was glad Rhoslyn was safely in Sabaah's care instead of here, watching the horror unfold.

Wil's eyes flashed as Falrey swooped toward the main gates. "Come on," he said through his teeth. Lanyon sounded his trumpet. An explosion rang out and broken rock sprayed into the air. With a roar, Falrey came to an abrupt halt, teeth bared as he searched for the cause of the blast.

The dust cleared, and the Steward sprang forth from the caverns.

Roaring as the sun struck its blind eyes, the serpent wrapped its tongue around the dragon's neck and clamped its jaws shut. Falrey shrieked and tore the snake's eyes out with his claws, wrenching himself free of the creature's teeth. Shouts rang out from the army and they shied back as the serpent struck again, dragging the dragon down to earth. The front lines of Falrey's forces bolted. The deafening cacophony roused the townsfolk from their homes and sent them screaming to cover.

Haeryn whistled and Taesyra alighted on the tower. He climbed into the saddle and helped Dovarul and Lanyon up. The cries of the two behemoths echoed in the open air. "Let's leave them to it. I'll take Lanyon to Caywen's position," Haeryn said, snatching up the reins as he turned to Eyoés.

Father and son locked eyes, and their lives passed in a flash.

Taesyra leapt from the battlements and soared down into the city below. Wil sprang for the open hatch and scurried down the ladder. A shot of panic raced through Eyoés as he found himself and Gwyndel alone. He whistled for Gibusil and climbed onto the griffin with her. A shriek drew his eye back to the carnage.

The serpent shot over the city ramparts and crashed down upon the wall with the dragon still in its mouth. Writhing in a nest of broken stone, the dragon latched onto the serpent's throat, amber eyes glowing bright as if backlit by flame. An explosion of fire burst through the its teeth, turning the serpent's head to ash. Falrey let out a screaming roar that rippled through the dust-laden air.

Gwyndel clapped her hands over her ears. The dragon rose to its feet, wings bloodied and bent at unnatural angles. With another roar, it threw its wings out, bones snapping back into place with sickening cracks as black mist seeped from his wounds. Gibusil plunged down from the Brothers, and Eyoés saw the ranks of Falrey's army move to encircle the walls.

"They're not all going to survive," Dovarul said. The cold realism of his words didn't reach his eyes.

The fleeing crowds trampled each other like frightened animals. Some were pinned against buildings and silently crushed. Haeryn couldn't believe what he was seeing.

Through the haze of smoke, Haeryn glimpsed Hjarti's broad shoulders as he shielded Jaaye and several of the Freechildren from the panicked crowd. A horn rang out as Caywen, Lanyon, and Erling clustered around a broad hatch at the base of the Brothers, helping people to the safety of the Steward's underground labyrinth. Haeryn instinctively ducked as violet flames blasted through the city. The crowd's hysteria grew tenfold.

As Taesyra landed beside Lanyon and the others, Haeryn caught sight of Gibusil shooting down from the sky and landing atop an overturned cart, shattering it to pieces. Gwyndel clung to Eyoés on the griffin's saddle. "Falrey's troops have broken into the city," she said, face pale.

Lanyon drew his sword. "They'll be bottlenecked in the streets. Keep the horses ready—when our chance for escape comes, we'll need them," he said, passing the reins of his horse to one of the soldiers as he made for where the Freechildren stood against the current of terrified townspeople. Neifon and Marc shouted a command and the Knights of the Lance dismounted, guiding their horses out of harm's way.

The scream of Falrey's roar turned Haeryn's blood cold. Another blast of fire shook the ground and the sound of fighting escalated. The horrified crowds leapt out of Wil's way as he thundered into the fray with a whoop, his men following with fierce cries.

Haeryn's daze broke as the fight for survival arrested his senses, heart racing out of his chest.

Falrey will pay for this.

Baring his teeth, Haeryn put on his helmet and wheeled toward the battlefront. A swarm of fur-clad warriors clashed with Wil's forces, beating them back to where the Rehils, Edeverans, and Freechildren mustered as one. A lone reindeer lead the charge, its rider yanking her spear free from the neck of an Edeveran knight. She wheeled on Wil and struck him with a fatal blow, knocking him into the carnage.

Merra. After all these years, her face was seared in Haeryn's memory. Along with other faces—children sacrificed to the gods, women dedicated to sorcery, men twisted into monsters by violent devotion. Hot, angry tears rolled down Haeryn's cheeks. This was the world he'd been rescued from.

The world I have yet to destroy.

Haeryn roared—and Taesyra leapt into the thick of the fighting. Merra's head shot up as the griffin's screech ripped through the din of battle. She leapt from the reindeer's saddle and fled on foot from the griffin's pursuit, leaving several spearmen to face the its rage.

Haeryn pressed Taesyra harder.

The roar of the great dragon sent chills up Gwyndel's arms. Loosing an arrow from a short bow, she watched it fell a Norgalokan and searched the skies. "He's coming!" she yelled.

Gibusil knocked aside several Norgalokans with his tail and clambered atop a nearby building with hobgoblins still clawing at his ankles. Eyoés gripped his sword in one hand and a broken spear shaft in the other as he looked up at the broad wings soaring toward them. He turned back toward the battle. "We need to warn the others," he said, throwing aside the broken shaft and taking up the reins.

The Sword Imperishable flared to life. "No—take me to him," Gwyndel said. "My peace is not his to take." Her father would have been proud to see them facing evil side by side.

The beast was closing in. Steeling himself, Eyoés spurred Gibusil and the griffin shot toward the dragon like a golden arrow. The dragon lunged at them and Gibusil lurched to avoid its bristling teeth. Gwyndel wildly swung the Sword Imperishable as the griffin bounced off the dragon's leg and she felt the blade sear through scales. Screams of agony tore the air. The great dragon thrashed, wings clawing at the air as it fled, fire spewing past its teeth. Eyoés cried out as the beast's tail caught Gibusil on his blind side and knocked them spinning through the air.

Floundering, Gibusil righted himself and the dragon fled over the city in a thundering crash. A large portion of the city wall lay in a heap left in the monster's wake. Eyoés sheathed his sword. "We can make it out!" he yelled. Gibusil regained his bearings and soared over the battle raging in the streets below.

Gwyndel caught sight of Taesyra among a swarm of Norgalokans, Haeryn and Dovarul lashing out furiously in every direction. Gibusil dove into the fray, scattering the fur-clad warriors as Gwyndel wielded the Sword Imperishable. "There's a way out Haeryn!" she cried. "Retreat while we have the chance!"

Haeryn bared his teeth. "I have to kill Merra! She's escaping!" he yelled back.

Gwyndel set her jaw. "Later," she yelled.

Dovarul grasped Haeryn's shoulder. "Come, lad. There are lives that need saving."

Glaring out from beneath his helmet, Haeryn gritted his teeth and left his revenge behind.

38

20th of Rotanos, 2211 SE

Santh stooped, picking up the remnants of a shattered halberd. Ash sifted through his fingers. Turning the weapon over in his hands, he wiped the ash from the blade in an attempt to see his reflection. He hefted the weapon on his shoulder and wandered from Thaydale's crushed gates, smelling a coming rain over the pungent odor of the fires. He threw the broken weapon onto a pile of burning corpses.

He turned his back on the flames. Across the fields, he could see more of them scattered about with their clouds of smoke heralding triumph for miles around. With the banner of Falrey O'Dyre flying securely over Thaydale's ruin, they had broken camp in favor of shelter in the abandoned buildings. Most of the fainthearted townsfolk surrendered to Commander Ros' forces, with only a scarce few choosing to resist. With his dreams coming to life before his eyes, Santh took no heed of such petty concerns.

He stepped over the broken remains of the gates and started down the main thoroughfare. In the distance, he heard a scream. One of the wounded, perhaps? As magnificent as it may have been, the battle had been costly. He smiled. Merra's Norgalokans had taken heavy casualties—and yet their sacrifice had proved useless at destroying the rebels.

War decides who is worthy. She's been measured and found wanting.

Santh spotted a familiar, disheveled figure weaving toward the Brothers. So Merra had been summoned as well. She stumbled as she walked, Winterhounds stalking behind her. It was a privilege to gloat from behind, to relish in her misery as she faced punishment. She wasn't worthy to serve the Great Cause. Too obsessed with her own self-image to care how their mission would affect generations to come.

His eyes narrowed as they entered the shadow of the Brothers to answer Falrey's summons. At the sight of Merra, the guards opened the door to the towers and shied back as the Winterhounds covered her approach. Santh followed alone and without pretense. He passed inside with a respectful nod to the guards and closed the door himself.

Santh opened the door to his sovereign's chamber with head bowed in homage. "Congratulations on your victory, my lord," he said, watching Merra from the corner of his eye. Steeling himself, he dared to lift his gaze.

Cradling a goblet of wine, Falrey turned to face them, fingering the back of an exquisite chair. The spoils of war. "Indeed," he said, setting aside the goblet with a sharp clink. "But this is only a taste of the end. In the days to come, our struggle will grow, testing the strength of all who fight for our cause. I trust you two will be among the loyal." He eased into the chair with a wince as he clamped a hand around his bandaged knee. His unexpected encounter with the two griffin riders had left him pale and limping, and the sight of his visible discomfort unsettled Santh.

Merra ignored the king's sign of weakness. "I am loyal—and you summoned *me* to speak with you, not this cur," she hissed. Santh said nothing to the contrary, looking down as he suppressed a smile. Her slander meant nothing to him.

Falrey's brow furrowed. "You'd be wise to reserve your judgment," he said softly. The man's voice thundered in Santh's ears despite his quiet words. Glimpsing the glow in his king's amber eyes, Santh looked at Merra. She bowed her head and stepped back. The dragon had spoken.

Falrey's look of disapproval lingered. "I wish to discuss the battle," he said, studying his two confidants with a searching glance that pierced to the heart of the matter. "Why did the insurgents escape?"

Santh paused, unnerved by the condemnation in the man's eyes. Merra shrank back, stuttering. "There were too many of them. My men were crushed and I almost lost my life!" she insisted. The words spilling out of her lips filled Santh with disgust.

Santh met Falrey's gaze and clasped his hands behind his back. "By the time I arrived at the far reaches of the city, the rebels were gone. If I may be so bold, my lord," he began, choosing his words with care. "What did Eyoés and Gwyndel do to you? Your strength is more than sufficient to crush them."

Falrey's eyes flashed. "An unforeseen complication," he remarked. "For now, it is none of your concern. Until I better understand my enemies, we must proceed with discretion." He cast a stray look to a pile of books stacked beside him. A copy of King Fohidras' Proverbs lay among them.

Santh nodded. "That's a just decision, my lord," he said.

The distant look in Falrey's eyes waned as he turned to Merra. "But discretion has its limits. Merra, I entrusted you with victory and you squandered your chances," he said. A chill raised the hairs on Santh's neck.

Merra fell to her knees. Head bowed to her chest, she trembled. "I'm sorry," she whispered. The sputtering of candles in the chandelier above crackled like bones in the silence.

Twisting his signet ring, Falrey watched her grovel. "I give you one final chance. The enemy has fled, and you will pursue. When you return to me, you will have redeemed yourself. Otherwise, you shall not return at all. Am I understood?" he asked with a pointed glare.

Merra sprang to her feet and bowed. "Yes, my lord," she said. In an instant, she spun on her heels and fled, throwing the door open and slamming it shut behind her.

Santh suppressed a grin as the nearby tapestry settled. The game was drawing to a close. For months, he had waited for Merra's alliance to collapse on itself. His patience had been rewarded.

He shook his head. "Such a pity," he sighed, eying Falrey to gauge his response.

Falrey caught his glance with a smirk. "Indeed. Her loyalty has not stood the test of time. Many are like her. Their fervor grows cold as the days go on, but there are those whose zeal grows stronger day by day, Santh," he said, rising from his seat with a grimace and taking the last sip of his wine. "You are such a one."

Santh raised an eyebrow. "I am hardly worth such praise. Our cause is what deserves admiration," he said.

Falrey shook his head. "No, Santh. You are the snake of the east, the pinnacle of man. Not a stagnant observer but an active partaker in change. I am privileged to call you my ally," he declared, locking eyes with Santh.

Falrey placed his hand on the man's shoulder. "I favor you over Merra. You have proven yourself not only loyal, but effective. For such a man, nothing is impossible," he said, presenting his signet ring. "You are like a son to me."

Santh's chest swelled. He'd done it. Basking in the triumph of securing royal favor, he kissed the king's signet ring. "Your will is mine," he said.

The rain chilled Merra to the bone, but she knew it wasn't only the rain.

Feet churning the mud, she ran down the broken street, dodging shards of shattered tile and stone. Under the grey sky, the abandoned city appeared its most forsaken, streaked with trickling ash as the rain washed it away. Blinking as raindrops dripped into her eyes, Merra fixed her eyes on the old stable and ran for it.

Her stomach twisted as Falrey's words returned to her memory in a constant cycle. She could almost feel his piercing eyes on her back as she ran, like a wolf slinking behind its wounded prey in anticipation of its sudden collapse. There was no escape. Only the steady plodding toward the inevitable.

Biting her tongue, Merra refused to accept that fate. Falrey anticipated her failure. Yet she would astonish him—*prove* to him that she was no longer the waif raised under Shaklun's dominance. That she had become something greater. The Queen of Norgalok.

Merra ground to a halt at the stable's entrance, pressing a hand against the doorframe as she shoved the door inward. In a world that despised her, the Winterhounds always stood by her side. The creatures crept toward her with snarls of greeting, emerging into the light of the doorway. Merra froze.

Their eyes no longer shone. Clouds of icy breath died on their tongues among pale, yellowed teeth. Merra could sense the difference in their presence. Shaklun's magic, the sorcery of Olthroc, was gone.

Falrey wished to prove her worth.

39

Pressing Rhoslyn to her chest, Gwyndel wrapped her cloak tight around herself to keep out the chill. She shivered, loosely grasping the reins of her horse as the sun glinted off the dew soaking her cloak. While the cold numbed her, she could smell the familiar perfume of decaying leaves. Even in nature, the world changed.

She withered in the saddle, hunched like a gnarled tree bent to the will of the tenacious elements. In her dreams, she had expected the end of all things with a certainty few seemed to share, yet she hadn't expected it to look like this. Persistent misfortune, not sudden catastrophe, would be the power that broke their world. The simplicity of it had blinded them all until it was too late.

Gwyndel craned her neck to peer at the coming dawn through bleary eyes. Brilliant streaks of light coated the scaly trunks like molten gold, trickling down the fissures in the bark like sap. As she squinted, she could make out the twinkle of frost upon the green boughs that hung down into their path, pointing out towards the hoary field that wound along the side of a steep hill. The long, weaving line of trodding soldiers stretched for what seemed to be miles, guarded by the ever present shadow of Gibusil and Taesyra as they kept vigil from the skies. Gwyndel smiled weakly. Some things, some people, didn't change.

She could hear the men's groans. Bloody bandages spotted the ranks like poppies against a canvas of torn surcoats and tarnished silver. The sound of their footsteps clashed in the odd rhythms of exhaustion to the lackluster tune of creaking wagon wheels. Gwyndel had no more tears to shed. The sight of suffering was a burden she had learned to carry well. It was the knowledge of their thwarted cause that kept her awake at night, fighting to preserve her sanity.

And underneath it all, her duty. Of all those suffering on this march to death, the Keeper of the Sword Imperishable was to be stalwart. The last one to doubt.

Gwyndel couldn't pull her gaze from them. These men had been entrusted to her like orphans. Desperate for guidance. She could read the plea in their eyes when they looked at her. They needed to know their efforts were not in vain. That their sacrifice would mean something to their children.

Gwyndel lowered her gaze. She too struggled to believe, and the admission pained her. Her duty as the Keeper of the Sword Imperishable was inescapable— one of her greatest reasons for living. Yet the sorrow spreading deep inside her threatened to numb her heart.

A piercing neigh startled Gwyndel. One of the horsemen struggled to calm his mount as a bobcat scurried away into the brush, pursued by arrows. Rhoslyn stirred under her cloak and whimpered.

Gwyndel slipped her hand inside her cloak and stroked her daughter's hair.

Falrey's roar will haunt her to her dying day.

The realization made her bristle.

I refuse to shrink back without fighting to undo the damage Falrey has done.

She gazed out over the weary ranks as they descended into a ravine, clinging to her waning courage.

I've seen hope and sacrifice drive out terror and evil. Whatever happens, we will stand upon our hope and stand by each other.

Gwyndel veered away from the rest of the column and rose in the saddle to peer down the winding line. Through the trees, she glimpsed the flutter of Caywen's banner as it glittered with hoary frost. She trotted down the hill, catching the weary eyes of the soldiers as she passed them. Rhoslyn grabbed a fistful of her mother's shirt to steady herself.

Gwyndel ducked as the low-hanging branches raked their leafless, spindly fingers through her hair. Leaves crackled under her horse's tramping feet as she slowed, winding around the gilded trunks of pines. She noticed Caywen among a copse of aspens, yellow leaves thick around her horse's ankles. Gwyndel brought her horse alongside and watched the soldiers pass by.

Caywen glanced at her as Gwyndel's horse snorted in the cold air. "Where's Vakros?"

Pulling back her cloak, Gwyndel stroked Rhoslyn's hair. "Guarding the rear with Hjarti," she said. "Making sure we keep our distance from the enemy."

Caywen shook her head and sighed, her breath steaming at her lips. "We can't distance ourselves forever. Eventually, we will have to make our stand," she said.

Crestfallen, she turned to Gwyndel. "What went wrong, Gwyndel?" she said, her once imposing presence crushed to dismay. "I've done what I could to ensure victory, only to watch it slip through our fingers. My ancestors flourished amid these same kinds of trials. I only flounder, wrestling for the chance to survive. I'm a disappointment to the Ambersters. Things cannot get worse." She turned away, suppressing a shiver as she wrapped her cloak around herself.

Gwyndel gazed out across the nearby valley, watching the sun paint the trees golden yellow and melt the autumn frost. "I don't know what the future may hold," she confessed, letting her thoughts speak freely. "I will not shower you with false hope or insist that we won't fail. That would be dishonest." As she spoke, Gwyndel felt the pain imminent in her words. But honesty was a better salve than bald-faced deception.

Caywen hung her head. "I know the truth of our predicament, and it frightens me. I don't know which is worse—to await the inevitable or deny it," she said.

The warmth of the Sword Imperishable dispelled the chill as it spread to Gwyndel's heart. "I've learned that it's by coming to terms with our weakness that we become strong. Perhaps we undermine our efforts by believing we can win the victory by our own strength," she said. "Throughout our lives, the Guide has noticed our plight and given us what we needed."

Caywen's face turned grim. "I'm not the same person the Guide gave the Amber Pendant to. It's been so long, it feels like a folk tale. I don't know if I have enough hope to believe," she confessed. "What if that proves a disappointment?"

Gwyndel's brow furrowed. "You don't mean that," she said. "He gave you purpose when he entrusted the blessed Amber Pendant to you. Without that, I would not be the Keeper of the Sword Imperishable."

Doubt glazed Caywen's eyes as she held Gwyndel's gaze. "What if it was an illusion? It took years before I realized the identity of the man who'd given the pendant to me. Perhaps I'm mistaken," she said. "Perhaps the Guide's blessing on my days was really only in my imagination."

Gwyndel clenched her jaw and pulled her horse back. She knew better than to let impulse guide her tongue—Norgalok's failed speeches had assured that. The simple memory made her cringe. Still, with Rhoslyn's warm body pressed against her chest, and the fate of the world hanging in the balance, the call of the Sword Imperishable beckoned her to speak. "We were meant to cross paths for such a time as this. There's a plan at work here. I'm sure of it. Hardship does not mean he is not with us. I will let you decide for yourself whether you choose to believe it," she said. "Vikar would be proud of your accomplishments."

Caywen stiffened, leather gloves crinkling as she clutched the reins. Turning back to Gwyndel, she pressed her trembling lips together with eyes glistening with tears. "He was," she said. Even in the ugliness of grief, the pride of her lineage showed on her face.

Gwyndel and Caywen eased their horses down a rocky slope, stirring up a trail of fallen leaves as they rode into a small vale nestled in the forest. Gwyndel caught the reflection of the sun shimmering off the smooth surface of a small lake.

A flash of color among the barren branches drew her eye. Pulling back on the reins, Gwyndel studied it from afar, patting her horse on the neck. The wind picked up, and she recognized the tremor of tattered canvas. Gwyndel lifted Rhoslyn with a grunt and passed her to Caywen's arms.

Caywen wrapped Rhoslyn in her cloak. "What is it?" she asked, peering into the forest with an untrained eye.

Gwyndel frowned and dismounted. "Perhaps nothing," she said, flinging open one of the saddlebags and removing an old short sword from inside. Buckling it to her waist, she ventured into the brush, keeping the vibrant blue canvas in front of her. Wings fluttered overhead and she looked up at a lonely crow drifting among the treetops. Its caws echoed. When she lowered her gaze, eyes stared back at her.

Huddled beneath the tattered remains of charred blue canvas, a small band of dwarves watched her in silence. Dirt and debris clung to their beards and darkened their clammy skin. They clustered around several pitiful campfires, the wisps of smoke dissipating in the morning mist. Their eyes rooted her in place. They were ghosts, pale and gaunt. The soiled symbol of Nubaroz hung in tatters.

"We thought you were *him*," a familiar voice croaked, raspy with the beginnings of sickness.

Gwyndel ventured a few steps forward, quickening as her eyes widened. "Brol?" she said.

Rising to his feet with effort, the dwarf lord hobbled toward her, leaning on a crutch for strength. A cough wracked his body. Kneeling before him, Gwyndel grasped his shoulders and turned to call out to Caywen.

"Don't," Brol said.

Gwyndel turned back to him and searched his eyes. "I can't believe you're still alive. Haeryn told me you vanished from North Iostan," she said, her face growing dark. "I know what you've seen. I've seen it too."

Brol shivered and coughed again. "Thousands of years, Gwyndel. Not for thousands of years have we seen anything like it," he said through a hoarse throat. "That monster—he let us escape. Like he was *toying* with us." With an uneasy glance over his shoulder toward his men, Brol lowered his voice. "We're all that survived."

Gwyndel grasped his hand and rose to her feet. "Come. I can lead you to food and a healer. Join us," she said. "You're not alone. No matter what comes, we will face it as family—"

Brol yanked his hand back. "Stop. The march of the dwarves has come to its end. Our brothers in Qelezal have been routed by Falrey's forces. There is no hope for us," he said, unwilling to look her in the eye. "Perhaps we can find our way home. Or die here." Brol turned his back on her dumbfounded expression and walked away, collapsing beside his comrades as they resigned themselves to fate.

Falrey had won his game of terror.

Gwyndel wiped her nose and lowered her gaze. Her steps came reluctantly. Returning the way she'd come, she pushed aside the brush and strode toward her horse.

Caywen shot a curious glance toward the forest. "What was it?"

Gwyndel paused, hands frozen on the saddle as she prepared to mount. "Nothing," she said.

4◊

24ᵗʰ of Rotanos, 2211 SE

Gibusil's reins chafed at Eyoés' icy hands as he twisted them in the cold alpine air. Everywhere he looked, the death of autumn covered the empty landscape. An endless sea of yellowed grass. Grey clouds hanging low over the patchwork of hills. Bare trees scattered over the ridges. Eyoés rode silent in the silence of a land drifting into sleep.

He blinked as his bleary eyes watered. He couldn't remember the last time he'd slept in peace. Wind gathered under Gibusil's wings and he brought the griffin gliding down the current. Clouds painted his face with water as he brushed through. The cold turned his thoughts rigid, and Eyoés rubbed at his tired eyes. Below, he could see the army as it traveled, mile after mile, step upon step. Eyoés grasped a small horn from his belt and blew a quick blast. A second call sounded from the ranks below as the army changed course to avoid the foothills of a snow-crested peak. Eyoés returned the bugle to his belt and swooped low, wind whistling in his ears. The sight of the army both warmed and chilled him.

They'd become his. Soaring above them, he watched their every move like a parent forced to watch the death of his child. Pride gripped him at their

endurance and perseverance. Their pain humbled him
with discouragement.

He'd heard deserters in the night—men stealing
away for a chance to preserve and establish themselves
in this new, wild world. Staring up at the stars from his
bedroll, Eyoés had been rankled by their decision. Yet
he understood. With rations growing lower by the day
and the miles bleeding their strength, escape tempted
them all.

Eyoés leaned forward, applying himself to his vigil
with greater focus.

*Endurance brings victory in the end. Breakthrough
may linger around any corner.*

He clenched his jaw to conquer a yawn.

I must press harder until I see victory.

Eyoés banked to the right, soaring around a
protrusion of rock to better see the land ahead. In an
instant, the yellow hills disappeared. Stone spires
spread for miles across the breadth of the landscape as
shards of rock crowded together so tightly that the
ground underneath was not discernible. Cedars filled
the gaps within the vast labyrinth. Eyoés tugged back
on the reins and landed Gibusil atop a nearby ledge of
granite. A faint, otherworldly whine raised the hairs on
Eyoés' neck as the wind whistled through the rock. The
sound reached past his thoughts into the depths of his
mind, unnerving him though he know not why. He
wheeled Gibusil around and fled.

He returned to the front lines and alighted on a
fallen tree, burned black by lightning. Caywen lifted
her hand and the heralds sounded the call to halt. Eyoés

beckoned Lanyon and Neifon and pointed in the direction of the distant grey stones. "There. I've never seen anything like it," he said, at a loss to describe what he'd seen.

Lanyon glanced in the direction Eyoés pointed. His expression hardened. "Seolta forest," he said.

Neifon checked himself. "Seolta? The legends say it's impenetrable."

Lanyon caught his eye. "Not entirely," he said, gazing out at the distant stones with suspicion. "It's a natural labyrinth—it has an uncanny way of deceiving both the eye and the mind. Time ceases to exist. Colors start to fade. All senses grow dull till the only sound one can hear is the screaming wind."

Eyoés' grip tightened on Gibusil's reins and he straightened, studying Lanyon. "I know we're desperate, but are we tempting fate?" he asked.

The Crimson Mark craned his neck to look Eyoés in the eye. "I've passed this way before. I know the risks," he said. "Falrey will not expect us to come near it, let alone venture into it."

Glancing toward Seolta forest, Neifon studied the rocks from afar. "If we entered a short ways into the labyrinth and lingered there until Falrey's forces pass, we could gain extra time. Perhaps even attack him from behind," he mused.

A raven's hollow croak echoed over their heads, and the bird glided in the direction of the forest like a bad omen. "It's not worth the risk," Eyoés declared.

Lanyon glared at Eyoés. "The battle for Alithell's soul is growing more critical by the hour. The side who dares to risk will prevail," he said.

Eyoés twisted his riding gloves in his hands. "We've risked enough already. You're asking for these men's deaths," he said.

Lanyon's eyes narrowed. "Without rest, they will collapse where they stand. Exposed. In the open. Nowhere to seek refuge except in death," he said. "Please. Scout out the forest, and you might find it changes your mind." The Crimson Mark turned his horse around and trotted back to the front lines without taking a second glance back.

Neifon sighed and followed Lanyon. "Hear him out, Eyoés," he said.

Eyoés shot a glare at the Crimson Mark's back. Catching sight of Taesyra, he whistled and motioned for Haeryn to follow him to Seolta forest.

Taesyra shot past him like a bolt of lighting. Eyoés caught a fleeting glimpse of Haeryn, his iron gaze fixed straight ahead with the single-minded focus of a soldier. A grin spread across Eyoés' face.

Gibusil threw himself into the chase. A gust of wind surged under the griffin's wings and pitched them about, threatening to dash them against the hillsides. Eyoés did all he could to hang on, ears popping. His skin tingled as his foot slipped out of the stirrup and dangled in the void. Holding his breath in the battering winds, he saw Haeryn. The gloom in his eyes was overpowered by a look of total freedom. Eyoés understood.

They'd been robbed of their time together, and this was a chance to get it back.

The sight of Seolta forest destroyed the moment. The dissonant screaming of the wind among the rocks hurt his ears. Haeryn dove into the maze without slowing. Urging Gibusil on in an effort to keep up, Eyoés plummeted after his son.

The forest swallowed them whole. Rising around them like teeth, the stone spires blocked out the weak grey light, leaving an eternal dusk within its depths. Eyoés could hear the sound of their wingbeats echoing off the rock. Gibusil pierced through the canopy of sprawling cedars and landed, wings snapping branches as he ground to a halt.

Eyoés stroked the griffin's neck and peered into the gloom. Light trickled down the stone walls and filtered dimly through the forest. He jumped as moss brushed against his face, hanging limp from the cedar boughs like the hair of the dead. As the trees stretched in crooked shapes, Eyoés imagined he saw hollow eyes gouged into the tree trunks wherever he looked.

He inhaled a breath of the stale, decaying stench of the place and turned to Haeryn. "Lanyon thinks Falrey wouldn't know we were here," he said, startled by the sound of his voice in the silence. "We could wait for him to pass, then appear when and where he least expects us." He shivered and gritted his teeth. "I'm not sure," he muttered.

Haeryn's fingers combed through Taesyra's feathers as he studied the shadows. "You don't know Lanyon like I do. He doesn't lead recklessly. If he thinks we will be safe here, I believe him," he said. He shook his head and his eyes settled on Eyoés. "So *dark*," he said. "Zwaoi—is this what it was like?"

A knot twisted in Eyoés' chest at the thought of Zwaoi's suffocating night, and as he eyed the sprawling arms of the cedars, he realized he'd expected to hear a long wail carried on the wind. He shook his head. "Nothing compares to that land of horrors," he said.

He wasn't so sure.

Gathering up Gibusil's reins, he swept a nervous glance across the terrain. "We should never have come here. If we hurry, we may gain a few more miles before we make camp," he remarked.

Haeryn bristled. "You don't trust him, do you?" he said with a sharpness to his words. "You think Lanyon's a fool but can't bring yourself to say it." Eyoés stiffened and he noticed his son grew quiet. With a sigh, Haeryn looked away. "I don't mean to insult you, Father," he said.

Eyoés closed his eyes and shook his head. "I know," he said, flexing his stiff fingers. "You're right. Lanyon's a capable leader. I know I should trust him and Caywen along with everyone else. But it's harder that you'd think, son. Once you've seen the worst life can do to you, you struggle not to doubt everything and everyone." The wind's screaming whine filled the silence. Haeryn didn't break it.

A flurry of horn blasts sent Eyoés' heart racing. Gibusil shot upward, bursting through the canopy in a cloud of debris toward the main army. Eyoés swerved around the nearest hill and was met with a rout.

The army's ranks shattered like glass under a hammer, fleeing in the direction of the hills with abandon while the banner of the Norgalokans streamed in pursuit. Eyoés looked for Caywen and the others and found them at the rear, desperately trying to rally their tired, hungry soldiers for a defense. The officers sounded their horns to no effect.

Eyoés swooped down upon the foremost ranks of the enemy and Gibusil tore through the riders leading the charge. In an instant, the Norgalokans were thrown into confusion. As he turned around for another pass, Eyoés watched Haeryn and Taesyra hurtle through the thickest column of the enemy. Eyoés lifted his eyes to his allies. Caywen and the others were just at the mouth of Seolta forest.

There was no turning back. Quelling the apprehension rising in the pit of his stomach, Eyoés dove at the Norgalokan ranks in another quick pass and then altered his course for the labyrinth. Gibusil and Taesyra both pulled away from the confused Norgalokans. Eyoés clenched his jaw as the last of their army vanished into Seolta's depths.

The decision had been made.

41

26th of Rotanos, 2211 SE

Haeryn tripped over a curling root and fell headlong into the underbrush. Stale leaves crunched like old bones as he came to his feet with a grunt, wiping the black paste of rotting foliage from his surcoat. He shivered as the cold air lingered deep in his bones. The splintering whack of hatchets and falchions beat a tired rhythm as the company blazed a trail through the web of barren limbs that blocked their path. In the eerie blue glow of dawn, branches were silhouetted in the fog, twisting and curving like limbs out of joint. The dead underbrush seemed to extend for miles in a sickly sea of brown.

Haeryn tensed when another wail echoed through the mist and faded back to an uneasy silence. The wind. Something so common shouldn't have sounded so—*pained.*

Picking up his fallen club, Haeryn clenched his teeth and continued to beat away at the brush. He could see his father out of the corner of his eye. A shadowy figure, familiar only by the way he held himself. In the murk, Haeryn could also hear Lanyon and Erling as they lent their aid.

Haeryn wiped at his nose and tried to spot the sun through the overcast clouds. He could only snatch glimpses. The trees blotted out the sky, blocking every path of escape he could think of. More lies. Seolta was full of them. It taunted him, reveling in his confusion. Haeryn jumped back as a stray branch nearly poked him in the eye.

This was an ageless place, untouched by the taming hand of man. A place better left alone.

Flexing his stiff fingers, Haeryn leaned up against a clammy, dead tree and squinted at the shadowy figure of his father. "Find anything?" he called out.

The figure stopped and turned to face him. "No sign of water," Eyoés replied. Haeryn couldn't understand how the murk twisted his voice, adding discordant notes to it.

Another voice rang out from the expanse. "Surely there's a stream of some kind—the legends speak of one that leads south, out of the maze," Lanyon shouted.

Rustling leaves sent Haeryn's heart pounding. He spun around, hair rising on his neck as Erling emerged from the fog like a specter. Worried lines creased the corners of his eyes. "The sun casts no shadows. The trees themselves don't show any of the normal growth patterns," he said, turning around in circles. "It's as if direction itself ceased to exist!"

Haeryn lifted his eyes to where the stone cliffs loomed on either side of the forest, hemming them in, leading them where they did not want to go.

A waft of smoke drifted to his nose. Haeryn turned, attempting to catch even a fleeting glimpse of their camp directly behind them. The fog had engulfed it, leaving Caywen, Dovarul, and Gwyndel to endure its miseries while they kept the troops calm. The Wardens of the Watch guarded their rear, their invisible presence offering a slight comfort. With the dangers of Seolta still unknown, they'd decided to keep the griffins grounded to avoid revealing their location. Hjarti had ventured into the forest alone. As one accustomed to the darkness of Zwaoi, he stood the best chance of finding a path out.

Provided Haeryn and the others didn't get lost themselves.

"Regroup!" Eyoés said, his echoing voice coming from a thousand directions as he trudged his way through the dead underbrush toward Haeryn. The rustling sound of footsteps filled the silence as they all emerged from the murk, the fog rolling off their clothes like steam.

With a sigh, Haeryn sat at the base of a stump and stared out into the furthest reaches of the mist. He distinctly sensed the vastness of their plight in the air like the morning dew. It sapped his strength.

Look at us now. Blind men, helpless as children.

The statement confronted him at the sight of his companions stumbling around. The glory that once filled his imagination was nothing like reality. Victory, the thrill that had emboldened his every thought, was only a dream.

I've thrown my life to a dead cause.

Haeryn couldn't bring himself to accept it. Their defeat was too keen. Too complete.

We don't deserve this. Are we the victims of some cruel destiny?

287

Leaning on a gnarled branch for a staff, Eyoés hung his head and closed his eyes as the others gathered around. "There must be a way out. We need time to think," he sighed.

Lanyon clenched his jaw. "I didn't anticipate a sudden attack to drive us this deep into the labyrinth. Maybe we could've defeated the Norgalokans on the plain," he said. He stuck his battered falchion into the earth.

Haeryn sat, throwing fistfuls of rotten leaves into the forest. "What's done is done. No one is coming to help us. We'll find a way out," he said.

Eyoés straightened. "The Guide himself will help us. He *must*," he said.

Haeryn shook his head. "Look at us. Our situation grows worse by the day. It's too late. If he was going to help, he would have showed himself by now," he sighed, crushing leaves in his fist.

Stifling a yawn, Eyoés gripped his staff. "In my experience, it's never too late," he insisted.

Haeryn clenched his jaw and studied his father. "Time to reconsider."

Lanyon planted his foot between them. "Division will be our death," he said.

Haeryn's eyes narrowed. "What does it matter? Do our chances look promising to you?" he said. The Crimson Mark held his tongue and turned away.

The sound of Erling's timid voice caught Haeryn by surprise. "I've looked death in the eye. My brother was going to kill me—and nothing I could do, or say, could stop him." Haeryn turned, watching the young scout stare at his feet. "My hour came. And yet I survive," Erling continued, squeezing a fistful of moss as he mustered the courage to look up. "That's the thing about the unexpected. It always seems impossible." Pressing his lips into a frustrated line, Haeryn forced himself to be silent.

Their rescue was beyond impossible—he was just the only one to see it.

42

28th of Rotanos, 2211 SE

Another bleak dawn, wreathed in fog. Huddled in the niche of a rotting stump, Eyoés watched the cycle begin. Again.

He shifted his position with a grunt to ease his stiff, numb legs. Shaking his head, he settled back against the stump. The cold seeped deeper and deeper into his joints like a disease, numbing his extremities one by one.

Working his fingers, he hunched over the small fire crackling by his side and added another twig to the small nest. The flames trembled weakly in the moist air. Eyoés could barely smell the wisp of smoke twitching above the fire, but it was warmth.

He blinked his bleary eyes and scanned the forest again. The wailing wind had run out of breath for the moment. His ears still rang from its pained cries. As Eyoés rubbed his numb jaw, he glanced back at the colony of tents crowded among the twisted trees. While they slept, their lives rested in his hands.

Swallowing, Eyoés tore a chunk of moss from the ground and twisted it in his fingers as he looked away. In the scheme of things, the responsibility was trivial. Since their arrival in Seolta, there had been no sign of life. During the night, Hjarti had discovered a hidden spring of fresh water, but no path of escape. Their water stores had been running dangerously low, so the discovery was a blessing in itself. Eyoés had spent one sleepless night, that was all. Yet even as the dawn brought an end to his vigil, his chest tightened.

Many lives rest in my hands. They will still be there even when this watch is over.

His gaze lingered over Haeryn's shelter at the far edge of the encampment. A piece of tattered canvas drawn between two trees, glittering with the recent rain. Eyoés could see his son curled up in a meager blanket underneath it. Despite Gwyndel's insistence to the contrary, Haeryn had purposely embraced the frigid nights of Seolta, exposing himself to the elements. He'd never pampered himself while others suffered—and for that, Eyoés was proud.

But Haeryn's bitter words against the Guide…

Eyoés' smile faded. With a heavy sigh, he rubbed his sore eyes. The thoughts he refused to embrace he'd found in his son's mouth. A gentle hiss drew his eye to the fire as the last flame died, sending its last breath of smoke into the misty air. Eyoés didn't bother to rekindle it.

Does the Guide not see we're losing our hope? We're all despairing, each in our own way.

A crack rang through the silence. Eyoés held his breath as he stared into the endless void of twisting branches and fog. Another snap, and footsteps caught his ear. Reaching for his sword, Eyoés huddled in the shadow of the stump and craned his neck to catch a glimpse of the intruder. The steps drew nearer.

Eyoés leapt from cover and drew his sword on a stunned Dovarul.

The dwarf backed away, hands extended. "Easy now!" he said.

Shaking his head, Eyoés sheathed his sword and studied the silent tents beyond. "I thought you were asleep," he sighed, taking a deep breath as he rubbed his bleary eyes.

The dwarf stifled a yawn. "I woke early to gather a report of the night watch," he explained, frowning as Eyoés tugged gruffly at his cloak. "You're a bit tense."

Eyoés avoided the dwarf's gaze. "I'm fine. Wishing for a better fire, that's all," he said.

Dovarul eyed him carefully, then moved on. Climbing up the sloped back of the stump, he sat down and pulled on a pair of gloves. "You're not fine—none of us are. Be honest with me, son," he said.

Placing a hand on the soggy stump, Eyoés slumped against it. "How much more can we take? Every turn leads us to disappointment and peril. When will it end?" he asked.

Dovarul glanced up at the soaring trees. "This forest has a way of making time obsolete. Makes a man feel he's doomed to be crushed with no end in sight. Remember," he said, turning to Eyoés, "our enemy is certain that if we're battered on the rocks long enough, we will yield. Will you prove him right?"

Clenching his jaw, Eyoés kept silent.

The hopeful smile on Dovarul's face waned. Hopping off the stump with a grunt, the dwarf sighed. "To tell you the truth, lad, I come to you with bad news. You know Erling was among the night watch. He wasn't with the others this morning," he said.

Eyoés turned. "What?"

Dovarul nodded. "Hjarti said he saw him venture off into the forest that way," he said, motioning to a convoluted tangle of trees that hurt to look at. "Before he left, Erling said something lay beyond that stand of trees. Whether he heard or saw something we don't know."

Dumbstruck, Eyoés looked in the direction the dwarf had pointed. A thick copse of gnarled branches stared back at him, silhouetted against the eerie dawn light. The night shadows still lingered. White bark peered out of the darkness like pale faces.

Eyoés frowned. "I'll find him. If I haven't returned by midday, leave us," he said.

Dovarul started. "Leave you?"

Eyoés caught the dwarf's eye and held it. "Don't risk losing more lives to find us," he insisted. Dovarul lowered his head with a sigh.

Scattering the ashes of his campfire, Eyoés wrapped his cloak tighter around his shoulders. He nodded at Dovarul and glanced back at the silent tents, then trudged off into the tangle of foggy trees with his sword bouncing at his side.

Eyoés stumbled as his foot slipped in the mud. The cold bit at his fingertips. Crooked branches caught his clothes and barred his path, snapping in a flurry of loud cracks as he forced his way through. He threw his arm up to shield his face.

As the brush thinned out, Eyoés grasped a low-hanging branch and stepped down into a tapering hollow. He looked around. Despite the sting of the cold air in his nostrils, the stagnant, decaying smell of Seolta Forest's depths still lingered. He spotted a boulder looming among the trees and crossed over to it. As he lingered in its shadow, Eyoés studied the forest. Every nerve tingled with the anticipation of an unwelcome surprise.

Where to start?

The sheer magnitude of the labyrinthine forest paralyzed him. They'd been lost for days. After relentless efforts to establish some sense of direction, their best scouts had deemed the place impassable. An impossibility that defied nature itself. And now he'd willingly volunteered to prove them wrong.

Eyoés jumped as the screaming wind started again. He could almost see Erling in his mind—a lonely specter doomed to wander in the darkness for the rest of eternity.

Taking his thoughts by the throat, Eyoés leapt to his feet and marched out of cover. He knelt in the center of the hollow and studied the ground. Evidence would present itself. The labyrinth was an illusion. No forest could defy nature. Such was the way of things, and Eyoés refused to accept the alternative.

He lifted his head and squinted to better capture the shape of the forest. The hollow wound away from him, like some ancient trail long forgotten to time. Looking back in the rough direction of their encampment, Eyoés continued down the hollow.

The ground sloped, drawing him further and further downhill as the trees closed around him. The wind chilled the growing sweat on his forehead. A strange restlessness settled over him and quickened his pace, sending him tumbling forward as his boot caught on a knobby root. Eyoés fell to his knees among the bushes.

The hollow had come to an end. Scraggly bushes now crowded around him, beaten into distended shapes by the elements. Grasping a low hanging branch, he pulled himself to his feet and wandered on.

Something caught his eye. He stopped, brow furrowed. Not far away, he noticed a broad trail weaving through the rotting leaves and underbrush. Eyoés ran to the path of overturned dirt, trodden into mud by many feet.

What passed through here?

A cold, clammy hand closed over his mouth.

Eyoés wrenched the hand from his face and leapt away, grabbing a fallen branch and swinging it blindly. The makeshift weapon whooshed through empty air as Erling leapt back. Pushing away his wet, matted hair, he threw a hand out to stay Eyoés.

Eyoés' club froze in mid-air. The surprise in his eyes quickly turned to a mixture of anger and relief as he threw the branch down. Letting out a forceful sigh in an effort to slow his speeding heart, Eyoés poked the young scout in the chest. "*Never* do that again!"

Erling's finger shot to his lips. "*Quiet!*" he hissed with a tense glance down the strange path.

The quiet scout's intensity caught Eyoés by surprise. He took a step back, straining to hear what lay beyond the silence. Eyes riveted upon the distant woods, Erling started down the muddy trail. Eyoés followed Erling with an uneasy glance at the trees behind him. He couldn't feel his toes anymore.

Erling drew up short, arms held tense at his sides as he looked off into the forest. Plodding to his side, Eyoés followed his gaze. The muddy path swerved among the briars and disappeared behind a thick stand of trees that impeded their view.

Erling fell to his knees behind some brambles and Eyoés followed his example. Erling held a finger to his lips and pointed. Something waited in the mist. Throwing his hood up, Eyoés squinted to better make out its shape. He caught his breath.

Tents. In the dawn mist, they nearly escaped his notice like some faint afterimage.

Erling's face twisted in a grim smile. "Merra's forces. They're just as lost as we are," he whispered. "There must have been another way in. I was headed back to tell Caywen when I found you."

Eyoés didn't dare to take his eyes off the enemy encampment. "Do they know we're here?" he asked, glancing at the scout to read his expression. Silent, Erling met Eyoés' gaze and shook his head with a twinkle in his eye.

Against all odds, Seolta Forest had delivered their enemies into their hands.

43

29th of Rotanos, 2211 SE

Gwyndel slunk through the shadows. Mingled with them. *Became* them.

Gliding soundlessly through the twisted branches, she alighted on an exposed rock and listened. As her glowing blue eyes pierced the gloom, she could hear them coming—faint crackles in the brush and the clink of armor jostled by their steps.

The morning cold settled in her stiff joints, and Gwyndel shifted her stance slightly as she tried to get a better view of the approaching soldiers. She caught the colors of their surcoats before she could completely make out the men themselves.

Gwyndel tugged her hood over her mud-smeared face and studied her quarry. In the eerie dawn light, she nearly lost the tents among the scraggly trees surrounding them. Two reindeer pawed at the frosty ground. The camp was dead silent. Even the watchmen made no sound, sitting huddled at their posts as though frozen there in the harsh winds.

Surveying the enemy lines one final time, Gwyndel slipped away and started back toward the scattered lines of Rehils and Freechildren weaving their way among the trees. The fog curled around her as she moved back to where the others waited.

The frontmost soldiers jumped at the sight of her. Gwyndel ran to Caywen and the others. "They're asleep. The forest bewildered the Norgalokans too— they don't know how close they were to us. I'm sure of it," she said, catching their eyes in turn.

Eyoés hung a hand from his belt. "How many sentries?"

"I counted seven, but there may be more," Gwyndel said. "I doubt they'll spot you until you're on top of them."

Leaning against a deadfall, Haeryn watched Gwyndel with intensity. "And Merra?" he asked, straightening in an effort to project some sense of patience. Gwyndel noticed his finger tapping restlessly on the pommel of his sword.

She nodded. "Her quarters are nestled in the thickest group of tents," she said, turning to Eyoés. "If you all direct the brunt of the fighting away from her, Haeryn and I can slip in."

Caywen's horse stirred and shied back from the mist. Speaking quietly to her mount, she gazed off in the direction of the enemy camp. She caught Gwyndel's eye. "Are you sure about this?" she asked in a whisper.

Haeryn interrupted. "We will capture Merra. Aunt Gwyndel and I will see to it. She'll be a valuable prisoner," he declared.

Jaaye pushed her way through with an impatient glare and thrust the butt of her glaive into the ground at her feet. Her restless fingers wrapped around the weapon's shaft as her eyes drifted to Haeryn. "The

Norgalokans will regret following us here," she said. A fierce smile lit up her face.

Gwyndel's brow furrowed. She eyed Haeryn, catching a hint of approval on his lips. Over the course of their march, she'd seen him and Jaaye walking among the tents in the late evening hours. They'd kept their discussion too quiet for Gwyndel to listen in. When she'd asked, Haeryn had merely insisted that Jaaye needed someone to confide in. For the moment, Gwyndel kept her misgivings to herself.

Haeryn shouldn't be around her. He's impulsive enough.

She checked herself. What right did she have to hold Jaaye in suspicion? The disaster at Thaydale and the haggard march to Seolta had divided them enough already.

Gently slipping between them, Lanyon caught Haeryn's eye and nodded, his hand resting on the neck of Caywen's horse. "We leave the horses here. The men are ready," he said as Marc came up behind him. "Sir Marc and I will lead them into position."

Eyoés nodded. Tightening his sword belt, he started past Gwyndel, then paused as he grasped her shoulder. "If there was anyone who could capture Merra, it'd be you and Haeryn," he whispered in her ear. "But be careful."

It started to snow. The wind surged into an unexpected storm, snapping branches exposed to the sky. The ground soaked Gwyndel's knees as she observed the Norgalokan camp from the shadows. Trees creaked overhead. Blinking to clear the snowflakes from her eyelashes, Gwyndel glanced to where Haeryn waited, a hunched shape nestled in the underbrush.

Eyoés, Lanyon, Jaaye, and the others were in position. Gwyndel could see the signs of their presence. A branch trembling where the wind could not touch it. A disembodied shadow. A foot snapping a branch—or was it the snow, crushing a weak bough? The ambiguity of Seolta forest grew as the snow fell. Clenching her jaw, she hoped they would remain unnoticed by the eyes of their enemies. The Wardens of the Watch, however, wouldn't be seen until it was too late. The Norgalokans slept. Gwyndel let out a slow breath and braced herself in the stillness.

A horn blast tore through the wind and sent Gwyndel's heart racing. The Norgalokan sentries leapt to their feet with startled cries and the tents exploded into life. The Freechildren and Rehils streamed into the clearing like a horde of ants. Steel rang out in the howling wind as the Norgalokans scrambled to resist, thrown into confusion by the unforeseen attacks of Uwéllor's gahrim. In moments, the enemy was forced back as Jaaye's men tore the tents to the ground.

Gwyndel saw an opening. She dove out of cover and dashed toward Merra's tent with Haeryn following on her heels. Her boots kicked up mud as she ran, swerving to avoid wild blades. When she arrived at Merra's tent, she didn't bother to slow down.

With a flash of blue fire, she tore through the side of the tent with the Sword Imperishable and leapt upon the first thing that moved. A yelp rang out and her weapon sliced through fur and bone. Her eyes fought to adjust to the darkness. Snarls and snapping jaws surrounded her and she lashed out, the Sword Imperishable illuminating a horde of eyes around her. The tent shook again and Gwyndel heard Haeryn's voice as he tripped over something with a grunt. Light streamed through the opening and revealed the scene.

Winterhounds.

Gwyndel scrambled back as one leapt at her, teeth snapping. Baring her teeth, she kicked the creature in the face with a sickening snap as it fell limp. The sight startled her and she scrambled back, brandishing the Sword Imperishable in front of her.

The Winterhounds—their eyes weren't glowing. The otherworldly breath steaming at their mouths was gone, and as Haeryn hewed them down, Gwyndel realized the advantage.

These beasts could be killed.

Gwyndel sensed movement and leapt back as a glistening spear passed in front of her nose. With a shriek, Merra leapt over the bodies of her fallen Winterhounds and plowed into Gwyndel, throwing her off balance. Haeryn rushed to her rescue and Merra wheeled on him, clubbing him across the face with her spear shaft.

Gwyndel scrambled to her feet. Before she could summon the Sword Imperishable again, Merra fled with Haeryn hot on her heels.

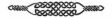

Haeryn gulped frigid air, crashing through the stale brush as he raced to keep Merra in sight. Through the snow and thick brush, he could barely see her, catching glimpses of a ghost flashing through the dark trees.

His cheek was still numb from Merra's blow. Gritting his teeth, Haeryn pushed himself harder, stumbling in his blind rush over treacherous ground. His heart leapt as his foot caught a sinkhole and sent him sprawling. Wresting his sword out of a tangle of branches, Haeryn tumbled into a winding hollow. He leapt to his feet in time to catch another fleeting glimpse of Merra. Breaking into a run, he ignored the snow working its way down his collar.

I won't be denied.

He'd returned to Norgalok. He could hear it in the howling wind. See it in the driving snow and smell it in the brisk air. Crows—he could hear them overhead, flocking toward the scene of battle. Violence was his world. It always had been.

As he ran, lungs bursting and heart pounding, Haeryn remembered. Screams. The wet cracking of bones. Snow glistening with blood in the quivering light of torches. The acrid stench of smoke rising to the song of incantations. Boats.

He remembered the story of his cruel kidnapping from the Wynrence settlement in Rehillon. The coast of Norgalok—a sudden snowstorm as the raiders prepared the sacrifice. The Kinsfolk had taken other prisoners besides himself.

They'd been sacrificed to the gods as tribute.

Haeryn's stomach turned and he gasped, tears burning his eyes as he ran. In a cruel twist of fate, those brutal men had whisked him into their world and conditioned him to violence, corrupting his childish innocence with their savagery. His attempt to estrange himself from Norgalok had only left the truth unaddressed.

He was one of them—a Norgalokan by *heart* and not by blood. And Merra was his final tie to their way of life.

Haeryn skidded to a stop, his ragged breath steaming. A giant wall of stone loomed over his head and extended out to either side in a broad cirque. Snow traced the crags on its surface. A dead end, and Merra knew it.

Standing at the base of the cliff, she kept her spear poised in front of her. They locked eyes as crows cawed overhead. Sword extended at his side, Haeryn took a step closer.

"Stay back, waif," Merra said, jabbing her spear forward.

Waif. The word enraged Haeryn and he took another step. "You don't know me," he said, pinning Merra to the stone with a cold glare.

Merra scowled, shooting a hasty glance at the cliffs encompassing her, seeking some path of escape. "Why should I? You're *nothing*—some orphan Eyoés Kingson stole to better his reputation. I saw you in Norgalok, at the Shrine. A child of the snows! How could you betray your people? Your gods?" she demanded.

Haeryn's eyes narrowed. "Why wouldn't I? A child, locked in a cage, expecting the priest's knife?" he asked, bouncing his sword in his grip. "The gods tried to kill me. They failed. And I will stamp them out."

Merra stiffened, realization dawning in her eyes. "You—you were destined for sacrifice?"

Haeryn refused to acknowledge the question.

He threw himself at Merra and she thrust her spear, the point finding the gap in Haeryn's armor and sinking into his shoulder. The force of the blow knocked him on his back and she moved to pin him to the ground. Batting away her spear, he sliced her leg open with his sword and knocked her off her feet. He leapt up, switching to a half-sword grip, and lunged at her. Stars flashed in Haeryn's eyes as the butt of Merra's spear cracked him over the head. She pounced at him, knocking the sword from his hand as she clawed at his face. With a strangled roar he lashed out with his dagger, blinded by Merra's fingers. He barely felt the knife land.

Haeryn tore himself away, dagger gripped in his trembling hand. Chest heaving, he staggered to his feet.

Merra didn't move. Haeryn tore his surcoat and staunched the blood flowing from his shoulder. He blinked to clear his vision, stooping over Merra as he picked up his fallen sword and sheathed it. Her dead eyes stared blankly into the sky. Haeryn paused to catch his breath, listening to the lonely wind scream against the rocks.

With a heavy sigh, he shook his head. "Norgalok is dead to me," he said under his breath. He left Merra's body for the crows and started back the way he'd come.

44

The troops greeted the clear sky with a shout. Sucking in a breath of fresh air, Gwyndel melted into her saddle and her cold skin tingled under the warm sun. The mist dissipated, revealing the path ahead as it stretched toward the nearby cliffs. There was no mistaking it—Seolta forest's strangling fist had loosened.

Rhoslyn bounced on her lap, waving at her father as he trailed alongside the meager supply train. It was a customary precaution, though with the Norgalokans utterly defeated, they were safe for now.

Gwyndel smiled until her cheeks hurt. She wrapped an arm around her daughter and squeezed her tight. With each step, the confusion of Seolta melted away and clear, hopeful thoughts returned like a lost friend.

A horn blast echoed in the open air and she looked up to the distant shape drifting back and forth on the horizon. Gibusil's feathers sparkled. At the head of the troops, Lanyon altered his course as Dovarul and Hjarti relayed the change in direction to the ranks. From the air, Seolta's maze was conquered.

Gwyndel abruptly yanked her horse's reins to keep him from feasting on the nearby shrubbery and came alongside Caywen and Jaaye. She eyed the two of them. "Truce?" she asked with a good humored smile.

Caywen caught her eye and raised an eyebrow. "Is that what you'd call it?"

Gwyndel's face reddened. "I'm sorry. I didn't mean to be rude—"

"No—please," Jaaye said. A rare smile brightened her face in a way Gwyndel hadn't seen before. "The Norgalokans fell because we worked as a *team*. I never imagined we could do that. Not with our differences." Hefting the glaive in her hand with a fierce glint in her eye, she admired the blade in the sunlight.

Caywen's brow furrowed and she studied Jaaye carefully. "You admit there are things we both can agree on," she remarked. Jaaye's eyes narrowed as she started to disagree.

Gwyndel cleared her throat. "We've all seen what unity can do in the face of uncertain odds. What good is it to insist on our own way?" she said. Twisting in her saddle, Gwyndel nodded to the valleys stuffed with dark behind them. "It was in our time of *weakness* that we laid hold of victory! This war is bigger than us. Until we decide to stand with each other and look beyond our own wants, we will be swept away," she declared.

Hope. Gwyndel could almost taste it in her mouth, pure and crisp like water from a sparkling brook. How long had it been since she'd known that burning in her chest? The surge of vigor that made her hands shake? As the army weaved between arching cliffs, Gwyndel's shoulders broadened. The burden of worry had lifted.

After all, the future was in greater hands.

It was Jaaye's look of doubt that broke the spell. With a huff, she turned away from Gwyndel with a smug grin. "No one *allowed* us this victory," she said. "We claimed it for ourselves."

The words pierced Gwyndel's ears like a discordant tune. She stared at Jaaye, catching the proud smirk on her face as she basked in a hollow sense of strength. Gwyndel turned to Caywen for support, only to catch a fleeting hesitation in her eyes.

She was afraid to believe.

A cackling screech made Gwyndel's ears ring and a gust of wind whipped her hair forward as Taesyra shot overhead, her broad wings dwarfing the armored rider huddled on her back. Cheers filled the air as the griffin's shadow passed over the ranks, followed by a flurry of blades thrust in the air in salute. Rhoslyn shouted and lifted her small fists.

They cheered for Haeryn Irongaze, the slayer of Merra. A living emblem of persistence and their victory in the face of hardship. The impossible had become reality. Not just for one, but for every soul marching under the open sky.

Straightening in the saddle, Gwyndel gripped the reins.

Caywen's doubts, Jaaye's foolishness—they'll both be proven wrong. The tables have turned. They'll see.

The blast of a horn drifted on the wind, and one by one the ranks ground to a halt like a rippling wave. Drawing back on the reins, Gwyndel frowned, weaving her horse around Caywen and Jaaye as she peered over the sea of helmets.

A horse thundered toward her, returning from the rise ahead. Drawing rein in a cloud of dust, Erling nodded at Gwyndel and turned to Caywen and Jaaye. "Falrey's waiting for us just over that ridge," he said, leaning forward. "He's flying a white flag."

45

Haeryn stared at the white banner shivering in tandem with the swaying grass. It dangled at a sharp angle from its pole thrust askew into the ground. A customary cry for mercy.

Only this flag of surrender was flanked by a host of cruel eyes.

The broad landscape displayed them in their glory. Battalions of disciplined, orderly ranks held their weapons at the ready. The wind bent to their will, rippling through the grass around them like water parting around a rock. In the silence of the wind, Haeryn waited for the roar of their shouts to rise into a united demand for blood.

It was the deciding clash. The confrontation he'd craved, yet Haeryn found himself hesitant.

The army had only just emerged from Seolta's throat. Haeryn jerked the reins to the side with a low whistle and Taesyra leapt off the rock face, gliding down to where the others waited. Eyoés dismounted as Taesyra landed on an old rockslide and clambered down to meet them.

Haeryn carefully dismounted, hand shooting to his bandaged shoulder as he tweaked it. Wincing, he remembered the prick of Dovarul's needle when he'd sewn the wound shut. He was lucky. The thrust from

Merra's spear had been clean and wouldn't cause lasting damage.

That is, once it healed. For the first time in years, a sword would be of no use to him.

Adjusting the sling to better nest his weak arm, Haeryn stroked Taesyra's neck. He could see the pity among the Knights of the Lance as they watched him limp. Blood flushed his cheeks and he quickened his steps. The empty space on his belt felt hollow without the perpetual tap of a scabbard on his thigh.

I refuse to be weak—ever. I'll prove Merra didn't have the last laugh.

Stroking Gibusil's broad chest as he passed, Haeryn stood tall to preserve his dignity. Lanyon didn't seem to notice him. Standing in absolute stillness, the Alcarthon general looked out over the plain, his gaze locked on the silent army staring back at them. There was no mistaking the tension creasing the corners of his eyes. Haeryn's stomach twisted.

Caywen's horse whinnied as she threw a tense glance at Falrey's white flag. "Perhaps we should double back into Seolta forest and find another path out," she said. Her voice faltered.

Lanyon wiped the sweat from his upper lip. "There is no other way out," he said, taking in a deep breath and looking Caywen in the eye. "Falrey knew we'd be here. He meant for this confrontation."

Jaaye dismounted, snatching her glaive from its sheath alongside her saddle. "Then we'd best not keep the cur waiting," she said, cheeks flushed red.

Gwyndel stood in her saddle with an irritated growl. "This is a trap! Surely you see it," she said, looking to the others for support. "Falrey wishes to lure us in."

Jaaye spun on her heels. "Lure us to what? He could kill us all where we stand, but he's avoiding a direct engagement and keeping his distance," she insisted.

Eyoés interrupted before Gwyndel could press her argument. "Jaaye's right. Falrey's giving us a chance to breathe and collect ourselves. He won't give us that chance again," he said, fingering his chin as he stared down at the ground.

Thridd gave a contented growl as Dovarul stroked her neck. "You really think Falrey's willing to talk?" he challenged.

Eyoés met the dwarf's eye. "There is only way to know for certain," he replied, squeezing the hilt of his father's sword. "If you think it's too dangerous, I'll lead a small party and speak with the usurper while the rest of you stay with the troops."

Haeryn caught the flash of worry in Lanyon's eyes. Seizing Eyoés by the shoulder, the Crimson Mark leaned close. "Falrey is a liar and a warmonger. If he keeps his word, it would be the first time. You may very well end up captive and be used to coerce us to surrender for your sake," he said in a fierce whisper.

"Falrey won't dare—not if the Wardens of the Watch have any say in the matter," Uwéllor declared, appearing in their midst out of thin air as his fellow gahrim took shape around him. Jaaye jumped back and

Caywen's horse threw its head back and danced in fright. Gritting her teeth, Caywen regained control of her steed as one of the gahrim stroked the horse's snout with quiet whispers.

Uwéllor removed his helmet and tucked it under his arm. "In the ancient days, Falrey was one of us—a lord among gahrim. He knows who we speak for. And we know what he is capable of. His silver tongue does not fool us," he said with a trumpeting voice.

The gahrim's words tore through Eyoés' heart like lightning. All eyes swung to Uwéllor as if compelled. Haeryn could feel it as well—a thrill electrifying every muscle in his body with a longing for action.

Victory. And not just a mere hope, but an *expectation*. The triumph of good wasn't just an ideal —it was an absolute certainty.

Lanyon stepped back, hand falling to his side. Taking a deep breath, the Crimson Mark bowed his head. "We ride to meet the enemy. Not as individuals, but as one people. United under one King," he said.

Haeryn leapt into the circle with a grin. "Falrey can't stand against us. The Norgalokans tried and paid the penalty!" he said, wheeling to the nearest common soldier he could see. "Summon a scribe! We make our demands plain in writing."

"Silence!"

Haeryn's heart skipped and he shied back, searching for the speaker.

The Knights of the Lance parted as Neifon rode through their midst on horseback with Sabaah behind him. Throwing his reins aside, he dismounted with the elegant grace of a well-bred nobleman. "Uwéllor is right," he remarked, his dignity captivating all who listened despite his hollowed eyes and dirty face. "But Falrey is also not so weak as to abandon his cause."

Haeryn's heart sank as the gahrim commander nodded in wholehearted agreement. Brow furrowed, he faced his companions in turn. They agreed. What had changed?

Did I misread their confidence?

Haeryn flushed and resisted the urge to wipe his sweaty palms. He felt exposed under their probing stares. Found out. In one moment, he thought they'd shared his passion. That they understood the yearning for victory that burned in his heart, inspiring him to rise each morning.

They didn't understand his passion—they never had.

Haeryn locked eyes with Neifon in brazen defiance. "Would you suggest crawling to Falrey in fear?" he said, ignoring the heavy stares of everyone around him.

Neifon stiffened. An indignant glint flared in his narrowed eyes and he held his chin high. "Not one of us will come to Falrey as beggars," he said through clenched teeth, "but this conference must be conducted with extreme care."

Eyoés stepped in. "We need to gather our words beforehand. Decide how we are going to approach this," he said, catching Gwyndel's nod of approval.

Neifon turned to Eyoés and Gwyndel with a sigh. "Falrey's intentions are unclear. Our ideal goal is to negotiate a compromise with Falrey and perhaps sow seeds of infighting among his ranks. That way we have time to truly recover our strength for a second bout," he explained. The exhaustion in his eyes betrayed the longing they all craved. The prospect of peace was a tender salve upon their strained souls. Even Haeryn suffered its allure.

Caywen and the others hesitated. Once they set foot in Falrey's jaws, there was no turning back. The decision would be final. "And if compromise is impossible?" Haeryn asked.

Neifon fingered the buttons of his frayed coat. He caught Gwyndel's eye and bowed his head. "Your touch made Falrey bleed. You speak words of light, and a silver tongue cannot deceive you. If the usurper bewitches us with his words, you can do what needs to be done," he said.

All eyes turned to Gwyndel. She clenched her jaw, looking to Vakros as he held Rhoslyn. He nodded. Swallowing the knot in her throat, Gwyndel took a deep breath. "With the Guide's wisdom, I will," she said.

Lanyon looked out at Falrey's forces. "We mustn't keep the usurper waiting," he said quietly.

Tearing his eyes from the white flag, he strode to his horse and took the reins from Dovarul's grasp. "Gwyndel, Neifon, and Eyoés will join me at the parley," he said, pulling himself up and into the saddle. Turning to Eyoés, he nodded toward the Wardens of the Watch. "The gahrim should be our guardsmen."

Eyoés nodded, and the Wardens of the Watch fell in without another word.

Caywen caught Lanyon's eye. "I'll muster the archers. If things go poorly, sound the horn and we'll provide a distraction," she said.

Haeryn's heart dropped. As his father clambered into Gibusil's saddle, Haeryn rushed to Lanyon and grabbed a fistful of his horse's mane. "Let me go with you!" he pleaded.

Lanyon shot a nervous glance toward the enemy lines. He leaned down and grasped Haeryn's wrist. "Haeryn, you are one of the strongest champions of our cause. Your determination has inspired us to resist despair—myself included. But this situation is delicate," he said. He cracked a weak smile. "Your passion blinds you."

The horse tore away from Haeryn's grip and started down the hillside. The Wardens of the Watch flew past him like a volley of arrows, keeping pace with Gwyndel and Neifon as they galloped alongside Lanyon—and above them, sparkling gold, Gibusil cast his shadow on the sweeping grass.

Haeryn's shoulders drooped. Numbness tingled his skin as his friends dwindled in the distance. His legs trembled beneath him and he sat on the cold ground, propping himself up with his good arm.

They left me to watch!

A fistful of sodden grass and earth squeezed out between his fingers. Through the dull ringing in his ears, Haeryn turned to see Erling and Marc sit on either side of him.

The breeze stirred Marc's hair as he looked out, squinting in the sunlight. "In life, there are many battles. Some of them are not ours to fight," he said, catching Haeryn's eye with a wistful smile. "That's the hard part—learning to let go and let someone else do what must be done."

Haeryn shot him a bleak scowl. "Let go?" he scoffed. "No one else will fight my battles. This is *my* world. I *can* do what must be done, Marc—"

Haeryn bit his tongue. As he heard himself speak, a hollow emptiness struck his core. If this war was a battle he could fight and win, why did his insistence sound so desperate? So contrived? He turned to Erling for support.

The young scout's eyes flicked in his direction and then darted away. Erling sighed. "This fight is beyond us," he said. In an instant, Haeryn knew. Light dawned in his mind, and for the first time in months, he saw clearly—like a child waking up to find himself caught in a duel of giants.

He was the child.

Eyoés *felt* Falrey's gaze before he saw the man.

As Gwyndel, Lanyon, and Neifon brought their horses to a trot, the enemy's front lines parted to make way. The movement rippled through the ranks, revealing the open-sided tent where the usurper waited, his eyes locked on them. Eyoés instinctively shied back. The very sight of the man's face was like a poison.

Letting out a measured breath, Eyoés landed Gibusil behind Lanyon's horse as the Wardens of the Watch flanked them on either side. A movement from Falrey's tent roused a sharp snarl from the griffin. Several tall figures slipped out of cover and spread out to either side, hands resting on the black longswords at their sides. After several nights spent listening to Haeryn's tales, Eyoés recognized the weapon.

Nightstone longswords. This must be the Baronsguard of Garifell—Falrey's bodyguards.

The Wardens of the Watch met the threat immediately, mirroring the movements of the Baronsguard and falling into an defensive position. None moved to break the impasse, and the tension lingered. Materializing out of thin air, horrid, misshapen gahrim lingered around Falrey and eyed the Wardens of the Watch with loathing. Gibusil crouched and Eyoés dismounted, his eyes fixed on Falrey as he wrapped the reins around the saddlehorn. Lanyon, Neifon, and Gwyndel dismounted along with him.

The usurper smiled and reclined in his lavish chair. "I'm honored that you all would heed my request to discuss terms," he said. His smoldering amber eyes fell on Gwyndel and lingered there, inspecting her with a gleam of hatred.

Bile burned the back of Eyoés' throat. "Speak, wretch," he spat. A warning glance from Lanyon cut him off.

A twisted smile spread on Falrey's face and he leaned forward in his chair. His gaze crawled over them. "I wish to commend you all," he said, glancing back toward Seolta forest. "In the face of my greatest conquests, you've persisted and refused to submit to my crown." Jaw set, he undid the bandage around his leg and peeled it back to reveal a deep cut. "You wounded me. And while entombed in a forest of no return, you crushed Merra. That is no easy feat."

Eyoés' blood ran cold. "How do you know about Merra?" he demanded, catching Lanyon's look of surprise before it was quickly masked.

With a quiet chuckle, Falrey sat back in his chair. "She owed *everything* to me—a truth she soon forgot in her craving for ambition. I didn't want her loyalty any longer, so I led her to you," he explained. "One must be willing to sacrifice the weakling to pacify the wolves. Consider your victory over her a sign of my goodwill."

The admission caught Eyoés by surprise. His stomach turned hollow.

Merra had no chance. A surprise raid was all it took to crush her. Our greatest triumph was spurious.

"You would be wise to consider his majesty's words," a familiar voice crowed as Santh Baklyn slithered out from the gathering soldiers and came alongside his king.

Eyoés fought to control himself. He deliberately ignored Santh and locked eyes with Falrey. "Why this sudden change of heart?"

Falrey gestured toward the surrounding landscape with a slight wave of his hand. "Autumn is upon us. Once the winter snows gather, making war over long distances will become difficult. Committing to a prolonged winter campaign will kill hundreds of men, both yours and mine," he remarked. "I'm willing to discuss terms." Catching Eyoés' eye, Lanyon motioned Neifon forward. His expertise would serve them well.

Neifon accepted the challenge. He stepped forward and formally acknowledged Falrey with a mere nod. "With your permission, I will express our wishes," he said. Eyoés could see even that show of deference irked him.

Falrey studied Neifon with a twinkle in his eye. He sat up straighter. "You may," he said.

Neifon cleared his throat. "We wish to negotiate a truce. As you've said, winter draws nigh, and war will benefit neither of us. Allow us to shelter in the Caverns of Nubaroz for the winter and return to fighting in the springtime," he said, watching Lanyon as he spoke. The Crimson Mark nodded his approval. Should they take refuge among the dwarves remaining in Nubaroz, they could better their chances of recovering their strength. Should Falrey break his promise, the caverns would provide a near impregnable stronghold. Eyoés glanced at Gwyndel and saw the uncertainty in her eye. Surely Falrey would recognize their advantage.

The usurper paused as the words sank in. A smile grew on his face and he folded his hands. "I'll offer you something better than a truce," he said, bowing his head with a sigh. "If you lay down your arms and disperse to Qelezal, Taekohar, and Rehillon, I swear by my crown that you will live in peace. You may govern those three territories as you see fit while the rest of Alithell enjoys peace under my reign. We can end this war here and now."

Eyoés couldn't believe his ears. Dumbstruck, Neifon turned to him and Lanyon for guidance. The Crimson Mark fingered the worn hem of his cloak as he wrestled. Peace had been offered to them by their greatest enemy. One who had pursued conquest with an effectiveness and zeal that rivaled their own.

Eyoés watched as the Baronsguard and the Wardens of the Watch stood locked in a silent clash of wills. The tension between them was rising. How long would this conflict endure—the old ways against the new? Perhaps this was the way of things. An endless wheel, an eternal hostility with no end in sight. Eyoés' shoulders slumped.

I don't have the strength to go on.

His heart leapt as Gwyndel shoved her way toward Falrey. "You've extended your offer. Now hear our answer," she declared, eyes ablaze with fire. The usurper gripped the armrests of his chair and the fallen gahrim shielded him from her advance.

Santh stepped into Gwyndel's path, hand falling to his sword. "How dare you address his majesty—"

Gwyndel seized him by the shirt. "Crawl back to the hole where you belong," she growled, shoving him away and turning on Falrey. "Full of glory, these three —the soaring griffin, the noble stag, the raging dragon. Crowned in majesty, the fourth—a king whose army is

with him heart and soul. The Proverb of Duegin."
Falrey recoiled.

The Baronsguard of Garifell started for her and the
Wardens of the Watch headed them off, shields raised.
Falrey raised his hand to stay his guardsmen and glared
at Gwyndel. "You expect your king to honor your
dedication? He always insists you give. Your lives,
your loyalty, and your blood. And in return he gives
you nothing," he said. "I offer you a peace Fohidras
refuses to grant you. Spurn it, and I will not extend it
again."

Gwyndel turned livid. "Peace?" she cried.
"Murderers like you are never satisfied with peace."
She wheeled on Santh as he backed away from her. "If
he wins this war, he will turn on you next." The Sword
Imperishable sprang from Gwyndel's hand and she
swung at Falrey. The blade passed inches from his face
and the usurper leapt backward with a roar, face
burned. Fallen gahrim shrieked and leapt back, staring
wide-eyed at the Sword Imperishable. As he tumbled to
the ground gripping his bleeding leg, the Baronsguard
threw themselves at the Wardens of the Watch. Seizing
Gwyndel by the arms, Eyoés and Neifon tore her away
from Falrey and ran for the horses as Lanyon sounded
the signal.

Eyoés heard a rustling carried on the wind and
looked up as a dark cloud of arrows soared through the
air from the bows of Caywen's archers. Leaping onto
Gibusil, he hauled Gwyndel into the saddle and took to
the sky, soaring under the black cloud as the Wardens
of the Watch shielded Lanyon and Neifon. Eyoés could

hear the volley land amid the cries of Falrey's men. He looked back as the last arrow fell and saw Neifon and Lanyon ride out, the Wardens of the Watch covering their rear as several hobgoblins tried to seize them.

There was no turning back.

46

Lanyon's horse skidded to a stop and he dismounted in a rush with Neifon. "Hobgoblins not far behind!" he cried as the front ranks closed the gap they'd ridden through.

"Shield wall!" Vakros bellowed, pulling on his helmet and yanking the strap to test it. At his command, the men rippled into motion, shields rising in arcs over their heads as the three foremost ranks locked shields with those in front.

Clambering down from Gibusil, Gwyndel mounted a horse and rode to where Vakros looked out over the horde of black figures throwing themselves against the hill. "Rhoslyn! Is she safe?"

Vakros reached over and pressed a firm hand to her cheek. "She's in Erling's care. Don't worry—focus!" he said.

The sound of the hobgoblins roaring in their harsh tongue made Gwyndel's skin crawl. As they closed the distance, she could make out the gangly limbs of monstrous steeds, bearing their riders as they clambered up the hillside. A full detachment of Falrey's cavalry followed on their heels, the horses' reins jingling as their necks jerked forward and backward. Rolling thunder shook the ground like a storm stirring under the earth. The very air seemed to vibrate.

"Lances!" Marc cried. The Knights of the Lance snapped into position, banners rippling from their lances as they lowered them over the shield wall.

Gwyndel's stomach twisted. She urged her horse back and peered through the bristling shafts. The enemy was losing momentum. Among the thundering hooves, she could hear the faint wheeze of horses struggling for breath. The enemy cavalry lost ground, yet the hobgoblins pushed on, unfazed. Clenching her teeth till her jaw hurt, Gwyndel urged her horse back as the Sword Imperishable surged to life in her hand, sending a radiant glow over those nearest to her.

Another volley of arrows soared over her head. It slammed into the oncoming enemy cavalry in a flurry of falling men and screaming horses. The hobgoblins slipped underneath the volley's arc and crashed into the shield wall.

The impact rippled through the ranks. Wood splintered as monsters plunged into the mass of bodies, tripping with horrid shrieks as lances plucked them up and hoisted them into the air with the impact. Blurs of metal whisked back and forth in a sudden explosion of desperate combat. Her ears rang with the piercing clang of metal and the screams of dying men and beasts.

The shield wall regrouped, trapping the hobgoblins in a sea of swords. A shout of triumph rose up. Followed by another. Then like the ocean's roar the cries of the victorious surged over the withering forces of Zwaoi. A thrill swelled in Gwyndel's chest and she joined their cry as her horse reared, bringing its hooves down on a Kélak estranged from the pack.

Falrey's heavy calvary plowed into the shield wall. The horses tumbled over the front ranks and lunged forward. Marc shouted an order and the infantry parted as the Knights of the Lance met the enemy head on.

Their lances splintered with a sharp *crack*. Gwyndel threw her shield up and a chunk of broken wood struck it. Fighting to regain control of her wild-eyed horse, she dodged a broken lance thrown in haste. The mounted knights wheeled back to face the enemy again with maces and hammers drawn.

Marc led the second charge with zeal. Whirling his mace over his head, he bashed in the nearest enemy's helmet and struck a second man squarely in the chest before the first rider hit the ground.

Gwyndel's throat clamped shut as Vakros joined Marc, ducking under an enemy's sweeping hammer and cleaving the man's arm with his axe. Several of Falrey's riders tore away from the Knights of the Lance and lunged after Marc and Vakros. Slapping her horse on the rump, Gwyndel intercepted them and swept the Sword Imperishable in a line of trailing flames.

The blade sliced through the nearest man's armor and sent him to the ground unconscious. The second rider yanked the reins and his horse leapt back in time to avoid the Sword Imperishable's shining tip. Vakros brought his mace down on the man's head before he could recover.

Eyes blazing, Gwyndel wheeled around to the cheers of the men as they attacked their foes with a renewed vengeance.

The tyrant's first charge had wrought nothing.

If he wins this war, he will turn on you next.

Santh raked a sweaty hand through his hair and spurred his horse to a fast trot. Around him, the rhythm of marching infantry thundered like drums and the sound of battle grew louder as they drew near. This desperate fight would decide the fate of generations. History would remember the victor. Santh double-checked the straps of his armor.

He will turn on you next...

Pulling on his sallet helmet, Santh cinched the strap and sighed, the sound ringing in his ears. What if she was right?

No! Falrey wouldn't dare execute his greatest asset. The Great Cause is dead without me.

The reassurance rung hollow. Santh clenched his jaw and fought to still his trembling hands. What guarantee did he have? For years, Falrey had craved this conquest. Such a thirst for power was unquenchable—Santh had felt its allure himself. And he knew it always hungered for more.

I have to protect myself. Make myself even more invaluable.

Santh looked up as the wind whipped Falrey's pennant, flashing the blue and purple colors against the cloudy sky. For now, there was one sure way to secure the king's favor. Falrey's parting command hung over his thoughts like a storm cloud.

Kill the Forester woman. The man who brings me her head will rule Alithell by my side. The one who fails will burn.

Santh ground his teeth as he caught sight of Commander Ros leading another contingent of hobgoblins up the hill. The man was a fraud, an opportunistic officer who didn't understand the grandeur of the Great Cause. Falrey had given them both the order, testing to see who would be the most loyal. Santh already knew the answer. He set his spurs and brandished an axe with a roar as his men clashed with the rebels.

Two piercing shrieks tore through the sky as Gibusil and Taesyra struck the ranks behind him. Cutting down the nearest rebel, Santh wheeled around in time to see furrows carved into his army as the two griffins banked for a second strike.

The trumpet blast and the thundering of hooves caught him by surprise as the Knights of the Lance crashed into both flanks of his men.

47

Haeryn clung to Taesyra as she tore through the enemy, bouncing like a plowshare in rocky ground. The impact rattled his teeth. With a shriek, the griffin shot into the air and Haeryn whipped back, fighting with white knuckles to keep his seat.

A laugh escaped him. There was no thrill of conquest like this. A sense of wonder and magnificence coursed through his limbs like fire. Upon a griffin's wings, he too was like the heroes of old. A legend.

Heart pounding, Haeryn leaned out from the saddle as Taesyra leveled her flight. Below, the squirming figures of cavalry and infantry spilled over each other like feuding ants. Santh was caught between three fronts, and even from this height, Haeryn could see the desperation growing in their attack. He grinned.

Now it's the traitor's turn to squirm.

A roar echoed through the skies, and Haeryn glimpsed a flash of gold as Gibusil dove for the kill. Eyes flashing, Haeryn spurred Taesyra into a plunging dive, heedless of the wind thumping in his ears or the wind biting at his skin.

Falrey was a fool to underestimate us.

Pain shot through Falrey's leg like lightning as one of his fallen gahrim cinched his bandage. He let it fuel his wrath, closing his eyes as he listened to the din of battle echoing from the hillside. After centuries of exile in the bowels of the earth, the sound of violence was sweet.

Heavy is the scepter that breaks the bones of rebellion.

Falrey O'Dyre fingered the crown upon his head, tracing the curving, thorny lines bordering the burns upon his forehead. The Sword Imperishable—he'd recognized the sting of purity at its first touch. He watched his blood stain the bandage upon his leg. Grinding his teeth, he caught the sharp clink of ballistas straining to load. Their wooden frames groaned with power.

The Scion of Asdale and his waif-son would pay the penalty for Gwyndel's insolence.

Caywen held her breath till her lungs burned. Twisting the reins in her gloved hands, she looked out over the battle as the Knights of the Lance pressed their assault, tearing deeper and deeper into the enemy's ranks. Their echoing shouts made the hair on her arms stand up.

Her horse grunted and shifted uneasily. With a shiver, Caywen stroked the creature's neck and glanced to where Lanyon and Neifon sat atop their horses. They talked among themselves as they studied the battlefield from afar, pointing out the enemy's movements and signaling the heralds to direct a counter-attack. Caywen tried to focus. She was an impostor among them. A high-minded noblewoman with little knowledge of war. What right did she have to command an army?

Lanyon's voice startled her. "Neifon and I think we should hold the cavalry back and tell the archers to release another volley. What do you think?" he asked.

A flash of heat rushed to Caywen's face. "If you think it best," she answered. Lanyon turned to the herald stationed at his side and the man relayed the order with a horn blast. The Knights of the Lance wheeled about and withdrew to retrieve fresh lances, lingering back as a dark cloud of arrows fluttered overhead, arcing down the hillside and pelting the enemy like black hail.

Caywen felt Lanyon's eyes on her. She briefly met his gaze and looked away. "You don't need my approval. Your judgment's better than mine," she said.

Lanyon's face softened. "We've discussed this. I want you here, Caywen. Your knowledge of these things will come in time. The men are bolstered by your encouragement and example," he said.

Neifon interrupted. "The hobgoblins are trying to break away from the front lines and support Santh's flank. The Knights of the Lance should ride out again and cut them off." The horn rang out and Rhoslyn let out a frightened squeal from where she sat in Erling's saddle. Wrapping his arm around the little girl, the young scout pressed her against his chest. Caywen grew queasy. Three generations would witness the day's fate and carry the scars to the grave.

Lanyon's horse stirred. Snatching up the reins, the Crimson Mark brought his mount forward and peered down the hill. "Something's changed," he said.

Caywen caught her breath and followed his gaze. "Where?"

Neifon pointed. The ranks of Santh's men shifted like sand, congealing into a thick crowd as the Knights of the Lance cornered the hobgoblins. Two quick blasts of a trumpet quickly followed. "They're regrouping," Neifon said. The words leapt from his mouth.

The trumpet sounded another blast and the enemy crawled back down onto the open plain—luring the Knights of the Lance and Rehil infantry down off the hill. A discordant roar of shouting voices swelled from the Freechildren and Rehil troops as they seemingly routed their foes.

Caywen's pulse spiked. "They're giving up the hillside advantage!" she said, wheeling her horse around to the nearest herald. "Command Lord Balston and Lord Crawbrand to hold their ground!" The herald's bugle sounded to no avail.

Lanyon drew his sword and lifted it high. "To me!" he shouted. A contingent of elves mustered to his side and he dug in his spurs, racing down the hill into the fray. Neifon held back and directed the archers to hold their fire. As Caywen rode to his side, she caught a fleeting glimpse of something black streaking through the air toward her.

Lighting struck her shoulder and her arm went numb. Caywen instinctively jerked back on the reins and her horse recoiled, throwing her off balance as she pitched from the saddle. "Lanyon!" she screamed. She hit the ground hard and stars flashed before her eyes.

Fire crackled across her chest and down her arm as she looked up at the arrow shaft sticking out of her shoulder, its fletching shivering in the wind. The world spun around her. Erling knelt beside her with Rhoslyn and quickly covered the child's eyes. His horrified expression blurred in Caywen's vision as he grasped the arrow shaft to pull it free.

"Don't!" Neifon cried as he stood over her and pulled Erling away. "She needs a healer." He yanked his gloves off with his teeth and tore off a chunk of his coat. Caywen winced in silence as he pressed the cloth around her wound to stop the bleeding.

Grabbing her chin with a bloody hand, Neifon looked her in the eye. "Try to breathe through your nose. Relax," he said, chin quivering. "Falrey's archers tried to pummel Lanyon as he rode down the hill. They overcompensated for the wind and struck you instead."

Tears sprang to Caywen's eyes and she clenched her jaw. She shivered, fighting to calm herself. Her head swam, and the sky turned brighter as Neifon's face dissolved into a blurry haze. With a weak sigh, Caywen watched the world disappear as she fainted.

Gwyndel shoved the enemy horseman off his saddle, the Sword Imperishable a blur of streaking blue as she spun and cut down the hobgoblin clambering onto her horse's flank.

She saw the battle through a haze of sapphire. Sweat trickled into her blazing eyes and hissed like water hitting hot coals. The battlefield shimmered with flashing blades. Men, elves, and hobgoblins crowded her horse's ankles like rats and the creature reared as Gwyndel clung to the saddle.

Gwyndel grunted as a sudden jolt turned the horse's whinny into a scream. Kicking her feet free of the stirrups, she leapt awkwardly as the creature tumbled to the ground with a halberd in its chest. Gwyndel rolled to her feet, swinging the Sword Imperishable in time to cut down the soldier who'd brought down her steed. She winced at a sharp pain in her knee.

Choking on the stench of death, Gwyndel snatched up a fallen kite shield. Figures gathered around her and she caught a fleeting glimpse of the Amberster crest on their surcoats as they joined shields with her. A bobbing raft of order in a wild sea of chaos. As Caywen's men crowded around her, Gwyndel refused the impulse to push them away. This was not Weomor.

A hobgoblin crashed into Gwyndel's shield and she fought back. Something had changed. As she strove to stem the tide, Gwyndel looked up to the empty hillside. Her heart sank. Falrey had lured them into giving up their height advantage.

Three deformed fiends of Zwaoi barreled over nearby horsemen with wails of glee, throwing the dead men like rags. Gwyndel stumbled back as the men shifted position around her and leveled their spears to catch the oncoming charge.

Long, disjointed limbs reached over their shield wall and tore the ranks apart. A slimy hand hammered Gwyndel in the chest and threw her backward. She landed in the mud with a grunt as the bodies of her men flew through the air, shields tumbling from their hands. Gwyndel rolled and swept the Sword Imperishable, feeling it hiss and vibrate in her grip as it cut deep. The beasts fell with teeth bared in frozen smiles.

Gwyndel leapt up, the Sword Imperishable poised in front of her. The battle around her kept its distance, leaving her to an unexpected rest. Chest heaving, she wiped the muddy hair from her eyes and blinked to clear her vision.

A horse snorted behind her. Gwyndel's heart jumped as she turned. Armor clinking, the black horse's rider faced Gwyndel, lifting the visor of his sallet helmet.

Santh smiled at the look of surprise on Gwyndel's face. "Hello witch," he said, eyeing the Sword Imperishable with a tense glare as he hefted his axe. He threw a quick glance over her shoulder—and his smile fled.

Brow furrowed, Gwyndel leapt aside. Sword bared, a tall man loomed before her atop a snorting warhorse, his face hidden by a helmet. Gwyndel glimpsed the commander's emblem upon his surcoat. "She's *mine*, Santh," he declared, his voice ringing in his helmet.

Santh sneered and slammed his visor down. "Then claim her over my corpse, Ros," he snapped.

Both men spurred their horses and Gwyndel threw herself out of the way, lashing out at Ros with the Sword Imperishable. The blade severed his leg and he tumbled from the saddle with a scream, dragged behind his charging horse into the chaos. Gwyndel ducked under Santh's axe, slicing the straps of his saddle and lunging out of the way as he fell to the earth. He leapt up with his dagger as another horseman thundered toward them.

Vakros' war hammer slammed into the traitor's back and Santh crumpled to the ground. Vakros brought his horse alongside Gwyndel, extending his hand.

Enemy riders charged to cut off their escape. Vakros spun to face them and grunted as a mace knocked him from the saddle. Gwyndel's heart leapt into her mouth and she sprang to his aid as the riders dismounted and dragged Santh away.

Cursing at the top of his lungs, Santh gnashed his teeth and glared hatred. "Leave me! She must die! The king wills it!" he screamed.

Gwyndel knelt by Vakros' side and placed a hand on his dented armor. "Did they break any ribs?" she asked.

Vakros shook his head, staring up at the sky with a look of horror and disbelief. "I—I can't move my legs," he stammered.

Gwyndel froze. The sounds of battle dimmed and her bleeding head spun as she prodded his legs. No response. She dashed to her husband's panicking horse and dragged the creature to where Vakros lay. "I'll get you out of here," she said through tears. A band of Freechildren drew rein alongside them with a shout, dismounting as they hastened to Gwyndel's side. They grasped Vakros and hoisted his limp frame across the saddle.

Mounting behind him, Gwyndel plucked up the reins and spurred the horse into an awkward trot up the slope away from the battle, flanked by men on either side. The shrieks of Gibusil and Taesyra tore the sky and she looked back, watching the griffins rip their way through the enemy on the open plain. Beyond, she caught movement from the rear of Falrey's line. Her face paled.

Through her tears, Gwyndel could make out the broad arms of ballistas.

"Arrows, Haeryn!"

Haeryn heard his father's shout echo above the battle. He pulled back on Taesyra's reins and brought her to an abrupt halt, rocking back and forth to the rhythm of her wingbeats as she hovered. Falrey's archers clustered like swarming wasps and raised their bows. Heart pounding, Haeryn smirked.

Let them try.

Gibusil shot past Haeryn to meet the arrows. Before Haeryn could snatch a glimpse of his father, Gibusil suddenly floated over the arcing volley like a cloud and plunged down toward the archers with the speed of a leaden weight. Haeryn's breath caught in his throat.

Impressive. Now my turn.

The reins hung limp in his hands for a moment as the volley of arrows streaked toward him. In an instant the spell broke and Taesyra shot forward. The arrows melted into a blur of black and Haeryn hastily judged the distance with a jerk of the reins. Taesyra clipped the top of the volley and growled in pain at the two arrows sticking her like thorns. Wheeling away from the stinging cloud, Taesyra took to open air and clawed at the arrows.

Haeryn's breath quickened and he leaned over the saddlehorn to inspect her wounds. They were minor. His heart started beating again.

He turned to watch the volley arch over the battlefield like a black rainbow and dig into the ranks below. Haeryn could hear them pattering on shields. The longer he stared down at them, the more he glimpsed crests he knew well—those of the Ambersters, the Knights of the Lance, and the Freechildren.

And here he flew, high above it all, free from pain, free from fear. This was not who he was.

A familiar, booming voice thundered below. Through the turmoil, Hjarti's massive shoulders glistened with sweat in the overcast light. The giant swung his billhook like a scythe, desperately clearing space as Dovarul and Thridd gathered about his ankles. Two horses careened toward them and Haeryn recognized Marc and Jaaye as they took refuge in the giant's shadow. All the while, over and over, the tide of war washed further and further into their fleeting haven.

The sight struck a panic within Haeryn he didn't see coming. Hjarti couldn't fight forever.

I have to save them.

Haeryn dug his heels into Taesyra's flank and the griffin dove. The wind brought tears to his stinging eyes and yet he refused to pull his gaze away. A cry tore from him as Jaaye tumbled from her horse. Haeryn braced himself for impact.

A streak of movement shot across his vision and struck Taesyra with the force of a charging bear, driving the griffin sideways. The impact tore Haeryn from the saddle and Taesyra shrieked in agony.

Haeryn was falling. As the wind whipped around his body and beat in his ears, Taesyra flailed with a ballista bolt lodged in her chest, crumpling in on herself with weak chirps. The griffin streaked like a fallen star, plowing into the ranks of Falrey's army in a final act of defiance.

"Taesyra!" Haeryn screamed, his lungs hoarse as his words were lost to the wind. Gibusil snatched him from the sky, carrying him off with the breath knocked from his lungs.

Eyoés threw himself against the saddle as another ballista bolt streaked over his head, its fletching rustling like feathers. Again, Gibusil cried out—an agonized, hoarse screech of grief as he tried to dive for Taesyra's broken body. Pulling on the reins with all his might, Eyoés blinked away tears and ignored Gibusil's cries. The sound made his stomach lurch.

The battle had become a rout. Falrey's banner beat in the wind as the Rehils and Freechildren scattered before it in confusion, the Knights of the Lance struggling to cover the rear. Hobgoblin war horns cried out in a discordant symphony and the black shapes bolted forward to cut off their escaping prey. Eyoés gritted his teeth and held Gibusil back with a pained glance down to where his son was clutched in the griffin's talons. They couldn't risk engaging the enemy. Not with Haeryn hanging exposed.

Eyoés choked back a sob as he caught sight of Sabaah and Hjarti—stranded in the middle of a swelling tide with swords flashing. The shields of Falrey O'Dyre buried them before his eyes, never to be seen again.

A flash of brilliant light blinded him. Gibusil came to a grinding halt, wings beating wildly as Eyoés fought to see what was happening below. His heart skipped as his eyes fell upon the lone figure standing between Falrey's horde and their fleeing prey.

The Guide.

Lifting his crook staff over his head, he struck the ground with a resounding crack that echoed like a thunderclap. The battlefield split open like yawning jaws to consume Falrey's advancing forces. An exhausted cheer rose from the Freechildren and Rehils.

Eyoés shielded his eyes from the light with his arm as Gibusil swooped low and set Haeryn down beside the Guide. "You came!" Eyoés shouted brokenly.

The Guide turned to him, face hidden by the cowl of his white cloak. "I never left," he said. "Turn south! Make for the mountains of Gald-Behn! In time I will meet you there."

Eyoés pulled Haeryn into the saddle and didn't look back.

48

Santh Baklyn kicked the dying man again, teeth clenched in a hard smile as he drove the last gasps of breath from the man's lips. With a grunt, he stepped back into the mud, the cold, churned wine of the battlefield gathering around his ankles. A gust of warm breath puffed across Santh's neck as his horse pawed at the ground, restless from the stench of death.

Santh mounted his horse and winced at the sharp ache racing up his spine. The armor had taken the brunt of the blow, though he could still feel the mace's strike afresh each time he moved. Wiping the sweat from his forehead, Santh chuckled to himself.

At least the scum got what he deserved.

He mounted his horse and watched the men sweep the battlefield. They wandered with the crows, spears cradled in their arms as they trudged through the mud and matted grass. Santh could hear the moaning pleas of the wounded wither away as the spears rose and fell, reaping tardy souls that hadn't the courage to give themselves up to death.

They'd found no sign of Gwyndel.

Santh shifted in the saddle, sick to his stomach. He let out a sharp breath. The battle alone had been costly enough. By the time the Guide had left, the chasm rent in the earth had claimed twice the number of men before it had stopped growing. It would take a long winter to recover from their losses.

Santh dug in his spurs and started for the king's tent. Chunks of mud sprayed up behind his horse as he rode. He clenched his jaw. These were delicate times, and the news of his failure would have to be delivered tactfully.

The thought chilled his blood as he eased back on the reins, trotting into the city of fires and tents clustered amid the sea of grass. He dared not lift his eyes to the banner swaying overhead. Santh sensed the stares of the men gathered among the tents. An uneasy smile twisted Santh's expression.

It's not my fault Gwyndel escaped. Had the Guide not shown himself, I would've had a second chance at her.

Santh's horse ground to a stop, throwing its head back as a gauntleted hand snatched the reins from Santh's grip. The slim, silent helm of a tall, armored killer stared back at him. Pulse racing, Santh lifted his eyes to see several others emerge from among the tents and draw their black, shimmering nightstone longswords.

The Baronsguard of Garifell.

Santh froze. His breath caught in his throat as one of the Baronsguard whisked Santh's sword from its scabbard. Santh dared not move his hands. As the silent knights closed in around him, he looked beyond them in search of an escape.

Terror sprang into his eyes.

A cruel smirk twisted Falrey O'Dyre's sharp features as he drifted out from among the tents, flanked by his fallen gahrim. Arms folded, he planted himself in full view. "Bring him to me," he commanded.

A swarm of hands seized Santh at once, pulling him from his horse and throwing him into the mud. With a grunt, Santh winced at the pain in his back and tried to crawl away, only to be dragged to his feet and thrown before the tyrant like a sack of grain. Coming to his knees, Santh swayed as he lifted his eyes. A cruel fire met his gaze as Falrey stared down at him.

Falrey bared his teeth. "You've heard what the men say of me, Santh. What my foes mutter in their weeping," he said, tilting his head with a mocking question in his look. Santh could hear the venom on his lips.

Santh swallowed the knot in his throat. "They—they say you are a god, your majesty," he replied in a hoarse whisper.

Falrey's bitter smile withered. Crouching in front of Santh, he glared down at him till the man looked away. "Mortals have no place in a battle between gods," he said, standing. "You've served my Great Cause well, Santh Baklyn. But you fell short in the end, like all mortals do."

Santh's honeyed tongue failed him.

Falrey smiled. "I share my victory with no one," he said.

Santh started as a sword was drawn. He grunted as one of the knights planted a boot in his back. Gritting his teeth, Santh struggled to rise. A kick to the side stilled him—and Santh glimpsed one of the Baronsguard hand a nightstone longsword to Falrey.

Falrey raised the blade, a sneer upon his lips. "There is only one King of Alithell, and his name is Death," he said. He swung the blade down on Santh's exposed neck.

49

9th of Rynéth, 2211 SE

Eyoés had never felt such cold. Freezing snow blasted at his exposed face like gravel, numbing his arms till they became like lifeless fetters tied around his chest. Sneezing, he pushed aside several low-hanging pine boughs. Snow hissed in a cloud around him as he looked back.

Men staggered out from under a rock outcropping like drunken men, throwing up white dust as they slipped in the new fallen snow and carried on. Rags and hoods shrouded the men, offering only a glimpse of their bright red faces. Snow crunched under their makeshift snowshoes. Huddled among the pines, Eyoés could see the pain in their stiff, waddling steps.

Beyond the mountains bordering Gald-Behn lay the flaxen fields of the King. Songs had been sung of them. Tales woven of them.

The trail they forged, they forged to paradise.

Eyoés grimaced, the icicles on his beard cracking like glass. A brittle sob choked in his throat and he marched on. It was too cold to think or feel.

A chirp drew his eyes upward as Gibusil alighted on an exposed rock, snow peppering his golden feathers. The griffin's feathers were fluffed to provide warmth. Gwyndel and Haeryn rolled off Gibusil's back, their movements impeded by stiffening cold.

Gwyndel cupped her gloved hands to her mouth. "There's a close patch of trees ahead nestled among the rocks! We make camp there," she shouted, her voice faint in the screaming winds.

Eyoés pulled the hood of his cloak down over his face and dabbed his tears before they could freeze. "No!" he said, voice trembling as he shivered, teeth chattering. Clenching his jaw, he quickened his pace.

When we die, we will die on our feet. I'll not fail my men by letting them die a disgraceful death. It's the least I can do after all I've done.

"Father!" Haeryn called out, his voice ringing clear as the wind paused. "Night is coming—and wolves gather!" A distant, echoing howl caught the wind and drifted into the valley, raising the hairs on Eyoés' neck.

He arrested his pace, lifting his eyes to the surrounding landscape. Darkness gathered. Over the small rise in their path, Eyoés could see the outline of a thick grove nestled among large rocks, their tops glistening with a hard crust of frozen snow. Eyoés' shoulders sagged. Warmth was within reach.

"Have—have the men make camp," he commanded with a sigh of resignation.

It will be our last night.

The men needed little prompting. Compelled by the hope of warmth, they surged forward in a last burst of strength, passing Eyoés and tripping over themselves as they disappeared into the shelter of the trees. Standing amid the stragglers, Eyoés gritted his teeth and dropped his gaze, planting one foot in front of the other till they carried him into the forest.

Placing a gloved hand upon the nearest tree, he sagged against it. The black shapes of the troops scurried across the blue-white snow, filling the air with the sound of snapping twigs. Flashes of firelight burst to life, illuminating the figure of Dovarul as he led Thridd about the camp to ignite the soldiers' stacks of firewood like a man distributing food among the needy.

Eyoés' pale face twisted behind the curtain of his steaming breath. A sea of emotion seized him and pulled him into the depths, holding him under like a drowning man. The sight of the camp lay before him like an artist's masterpiece—imprinted upon his memory with all the emotions and sensations of the moment.

The night Alithell's hope died.

With a sigh, Eyoés accepted it. Tears fell as the hope of freedom drifted away, carried with his steaming breath into the boughs above. Despite their sacrifice—*his* sacrifice—their quest for a free Alithell had withered. Alithell did not want saving.

We did what we could.

Squinting at the hot flames of a campfire, Eyoés trudged toward it. Men scurried about him with tent poles and canvas in hand, working furiously to set up the structures as night tightened its grip. As he seated himself by the fire, Eyoés pulled his eyes away from the flames.

Caywen Amberster lay beside the crackling heap, shrouded in blankets like a dead woman wrapped for burial. With a groan, she stirred in her sleep. Throwing back his hood, Lanyon rushed to her side and knelt.

Eyoés looked on with a dull stare. "How is she?" he asked.

"She's weak. The wound will take weeks, if not months, to heal. Hopefully I've immobilized her well enough," Lanyon said. "The camp surgeon fears that changing her dressings in these conditions will increase the chances of infection. It's a miracle it hasn't already set in."

A miracle. Sickened, Eyoés turned back to the fire. "Lanyon, can I trust you?" he asked.

Firelight sparkled in Lanyon's eyes. "I've fought at your side. Suffered with you. Bled with you. Is that not assurance enough?"

Eyoés met his gaze. "I'm not speaking to Wyndar Alcarthon, the general. I'm speaking to Lanyon, my friend," he said.

Lanyon sank back against a fallen log bathed in an orange glow. "You are a man I am pleased to serve, Eyoés," he said, turning his eyes away. "You and Haeryn. A wanderer like me would count himself lucky to call either of you his friend." The words were hushed and pondered.

With a sigh, Eyoés brought a hand to his brow, folding over in his seat. "We know death when we see it, Lanyon. Why do we preserve the facade?" he muttered with frigid lips.

Lanyon's brow furrowed. "Don't say that," he insisted. "If we can make it over the next ridge tomorrow—"

"There will be another ridge after that. One after another. These men have proven their worth and fought till the end. Shouldn't we be honest with them?" Eyoés asked, batting the snow from his eyelashes. "The Kingdom above the Stars is waiting for us, and they need to remember that." Eyoés swallowed the lump in this throat as Erling carried Rhoslyn to one of the fires, followed by several men as they carried Vakros on a travois.

Lanyon leaned forward, hands outstretched to the flames. "Our defeat's nothing to be ashamed of," he said. "We fought a good fight, and we should be proud of that."

Eyoés grabbed a handful of snow in his gloved fist. "But look at the world we're leaving behind. There will never be peace again," he said. "We move on to something greater while the rest of the world suffers. What good is there in that?"

Wiping at the melting ice around his mouth, he stood. "I'll find Gwyndel and fetch the healer. It's time we check Caywen's wound," he said.

Snow gathered about Haeryn's ankles and clung there like weights. Dragging his feet, he gritted his teeth and pulled his Norgalokan cloak further over his wounded arm. The night was growing darker. Scattered fires crackled among the trees like beacons of safety, illuminating those gathered around them. Snow hissed down from the boughs overhead as the warmth reached them.

Haeryn crawled to no man's fire. Gathering his cloak about him, he trudged through the camp in silence.

He refused to think. Refused to speak. He could only *feel*—feel the rancor settle in his stomach like an illness, the bitterness of failure settle on his tongue. It was the only course left to him, a wounded knight dying in the far reaches of the mountains like a man stranded.

Helpless—in a way he'd never conceived possible. His face twisted in disgust and he spat in the snow.

I never thought we'd die like this. In shame.

The thought slipped into his mind like a dagger through armor. Clenching his teeth till his jaw ached, Haeryn drove his fist into the nearest tree, sending a spray of snow cascading down. He sank against the knobby pine and closed his eyes.

The Guide allowed this.

Snow crunched as footsteps dragged toward him. Haeryn didn't bother to open his eyes. Wrapping a numb hand around a branch, he squeezed it till his arm trembled. "Leave me," he commanded through his teeth. The tree shuddered and snow thumped to the ground as a glaive was laid against the branches. Haeryn recognized it out of the corner of his eye.

"You can't command me," Jaaye said, grasping Haeryn's shoulder and pulling him away from the tree.

He wrenched away in a half-hearted attempt to free himself from her grip. Jaaye yanked him again, fist tightening around the wad of fur as she retrieved her glaive. "You sulk too much, Haeryn. In times like this a man needs friends and a warm drink," she said. Leaning against her glaive, Jaaye set off into the camp, dragging Haeryn behind like a disobedient child.

Shooting a wounded glare in her direction, Haeryn fell in step with her and pulled the fur-lined hood of his Norgalokan cloak over his head. "Thought you'd consult your blessed phial tonight. Considering the circumstances," he remarked.

Jaaye didn't look him in the eye. "A wise friend of mine told me that I was too brave for slavery. That he knew my pain and would walk alongside me through it all," she said. "It's time I repay the favor."

Warmth kissed Haeryn's cheeks as they neared one of the campfires. The bright glow turned the snow to the color of sunset. As he tore himself from Jaaye's grip, Haeryn threw himself down on a patch of bare ground as a rabbit turned on a spit over the flames, sizzling and sputtering. The night didn't feel so cold anymore.

Pushing back his wool hood, Erling slipped into the firelight across from him. "It's good to have you with us, Haeryn," he said, steam rising from his skin in the fire's warmth.

Haeryn bit his tongue. Removing the glove from his free hand with a yank, he bared his swollen, numb fingers to the flames, biting down a curse as they flared to life in stinging pain. His sullen look deepened as Jaaye sat beside him.

I don't want their comfort. Or their company.

352

He snatched up his glove and stood to leave.

Erling lifted his pained gaze. "Don't leave us, friend," he implored.

Haeryn pinned both of them to the spot with a scowl. "What do you want from me? Determination? Hope?" he growled, peering down at them with a snort of disgust. "I have nothing to give, and no patience to give it."

He started off—and found himself facedown in snow as Jaaye shoved him into a snowbank. She wiped the powder from his gasping face with a smirk. "We want you to eat and warm up, you belligerent churl," she said. Jaaye carved off a chunk of rabbit with her knife and shoved it at him. "Eat."

Blinking the snow from his eyelashes, Haeryn looked down at the steaming meat in his hands. His stomach grumbled. With a sigh of defeat, Haeryn shot a final glare at Jaaye and dug in.

Erling watched him through the flames with bleary eyes. "We did our best. Outside Seolta," he said.

Haeryn's fingers paused above strips of rabbit. "I know you did," he said.

Jaaye shook her head. "I gave up the hill. They lured us onto open ground, and I fell for it," she said.

"Falrey saw our desperation and twisted it to his advantage. That, at least, is not our fault," Erling said. Gathering the folds of his cloak, he reached underneath and slipped out a small knife from his belt. He carved off a piece of meat for himself and studied Haeryn. "You and—Taesyra. Worthy of remembrance. You both fought well. We're proud of you," he said.

Haeryn downed the last of his meat. "Worthy of remembrance," he scoffed. "*Remembrance* is for failures. It's a paltry compensation. And yet Falrey will still wipe us from history."

The thought silenced Jaaye and Erling for a time.

Blowing on his cold fingers, Erling reached back and grabbed a fistful of twigs from their scant pile. "Hard times make for grand victories," he mused. "Perhaps there is a chance—"

Haeryn laughed—a bitter, choking laugh shaped from suppressed sobs. "You can't even *fathom* the possibility that our greatest efforts have come to nothing! We were hopelessly naive. None of us will survive this. That is our punishment."

A single footstep crackled in the frozen snow behind him.

Men pounced from the hoary gloom and barreled past Haeryn in a spray of snow as they fell upon the sizzling rabbit with desperation in their eyes. Jaaye and Erling sprang to their feet and were thrown aside as the men tore the spit to pieces. One of them screamed as flames licked up his rags.

Haeryn struck out blindly, taking the nearest man to the ground. He snatched up a branch in his quaking fist and wheeled on the others. Jaaye's muffled voice warbled in Haeryn's ear as he swung, eyes growing wilder with every jarring blow.

He threw his arm back for another strike. Hands seized him from behind and threw him backward. Pain shot through Haeryn's wounded shoulder and he choked back a cry, scrambling to his knees in time to see the brigands run off into the night with the mangled rabbit trailing steam in their wake. Voices rose up in camp as soldiers grabbed their weapons and rushed to their aid too late.

Haeryn brandished the broken branch in his shaking fist. "You held me back!" he yelled. "What's come over—"

Jaaye slapped the branch away and locked eyes with him. "This isn't your fault!" she said, spreading her arms wide. "No one is to blame! We have no say in what fate decides to afflict us with. Why can't you see that? What are you afraid of?"

Haeryn's arm fell to his side. He looked over Jaaye's shoulder to the soldiers watching him. They visibly shivered as the night grew dark.

Swallowing, he caught the glimmer of firelight in Jaaye's eyes. "I'm afraid that my strength isn't enough," he said.

5◊

Haeryn woke to the touch of a finger on his forehead. As he opened his eyes, he could still feel it, pulsing deeper and deeper with an ever growing clarity. He grasped the collar of his Norgalokan cloak to pull it further over his face.

He felt the touch again. Stronger this time. His pulse quickened as he realized he hadn't seen anyone nearby.

Bracing himself for the cold, Haeryn sat up, making out the shapes of Erling and Jaaye lying under the pine boughs alongside him. Needles gathered in the fur of his cloak as he huddled underneath the low, arched arms of the tree.

Someone sat outside. Haeryn could see him through a gap in the prickly boughs laden with ice and snow—a silent visitor, watching him as he'd slept. Picking up his sheathed dagger, Haeryn crawled over Erling and pushed his way out of their sanctuary.

The man stirred, peeking out from under his white cowl. "Haeryn Irongaze. Justice-bringer. Will you speak with me?" he asked, cradling the crook staff in his arms.

Haeryn froze in the cloud of his own breath. The two of them locked eyes. "It's you," he said, the bitterness in his voice tempered by the fear quickening in his heart.

The Guide's serene expression did not change. "Will you speak with me?"

Swallowing, Haeryn nodded.

A hint of a smile touched the Guide's face and he motioned with the tip of his staff. "I'm not here to punish you," he insisted.

Haeryn crept forward, heedless of the growing numbness in his gloved hands. "Then you know my thoughts," he said.

"You are not the only one who blames me for their troubles," the Guide answered. As he passed the crook of his staff over the ground, the snow melted. Haeryn pulled off a glove and touched the bare, dry earth, wondering at its warmth.

He paused, then sat across from the Guide, pulling his knees to his chest as his eyes flitted up to meet the gaze of a god. Despite the bitterness lingering within, Haeryn couldn't understand the vulnerability he felt in any other way.

That's foolishness. Nothing more than a wise man.

Haeryn's heart skipped as the smile grew on the Guide's face. "Truth becomes undeniable when it looks you in the eye, does it not? Yet it is even greater to believe in truth when it is at a distance," he said.

Haeryn lowered his eyes. "A man can't put too much faith in the gods or in wise men," he said.

"I am not like your old gods," the Guide said. The man's quiet words thundered in Haeryn's chest.

Squeezing the glove in his hand, Haeryn pursed his lips in a grim scowl. "You threw us into Falrey's jaws. Left us to crawl away, starving and dying. And you say you're not like the other gods?" he snarled.

The Guide's gaze probed like a healer gauging a wound. "Did I destroy Asdale? Did I harry you like a hound nipping at your heels? Were Falrey and Santh innocent of these things?" he replied. "You cannot blame me for the actions of wicked men."

Haeryn's eyes narrowed. "But you allowed it," he said. "You let Falrey rampage without consequence. Without *justice*."

A sudden coldness twisted Haeryn's gut as soon as the words left his mouth. Trembling, Haeryn flinched back. He watched with held breath as the Guide lowered his head.

The Guide's fingers tightened around the heft of his staff, turning a clammy white as they twisted around the wood. He fell silent, and the moonlight glinted off tears on the man's cheek.

A weeping god.

When the Guide lifted his head, his eyes burned like fire. "The proper time has not yet come," he said. The words tolled with a finality that sent a chill racing up Haeryn's back.

Haeryn rose to his feet, crushing his glove in his fist. "Proper time?" he snapped. "The proper time is now! I would rather fight and die to bring justice than wait, *languishing*, for the proper time."

The coaxing look in the Guide's eyes struck a chord of doubt. Haeryn rubbed his cracked lips with the back of his hand and looked away. Unsettled, he examined his own words—and his stomach twisted.

Shrinking back, Haeryn wrapped his arms around himself. "I can never bring it about, can I?" he said, avoiding the Guide's probing look. "I've lived my life for a goal I can never attain."

The Guide leaned forward and placed a gentle hand on Haeryn's shoulder. "Righting all the wrongs of the world is beyond anyone," he said with the gentle truthfulness of a father. "Surrender your zeal for control, and you will see the impossible come to pass." The Guide stood, leaning upon his crook staff.

Haeryn peered at him, blinking to clear the tears from his eyes. "Why did you come to me? Father and Aunt Gwyndel need you more than I do," he said.

The Guide paused, and Haeryn's breath caught as he glimpsed a look of grief pass quickly over the man's face. "In time, you will know," he said. "Come."

Throwing his hood over his face, the Guide tapped the butt of his staff on the ground and started off through the forest. Haeryn squinted as the light glowing from the crook of the staff lit the way. He followed in a daze, staring at the man's white cloak as it billowed over the blue tinted snow.

I devoted myself to something I could never fulfill myself.

His mind still reeled. The blatant truth faced him openly, and as he walked along a path through melted snow, Haeryn couldn't decide how he felt. Pain at his naivety. Relief at his new clarity. Wariness that perhaps, despite appearances, all this was a lie meant to distract him with naive hope. Haeryn sighed.

Perhaps a naive hope is better than despair.

At the sound of Gibusil's rumbling breath, Haeryn stopped. He could see the griffin's massive form in the darkness, tucked beside the tattered walls of his father's tent. Haeryn lingered in the shadow of a fallen tree, watching with a sad smile as the griffin's sides rose and fell.

Gibusil's eyes shot open the moment the Guide approached the tent. He didn't growl. With a quiet laugh, the Guide stroked the griffin's broad forehead and looked toward the tent flap.

A gloved hand flung it aside, and Eyoés stumbled out into the night, a wool blanket bundled around him. Gwyndel followed on his heels, her hair poking out in clumps around the edges of her hood. Sleep still clung to their eyes. In the shadows within the tent, Haeryn could see Vakros and Rhoslyn watching intently from where they lay.

Eyoés saw the Guide and the blankets dropped from his shoulders. "You came for us," he said. The brokenness in his voice unsettled Haeryn.

Gwyndel collapsed to her knees. "Please—*please!* What do we do?" she implored.

The light from the Guide's staff shone brighter. "Your work and suffering is not in vain. Hear this— Falrey's cause will die upon the Sword Imperishable," he declared. Turning to Haeryn, he nodded. "Heed well what I've said."

Haeryn met the stares of his father and aunt with an uncertainty equal to their own. The path they walked, they did not walk alone.

"So be it," he said.

51

14th of Rynéth, 2211 SE

Gathering the reins in his hand, Eyoés looked out across the broad, flaxen fields of Gald-Behn, the honeyed air sweet on his tongue. Under the bright, open sky, hope seemed truly alive. Like a dead soul resurrected in paradise. Eyoés smiled, a chuckle springing to his lips.

If this was to be their last stand, there was no better place for it.

As Gibusil alighted amid the surging sea of grass, Eyoés turned to face Haeryn with a grin. "I'd always hoped you'd see this," he said, looking up as two birds passed overhead in song. The bubbling of water sang in his ear and he pointed to a sparkling river nestled in the endless fields. "The end of the River of Larimar. The waters come all the way from the ocean to become the purest drinking water," he said.

Eyoés knew the look of speechless awe and serenity on his son's face. It was a moment he'd revisited time and time again, and each time, he understood that it was brought about by something greater than the broadness of the landscape.

Haeryn gazed off into the distance, making out the white walls of Hargalion sparkling like gems on the horizon behind them. His hand moved to unbuckle himself from the saddle and hung there. "I must see it all," he whispered to himself.

Eyoés grasped his son's hand. "When the day is won, perhaps you'll have your chance," he said.

Banners whipped in the sweet winds. Alcarthon. Freechildren. The standards of Edeveros and Rehillon. All flew together as equals in a united line. As the armies of Alithell waited in silence, Eyoés singled out Gwyndel at their head, flanked by Jaaye and Lanyon. Despite the knots in his stomach, hope lived on.

Hear this—Falrey's cause will die upon the Sword Imperishable.

It was enough. With the Guide's words in his thoughts, Eyoés checked the straps fastening his armor.

Gwyndel will kill the tyrant. Of all of us, at least she will survive.

"Enemy spotted."

Eyoés peered down to where Uwéllor stood in the shadow of Gibusil's wing, the Wardens of the Watch joining him as they encompassed the griffin as an honor guard.

Rising up from a shallow dip in the land, Falrey's banner greeted them, leading a host of men and beasts in its wake. Gibusil's ears flattened and Eyoés pulled back on the reins to keep the griffin in check. He could hear their marching song on the wind—a driving, regal song with a menace that silenced the birds. As the enemy formed ranks with a blast of the trumpet, Eyoés saw the lone figure leading them on foot. The tyrant himself.

Hooves beat the ground as Erling, Marc, and Dovarul thundered to Gibusil's side. Marc removed his helmet. "The odds are slim, sir. On such level ground, a committed charge at the enemy will shatter us like waves upon the rocks," he said.

Eyoés frowned. "What about the archers, like we discussed?"

Hefting a partizan spear on his shoulder, Erling shook his head. "Falrey learned his lesson from Seolta. His ranks are deployed so his men can hide behind shields if we attempt a volley. They'd suffer minimal losses," he said.

Leaning out from the saddle, Haeryn reached back to adjust the sling on his opposite arm. "What does Lanyon think?" he asked.

Marc and Erling shot each other a reluctant glance. Dovarul peered over Marc's shoulder. "Frankly, he thinks we'll be dead within the hour. Don't believe him. I'd give it *two* hours," he said. Marc gave a grim chuckle.

The dwarf's face turned serious. "In all honesty, whether we live or die no one knows. Not even the great Wyndar Alcarthon. But if the Guide has declared Falrey's doom, then his fate is sealed," he said.

Wetting his dry lips, Eyoés glanced to the rear of the army. "And the others?"

Dovarul nodded. "Vakros, Rhoslyn, and Caywen? They're on a cart headed for Hargalion. Don't worry about them," he said.

Eyoés closed his eyes and let out a slow, controlled breath. "We end this today. Under the blessed sun." He opened his eyes. "It's time Falrey tasted fear for himself."

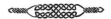

The horse next to Gwyndel shied back, eyes rolling back in terror as it chomped at the bit. Its rider muttered in his helmet and fought to right the beast.

None of the others passed judgment. Tugging at the collar of her armor, Gwyndel placed her helmet on the saddlehorn and adjusted the strap. The air was still and silent, leaving only the sound of her heart pounding beneath steel.

The enemy looked on with quiet expectation.

She glanced at Lanyon and Jaaye, probing their steely expressions with a growing envy. Neither met her gaze. Did they fear to admit what they all felt? Turning her helmet over in her hands, Gwyndel heard the clack of lances as the Knights of the Lance readied themselves. The total stillness, the anticipation of what was to come—it compelled her to savor every second of this moment.

And yet, I will survive.

The Guide's declaration twisted her gut. She was to be the tyrant-killer. By now, the news had spread through the ranks, and in a matter of days, she had come to bear the burden of victory on her shoulders. It was her fate, and Gwyndel trembled at the thought of facing it head on.

Gritting her teeth, she put on her helmet.

Everything for this moment. The greatest victory truth could ever claim.

She could see Falrey through the slits of her helmet, poised like a tournament champion at the end of the lists. He wore no armor. No helmet. Only fists clenched at his side. His eyes bored into hers from afar, daring her to make a move.

A hand grasped her arm and she turned to see Marc at her side, his armored arm wrapped around his helmet. He flashed her a soft smile. That was all.

"Andíamas Radem!" Gwyndel cried, her voice ringing clear across the open plains like a pealing bell.

The ranks erupted into a deafening roar and the horns sounded the charge as the armies of Alithell surged forward as one, streaming banners above them and thundering ground below them. A screech echoed from the sky as Gibusil passed overhead in a broad shadow.

In a blink of an eye, Falrey transformed, leaping into the air and taking flight with a discordant scream that set Gwyndel's teeth on edge. His hordes followed on his crimson-scaled heels. Surrounded by a sea of lances and pikes, Gwyndel braced herself for bone-jarring impact as the distance between them shrank.

The deep clang of a single bell made the very air tremble. In an instant, Gwyndel saw the crown upon the dragon's head shatter like glass and the monster twisted in agony, plummeting to the earth in a cloud of dust.

Gwyndel heaved back on the reins and skidded into the dust cloud along with her fellows—and through the drifting haze, she glimpsed horses galloping across the plain in their direction.

The banner of King Fohidras flew above them.

52

Like peals of thunder, the royal trumpets sounded a song of victory, shaking the skies and the earth and the very breath in Eyoés' lungs. The King himself charged down the hill, his robes streaming behind him like ribbons as a roaring sea of gahrim followed his lead.

Haeryn shouted as Eyoés dug in his heels and Gibusil plunged at the enemy. Falrey's forces ground to a halt and scrambled to regroup. Whoops of joy erupted from the armies of Alithell and they threw themselves headlong at the enemy, colliding with the broken ranks of hobgoblins before the creatures could make a stand.

Eyoés blinked away the tears blurring his vision as Gibusil struck Falrey's ranks with a thud, throwing shields and weapons into the air among clods of torn earth. With a tug on the reins, the griffin wheeled and fell upon one of Falrey's ballistas, tearing the wood apart with talons and beak. Through the settling dust, Eyoés saw the Wardens of the Watch charge past, piercing through the disarray and confusion as they fought by his side.

Throwing himself from the saddle, Eyoés joined them. He drew his father's sword and looked up at Haeryn as his son clambered to the front of the saddle. "Make them pay, son!" he cried. Face beaming, Haeryn snatched the reins in his free hand and took flight, plowing through another ballista crew as he went.

Eyoés spun as Uwéllor grasped his shoulder and caught his eye from within his helmet. "Hope is a miracle!" he declared, motioning for Eyoés to follow as the Wardens of the Watch changed course to cut Falrey's forces in half.

Eyoés plunged into the fray, ducking under a sweeping halberd as he slammed his shoulder into the enemy soldier, cutting him down and turning on a pack of wild-eyed hobgoblins. Even as the turmoil of warfare raged around him, Eyoés struggled to hold back sobs. He'd forgotten what victory felt like.

Brandishing a spear in one hand and his father's sword in the other, he unhorsed a passing cavalryman and grunted as the momentum yanked the spear from his hand. He spun to face a flicker of movement too close for his liking.

The smile froze on his lips as he locked eyes with Falrey O'Dyre.

Falrey glared back at him with amber eyes full of rage. Blood and dirt soiled his fine uniform, and the twisted remains of a broken crown clung to his skull. Shouts rang out behind Eyoés as the Wardens of the Watch hastened to his aid.

Plucking a nightstone broadsword from a hobgoblin corpse, Falrey smiled.

Gwyndel's ears rang from the sound of her own breathing echoing inside her helmet. She urged her horse to a gallop and summoned the Sword Imperishable in a flash of light. The flaming blade swept among her fleeing enemies, claiming lives and showing mercy where truth demanded. Gwyndel didn't look back.

She sought a bigger prize.

Eyes stinging with sweat, she combed the battlefield for sign of Falrey, the clarity of her vision piercing through the chaos with a hunter's focus. The longer the minutes stretched, the faster her heart pounded. A shout rang out behind her. Uwéllor—she could recognize his voice even in her helmet. Wheeling her horse about, she looked in the direction of the sound. Her hunter's gaze found its target.

Falrey fought alone—and he was fighting Eyoés.

Panic gripped her as the Wardens of the Watch raced to Eyoés' aid, throwing themselves toward Falrey like a pack of wolves attacking a bear. Gwyndel spurred her horse, the beast's breath coming in ragged gasps.

Gibusil shot over her head toward Eyoés as Haeryn rushed to his father's aid. A ballista bolt streaked past and the griffin drew up short, forced to withdraw as a second ballista locked its sights on them. The Wardens of the Watch cried out as one of the gahrim fell under Falrey's blade.

Gwyndel froze, her heart torn in two—then galloped for Eyoés. The chaos of the battle slowed her down. She fought her way through as the Wardens of the Watch fell, one by one, under Falrey's sweeping nightstone broadsword. Eyes blazing, Gwyndel pushed harder and lifted the Sword Imperishable.

The dazzling blue blade vanished in her hand.

Eyoés landed in the matted grass with a grunt, wincing as he clambered back to his feet and grabbed his sword from where it had fallen. Immediately he leapt back as the tip of Falrey's blade flashed past his nose. Uwéllor pushed past him and leapt into the gap, driving his shoulder into Falrey's side. The two went sprawling and Eyoés pounced, gripping his blade in a half-sword grip as he tried to pin Falrey to the earth.

A kick to the leg knocked him down as Falrey escaped Uwéllor's grasp. Eyoés sprang to his feet and swung blindly, a shock coursing down his arm as his weapon bit into Falrey's chest.

The tyrant stumbled back, pressing a bloody hand to his chest as he held his nightstone broadsword in front of him to ward them off. Uwéllor batted it aside and closed in. Falrey bashed the pommel of his sword into the gahrim's helmet and flung him to the ground, unconscious. Eyoés' heart skipped as he saw the ghastly wound on Falrey's chest vanish under a cloak of black mist. Chest heaving, the tyrant turned to Eyoés.

Eyoés leapt back and warded him off with his sword, heart pounding in his mouth. The gleaming tip of his blade trembled in his grip.

Falrey pounced. Eyoés was forced to retreat as sweeping strokes collided with his blade with a power and precision that battered him. His teeth rattled and he darted into the first opening he saw.

His blade glanced across Falrey's cheek and the tyrant knocked the sword from his grasp. Face half shrouded in black mist, Falrey shoved Eyoés to his knees.

A sudden coldness spread through his chest, then turned to fire. He followed Falrey's arm to the sword buried in his own chest. The sweet air of Gald-Behn began to wane in his lungs.

A thousand faces returned to him at once, and with them a deep yearning that wounded him deeper still.

Eyes bright with hatred, Falrey clenched his jaw. "Your life was a mistake. A consequence of Skreon's failure to finish what he started," he said, searching Eyoés' eyes. "You die in disgrace."

A flash of blue light startled Eyoés, and he looked down to see the Sword Imperishable appear in his hand.

Blinking back tears, Eyoés bared his teeth and drove the flaming blade into his enemy's chest. Falrey froze, the hate in his eyes melting into terror as he shuddered. Eyoés drove the Sword Imperishable deeper. "If this is disgrace, I accept it," he said.

A howl erupted from Falrey and he threw himself backward, yanking his nightstone broadsword from

Eyoés' chest. His harsh, chiseled face shriveled, seeping black mist as his amber eyes turned a milky white. While spots flashed before Eyoés' eyes, Falrey burst into a thousand fragments of black. The tyrant's sword fell to the ground and was lost in the grass.

The sounds of battle grew dim in Eyoés' ears and he fell onto his back, gazing up into the broad, clear sky where the sun shone and the air tasted of paradise.

With his final breath, he smiled.

53

The world swam as Gwyndel fell to her knees beside the body of her brother. Tearing off her helmet and throwing it aside, she stared at his vacant eyes, hands trembling. His face—it carried such *peace*. The tears came in a rush.

Sobs shook her and she fell across her brother's chest, oblivious to everything but her pain. The waning sounds of battle grew faint and distant in the wholehearted blindness of her stricken heart.

A shadow covered her as she sensed Haeryn's running footsteps more than heard them. Throwing himself on his knees, Haeryn looked down at his father's still face. His breathing grew ragged. He sat back on his heels, his iron gaze glistening as tears poured down his face and dripped from his chin.

Gwyndel choked on her words as her face contorted in grief. "He did it," she said.

Haeryn pressed his trembling lips together and looked at the bodies of the Wardens of the Watch scattered in the grass. "He died a hero. A hero among heroes," he said.

Gwyndel nodded and bit her lip. "Father would be proud. The scion of Élorn, defender of the world," she said. As she looked at her brother's face, the sunlight danced across his eyes. The wind brushed her face and she looked up, watching it ripple through the golden fields of Gald-Behn. Birds chirped out of sight in the sky above. With a trembling sigh, Gwyndel smiled.

Eyoés died tasting the peace he's craved for so long. The peace that Asdale once carried.

Something pushed her aside and Gwyndel turned to see Gibusil's head lingering above his master's body. With a weak chirp, the griffin nudged Eyoés with his beak. A sob tore from Gwyndel's throat and she embraced the griffin's neck, seizing fistfuls of feathers and fur as she wept.

"Weep no more. The day is won, and your brother yet lives among the stars."

Gwyndel peered up at the King through her tears. Flanked by three towering gahrim in resplendent armor, King Fohidras placed a gentle hand on her shoulder and knelt by her side. Crimson mud splattered the golden robes that hung from his broad shoulders.

Gwyndel choked back a sob as she saw the tears welling in his eyes. "Why did it have to end this way?"

Royal tears freely fell. "For years Eyoés wished he could do more to pull this blind world from the flames. He also wished to leave a legacy worth remembering," he said, catching Haeryn's eye. "There is no better love than to sacrifice for one's friends."

Haeryn trembled. "But *he* wielded the Sword Imperishable," he said, voice quaking.

"It is mine to use how I will," Fohidras answered, squeezing Gwyndel's arm, "and I will continue to entrust it to your stewardship."

They fell silent for a time as the last strains of battle waned and the exhausted cheers of the victors rose. With a trembling sigh, Haeryn surveyed the battleground as he stroked Gibusil's neck. "What do we do now?" he asked, turning to the King for direction. "Lead the way and I will follow."

The King paused, stroking Gwyndel's hair like a father comforting his daughter. "The world has changed, Haeryn Irongaze. I do not desire the wealth, words, or lands of my people—I wish to capture their hearts," he said, rising to his feet. The gahrim stood at attention.

King Fohidras laid a strong hand on Haeryn's shoulder and shook him with a sad smile. "You've seen the people. Falrey's poison works deep, and their hearts are corrupted. They will not accept my rule," he said.

Gwyndel's head shot up and she turned to the King with eyes cold with shock. "You're leaving," she said. There was no question of it, and as her gaze fastened on the King's grieved look, she knew it to be true.

The King lowered his head. "A kingdom forced upon its subjects only inspires strife and hatred," he said. "In time, they will hear my call anew and bend their knees willfully."

Haeryn trembled. "We are alone then," he said.

A smile broke across the King's face and he placed a hand on Haeryn's cheek. "You are never alone, whether you see me or not. We will be together again," he declared, catching Gwyndel's eye. "You are never forsaken. Never forgotten."

A chirp startled Gwyndel as gahrim came forward, two baby griffins cradled in their arms. Gibusil rushed forward and nudged them with his head. The King smiled at Haeryn. "Taesyra and Gibusil's offspring. Restored to you after their capture during Asdale's fall," he said. "I understand the pain of your loss, and I would see you healed of it." Tears sprang to Haeryn's eyes as the griffins leapt down and rolled around his ankles.

Squeezing her eyes shut, Gwyndel wiped her cheeks. She opened her eyes, watching the King and his gahrim vanish like the last vestiges of a dream.

54

25th of Rynéth, 2211 SE

In the shadow of Gwyndel's treehouse, Haeryn watched the last spadeful of soil scatter across his father's grave. The breeze caught the dust and carried it in a faint cloud across the sun-speckled forest floor, sprinkling it upon the dead leaves.

It was done. Haeryn lingered there, listening to the silence of the forest under the distant winter sun. The breeze faded and the birds held their tongues. Gritting his teeth, Haeryn scooped up a handful of dry leaves just to hear them crackle. Without his father's voice, the silence was too vast. Too empty.

He glanced to where Lanyon stood, head bowed in respect as he studied the memorial stone. After a life of wandering through shadows, he'd laid hold of his birthright as Wyndar, heir of the Alcarthon name. The bracing cold bit Haeryn's cheeks. That sense of certainty still eluded him.

The world I knew is gone. What's my purpose now?

Falrey O'Dyre, the infamous Llumiael of old, was dead. Gald-Behn lay empty, shrouded in a deep magic that refused entry to anyone. Borders, territories, and alliances no longer existed. Gwyndel sobbed quietly and Rhoslyn squeezed her mother's hand, eyes red with tears. With her father disabled and her mother foraging for food, the girl struggled to help wherever she could. Before long, she wouldn't remember the better times.

Haeryn shook his head and rose to his feet. "May the Guide and King ever watch over this place, and may the dead find peace here," he declared. It was an old blessing his father had adopted during his short time in Amiranoor. Sometimes, Haeryn wondered whether Eyoés had guessed the kind of fate that would befall him. The formality and sentiment of the words offered a small refuge.

Snatching up their spades, the servants left to allow the small group their privacy. Haeryn turned as Gwyndel approached him, holding Rhoslyn's hand in a tight grip. She embraced him. "Your father would be proud," she said.

Haeryn met her eyes with a flat smile and nodded. What else was there to say?

Every step of their return journey, the uncertainty had grown stronger—at first, a mere glimmer overshadowed by grief. Now, as he stood under the bare trees standing guard over his dead father, he found it difficult to turn his mind to brighter things.

"Is this what it feels like?" he asked. "The uncertainty. Is this how it felt to became the Baron of Taekohar?" Haeryn's heart twisted as he realized he'd spoken not to his aunt, but to his dead father.

Gwyndel paused, looking at her brother's grave mound. "Yes. There were many days where Eyoés and I felt the weight of Asdale's future in our hands. But it doesn't last forever," she said.

Watching Lanyon, Caywen, and Jaaye as they talked to each other, Haeryn grasped Rhoslyn's other hand and started for them. He sighed. "Asdale is still occupied by the enemy, and winter is upon us. Alithell is a lawless wilderness," he said.

Gwyndel caught his gaze and held it. "We are the scions of Taekohar now. The scions of Alithell. This world is ours to protect and rebuild," she said.

Haeryn stopped and searched her eyes in silence. His uncertainty remained, and yet as he considered his duty, he found a strength hidden in the tension. Releasing Rhoslyn's hand, he stroked her head with a smile. "So be it," he said.

With a nod, he threw up his hood and strode toward Lanyon, rubbing at the wound healing in his shoulder. "Friends, Asdale is ours for the taking. Our lands are broken and scattered," he said. "And from these ashes, we *rise*."

To access exciting Sword and Scion freebies,
please visit the Exclusive Content page on my
website:

www.jacksonegraham.wix.com/jackson-e-graham

Password: AndiamasRademSS